The Spoilers
&
The Warlords

St. Martin's Paperbacks

The Spoilers

"A HUNDRED VIRGINS WON'T COME CHEAP."

"No problem," Starbuck said equably. "I'm loaded and willing to pay plenty."

O'Brien eyed him craftily. "What about me? Here in Frisco, a go-between don't come cheap either."

Starbuck ventured a smile. "How does five percent strike you?"

There was a moment of weighing and deliberation. O'Brien hadn't the vaguest idea of the asking price for a hundred slave-girl virgins. Whatever the amount, it would be steep. . .too tempting to resist.

"You're on."

Starbuck flashed his gold tooth in a nutcracker grin. Today was only a first step, but his instinct hadn't played him false.

Denny O'Brien had swallowed the bait whole.

The Spoilers

MATT BRAUN

St. Martin's Paperbacks

This is a work of fiction. All of the characters, organizations, and events portrayed in this novel are either products of the author's imagination or are used fictitiously.

THE SPOILERS / THE WARLORDS

The Spoilers copyright © 1981 by Matt Braun.
The Warlords copyright © 2003 by Winchester Productions, Ltd.

For information address St. Martin's Press, 175 Fifth Avenue, New York, NY 10010.

ISBN: 978-1-250-30856-6

Our books may be purchased in bulk for promotional, educational, or business use. Please contact your local bookseller or the Macmillan Corporate and Premium Sales Department at 1-800-221-7945, ext. 5442, or by e-mail at MacmillanSpecialMarkets@macmillan.com.

Printed in the United States of America

The Spoilers St. Martin's Paperbacks edition / November 2002
The Warlords St. Martin's Paperbacks edition / July 2003

St. Martin's Paperbacks are published by St. Martin's Press, 175 Fifth Avenue, New York, NY 10010.

10 9 8 7 6 5 4 3 2 1

To

BETTIANE

the source of all

that matters

Author's Note

The Spoilers is for the most part a true story. In 1882, San Francisco was the wildest, the wickedest, and certainly the most dangerous city in the West. The cowtowns and mining camps, by comparison, were tame stufff. Host to the Barbary Coast and Chinatown, not to mention a waterfront steeped in infamy, the city by the bay was a cosmopolitan hellhole. In that day and time, it was considered the roughest, and by far the most depraved, metropolis on the North American Continent.

Yet, during this same era, San Francisco was the premier city of the Old West. A financial center, a place of sophistication and culture, it was already a mythical wonder famed for its natural beauty and idyllic setting. Beneath the surface, however, there was an unholy marriage between underworld vice lords and corrupt politicians. Their alliance, bolstered by savage methods and a callous disregard for human life, was to rule San Francisco for nearly a quarter-century. Their downfall, when it came, happened very much as described in the story that follows.

The characters who people *The Spoilers* are real. Their names are unchanged, and the diabolic manner in which they pillaged San Francisco required no invention. Some license has been taken with events and dates, but the spoilers themselves are, if anything, less formidable than they were in real life. Luke Starbuck represents a breed apart. A detective and manhunter, he relied on wits and guts, and when necessary, a fast gun. His assignment in *The Spoilers* borders more on fact than fiction.

CHAPTER 1

A brisk October wind swept across the bay. The ferry plowed toward San Francisco, buffeted by the choppy waters. Directly ahead lay the waterfront, a sprawling collection of wharves and warehouses below the hill-studded city.

Luke Starbuck stood alone at the railing on the bow. The other passengers, crossing on the morning ferry from Oakland, were huddled inside the warmth of the main-deck cabin. Face to the wind, Starbuck appeared heedless of the damp chill and the spray that peppered him as waves slapped against the hull. His eyes were fixed on the harbor and the city beyond. He thought it the damnedest sight he'd ever seen.

Telegraph Hill, towering prominently above the waterfront, was cloaked in fog. Around the curving shore of the bay, the terrain formed a bold amphitheater, with inland hills surrounding the center of the city. The bay itself, perhaps the finest landlocked harbor in the world, was crowded with ships. At anchor were vessels of all nations, mast upon mast, their flags fluttering in the breeze. Westward, hidden by the fog-bound peninsula, was the Golden Gate. Through its channel, and into the harbor, sailed the ships of the China trade. Their cargo holds were filled with copra and raw silk, coconut oil and sugar, and myriad imports from the exotic Orient. The trade had transformed San Francisco into one of the richest ports on earth.

To Starbuck, who was not easily impressed, it was grander than anything he'd imagined. A former cowhand and rancher, he had grown to manhood in the Texas Panhandle. Circumstance had thrust him into the role of range detective, and several years were spent in the employ of Cattlemen's Associations across the West. As his reputation grew, he'd been hired by diverse organizations, like banks and mining companies. He was known to have killed at least twenty men, and among outlaws, he was considered the deadliest of all manhunters. Yet his skill as a detective by far exceeded his renown with a gun. His services were in constant demand, and though he was something of a lone wolf, his credentials were on a level with those of the Pinkerton Agency. He was celebrated as a man who never quit, that rare blend of bulldog and bloodhound. He got results.

For all his experience, however, Starbuck was not widely traveled. His work had been confined primarily to the Rocky Mountains and the Southern Plains. To him, Denver was a metropolis, and any body of water wider than the Rio Grande was beyond his ken. The sight of the bay, with tall-masted clippers and ocean-going steamers, was therefore a marvel to command attention. San Francisco, wondrously situated in a ring of hills, and several times the size of Denver, was like a storybook come to life. A profusion of cultures, cosmopolitan and sophisticated, it was the premier city of the West.

Watching it from the bow of the ferry, Starbuck felt a keen sense of exhilaration, and a quickening excitement. He told himself he'd been wise to accept Charles Crocker's summons. Whether or not he accepted the assignment was another thing, and suddenly not too important. Simply being here—San Francisco itself—was well worth the trip. He thought he might stay a while.

Only a week before, he'd been on the verge of accepting another assignment from Wells, Fargo. Then, out of the blue, he had received a wire from Charles Crocker, president of the Central Pacific Railroad. The message was terse, lacking specifics, but urgent in tone. Crocker requested Starbuck's presence in San Francisco, stressing the need for his professional services, and offered to pay all expenses.

Headquartered in Denver, Starbuck had never been retained by a railroad, and the idea intrigued him. He wired an affirmative reply and caught the next westbound. Arriving in Oakland yesterday evening, he had spent the night in a lodging house. Crocker's summons had indicated no need for secrecy, but by now it was second nature. He was entering San Francisco unknown and unannounced, one of the crowd.

When the ferry docked, he was the first to step ashore. He walked along the wharf and stopped on the corner of Market Street. The main thoroughfare of the city, Market began at the waterfront and bisected the business district. He stood for a moment, feeling somewhat like a hayseed, and simply stared. There was no question that San Francisco put Denver to shame. The buildings were taller. The people were more fashionably dressed, and crowded the sidewalks in greater numbers. There was a greater profusion of carriages and hansom cabs, blocking the street as far as the eye could see. The clamor and hubbub were deafening, and the whole scene put him in mind of an ant heap busily swarming with activity. Everything was bigger and louder, and somehow larger than life. He suddenly understood why the city by the bay was spoken of in awed terms.

Still, nothing daunted Starbuck for long. He took it all in stride, and quickly decided there was no reason to gawk. People were people, and ant heaps were all much alike, some merely larger and louder than others. Stepping off the corner, he dodged in front of a carriage and hopped aboard a horse-drawn streetcar. He paid his fare, asking the conductor for directions, and found a seat in the rear. Several blocks uptown, he spotted the triangle where Montgomery and Post intersected Market, and jumped down. He joined the crowd and walked north along Montgomery.

Crossing Sutter, he saw the Wells, Fargo Building kitty-corner across the street. He was tempted to step inside and pay his respects. Only four months ago, while working undercover for the stage company, he had been instrumental in running Wyatt Earp out of Arizona. With Earp's departure, stagecoach robbery in the Tombstone district had all but ceased. The company had awarded Starbuck a generous bonus for his part in routing the gang. Now, however, he resisted the impulse to stop by Wells, Fargo. He wasn't a tactful man, but neither was he a dimdot. Having hedged on accepting a new assignment, it wouldn't do to let them know he was in town to see Crocker. Wells, Fargo could wait.

At the next corner, in the heart of the financial district, he found the Mills Building. The corporate offices of the Central Pacific Railroad occupied the entire third floor. A rickety elevator deposited him in the waiting room, and he gave his name to a man seated behind a reception desk. An office boy scurried off to announce his arrival, and he took a chair. Several minutes later, a young man with thick glasses approached, introducing himself as Crocker's secretary. He led Starbuck down a long hallway and ushered him into a corner suite.

Charles Crocker's office was lavishly appointed. Overlooking the intersection of Montgomery and Bush, it was furnished with wing chairs and a sofa crafted in lush Moroccan leather. The floor was covered by an immense Persian carpet and the walls were lined with oil paintings of the California coast. At the far end of the room, framed between two windows, was a gargantuan desk that looked to be carved from a solid piece of teak. The room seemed somehow appropriate to the man who rose from behind the desk.

Starbuck was reminded of a whale. Charles Crocker topped six feet and weighed not a stone less than three hundred pounds. Age had begun to thicken his girth, and his muttonchop beard was flecked through with gray. Yet he moved with vigor and held himself in a posture of ramrod self-assurance that bordered on arrogance. His voice was deep and resonant, with a booming, organ-like quality.

"Welcome, Mr. Starbuck!" He extended an arm the size of a log. "Welcome to San Francisco."

"Mr. Crocker." Starbuck found his handshake only slightly less powerful than a bear trap. "Glad to be here."

"How was your trip?"

"No complaints. You run a pretty fair railroad."

"None better!" Crocker said affably, waving him to a chair. "We pride ourselves on that. Indeed, we do!"

Starbuck seated himself in one of the wing chairs. The secretary, without being asked, took the other chair. Adjusting his glasses, he pulled a pad and pencil from his pocket, and waited at stiff-backed attention. Crocker crossed behind the desk and lowered his bulk into a tall swivel chair.

"Well, now," he said in his orotund voice, "down to business. You haven't come all this way for chit-chat, correct, Mr. Starbuck?"

"I'm all ears, Mr. Crocker. Fire away."

"Excellent!" Crocker gestured toward his secretary. "I'll just have Higgins take notes on our discussion. For the record, so to speak."

"Why do you need a record?"

"Standard practice," Crocker explained. "I trust you have no objection?"

Starbuck looked at him without expression. "I'm not much for talking on the record."

"May I ask why?"

"Things put down on paper sometimes come back to haunt you."

"Aren't you being overly cautious, Mr. Starbuck?"

"We all protect ourselves in different ways."

"Indeed?" Crocker said gruffly. "Well, suffice it to say, I never enter into an arrangement without a written record."

"Your privilege," Starbuck remarked in a dry, cold manner. "I never make a deal in writing. A handshake does it, or it doesn't get done."

"Suppose I break my word, decide not to pay you when the assignment's completed?"

Starbuck gave him a slow, dark smile. "You won't."

Starbuck was a rock of a man. He was sledge-shouldered, with lithe catlike reflexes, and taller than he appeared. His hair was sandy colored and his pale blue eyes took another man's measure in one swift glance. His gaze, now centered on Crocker, was steady and confident. The result was striking, somehow cold and very impersonal.

Crocker met and held his gaze. He was aware he'd underestimated the younger man. From all reports, Starbuck was a crackerjack detective; but those same reports indicated he was a mankiller, devoid of compassion or mercy when pushed beyond certain limits. After a moment's reflection, he was forced to admit Starbuck had a point. Today they wouldn't be dealing in vague abstractions. Their discussion, by necessity, would touch on the subject of death. That was something better left out of the record. A handshake would do very nicely.

"That's all, Higgins." He dismissed the secretary with a curt nod. "I'll call if I need you."

Higgins rose, looking slightly bemused, and walked from the room. There was a long, strained silence until the door closed. Then Crocker leaned back in the swivel chair, which creaked ominously under his weight.

"You're a cool one, Mr. Starbuck."

"No offense," Starbuck said woodenly. "A man in my line of work can't afford to take chances."

"I daresay," Crocker agreed, quickly moving on. "Now, as to the reason I asked you here. The Central Pacific has a problem with train robbers. I want it stopped."

"How serious a problem?"

"Very close to ruinous, Mr. Starbuck. Our express cars carry gold from the San Francisco mint and currency shipments from the banks throughout California. Over the past year we've been robbed on an average of twice a month. The losses, as you may well appreciate, have been staggering."

"No idea who's behind it?"

"None."

"The same gang every time?"

"We think so, but there's no way of knowing for certain."

"Any pattern?" Starbuck ventured. "Do they favor a certain section of the line? Or maybe strike at a certain time of the month?"

"Yes to both questions. More often than not they raid the southern line, somewhere between here and San Jose. As to timing, they *always* strike when we're carrying a large shipment."

"Always?" Starbuck regarded him with impassive curiosity. "Are you saying they know exactly which trains to hit?"

"I am, indeed," Crocker said in an aggrieved tone. "That's why I summoned you, Mr. Starbuck. We have a Judas in our midst—someone who supplies them with our shipment schedules. No matter what precautions we take—despite the utmost secrecy— they always know. Always!"

Starbuck's eyes were hard, questing. "What about your own security force? With the pattern established, they could've pulled a switch and waylaid the robbers."

Crocker looked painfully embarrassed. "We tried that on two separate occasions. In both instances, the train wasn't robbed."

"Your Judas tipped them off in advance?"

"Precisely."

"So you're asking me to ferret out the Judas?"

"The Judas," Crocker said, watching him carefully, "and the gang leader. I want it stopped—permanently."

A stony look settled on Starbuck's face. He'd heard the same message many times before. Always phrased discreetly, never in the form of a direct order, it was nonetheless obvious. Someone needed to be killed, and he was being asked to do the job. He gave Crocker an evaluating glance, then shrugged.

"I work at my own speed and I do it my own way. If I take the assignment, then I'll report directly to you and no one else."

"Does that include Tom Kelly, our security chief?"

"That includes everybody and anyone. Either our meeting today stays inside these four walls or I want no part of the deal. One little hint, and your Judas would most likely punch my ticket."

"Where would you begin?"

"Where it's least expected," Starbuck said stolidly. "I'll let you know after I've had a chance to nose around."

Crocker's expression was speculative. "How would you report to me?"

"Never here," Starbuck told him firmly. "I'll figure a way to get word to you. If it's necessary that we meet, then it'll have to be somewhere else. Somewhere damn private, and always by yourself."

"In other words, you would operate independently and keep me informed as it suits your pleasure. Is that essentially correct?"

"That's the way I work," Starbuck said levelly. "So far it's kept me alive."

"An admirable record," Crocker observed with a tinge of irony. "Now, as to your fee. I presume you have a standard rate?"

Starbuck had done his homework on the Central Pacific. In 1862, two companies were awarded federal charters to build a transcontinental railroad: the Union Pacific, building westward from the Missouri River, and the Central Pacific, building eastward from California. Crocker and three business cronies—Leland Stanford, Mark Hopkins, and Collis Huntington—were the sole stockholders of the Central Pacific. Thereafter, they were known as the Big Four, and with reason. The government granted them nine million acres of land, $24,000,000 in federal bonds, and no strings attached. For four years, three thousand Irishmen and ten thousand Chinese coolies labored to build their railroad. One of the end results was San Francisco's fabled Chinatown. The other was a separate construction company, which had exclusive rights to purchase material and build the

Central Pacific. Crocker and his cohorts, once again the sole stockholders, raised $79,000,000 in bonds and cash from the government and private investors. Of that amount, $36,000,000, not counting river frontage and ocean property, was siphoned off into their own pockets. The facts had slowly come to light, and now, in 1882, the holdings of the Big Four were conservatively estimated at $100,000,000 or more.

The newspapers of the day, never overly fond of robber barons, had characterized Crocker as "ruthless as a crocodile" and a man who believed in "the brute force of money." Having briefed himself on the Big Four in general, and Crocker in particular, Starbuck saw no reason to be charitable. He had come to the meeting fully prepared to deal with a crocodile, and he hadn't been disappointed. Then, too, having heard the assignment, he now had fewer qualms about holding Crocker's feet to the fire.

"One hundred dollars a day," Starbuck said at length. "All expenses paid and a minimum guarantee of a thousand dollars. That's my standard rate."

"Awfully steep, isn't it?" Crocker complained. "The Pinkerton Agency only charges half that amount."

"The Pinkertons won't do the job you want done, otherwise you would've hired them to start with."

"I'm afraid I don't follow you."

"It's simple enough," Starbuck said in a deliberate voice. "You want your Judas and the gang leader

killed. No arrest, no trial, just a couple of quick fu-
nerals and the less fanfare the better."

"I didn't say that."

"Naturally." Starbuck cracked a smile. "If you
had to say it, then I'd be the wrong man for the job.
Tell me it's not so and I'll head on back to Denver."

Crocker gave him a faint nod of satisfaction.
"Your terms are acceptable."

"I'll be in touch."

Starbuck heaved himself to his feet. Crocker rose
and they shook hands, staring gravely into each
other's eyes. Then, with no parting word, Starbuck
turned and walked out. He closed the door softly
behind him.

Crocker slumped back into his chair. His palms
were sweaty, and he breathed a heavy sigh of relief.
There for a moment, looking into Starbuck's eyes,
he had experienced the sensation of fear. He knew
it was justified, and he felt no shame.

He had the distinct impression he'd just struck a
bargain with the Devil himself.

CHAPTER 2

Starbuck arrived at the depot shortly before boarding time.

The morning train for Los Angeles departed at seven o'clock, and by his watch he had a quarter-hour to spare. He purchased a ticket for Salinas, then crossed the waiting room to the departure gate. He carried no luggage, but he was nonetheless prepared to travel. A Colt sixgun, hidden by his suit jacket, rode comfortably in a crossdraw holster.

Outside, he paused on the platform and pulled out the makings. He creased the paper, sprinkling tobacco, and rolled himself a smoke. A flick of his thumbnail struck a match and he lit the cigarette. Moving to one side, he propped himself up against a wall, quietly watchful. His eyes slowly scanned the crowded platform.

The San Francisco-to-Los Angeles run was clearly profitable. A large throng of passengers had already boarded, and others were saying their last goodbyes to family and well-wishers. Everyone looked perfectly ordinary, businessmen and drummers, working stiffs and farmers, and a dithering assortment of women and children. None of them appeared to be packing a gun, and there wasn't a suspicious face in the crowd. Insofar as he could determine, it was simply another day on the Central Pacific. Nothing out of place, no reason for alarm.

His attention moved to the train itself. There were four passenger coaches, normal for the morning run to Los Angeles. Down the line, the locomotive chuffed and belched steam. The tender was freshly loaded with coal, and directly behind, the last of the mail sacks were being loaded aboard the express car. A mail sorter and two guards, both armed with pistols, were visible through the door. Coupled to the rear of the train was a slat-sided boxcar. While unusual, for livestock was normally hauled by freight trains, its presence today was wholly unavoidable. The boxcar was part and parcel of Starbuck's plan.

On the platform, near the open door of the boxcar, a man stood smoking a pipe. He was tall and lanky, almost cadaverous in appearance, and he wore the rough-garbed clothing of a stockman. He was watching the crowd with no apparent interest, puffing cottony wads of smoke. His manner was somewhat resigned, almost bored. The look of a hired hand stuck with an unpleasant chore.

Starbuck sauntered over, the cigarette stuck in the corner of his mouth. He stopped in front of the man, nodding amiably.

"Howdy."

"Mornin'," the man replied. "Do something for you?"

"Well, neighbor, my curiosity's workin' overtime. Thought mebbe you'd oblige me by answerin' a question."

Starbuck easily slipped into the lingo of the range. His boots and wide-brimmed hat, the roll-your-own dangling from his lips, all did the trick. The man brightened and responded in the slow drawl common to south Texas.

"You're a long ways from home, ain't you?"

"For a fact," Starbuck grinned. "Hail from the Panhandle, couple of days ride north of San Angelo."

"Damnation! Ain't that one for the books! I'm from down around Laredo myself."

"Pegged you for a Texican! Yessir, I was standin' over there and I says to myself, that feller's got the look of homefolks. Figgered I'd just mosey over and see."

"Glad you did! Shore good to hear a man speak plain English again."

Starbuck held out his hand. "Name's Joe Dobbs."

"Hank Noonan." After pumping his arm, Noonan gave him a quizzical look. "What brings you out here?"

"Aww, just rubber-neckin'," Starbuck chuckled. "Fell into a little *dinero* and thought I'd take a gander at the ocean. Never seen one a'fore." He paused, took a drag on his cigarette. "What about your ownself?"

"Horse trainer." Noonan puffed importantly on his pipe. "Feller name of Crocker—owns this here very railroad—come down to the King spread a few years back and bought hisself a string of thoroughbreds. I was head wrangler there at the time and he hired me to wetnurse his stock. Been out here ever since."

"Got a nice outfit, does he?"

"Fair to middlin'," Noonan allowed. "Thousand acres or so down along the coast. But he's got an eye for racehorses, and the pay's good too."

"That's what got my curiosity whetted. Wondered why they had a stockcar hooked onto a passenger train."

"Have a looksee." Noonan jerked a thumb at the boxcar. "Takin' one of Crocker's mares down to a breedin' farm in the San Joaquin Valley. Him ownin' the railroad, he can pretty damn much do what he pleases. That's how come she wasn't put on a regular freight run."

Starbuck crushed his cigarette underfoot, then stuck his head through the boxcar door. A chestnut mare, haltered and tied in a stall, stood munching hay. His gaze shifted quickly around the car and abruptly stopped. He spotted an old saddle and some bridle gear piled near a water barrel. He grunted softly to himself, satisfied.

"Aboard! All aboard!"

The conductor's voice rang out in a last call to

passengers. Starbuck turned, clapping Noonan on the shoulder, and gave him a parting handshake. Then, as the Texan scrambled into the boxcar, he hurried forward. Bypassing the rear coaches, he walked along the platform. The train lurched and he swung aboard the first coach, directly behind the express car. The conductor gave him a dirty look and signaled the engineer. Moments later, the train gathered speed and rolled southward out of the switching yard.

Starbuck found a window seat toward the front of the coach. A sundries drummer was seated beside him, and they passed the next few minutes in idle conversation. Presently, a candy butcher came through hawking sweets and sandwiches. The drummer, commenting he'd missed breakfast, bought a ham and cheese that looked stale as sawdust. Then the conductor passed by, punching tickets, and announced an upcoming stop. Starbuck yawned a wide jaw-cracking yawn, and settled deeper into his seat. He pulled his hat down over his eyes, and left the drummer to his sandwich.

Feigning sleep, he mentally reviewed all he'd learned over the past three days. Even now, he was looking for holes in his plan, something he might have missed. However careful, no man was infallible. He'd made mistakes before, and he would likely make some this trip out. But in his view, that was no excuse for sloppy planning. He especially wanted no miscues today.

After his meeting with Crocker, he had holed up

in a seedy Mission District hotel. There, sprawled out on the bed, he had analyzed the various approaches he might take. On balance, he'd concluded that the place to start was with the robbers themselves. To go undercover within Central Pacific would have proved time-consuming, and perhaps not all that productive. The railroad's organization—the sheer number of people—was simply too vast and too segmented. It would have taken him weeks, maybe even months, to establish himself and work his way through the organization. The time span might have been shortened by limiting himself to upper-echelon departments; but that approach had serious drawbacks, as well. There were too many people, from clerks to vice-presidents, with access to express-car shipment schedules. And the Judas, obviously a slippery customer, would not be caught napping.

All in all, it seemed to Starbuck that the fastest and most direct approach was the gang itself. Once he identified the ringleader, and had him under surveillance, it wouldn't take long to isolate the Judas. Barring that, he could, as a last resort, pass himself off as a hardcase and infiltrate the gang. He'd done it with cattle rustlers and stage robbers, and he had no doubt it would work with train robbers. Yet that, too, would consume time—perhaps a month or longer—for outlaws were slow to accept a stranger into their ranks. By far, the better plan was to let the gang leader lay a trail to the Judas. Then, in a manner of speaking, he would kill two birds with one stone. Or at the very least, a couple of .45 slugs.

That much decided, Starbuck had contacted Crocker the next evening, slipping unobstrusively into his mansion on Nob Hill. He obtained a map of the Central Pacific railway lines and pinpointed the exact location of all previous robberies. A detailed study of the map proved illuminating. While a few of the holdups had occurred on the run to Sacramento, the majority had taken place in the fifty-mile stretch between San Francisco and the Santa Cruz Mountains. He put himself in the robbers' boots—a feat of mental gymnastics he'd learned as a manhunter—and arrived at a gut-certain hunch. The gang was quite probably operating from a hideout within a twenty-mile radius of Los Altos, a sleepy whistlestop some thirty miles south of San Francisco. Telegraph had improved communications among law officers, and the gang leader was clearly no dimwit. After pulling a holdup, the robbers had never been sighted, much less pursued. That strongly indicated they had a hideout that was within two hours' ride of the jobs they'd pulled to date. He determined that the first step was to unearth their hideout.

The following night he had again contacted Crocker and outlined his plan. An unusually large express shipment was to be arranged two days hence, on the morning train to Los Angeles. Everything was to appear routine, and standard security measures were to be employed. Crocker had bellyached long and loud, demanding extra guards to prevent loss of the money. Starbuck remained adamant, arguing that the gang must be lured into a holdup and thereby afford him the advantage of a fresh trail. In the end, common sense prevailed and he'd got his way. His last request, more so than the money, had brought on a fit of near apoplexy. Using some plausible cover story, one of Crocker's racehorses was to be shipped south on the same train. A hot shouting match ensued, but in that, too, he had prevailed. He left Crocker to work out the necessary subterfuge.

Now, scrunched down in his seat, he concluded he'd left nothing undone. All was in readiness, and it remained only for the gang to take the bait. Some inner voice told him he wouldn't be disappointed. He closed his eyes and almost instantly, like an animal, he was asleep.

The train passed through Los Altos an hour or so later. Awake and watchful, Starbuck began to wonder if he'd bet a loser. The next stop was San Jose, some twenty miles down the line. The gang, according to the information provided by Crocker, had never robbed a train south of San Jose. Which meant it had to happen soon or not at all.

Long ago, Starbuck had determined that outlaws were essentially lazy. For all their cunning, those who rode the owlhoot were unimaginative and generally possessed more balls than brains. Unlike highclass crooks, such as con men and grifters, the average desperado was a creature of habit. Unwittingly, because he was shiftless and indolent, he took the path of least resistance. Once he stumbled upon a method that worked, he seemed to fall into a rut, seldom attempting anything new or novel. A pattern invariably emerged, and his actions thereafter became somewhat predictable. All of which gave Starbuck reason for concern.

Unless the gang struck soon, his plan would very likely prove a washout. There was always tomorrow, and another plan, but he much preferred today. He prided himself on outguessing crooks—the first time around.

Starbuck's judgment was vindicated some five miles south of Los Altos. On a dogleg curve, a tree had been felled across the tracks. The engineer set the brakes and the train jarred to a screeching halt. The sudden jolt caught the passengers unawares, and there was a moment of pandemonium in the coaches. Women screamed and men cursed, and luggage from the overhead racks went flying down the aisle. Untangling themselves, the passengers were dazed and not a little fearful. Their voices verged on panic.

Then, suddenly, a collective hush fell over the coaches. A gang of masked riders burst out of the woods bordering the tracks. Four men rode directly to the express car, pouring a volley of shots through the door. The three remaining men, spurring their horses hard, charged up and down the track bed. Their pistols were cocked and pointed at the passengers, who stared open-mouthed through the coach windows. No shots were fired, but the message was clear: *Stay on the train or get killed*. Which made eminent good sense to the passengers. The Central Pacific, like most railroads, was not revered by the public. A holdup, according to common wisdom, was a matter between the railroad and the bandits. Only a fool would risk his life for the likes of the Big Four. And there were no fools aboard today.

Starbuck had a ringside seat. From his position in the front of the coach, the four men outside the express car were plainly visible. Watching them, he had to admire their no-nonsense approach to train robbery. One of the riders produced a stick of dynamite and held the fuse only inches away from the tip of a lighted cigar. Another rider, his voice raised in a commanding shout, then informed the express guards that they had a choice: *Open the door or get blown to Kingdom Come!*

The guards, much like the passengers, were unwilling to die for the Central Pacific. The door slid open and the guards dutifully tossed their pistols onto the track bed. Three of the robbers dismounted and clambered inside the express car. The other three, still menacing the passengers with pointed guns, held their positions outside the coaches. The seventh man, the one with the foghorn voice, directed the operation from aboard his horse. His tone had the ring of authority, brusque and demanding. His attitude was that of a man accustomed to being obeyed.

Starbuck immediately tagged him as the gang leader. He looked to be of medium height, powerfully built, and he was dressed in the nondescript workclothes worn by the other men. A slouch hat covered his head, and a wide bandanna, pulled up over his nose, effectively masked his features. Yet, upon closer observation, Starbuck spotted something that couldn't be hidden. A thatch of red hair, brilliant orangey-red, spilled out from beneath the slouch hat. Bright as a sunset, it was a head of hair that would stand out in any crowd.

From start to finish, the holdup took less than five minutes. The robbers inside the express car emerged with mail sacks stuffed full of cash and quickly mounted their horses. On signal from their leader, the gang opened fire and raked the length of the train with a barrage of lead. The shots were purposely placed high, but windows shattered and wall panels splintered and the angry snarl of bullets ripped through the coaches. Everyone dove for the floor and prudently stayed there. A moment later the gunfire ceased and the thud of hoofbeats drummed the earth.

Starbuck peeked over the windowsill just as the gang disappeared into the woods. He jumped to his feet, hopping over the drummer, and moved through the door. Outside, he went down the coach steps and sprinted toward the rear of the train. Not ten seconds elapsed from the last gunshot to the time he pulled up in front of the boxcar. He hammered on the door with his fist.

"Noonan! Hank Noonan! Open up!"

"Who's there?"

"Joe Dobbs! C'mon, get the lead out! It's life or death!"

"Hold on, Joe!" The door flew open and Noonan gaped down at him with a look of fright. "Lord God A'mighty, they didn't shoot you, did—"

Starbuck showed him a cocked sixgun. "Hank, I want you to listen real close and do exactly what I say. Savvy?"

Noonan bobbed his head, eyes popped out like a pair of fried eggs. Following Starbuck's instructions, he muscled the loading ramp to the door and dropped it into place. Starbuck climbed inside, noting out of the corner of his eye that a crowd of men had gathered around the express car. He ordered Noonan to saddle the mare. The Texan suddenly pulled up, his features twisted in a mulish frown.

"No sir!" he muttered hotly. "You ain't gonna steal—"

Starbuck wagged the snout of the sixgun. "Don't play hero, *compadre*. Just get it done—*muy pronto!*"

Grumbling under his breath, Noonan went to work. He saddled the mare, afterward fitting the bit into her mouth and slipping the bridle over her head. Then he backed her out of the stall and walked her to the door. With an unpleasant grunt, he tossed the reins to Starbuck.

"I dunno your game, but you shore picked the wrong horse. Old man Crocker's gonna hang your ass a mile high."

"Obliged for the warning, Hank. Now step aside and don't make any sudden moves."

Starbuck holstered his gun and looped the reins around the mare's neck. He stepped into the saddle, tugged at the brim of his hat, and gave Noonan a sardonic smile. Then he feathered the mare in the ribs and reined her down the loading ramp. Once clear of the track bed, he gigged her hard and rode off at a gallop.

A moment later he vanished into the trees.

CHAPTER 3

The chase lasted almost three hours.

From the outset, it was apparent to Starbuck that he'd underestimated the gang leader. He had expected a furious dash, speed rather than deception. That view had been reinforced when the job was pulled scarcely five miles south of Los Altos. An hour's hard ride, on a direct beeline to the hideout, was how he had visualized it upon taking the trail. He'd never been more wrong.

Instead of a beeline, the robbers zigzagged all over the countryside. A mile or so north of the holdup scene, they suddenly changed course and circled west of Los Altos. In the process, they crisscrossed several creeks, and at one point held their horses to mid-stream for something more than a half-mile. Then they switched directions and again turned due north. Their path, however, was meandering and uncannily deceptive.

At all times, the gang warily avoided open

ground. While they never doubled back, they stuck to redwood forests and scrub-choked hills wherever possible. Upon encountering lowlands, they veered off into rocky defiles latticed with brushy undergrowth. Their general direction was always north, but the winding route followed a network of harsh and seemingly predetermined obstacles. Quite clearly, they knew the terrain and had developed evasive stratagems to throw off pursuit. To all but a skilled tracker, their trail would have been lost within a few miles.

Starbuck's years as a manhunter served him well. Early on in his career, he had worked solely as a range detective. His principal targets were cattle rustlers and horse thieves, men schooled in plains lore and the artful dodges of hiding a trail. By necessity, he had become a tracker of surpassing skill, able to read signs practically invisible to the naked eye. Today, those skills permitted him to follow a crazy-quilt path that would have defeated ordinary lawmen. Several times he lost sight of the gang, but he never lost their trail. He stuck to their tracks like a born Apache.

An hour into the chase Starbuck realized he had committed another error. Having underestimated the gang leader, he had thoughtlessly compounded the problem by choosing the wrong mount. The thoroughbred mare was built for speed, not endurance. Unlike common saddle horses, she had no bottom, no staying power over the long haul. North of Los Altos she began to play out, and he had no choice

but to conserve her stamina. His pace was slowed
even further, and with each passing mile, he found
himself falling farther behind. Once again, his ability
to read sign and track on hard ground kept him in
the race.

Yet, for all his skill, he barely avoided disaster in
the end. Shortly after midday, he was tracking
through a low range of mountains. His eyes were on
broken twigs and crushed vegetation, and the sign
indicated he was perhaps twenty minutes behind the
gang. He topped a ridge, and spread out before him
the mountains dropped off to a rolling plain. At the
bottom of the ridge was a creek, bordered by trees,
and on the far side was a farmhouse and a small
barn. For a moment, looking down with surprise,
nothing registered. Then he saw the corral, and the
horses. And gathered outside the farmhouse, a group
of men.

Suddenly it dawned on him that he was skylined.
Wondering if he'd been seen, he sawed at the reins
and whipped the mare back over the ridge. A short
distance north, he dismounted and left the mare tied
in a grove of trees. He walked quickly to the ridge,
removing his hat, and went belly down. Below, not
a hundred yards away, he had a commanding view
of the farmhouse. The men were still bunched near
the front door, and there was no apparent sign of
alarm. He thought it was his lucky day. Goddamned
lucky!

A closer look confirmed that the chase had indeed
ended. He spotted the red-haired gang leader, clearly

a standout even at a distance. The men were gathered around a water pump, taking turns sluicing off the grime of a long and dusty ride. Apparently in good humor, their leader was gesturing and talking in a loud voice. The sound of laughter carried distinctly to the ridge top.

Starbuck's attention was abruptly drawn to the corral. He saw a man, dressed in bib overalls, forking hay to the horses. A quick count verified that he was not one of the original seven who had robbed the train. Upon closer inspection, Starbuck realized there was more to the farm than he'd seen at first glance. Beyond the house, several acres were fenced and planted with a variety of vegetables. Off in the distance, a herd of some twenty dairy cows grazed placidly in the noonday sun. No hardscrabble operation, the farm had a look of substance and prosperity. The abundance of produce, and the presence of milk cows, meant only one thing. There was a marketplace nearby, probably no more than a few hours' ride away.

A woman suddenly stepped through the doorway of the house and called to the men. She wore a checkered apron, and from her scolding manner, Starbuck sensed she was summoning the men to a hot meal. For the first time, he noticed the mail sacks piled beside the door. As the gang trooped inside, the burly redhead and another man each hefted one of the sacks. From all appearances, more than a hot meal would be divvied up over the dinner table.

Something bothered Starbuck about the setup. A

dairy farmer and his wife seemed unlikely accomplices for a band of train robbers. Nor was the farm itself the hideout he'd expected to find. One somehow didn't dovetail with the other.

The thought prompted another question. He wondered where the hell he was. He had some general idea, for he knew the chase had carried him far north of Los Altos. But he had no notion of where it had ended, or exactly how far north.

He pulled the map from his inside coat pocket and spread it on the ground. Turning, he studied the mountain range, noting rises in elevation and dominant peaks. With one eye on the terrain, he slowly scanned the map. Suddenly he blinked and his finger jabbed at a spot that marked the flatland below. The farm was on the western slope of the San Bruno Mountains, roughly in the center of the peninsula. The hairpin bend in the creek pinpointed his precise location.

He was less than ten miles south of San Francisco.

The sheer audacity of it was stunning. No one would believe a gang of train robbers would operate that close to a major city. Nor would anyone suspect that a tranquil dairy farm was an outlaw hideout. It took the cake for nerve, and it proved that there was always an exception to any rule. The red-haired gang leader not only had a big set of balls; he had brains, as well. The whole operation had been planned with a sort of tactical genius.

On impulse, Starbuck was struck by another of his hunches. The farmhouse was a rendezvous, not a hideout. A meeting place and a way station for the horses. A stopover for the gang before they rode on to somewhere else.

He smiled, nodding to himself, and returned the map to his coat pocket. Then he settled down to wait.

A short time later Starbuck got still another surprise. The train robbers, followed by the farmer, emerged from the house. Yet they were now an altogether different group of men. Their workclothes had been exchanged for city suits and bowler hats; the transformation was startling. No longer was there any resemblance to the gang that had stopped the morning train.

The barn doors were opened and two carriages were rolled outside. A team of bays and a team of chestnuts were then led from the barn and hitched to the carriages. Four men climbed aboard the first carriage and took off along a wagon trail that snaked westward. The gang leader and the others waited, talking quietly amongst themselves, until some ten minutes had passed. Then they stepped into the second carriage, waving to the farmer, and drove off in the same direction. To all appearances, they might have been businessmen or land speculators, or even a crew of Bible salesmen canvassing the countryside. By no stretch of the imagination would anyone connect them to the train holdup.

Starbuck quickly checked his map. He located the wagon trail and saw that it intersected a main road, running north-south along the peninsula. The only other road, some miles to the west, skirted the coastline. There were fishing villages along the ocean, and a few small settlements dotted the bay side of the peninsula; all the land in between appeared to be sparsely populated, mainly farms. The relative isolation of the area merely enhanced his respect for the gang. Their rendezvous point, though close to San Francisco, was nonetheless remote. The concept was masterful and the execution flawless. The work of a man who knew his business, a professional.

Waiting until the carriage was out of sight, Starbuck mounted the mare and rode north. He forded the stream a mile or so above the farmhouse, then turned due west. Presently he crested a rise of ground and spotted the main road. He walked the mare to a grove of trees, staying hidden in the shadows, and rolled himself a smoke. Before he had time to finish his cigarette, the carriage appeared from the south. The gang's destination, much as he'd suspected, was San Francisco. Allowing them a five-minute lead, he left the trees and reined the mare toward the road.

He easily kept the carriage in sight.

Once inside the city limits, Starbuck was able to close the gap. By then it was late afternoon, and he was just another horseman on streets clogged with traffic. He had no fixed plan in mind, but he'd set himself a task that was essential to any further action. Before the night was out, he meant to establish the gang leader's identity.

The carriage led him across town, to the intersection of Jackson and Sansome. There, the team and carriage were dropped off at a livery stable. He dismounted, hitching the mare outside a saloon on the opposite corner. The four men in the first carriage were nowhere in evidence, but that gave him no reason for concern. After a robbery, very likely wearing money belts stuffed with cash, it figured they would scatter. Shortly, the thought was confirmed when the burly redhead talked with the two men a moment, then waved and walked off. He turned north on Sansome.

Starbuck followed, strolling casually along the opposite side of the street. The sidewalks were thronged with passersby, and he readily blended into the crowd. Having spent three days in San Francisco, he'd gotten his bearings, and the direction of the surveillance came as no great surprise. The gang leader was moving at a brisk pace toward the Barbary Coast.

A hellhole, infamous throughout the world, the Barbary Coast was not for those of faint heart. On the bay side, it was bounded by the waterfront and Telegraph Hill, and extended several blocks inland along Pacific and Broadway streets. A wild carnival of depravity and crime, the area was devoted to dancehalls and brothels, gambling casinos and groggeries, and sinister crimping joints where sailors were drugged and shanghaied for brutal voyages at sea. Vice and debauchery were the district's stock-in-trade.

Local legend attributed the name to the African coastline of earlier notoriety. Whatever its ancestry, the Barbary Coast transformed the dreams of sailors and landlubbers alike into wicked, and sometimes deadly, reality. On average, there were several murders a night, with seamen the most common victims. After voyages lasting two to four years, the sailors were ripe for women, alcohol, and some of the gamier pursuits known to man. The Opera Comique, a dive billing carnal entertainment, presented live shows involving feats of copulation that ranged from acrobatic couples to onstage orgies. Not to be outdone, the Boar's Head staged a show-stopper in which the buxom star was mated on alternate nights to a Shetland pony and bull mastiff. No man, however low his tastes, failed to get his money's worth on the Barbary Coast.

Starbuck trailed the gang leader to the Bella Union. A somewhat higher-class establishment, it was located at an intersection humorously dubbed Murder Corner. Offering all things to all men, it provided women, gaming tables, and risqué stage shows. A billboard out front ballyhooed the attractions inside:

PLAIN TALK AND BEAUTIFUL GIRLS!
Lovely Tresses! Lovely Lips! Buxom Forms!
At the
BELLA UNION.
And Such Fun!
If You Don't Want to Risk Both Optics
SHUT ONE EYE.

The batwing doors opened onto a large barroom and gaming parlor. Beyond the bar was a spacious theater, with an orchestra pit and a stage ablaze with footlights. The floor was jammed with tables, and a horseshoe balcony was partitioned into ornate, curtained boxes. Songs and dances were performed, pandering to the profane nature of the clientele, and the atmosphere fell somewhere between licentious and obscene. After their acts, the girls mingled with the customers in a crush of jiggling breasts and fruity buttocks. The sofas in the boxes were reserved for private entertainment, and along with the mandatory bottle of champagne, added greatly to the income of all concerned. A pretty little *danseuse* from the show went for a ten spot, and chilled bubbly doubled the tab. The girl kept half the charge for her services and the balance went to the house.

Sunset was still an hour away, but the Bella Union was already jam-packed. Starbuck shouldered a place at the bar, wedging himself in between a bow-legged sailor and a whiskery miner. He ordered rye and kept one eye on the red-haired robber, who had taken a position at the end of the bar. A close-up look revealed that the man was ugly as a toad, with pockmarked features, nut-brown eyes, and freckles almost the exact color of his hair. Starbuck committed his face to memory.

So far the gang leader had spoken to no one but the bartender. He stood with his elbows hooked over the counter and watched the show with a vacant expression. Onstage, a screeching troupe of dancers was romping through a version of the French *can-can*. Their frilly drawers and black mesh stockings exploded into view as they went into the finale and flung themselves rump first to the floor in *la split*. Then, screaming and tossing their skirts, they leaped to their feet and raced offstage as the curtain dropped. The spectators rewarded them with thunderous applause, which prompted a caterwauling curtain call. Then, awaiting the next act, everyone went back to drinking.

On his second shot of rye, Starbuck saw the gang leader straighten up and nod to someone pushing through the crowd. The man who joined him was stocky and muscular, with a square, tough face and a handlebar mustache. He was dressed like a dandy and carried himself with the cocky poise of a prize-fighter. He spoke to the gang leader, who beamed a wide grin, and rapidly bobbed his head. The transformation in the train robber was immediate, and curiously out of character. He looked not just respectful, but somehow servile. A hardass bandit suddenly turned boot-licker.

Starbuck signaled for another drink. While the barkeep was pouring, he ducked his chin toward the end of the counter. "Shore wouldn't wanna tangle with that pair."

The barkeep followed his gaze, and chuckled. "You'd sure as Christ regret it if you did, cowboy."

"Why? They somebody special?"

"Well, the one with the mustache is Denny O'Brien. Owns the Bella Union and half the Coast.

The other one's Red Ned Adair, and claims he's meaner'n tiger spit. For my money, they both are."

"I don't reckon I'd care to argue it either way."

"You've got lots of company, cowboy."

The barkeep hustled off, and Starbuck silently repeated the names to himself. Then he saw the one named O'Brien turn and walk toward a staircase near the entranceway to the theater. The gang leader downed his drink and quickly followed along. Together, they mounted the stairs and disappeared from view.

Starbuck had a visceral instinct for the truth, some sixth sense for divining what lay beneath the surface. He was suddenly struck by the thought that the operation was bigger than he'd suspected. Quite probably an organized mob, with Denny O'Brien calling the shots and Red Ned Adair pulling the holdups. Something told him it was so, and he'd learned long ago never to go against his instincts.

He decided it was time to go undercover.

CHAPTER 4

Early the next morning Starbuck set out to explore San Francisco. His knowledge of the city was thus far general, and what he needed now was specifics. Every town, much like a timepiece, had inner working forever hidden to the casual observer. He meant to determine Denny O'Brien's place within the underworld mechanism.

Last night, upon leaving the Bella Union, his thoughts were disjointed and without order. He knew essentially what must be done, but he hadn't yet decided *how* it would be done. With some stealth, he had retrieved the mare and left her tied in the courtyard of Crocker's mansion. All the way back down Nob Hill, he had puzzled over the new turn of events. By the time he reached his hotel, he'd arrived at what seemed a logical first step. Before going undercover, he had to establish who was who on the Barbary Coast, and where the owner of the Bella Union fitted into the larger picture. Only then could he develop a workable approach to Denny O'Brien.

Today, like a wolf prowling unfamiliar territory, he made a personal reconnaissance of downtown San Francisco. The sporting crowd seldom awakened before noon, so he spent the morning on a sightseeing tour. He crisscrossed the Barbary Coast, gaining a sense of direction and a feel for the lay of the land. The seedier dives along the waterfront were of little interest, but the larger establishments, located primarily on Pacific and Broadway, held his attention. These were the joints that competed directly with the Bella Union, and he catalogued them for future reference. In the course of his wanderings, he gave Chinatown a brief once-over, then turned uptown. There, somewhat to his surprise, he found still another vice district. Though tightly contained, and considerably smaller than the Barbary Coast, it had the look of flourishing nightlife. He thought to himself that it merited further investigation.

By noontime, he'd seen enough to satisfy his immediate needs. The saloons were open, and he made his way back to the Barbary Coast. He picked a watering hole directly across from the Bella Union, one with a crowd of heavy drinkers and careless talkers. A schooner of beer entitled him to a free lunch, and he helped himself to cold cuts and cheese from the trencherman's counter. Then he bellied up to the bar and went to work.

A master of subtle interrogation, Starbuck had the knack of engaging total strangers in conversation. He was a good listener, and seemed raptly interested in the other man's opinion. He also played on their vanity, professing ignorance of the subject at hand, and got them to reveal more than they realized. With adroit prompting, he kept them talking and guilefully steered the conversation along the course he'd planned. When they parted, he had drained them dry of information while saying almost nothing about himself. He left them full of boozy good cheer and a profound sense of their own importance.

Before three o'clock, Starbuck had hit four saloons. At each stop he put away several schooners of beer and generously stood drinks for those he gulled into conversation. He talked with bartenders and pimps, gamblers and street-corner grifters, and one old barfly who supplied a wealth of Barbary Coast gossip. When he walked out of the fourth saloon, he had unearthed everything and more he'd hoped to learn. His view of San Francisco's underworld was by no means complete, but he knew who was who and precisely what it was they controlled. And with one possible exception, he had their names.

The city was split into three very distinct areas of vice and crime. There was a fine line of demarcation separating the areas, almost as though the boundaries had been staked and mapped. Curiously, there was no spillover of activities, even though the three areas abutted one another like wedges sliced from a pie. The city government, from the mayor's office down to the corner policeman, turned a blind eye to the whole affair. The payoffs, everyone agreed, had made rich men of those in public service.

Denny O'Brien was the acknowledged boss of the Barbary Coast. Nothing happened without his sanction, and he maintained a squad of plug-uglies to enforce his demands. He collected a percentage off the top, and no operation was too small to escape his attention. Even the lowly crib whores and crimp joints paid tribute.

His counterpart in Chinatown was Fung Jing Toy. A tong leader and supreme vice lord, he ran Chinatown with godlike impunity. His *boo how doy* hatchet men collected fees from all underworld enterprises, including gambling, opium dens, and bordellos. He also extorted protection money from legitimate businesses, using intimidation and threats of violence. Finally, with all his rivals killed or whipped into line, he controlled the market in Chinese slave girls. The trade reportedly did a brisk business with Occidental and Oriental alike.

There remained only the area Starbuck had surveyed late that morning. Known as the Uptown Tenderloin, it was a district reserved for swells and the upper strata of San Francisco society. Theaters and opulent restaurants vied with cabarets and plush gambling casinos for the gentry trade. The nightlife was almost decorous, the only exception being the high-priced parlor houses. Discreet madams and beautiful whores served the monied class with all the attention accorded the master of a harem. A parlor-house whore was the *crème de la crème* of her trade, and a bright girl occasionally snared herself a millionaire. According to those who knew, more than one matron on Nob Hill had begun her career in the Tenderloin.

Yet there was an apparent contradiction to the Uptown Tenderloin. All afternoon Starbuck had tactfully posed the same question: Who controls the Tenderloin? Each time the question was asked, he'd drawn a blank. The men in the Barbary Coast saloons had scratched their heads and appeared stumped. So far as they knew, the Tenderloin had no boss. Something of a neutral zone, it seemed to run itself. The police kept it cordoned off for the gentry, and the lowlifes avoided it on threat of a billy club upside the head and a night in jail. The playground of the rich, it was thought to be immune to the overtures of crime bosses and vice lords.

Starbuck thought otherwise. A suspicion began to form sometime that afternoon. Vague at first, it slowly blossomed, and by the time he walked from the fourth saloon, it had taken form. Despite all he'd heard, he believed there was most definitely a boss of the Tenderloin. Further, he thought it quite likely that the same man was the underworld czar of San Francisco. An overlord who dictated to both Denny O'Brien and Fung Jing Toy.

He'd seen it happen closer to home. For the past decade, a shadowy, unobtrusive man named Lou Blomger had ruled Denver from behind the scenes. It made sense that a similar situation existed in San Francisco, where the pickings were riper and vice even more prevalent. The temptation was simply too

great. With the amount of money involved, someone
who dealt in grand schemes would have built himself
an underworld empire. That he stayed out of the
limelight, operating in the dark, made it no less real.
To Starbuck, it seemed undeniable, chiseled in stone.
All he had to do was prove it.

However it turned out, everything he'd learned
had merely reinforced his original thought. The place
to start was Denny O'Brien. He even had a cover
story in mind, and instinct told him the Barbary
Coast boss would go for it bait and all. From there,
it was simply a matter of allowing nature to take its
course. Red Ned Adair had the balls, and Denny
O'Brien called the shots, but they both danced to
another man's tune. Time, and a bit of luck, would
reveal his name.

That evening Starbuck caught the night train for
Los Angeles.

The city of angels was somewhat provincial and
backwoodsy compared to San Francisco. Yet, while
it lacked a cosmopolitan flavor, Los Angeles was
nonetheless prosperous. Certain shops in the downtown area catered to those with money to burn. However excessive the demand, a man willing to pay the
price could indulge almost any whim. All within a
matter of hours.

Starbuck went directly from the train station to a
men's haberdashery. He knew little about Los Angeles itself, but he had developed contacts throughout the West. In his business, the tools of the trade

were dictated by the nature of the case, and time was often a factor. From his contacts, he knew where to go and who to see, no matter how strange the request. While he could have satisfied the same needs in San Francisco, it might very well have compromised the case. Secrecy and a whole new identity were essential to his plan. He would depart Los Angeles a different man from the one who had arrived on the morning train. And no one in San Francisco the wiser.

At the haberdashery, Starbuck spoke privately with the proprietor. He indicated that money was no object, so long as the service met his demands. He wanted a complete wardrobe—expensive clothes with the look of hand-tailored garments—and he wanted it no later than four o'clock that afternoon. The proprietor, with a nose for profit, assured him the deadline was no problem.

A clerk materialized at Starbuck's elbow, and a tailor was summoned from the back room. Under the proprietor's watchful eye, an array of clothing was selected from the racks and paraded before Starbuck for his approval. He chose four single-breasted suits, all fashionably cut and dazzling in color, ranging from pearl-gray to lush chocolate. He next selected several brocaded vests, gaudy to the extreme and color-coordinated with the suits. Then he picked out ruffled linen shirts, cravats and string ties, and a half-dozen sets of silk underwear. A brown derby and a gray fedora, along with three pairs of kidskin boots, were added to the pile. His last purchase was a matched set of hand-rubbed leather luggage.

A meticulous fitting session followed. One at a time, Starbuck changed into the suits and stood before a full-length mirror. The tailor, his mouth stuffed full of pins, took a nip here and a tuck there. When he finished, the suit jackets and trousers draped perfectly, with the rich appearance of clothes crafted stitch by stitch. Once more in his old suit, Starbuck paid the bill and added an extra hundred for good measure. The proprietor, bowing profusely, escorted him to the door. His wardrobe would be packed and waiting at the appointed time.

On the street, Starbuck hailed a hanson cab and gave the driver the name of a local dentist. Pleased with his progress thus far, he rolled himself a smoke and settled back in the seat. He'd spent somewhat more time than intended at the haberdashery, and he quickly calculated the cash left in his money belt. He judged the amount—$3,000—adequate for what remained to be done. If not, then he would wire his bank in Denver and arrange a speedy transfer of funds. Bankers, very much like whores, would always accommodate their select clientele.

Starbuck worked at his profession by choice rather than need. He was a man of considerable means, with a portfolio of municipal bonds and commercial real estate valued in excess of $250,000 on the open market. Not quite two years ago, he had inherited the largest cattle spread in the Texas Panhandle. The owner of the ranch, who was his closest friend and something of a surrogate father, had no family and had therefore designated him sole heir. Forced to choose between ranching and the detective business, he'd found it to be no contest. He sold the ranch for $200,000 and worked out an arrangement whereby the bank would manage his holdings for a fixed fee. So far, he had no complaints. The bank had shown a respectable return on his investments, and the financial independence enabled him to accept only those cases that piqued his interest. His net worth was a matter he thought of only rarely. He considered manhunting a far more rewarding endeavor.

The dentist was a slender man, completely bald, with innocent brown eyes. After being ushered into his office, Starbuck explained precisely what he had in mind. He wanted a gold sleeve fitted over his right front tooth, and anchored securely. Once in place, he concluded, it must appear to be a genuine gold tooth.

"A fake tooth?" the dentist asked, as if he couldn't have heard correctly. "You want a fake *gold* tooth?"

"A fake tooth," Starbuck corrected, "that looks like the real article."

"Why?" the dentist said, bewildered. "To what purpose?"

Starbuck smiled. "Ask me no questions and I'll tell you no lies. Can you do it?"

"I suppose so"—the dentist shrugged, eyebrows raised—"assuming you're willing to pay the price."

"How much?"

"A hundred dollars, plus the cost of the gold."

"Done." Starbuck pulled out his wallet. "One

more thing. It has to be ready by four this afternoon."

"Impossible! I'll need at least a week."

Starbuck extracted three hundred-dollar bills from
his wallet and spread them on the desk. "A day's
work for a week's pay. Interested?"

The dentist pocketed the bills and pointed to a
high-backed operating chair. "Have a seat. I'll have
to take some measurements."

"You come highly recommended, Doc. Don't disappoint me."

"Recommended by whom?"

"Like I said, ask me no questions—"

"Very well, no more questions. Let's get on with
it."

Starbuck moved to the chair and seated himself.
The dentist selected several instruments from a cab-
inet, then pried Starbuck's mouth open and began
taking measurements. Ten minutes later he walked
from the office and flagged another hansom cab.

The next stop on Starbuck's itinerary was a posh
jewelry store. His shopping list was itemized, though
flexible, and the purchases required only a few
minutes. He selected a diamond pinky ring, with a
stone only slightly smaller than a sugar cube. Then
he chose a garish horseshoe-shaped diamond stickpin, with matching cuff links. His last purchase was
a diamond-studded pocketwatch the size of a teacup.
When the lid was opened, it chimed a musical ren-
dition of *"Darling Clementine."*

There was no haggling, and he again paid in bills

of large denominations. He stuffed the new watch into his vest pocket and threaded the heavy gold chain through a buttonhole. The old watch, along with the other items, were casually dropped into his jacket pocket. The jeweler watched the whole procedure with an expression of bemused wonder. He was still clutching a fistful of hundred-dollar bills when Starbuck hurried out the door.

One last stop completed Starbuck's shopping spree. The store was located on a sidestreet, with a small wooden sign pegged to the wall. The gunsmith's name was John Bohannon, and his work was known to lawman and outlaw alike. He was a master craftsman of the concealed weapon.

The inside of the store looked like an ordnance depot. The walls were lined with pistols of every description, and a double-shelved showcase was filled with pocket derringers and cut-down revolvers. Bohannon rose from a workbench at the rear of the store and moved to the showcase. He was a short, rotund man, with a shock of white hair and metal-framed glasses that magnified his eyes like a telescope. He greeted Starbuck genially.

"Afternoon. What can I do for you today?"

"I need a couple of guns," Starbuck told him. "One belly-gun and one hideout, the smaller the better."

"What caliber?" Bohannon asked pleasantly. "I've got everything from twenty-two to forty-five."

Starbuck's mouth curled. "Large enough to stop a man when he's centered the first shot."

Bohannon's eyes gleamed behind the bottle-thick glasses. "I take it you're an experienced shootist?"

"I generally hit the mark."

"Then something in forty-one ought to do the trick."

Bohannon bent over the showcase and took out a Colt Lightning. Only recently introduced, the revolver was double-action and fired a .41-caliber slug. The barrel and ejector rod had been trimmed to three inches. For a hideout gun, he suggested the Colt New House Model. A stubby five-shot revolver, it was chambered for .38 caliber. The birdshead grip was framed with ivory handles, and the sheathed trigger was activated by cocking the hammer. The barrel length was one and a half inches, and the entire gun could be covered by a normal handspan.

Starbuck handled the guns, testing them for balance and smoothness of action. The workmanship was flawless, and he quickly approved both selections. Bohannon outfitted him with a shoulder holster for the Lightning, and a clip-on boot holster for the hideout gun. A box of cartridges for each gun completed the deal, and Starbuck gladly forked over nearly two hundred dollars. They shook hands and parted, never once having exchanged names.

Outside, Starbuck checked his new timepiece. The watch chimed three and merrily trilled "Darling Clementine." He smiled and mentally reminded himself to wire Mattie Silks, a Denver madam who owed him a favor. Once the message was sent, all that remained was to collect his wardrobe and the gold tooth. His disguise was set and his cover story would bear scrutiny. The northbound train departed at six, and from there it was on to San Francisco and his next stop.

The Barbary Coast and Denny O'Brien.

CHAPTER 5

Starbuck arrived at the Palace Hotel late the next morning. A doorman approached, but he bounded down from the hansom cab without assistance. Slipping the man a five spot, he jerked his thumb at his luggage. Then he stepped back, craning his head upward, and ogled the architecture.

Considered San Francisco's finest, the hotel was a structure of Olympian proportions. The building occupied an entire city block, and construction costs were reported to have exceeded $5,000,000. The entrance-way was an immense courtyard, surrounded by galleries lofting seven stories high. Overhead, a domed skylight flooded the courtyard with a brilliant rainbow of colors. Already a legend to world travelers, the Palace was a home-away-from-home for visiting royalty and other people of wealth.

With the doorman at his heels, Starbuck swept into the lobby. He was attired in a getup of spectacular vulgarity. He wore a pearl-gray suit, with a

sapphire-blue cravat and a brocaded vest to match.
Diamonds sparkled from his ring and cuff links and
stickpin with tawdry opulence. A cigar was wedged
in the corner of his mouth, and his gold tooth
gleamed like a lighthouse beacon.

Halfway to the front desk he suddenly stopped.
The lobby floor was paved with silver dollars set in
dark marble, and he gazed down on the sight with a
look of pop-eyed wonder. The fashionably dressed
men and women strolling through the lobby meanwhile paused and stared at him like a sideshow freak
escaped from a circus. An interval of absolute silence stretched to several moments. Then, with a
loud snort, he shook his head.

"Jeeezus Christ! Flat knocks your eyes out!"

Puffing clouds of smoke, he munched his cigar
and proceeded across the lobby. He halted at the
desk and knuckled his fedora onto the back of his
head at a rakish angle. Grinning broadly, he nodded
to the clerk.

"Harry Lovett's the name. I want the classiest
suite you've got."

The clerk peered down his nose. "Do you have a
reservation, sir?"

"Hell, no!" Starbuck trumpeted. "Harry Lovett
don't need no reservation. Now hop to it, sonny! Fix
me up, and none of your sass."

The clerk flushed and quickly produced a registration card. Starbuck signed his alias with a bold
stroke and then dropped the pen on the desk. With

obvious distaste, the clerk picked up the card and studied it at length.

"Have you stayed with us before, Mr. Lovett?"

"Nope," Starbuck said briskly. "This here's my first trip to Frisco."

The clerk flinched. Only seamen and people of low station referred to the city by the bay as "Frisco." By his expression, it was apparent he had already relegated Harry Lovett to that category. He tapped the registration card on his fingertips.

"One moment, please."

Turning away, he walked to a door at the end of the desk. A small sign identified the room beyond as the manager's office. He knocked softly and entered. Starbuck rolled the cigar to the opposite side of his mouth and looked bored. Then he noticed a stack of brochures on the counter, emblazoned with the hotel's name. He took one off the top and made a show of moving his lips while he read.

The brochure, meant to delight and inform, was a compendium of statistical trivia. Built by William Ralston, one of the city's leading industrialists, the Palace was an eclectic blend of rococo Victorian and ornate Louis XV. The hotel could accommodate twelve hundred guests and there was a fireplace in every room. A total of twenty thousand silver dollars were inset into the lobby floor, and there were nine hundred cuspidors scattered throughout the hotel. A hallmark of service, there were four hundred thirty-nine bathrooms, which provided the luxury of one bathroom for every 2.7 guests. In keeping with the overall decor, the toilet seats were specially crafted by Chippendale, that most revered of British imports. The cost of the toilet seats alone exceeded—

Starbuck stopped reading. He thought to himself he really wasn't out of place at the Palace. He was acting the part of a coarse, loud-mouthed vulgarian. The hotel, bragging about its toilet seats, was somewhat in the same league. For all their pretensions, the rich crowd wasn't above flaunting their built-for-a-king crappers.

The office door opened and the room clerk bustled forward. He stopped and carefully laid the card on the desk. His expression was dour.

"Mr. Lovett, the manager has asked me to inform you of hotel policy. A guest who hasn't stayed with us previously is required to pay at least two days in advance. As you can appreciate, our suites are commodious and therefore quite expensive. So if you would care to look elsewhere—"

"Sounds fair." Starbuck took out his wallet and fanned ten one-hundred dollars bills across the counter. "A thousand ought to do for openers. You tell me when that runs out and I'll pony up some more."

The clerk sighed and reluctantly scooped the bills into a cash drawer. Without a word, he walked to the letter boxes, fished out a room key, and returned to the desk. He snapped his fingers, signaling a bell-boy.

"Bellman! Suite four-o-six for Mr. Lovett."

Starbuck started away, then turned back. "Say, al-

most forgot to ask. Which way's the Barbary
Coast?"

The clerk looked aghast. "Simply walk in the direction of the waterfront, Mr. Lovett. I'm told it's
difficult to miss."

"You mean to say you've never been there?"

"No." The clerk drew himself up stiffly. "Never."

"Damn shame," Starbuck said with a waggish
grin. "You ought to turn loose and live a little. We
only pass this way once, and that's a mortal fact."

Starbuck pulled out his diamond-studded watch
and popped the lid. The strains of "Darling Clementine" tinkled across the lobby. Hotel guests standing
nearby turned to stare and the clerk rolled his eyes
toward the ceiling. Starbuck snapped the lid closed
and replaced the watch in his vest pocket.

"How long does it take to walk there?"

"A matter of a few minutes, no more."

"Much obliged."

"All part of the service, Mr. Lovett."

Starbuck flipped him a salute and strode off toward the elevators. The bellboy hefted his luggage
and hurried along behind. Watching them, the clerk
passed his hand in front of his eyes, and slowly
shook his head.

Shortly after one o'clock Starbuck pushed through
the doors of the Bella Union. The noontime rush had
slacked off, and there were perhaps a dozen men
strung out along the bar. He hooked a heel over the
brass rail and nodded pleasantly to the bartender.

"Your boss a fellow by the name of Denny O'Brien?"

"Six days a week and all day on Sunday."

"Where might I find him?"

The barkeep ducked his chin. "See that gent down there?"

Starbuck glanced toward the end of the bar. A man stood hunched over the counter, staring dully into a glass of whiskey. He was wide and tall, with brutish features and a barrel-shaped torso. His head was fixed directly upon his shoulders, and he appeared robust as an ox. Starbuck recognized him instantly as a bruiser. One of a breed, bouncers and strongarm men, who maintained order with sledge-hammer fists.

"Yeah, so?" Starbuck asked. "What about him?"

"You want to see Mr. O'Brien, you start with him. His name's High Spade McQueen."

"Sounds like a gamblin' man."

The barkeep smiled. "If I was you, I wouldn't bet against him. You might try talking real polite, too."

"That tough, huh?"

"Mister, he's a cross between a buzz saw and a grizzly bear. You never seen anything like him."

"Thanks for the tip."

Starbuck shoved away from the bar and walked toward the rear of the room. He braced himself to appear bluff and hearty, a man of dazzling good humor. Working undercover, he always turned actor, assumed a role, and it wouldn't do to slip out of character. He rounded the end of the bar and halted.

Smiling affably, he showed High Spade McQueen his gold tooth.

"Mr. McQueen?"

"Who're you?"

"Name's Harry Lovett," Starbuck replied. "I've come all the way from Denver to see Denny O'Brien. The barkeep told me to check with you."

McQueen swiveled his head just far enough to look around. An ugly scar disfigured one cheek and his eyes were like ball bearings. He fixed Starbuck with a sullen stare.

"You got business with Mr. O'Brien?"

"I bear greetings from a mutual friend, Mattie Silks. She was of the opinion Mr. O'Brien and me might do one another a favor."

"Such as what?"

"I'm here to buy some whores. I need advice, and I'm willing to pay handsomely to get it."

McQueen's mouth split in a grotesque smile. His teeth were yellow as a row of old dice, and the scar distorted his features. He pushed off the bar.

"You should've said so to start with. C'mon, I'll take you up to the office."

He crossed the room and mounted the staircase. Starbuck obediently tagged along. From the rear, he was even more aware of the man's massive shoulders. He reminded himself to strike the first punch if ever he locked horns with High Spade McQueen.

Upstairs, McQueen turned into a small alcove off the central hallway. There was a door at the end of the alcove, and the balcony afforded a commanding view of both the theater and the barroom. He rapped on the door and a muffled voice from inside responded. Entering, he waved Starbuck through the door.

Denny O'Brien was stooped over a steel floor safe. He shot McQueen a look of annoyance, then quickly closed the safe door and spun the combination knob. Before the door swung shut, Starbuck caught a glimpse of several ledgers and neatly stacked rows of cash. His expression betrayed nothing.

"Sorry, boss," McQueen apologized in a low rumble. "Thought you'd be done by now."

"You're not paid to think!" O'Brien said curtly. "What do you want?"

"This here feller's named Lovett. Says he come all the way from Denver to see you."

"Yessir, Harry Lovett." Starbuck moved forward, hand extended. "And let me say it's an honor to meet you, Mr. O'Brien! Heard lots about you, and all of it good."

O'Brien held out a square, stubby-fingered hand. He shook once, a hard up-and-down pump, then let go. He gave Starbuck's getup a swift appraisal, noting the diamonds and the dapper cut of the clothes.

"Who's been telling you all these good things?"

"Mattie Silks," Starbuck lied heartily. "She says there's only one man to grease the wheels in Frisco, and that man's your very own self."

"Did she, now?" O'Brien sounded flattered. "I

haven't laid eyes on Mattie in four, maybe five, years."

"Well you made an impression on her, Mr. O'Brien. I'm here to tell you she tagged you for a real stem-winder."

"Have a seat."

O'Brien crossed behind the desk and lowered himself into an overstuffed judge's chair. His churlish manner seemed to moderate. His ruddy features thawed slightly and his eyes were friendly but sharp. Very sharp.

Hat in hand, Starbuck took a chair directly before the desk. Once more he marked that O'Brien's whole being was charged with energy, alive and very shrewd. Up close, there was a strong sense of animal magnetism about the man. A sense of lightning intelligence and feral cunning, underscored by a sharp odor of danger. Starbuck was also aware that O'Brien's gorilla had taken a position by the door, immediately behind him. Apparently a stranger was to be trusted no further than arm's length.

O'Brien eyed him in silence for a moment. "You a friend of Mattie's?"

"Yessir, I am," Starbuck said stoutly. "Mattie and me go back a long ways."

"You're from Denver, then?"

"On again, off again." Starbuck flipped a palm back and forth. "I drift around, generally the mining camps. A man in my line's got to go where the action's the hottest."

"What line would that be, just exactly?"

"Confidence games. Leastways, it was. You might say I've retired from the profession."

"Oh?" O'Brien said lazily. "How so?"

Starbuck gave him a jolly wink. "Hooked myself the prize sucker of all time. Took him for a bundle and figured I'd make a clean break, put my flim-flam days behind me. So I decided to go legit."

"I get the feeling legit doesn't mean reformed."

"You bet your socks it don't!"

"You've got a new line in mind, is that it?"

"Yes, indeedee!" Starbuck said with great relish. "I aim to open a string of cathouses like nothing nobody's ever seen. Corner the market, in a manner of speaking."

"Corner the market where?"

"The mining camps." Starbuck lit a cigar, puffing grandly. "Leadville, Cripple Creek, four or five of the bigger camps. I'll make an absolute goddamned fortune!"

"Yeah?" O'Brien looked skeptical. "Last I heard, there wasn't any shortage of whores in the mining camps."

Starbuck woofed a bellylaugh. "Mr. O'Brien, them miners are queer birds. They'll pay double for anything that speaks foreign or looks the least bit different. So I figure to give 'em a crack at something besides white women."

"Like what?"

"China whores."

"Wait a minute!" O'Brien said bluntly. "Are you saying Mattie sent you to see me about slant-eyes?"

"She sure did," Starbuck acknowledged. "I don't know my ass from a brass bassoon about Chinamen. Never dealt with one in my life. She thought maybe you'd act as a go-between for me."

"A middleman?"

"No, not exactly. I'll make my own deal, but I need someone to open the door. Way I hear it, them Chinamen won't traffic with just anybody when it comes to slave girls."

"You plan to buy them outright, then?"

"For a fact," Starbuck said with cheery vigor. "An even hundred."

"A hundred?" O'Brien repeated, suddenly dumbstruck. "You mean to buy *one hundred* slave girls?"

"I like round numbers. Course, I'm not after just any girls." Starbuck paused, admired the tip of his cigar. "They've got to be virgins."

"Virgins!" O'Brien stared at him with a burlesque leer of disbelief. "You want a hundred *virgins?*"

Starbuck let the idea percolate a few moments. "All virgins—and the whole kit and caboodle ages twelve to sixteen."

A smile formed at the corner of O'Brien's mouth, then broke into laughter. "By God, you think big, don't you? A hundred little China dolls!" He threw back his head and roared. "With their cherries intact, for Chrissake!"

Starbuck gave him a foolish grin. "Well, don't you see, them miners will really go for little girl whores, specially the innocent kind. By kicking things off with Chinee heathen virgins, I'll put the other cathouses in the shade damn near overnight. After that, nobody'll be able to touch my operation."

"Hell, I believe you!" O'Brien shook his head with admiration. "But you're talking about a shit-pot full of money. A hundred virgins won't come cheap."

"No problem," Starbuck said equably. "I'm loaded and willing to pay plenty, just so long as I get what I want."

O'Brien eyed him craftily. "What about me? Here in Frisco, a go-between doesn't come cheap, either."

Starbuck ventured a smile. "How does five percent strike you?"

"It gets my attention." O'Brien shrugged noncommittally. "I'd listen a lot closer if you were to say ten percent."

"One of the last things Mattie told me was that you wouldn't try to stiff me. You open the right door and you've got yourself a deal."

There was a moment of weighing and deliberation. O'Brien thought it the most outlandish idea he'd ever heard. Yet that very oddity gave it a certain credibility. Nobody but a dimwitted fool would invent such a weird and grandiose story. While Harry Lovett was a smooth talker, he was clearly no simpleton, and everything about him reeked of money. O'Brien hadn't the vaguest notion of the asking price for a hundred slave-girl virgins. Whatever the amount, it would be steep, approaching the six-figure mark. A piece of any action that sweet was too tempting to resist.

"You're on," he said at length. "I'll set up a meeting with the head Chink in Chinatown. His name's Fung Jing Toy."

Starbuck flashed his gold tooth in a nutcracker grin. He looked pleased as punch and it was no act. Today was only a first step, but his instinct hadn't played him false.

Denny O'Brien had swallowed the bait whole.

CHAPTER 6

Chinatown was a world apart.

Upon crossing the intersection of Dupont and Washington, the white man's domain abruptly ended. From there, as though transported backward in time, the outsider had a sense of having entered Old Cathay. An ancient culture, unchanged for thousands of years, made only surface concessions to the blue-eyed white devils. Underneath, the old ways still existed.

In the lowering dusk, Starbuck walked along Washington Street. His appointment with Fung Jing Toy was for seven o'clock. All afternoon messages had passed back and forth between the Chinatown vice lord and Denny O'Brien. The working arrangement between them was apparently civil, but larded with distrust and an element of rivalry. Fung's initial response, relayed by High Spade McQueen, had expressed cautious interest. Then, as the negotiations progressed, further information had been requested with respect to Harry Lovett's background. Finally, with O'Brien's assurance that the slave girls were intended for Colorado brothels, the vice lord acceded. Late that afternoon, a time had been set for the meeting.

Starbuck, meanwhile, was pumping Denny O'Brien. He'd spent the afternoon with the Barbary Coast boss, still play-acting the glib and garrulous con man turned whoremaster. His questions were reasonable, and framed in a manner that made O'Brien his ally, something of a conspirator. To dicker successfully for the slave girls, he explained, he needed some general idea as to whom he was dealing with and what sort of reception he might expect. O'Brien, who evidenced no great charity toward Chinatown's vice lord, was only too happy to oblige. He spoke at length, and with considerable authority, on Fung's rise to power. What he had to say was revealing, and recounted with a certain grudging admiration. He described a man of obsessive ambition and savage methods.

Fung Jing Toy had immigrated to America at the age of five. As a child he witnessed the early tong wars on the streets of Chinatown, supporting himself as an apprentice to a shoemaker. A quick learner, ever willing to bend the rules, he displayed a compulsive drive to get ahead. At twenty-one, cloaked by a lily-white front, he began manufacturing shoes under the name of J. C. Peters & Company. The firm, however, was merely a legitimate base for criminal intrigue. He soon expanded into fan-tan parlors, opium smuggling, and prostitution. All the while, his horizons continued to broaden.

Early in 1876, Fung seized power of the Sum Yop tong. His next move, an open challenge to the other tong leaders, seemed suicidal. His gang began high-jacking shipments of slave girls and assorted contraband being smuggled into San Francisco by the opposing factions. With little regard for human life, he provoked the bloodiest street war in Chinatown's history. Over a period of four years, his *boo how doy* hatchet men butchered more than a hundred of their rivals. By 1880, the other tongs were whipped into submission. A truce conference was convened, and Fung emerged the absolute ruler of Chinatown.

Since then, he had consolidated his power with ruthless efficiency. Once a week, his henchmen collected a percentage of gross receipts from all vice enterprises. Those who welched, or attempted to hold out, were swiftly raided by the police. Or in extreme circumstances, they were murdered as an object lesson. All legitimate businesses, importers and merchants alike, were required to pay weekly tribute for protection. The alternative was an unexplained fire, or a midnight visit from a squad of hatchet men. The slave girl trade, once an open market, was now Fung's province alone. Only those who obtained his sanction were allowed to traffic in human cargo.

A traditionalist, Fung still observed the old customs. He dressed like his forefathers, affected humility, and lived in a modest house on Washington

Street. He was a student of art and ancient scrolls, and his own poetry was said to contain such subtle nuances that it could not be translated into English. A playwright as well, he wrote dramas which were performed at the Chinese Theater on Jackson Street. According to rumor, he subsidized the theater and was a patron to those who displayed artistic merit.

Yet, for all his benevolent mannerisms, he had the killer instinct of a cobra and a barbaric sense of survival. Assassination by other tong leaders was an ever-present danger, and his personal living quarters were virtually impregnable. The barred steel door, leading into a suite of rooms without windows, was guarded by a pair of Tibetan mastiffs. At all times, night and day, he was also accompanied by two *boo how doy* hatchet men. Not surprisingly, his death was widely contemplated but rarely attempted.

Starbuck was intrigued by the man. From all he'd been told, Fung was an enigma, the inscrutable Oriental of legend. A vicious killer who wrote poetry and performed masterfully on the zither. A philanthropist who traded in slave girls and extorted tribute from his own countrymen. A throwback to the warlords of old, at once civilized and savage. In short, a man of many parts, and worth meeting.

Chinatown itself seemed no less a paradox. Walking along Washington, Starbuck thought to himself that it was actually a city within a city. One big tenement, it was dirty and overcrowded, squalid and diseased. The people lived in cellars and back-alley rabbit warrens, musty wooden cubicles. The women were dressed in black pantaloons and long smocks, and the men, their hair braided in pigtails, wore floppy jackets and baggy pajama pants. Most spoke only the dialect of their native land, and those who could converse with a Westerner resorted to pidgin English that was all but incomprehensible. A stranger asking directions might as well have talked to a deaf mute.

Washington Street, otherwise known as the Street of the Thousand Lanterns, teemed with people. The sweet smell of opium and the stench of sweaty bodies intermingled in an oppressive odor. The shops and stores, displaying their wares, added to the rank aroma. Dried sea horses and pickled squid were heaped in a herbalist's window. A grocer's storefront exhibited row upon row of plucked chickens and skinned ducks, dangling from overhead beams. Sidewalk bins overflowed with winter melons and rotting vegetables, and a fish peddler operated from an open cart on the corner. Amid the din of commerce, there was human barter, as well.

Crib whores, imprisoned behind barred windows, talked up their trade. The lowest form of slave girls, they wore only short blouses, naked from the waist down. Chinese men were addressed in the native tongue, and offered unknown splendors at reduced rates. White men, thought to be ignorant and lavish spenders, brought on a frantic singsong chant.

"Chinee girl velly nice! Looksee two bits, feelee floor bits. Dooe only six bits!"

Hurrying past, Starbuck was reminded that the

plumbing of Oriental women was thought to be different from that of white women. To the uninitiated, it was commonly believed that their private parts went east-west instead of north-south. The debate, actively fostered by the Chinese, had produced a thriving, if somewhat bizarre, sideline to the oldest profession. A curious customer could have a looksee for two bits, a mere twenty-five cents. Or if he cared to check out the plumbing personally, he could have a feelee for four bits. That served to settle the east-west question, and often led to an additional sale. For another quarter, a total of six bits, he could actually doee. Quick as a wink, for the crib girls were also velly fast, all doubt was then removed.

Starbuck was something of a novice himself. He'd talked countless girls, from schoolmarms to saloon tarts, out of their drawers and into bed. Yet he had never been in the sack with an Oriental woman. He knew the east-west question was sheer tomfoolery, but he thought it might be worth a try while he was in Frisco. Whichever direction the plumbing ran, it would be worth the price of admission. A little doee now and then kept a man from going stale.

A couple of minutes before seven, Starbuck located Fung's house. As he'd been told, it was the only three-story building in all of Chinatown that wasn't swarming with a hundred or more occupants. He rapped on the door and almost instantly it swung open. A servant bowed him inside, quickly closing and bolting the door. Without a word, the man turned and walked along a central hallway.

Starbuck followed. He checked left and right, naturally curious about the inside of a Chinese home. Yet there was little to see; the rooms off the corridor were dark; except for dim candles and several large vases, the hall itself was bare. He had the sense of being watched, which was reinforced by the servant's casual manner. He wondered how many hatchet men silently waited in the darkened rooms.

At the end of the hallway, the servant stopped and bowed him through a door. Stepping onto a small landing, Starbuck saw a lighted staircase leading to the cellar. He went down the stairs, which turned sharply at the bottom, and emerged in an underground chamber. One look and he understood immediately why Chinatown's vice lord still survived.

The chamber ran the width of the house. Ornate candle fixtures were attached to the walls, and a steel door stood opposite the staircase. Before the door, chained to the wall, were two beasts that vaguely resembled dogs. Huge as tigers, the mastiffs looked as though they would happily devour a man for breakfast. The dogs snarled in unison, and showed him fangs the size of tusks. He remained very still.

A Chinaman appeared in the doorway. At his command, the mastiffs dropped to the floor, silent but watchful. Another man came through the door and paused, hands stuffed up his sleeves. Tall men, muscular and hard-faced, they both wore broad-brimmed flat hats, their hair twisted in long queues. Their robes were black and their rubber-soled shoes made every movement silent as a whisper. From the look of them, there was a hatchet up every sleeve.

Starbuck thought he'd never seen men who so thoroughly fitted the part of assassins. The first one expertly patted him down, and removed the Colt Lightning from his shoulder holster. The hideout gun in his boot top went undetected, and knowing it was there gave him some degree of comfort. Still, even though he was armed, he warned himself to play it fast and loose. A bold front and quick wits were the key to leaving the chamber alive.

The hatchet man in the doorway moved aside and motioned him through. Starbuck gingerly stepped past the mastiffs and entered a spacious room. Spartan as a monk's cell, the room was furnished with floor cushions and a low teakwood table. To his immediate left was another steel door, which he assumed led to the living quarters. The hatchet men took up positions directly behind him, one on either side of the entranceway. He needed no reminder that it was also the only way out.

The side door opened and Fung Jing Toy whisked into the room. He wore a silk mandarin gown and a black skullcap. A slender man, with a long mustache and skin the texture of parchment, his bearing was that of someone who spends his life remote from the world of people. His eyes were impersonal.

"Mr. Lovett." His head dipped in a bow. "Please be seated."

"Thank you kindly."

Starbuck lowered himself onto one of the cushions. His legs were too long to fit under the table, and he awkwardly twisted around sideways. Fung moved to the opposite side of the table and took a seat, legs crossed. A moment passed; then he nodded with grave courtesy and spoke in a reedy voice.

"I am told this is your first visit to our city."

"That's a fact. Got in late this morning."

"Have your expectations been fulfilled?"

"Well . . ." Starbuck smiled lamely. "I've been pretty busy. Haven't had much time to catch the sights."

"A situation not without remedy. You must allow us to show you something of Little China during your stay."

"Little China?"

"A colloquial expression," Fung said with a patronizing smile. "Your people call it Chinatown. We find our own name more suitable."

Starbuck realized the vice lord's smile was closer to a grimace. A cold rictus that touched his lips but never his eyes. The serpentine charm and oily manner also failed to hide the hauteur in his voice, the deep arrogance. Still, there was no faulting the man's command of English. He spoke with only a slight accent, and he used three-dollar words. Starbuck thought "colloquial" was a real piss-cutter. He made a mental note to look it up in the dictionary.

"Now, as to business," Fung went on blandly. "Denny O'Brien informs me that you are interested in a purchase of some magnitude."

"All depends," Starbuck said tentatively. "The

merchandise would have to be prime stuff, pick of the litter."

"Ah, yes." Fung permitted himself an ironic glance. "Pick of the litter meaning virgin girls, is it not so?"

"Nothing less," Starbuck affirmed. "Virgins will be the come-on, if you get my drift. I'll use 'em to start the operation off in real style."

Fung gave him a thoughtful stare. "I believe you plan to open several houses, all at the same time. To one of humble aspirations, that seems a grand and daring concept."

Starbuck beamed like a trained bear. "I think big and I'm willing to put my money where my mouth is. Four or five houses—all stocked with virgins—it'll flat knock their eyes out! No way it'll fail, and there's the God's own truth."

Fung studied his nails. "An ancient proverb advises us that truth wears many faces." He suddenly looked up, eyes gleaming icons. "I understand you are a man of some influence in the Colorado mining camps?"

"Well, let's just say I've got pull with all the right people."

"Then you must know my associate, Wong Sing? He resides in the town called Leadville."

"No." Starbuck sensed danger. "Never made his acquaintance."

"How is that possible?" Fung's eyes were now veiled. "He leads the Sum Yop tong in Leadville."

"What's his front?" Starbuck asked evenly. "What's he do for a living?"

"I am told he operates a laundry."

Starbuck opened his hands, shrugged. "Not too likely we would've met. See, I don't care much for starch in my shirts." He paused, flashed his gold tooth in a crafty smile. "I generally find a woman willing to do my wash."

The statement was entirely plausible. In mining camps, white men were fond of saying all Chinamen looked alike. Moreover, those Chinese who owned businesses invariably ran a laundry or back-alley café. So it was understandable that the one who called himself Harry Lovett would have no knowledge of Wong Sing. Yet Fung was not wholly satisfied with the answer. He survived by trusting no man, most especially a blue-eyed devil endorsed by Denny O'Brien. He concluded the matter would bear further scrutiny.

A smile appeared at the corner of his mouth. "Upon your return, you must make yourself known to Wong Sing. He would be honored to be of service . . . should the occasion arise."

"I'll do that very thing," Starbuck said earnestly. "Who knows? Maybe we'll be able to swap favors here and there."

Fung laced his fingers together, considered a moment. "Your request is most unusual. A hundred virgins, all of such tender age, are not easily obtainable."

"No, I suppose not." Starbuck feigned a sly look.

"Course, if I made it worth your while, you likely wouldn't have any trouble, would you?"

Fung nodded wisely. "I believe it could be arranged."

"How much?"

"One thousand dollars a girl."

"Holy Christ!" Starbuck appeared shocked. "That's a little steep, isn't it?"

"Perhaps," Fung intoned. "On the other hand, where else would you turn? I alone govern the trade in slave girls."

"You've got a point." Starbuck hesitated, his features screwed up in a frown. "How would I know they're all virgins?"

"You have my word," Fung said in a voice without tone. "Or if you wish, you may have them inspected by a doctor. Such matters are readily arranged."

Starbuck pondered a moment, then laughed. "What the hell, it's only money! When can you make delivery?"

"Hmm." Fung nodded to himself as though possessed of some secret knowledge. "I will consult with my associates and advise you. These affairs must be conducted with a certain delicacy."

Starbuck found the statement too cryptic for comfort. "Don't hang me up too long. I'm already short on time."

"I beg your indulgence," Fung said politely. "In the meantime, allow us to entertain you. The treasures of Little China are many and varied . . . and quite often memorable."

Fung rose to his feet. Starbuck was assured he would be contacted, and on that note, the meeting ended. Bows were exchanged, then one of the hatchet men escorted Starbuck past the dogs and up the stairs. Once they were out of sight, Fung turned to the other guard with a look of sharp concern.

"Find May Ling!" he ordered. "Bring her to me now."

CHAPTER 7

Starbuck had no illusions about the girl. She was a gift from Fung, a young seductress meant to please and delight him. Yet she was also a spy, an enchanting interrogator with both the beauty and the thorns of a rose. He had no doubt his every word was reported directly to her master.

The invitation was extended the morning after his meeting with Fung. At first, aware of the danger, his reaction was to politely decline. Denny O'Brien had already offered him one of the Bella Union girls, and that was excuse enough to beg off. Then, wary of insulting Fung, he thought it wiser to accept. There were grave risks entailed, but he was an old hand at guarding himself in the clinches. Besides, he was horny as a billy goat and still extremely curious about Chinese women. Until he verified it for himself, the question of their east-west plumbing would always stick in his mind. He accepted, and the engagement was arranged for that evening.

Shortly after sundown, one of Fung's men met him outside the hotel. He was led to a building in the heart of Chinatown, then upstairs to an apartment on the second floor. The man knocked three times, bowed from the waist, and disappeared down the stairs. He was left alone before the door.

Whatever he expected, Starbuck was not prepared for the girl's loveliness. May Ling was tiny, with a doll-like figure and large almond-shaped eyes. Her features were exquisite, with bee-stung lips and high cheekbones, all framed by a mass of hair black as obsidian. Her voice was odd and vibrant, and there was about her an aura of innocence destroyed. She smelled sweet and alluring, and gave off a sensual radiation as palpable as musk. He judged her age at somewhere between eighteen and twenty. A child-woman of evocative beauty.

Her apartment was small but richly furnished. The walls were decorated with silk prints and the floors were lushly carpeted; the bureau and several squat chests were finished in black, heavily lacquered, and trimmed with brass fittings. A tall Oriental screen separated the living area from the bedchamber, and a miniature kitchen was partitioned off by yet another screen. A low table, used for both entertaining and dining, was surrounded by plush floor cushions.

May Ling was dressed in a milk-white kimono that seemed to mold her body in melted ivory. Her English, like Fung's, was remarkably correct, with only a trace of an accent. She greeted Starbuck with a cordial bow, and showed him to the place of honor at the table. In deference to his Western tastes, she served whiskey and provided a porcelain ashtray for his cigar. She was gracious, drawing him out with small talk, and gave no hint of embarrassment at the arrangement. She was there for his pleasure, and quite clearly eager to please.

Starbuck was indeed pleased. She was a creature of surpassing beauty, and the atmosphere was conducive to thoughts of erotic Oriental mysteries. The scent of joss sticks and sandalwood was heady, somehow intoxicating, adding to the sensation of her nearness. When she spoke her lips moved like moth wings, and she seemed to have an infinite variety of smiles, all suggestive of the night ahead. He watched, sipping whiskey, while she glided spectrally from the kitchen to the table. His hunger, mounting steadily, was not for food.

Dinner was one surprise after another. She served prawns simmered in a sticky, sweet sauce, and something that vaguely resembled pork, swimming in a thick black gumbo. Steaming bowls of vegetables, similar in appearance to seaweed, complimented the meat dishes, and with each course there appeared another mound of snow-white rice. Herbal tea and delicate cookies, tasting faintly of ginger, finished off the meal.

Starbuck thoroughly stuffed himself. He'd never tasted prawns, and the other dishes, though equally unfamiliar, were nonetheless savory. After dinner, he loosened his belt a notch and lit a cigar. May Ling cleared the table and poured him another whiskey.

Then she took a zither from a wall peg and seated herself across from him. Her fingers flew over the instrument like darting birds, producing a strange and haunting music. The sound was discordant to his ear, not unpleasant but seemingly without melody. To his amazement, she opened her mouth and began to sing. The words were meaningless, but the timbre of her voice was almost hypnotic, curiously intimate. Her gaze never left him, and he felt certain the song was meant to convey some seductive message. When she finished, he stuck the cigar in his mouth and applauded heartily. She blushed and modestly averted her eyes.

The evening thus far was beyond anything he had imagined. The lavish meal and the haunting song were unaccustomed preliminaries to the mating ritual he normally practiced. Yet the girl herself was by far the greatest surprise. She had asked no questions and made no reference whatever to his dealings with Fung. Nor had she displayed even passing interest in who he was or where he came from, or the nature of his business. In short, she'd made no attempt to grill him, and seemed content merely with his company. He found himself somewhat bewildered, and more than a little curious. Tactfully, choosing his words, he asked her about herself. His interest was genuine, and from the expression in her eyes, he knew it was a question she'd seldom been asked. He prompted her, gently insistent, and she slowly began to talk.

Her life, she told him simply, had been ordained

by circumstance. Her parents were poor, struggling to eke out an existence. Like many peasant girls, governed by a centuries old custom, she had been sold into bondage. The contract took effect on her tenth birthday, and by then she'd shown promise of beauty. One of Fung's agents ultimately bought her, and she had arrived in San Francisco not quite a year later. Unlike ordinary slave girls, Fung had taken a special interest in her. A tutor had been retained to teach her English and the art of conversation, and still another mentor had trained her in music and song. A woman of great wisdom had instructed her in lovemaking and the many exotic acts pleasurable to man. At age fourteen she had been accorded a great honor. Fung, her master and patron, had himself taken her virginity.

With a note of pride, she observed that since that time she had lived the life of a courtesan. She entertained those men, both Chinese and American, who were of special interest to her master. In return, she had been given her own quarters and the freedom to travel Little China as she pleased. Over the years many wealthy men had attempted to buy her, offering thousands of dollars above the price normally paid for even the most beautiful virgin. Yet, declaring her beyond value, her master had refused in each instance. That refusal had bestowed great honor on her, and wherever she went the people of Little China treated her with the respect reserved for one of position and rank. Few slave girls rose so high, and she considered herself the most fortunate of women. Not yet twenty, she had found serenity and purpose in life. She existed to serve her master, and her days were filled with happiness. She was content.

Starbuck believed her. She was a slave, and whether she called herself courtesan or whore, she would live out her days in bondage. All the same, she was happier than any white whore he'd ever known. She was at peace with herself and her world, and the serenity she spoke of was no act. Her voice, the expression in her eyes, told the story. She had found something in life that few people attain. Her mirror reflected the worth of her own esteem.

May Ling smiled and sang him another song. He lay back on the pillows, sipping whiskey and puffing his cigar. After a time, she put the zither away and held out her hand. He climbed to his feet, all but bewitched by her loveliness, and allowed himself to be led to her bedchamber. There she undressed him, and after stepping out of her kimono, she let him gaze a moment upon the golden swell of her breasts.

Then she showed him that Chinese girls were, after all, no different from white women. Some were simply better than others, and she skillfully persuaded him that she was the best.

May Ling never questioned her master's orders, or his motives. To her, a man's body was like a zither, an instrument to be strummed and caressed. Several times during the night, using her own body to strike responsive chords, she had taught Starbuck exquisite harmonies known only to a trained courtesan. Early the next morning, she undertook the balance of her assignment.

After a late breakfast, she suggested a personally conducted tour of Little China. Starbuck was feeling a bit frazzled, his juices sapped by her arduous and sometimes gymnastic lovemaking. Under normal circumstances he might have hesitated, but his brain was muzzy and he suspected nothing. Chinatown was Fung's domain, and seeing it through May Ling's eyes seemed very much in order. He immediately approved the idea.

On the street, she took his arm and guided him toward the center of Little China. As they walked, she chattered on gaily, explaining that the district was the largest Chinese settlement outside the Orient. Within a dozen square blocks, some thirty thousand people lived and worked, rarely ever setting foot in the white sections of San Francisco.

The Chinese, May Ling noted proudly, were an industrious people. Some twisted cigars for a living, others worked in clothing and shoe factories, and many served in white homes as cooks and houseboys. For the most part, they were frugal, followed the ancient religious rites, and kept very much to themselves. Yet they were not the simple peasants, ignorant and humble, so commonly portrayed by whites. Almost all were fanatic gamblers, playing the lottery and fan-tan, and even a variation of poker. Opium smoking was widely practiced, and the trade in *gow* pills, pipe-size balls of opium, had evolved into a thriving industry. There were even exclusive establishments for white gentlemen and their ladies. Unlike common opium dens, the service there was discreet and costly, the *gow* pills of superb quality.

Still another misconception, May Ling went on, was the belief by whites that Orientals were sexually backward. To the contrary, the Chinese were a very sensual people, connoisseurs of the flesh. A Chinese man seldom limited himself to one woman, even if he was married and had a family. Nor was it considered shameful for a Chinese woman to enjoy the act, and express that joy through inventive byplay passed down from mother to daughter. In fact, the Oriental preoccupation with sex manifested itself in many forms. The most widely known was the flourishing trade in slave girls. Nowhere else on earth was the appreciation of eroticism so vividly demonstrated.

May Ling suddenly stopped. Her eyes seemed to sparkle with secret amusement. "Would you care to attend a slave-girl auction?"

"Would I!" Starbuck said, astonished. "I'd like nothing better."

"I believe one is being held this morning."

"You really think they'd let us watch? I've heard these things are sort of private, invitation only."

"Oh, yes," May Ling trilled happily. "You are with me, which means you are a very special friend of the master. We would not be turned away."

"Well, what are we waiting for? Hot damn, a real

live slave-girl auction! You're just a sackful of surprises."

"Perhaps we shouldn't." May Ling mocked him with a tiny smile. "These girls are not virgins, and much older than those you wish to purchase. You might be disappointed."

Starbuck laughed. "Don't worry your pretty head about that. C'mon, chop, chop! Let's go!"

With a minxish giggle, May Ling took his arm and led him to the corner. There they turned onto a side-street, then walked toward a warehouse halfway down the block. A squad of hatchet men, uniformed in the regulation pajama suits and black hats, stood guard outside. Approaching them, May Ling let go a volley of Chinese, her tone gracious, yet somehow imperious. The men bowed respectfully, and one of them rushed to open the door. She stepped through, followed closely by Starbuck, and directed him to a vantage point along the wall. From there, they had an unobstructed view of the entire warehouse.

Starbuck was reminded of a livestock auction. A large crowd of men, both Chinese and white, were ganged around a wooden platform. The auctioneer, a jolly-eyed Chinaman with a loud mouth and a winning smile, walked the platform like a captain commanding the bridge of a ship. Beyond the platform, huddled together in a forlorn group, were a hundred or more Chinese girls. One at a time, they were brought forward by the auctioneer's assistants and stripped naked. Shoved onto the platform, they were then forced to parade before the crowd like prize broodmares. The prospective buyers were allowed to examine each girl before the bidding began.

May Ling briefly explained the complex system underlying the slave-girl trade. Her master placed an order with procurers in China for delivery in San Francisco on a certain date. Upon arrival, the girls were secreted in padded crates, invoiced as dishware, and American customs agents were bribed to pass the bales without inspection. While special orders were often filled for wealthy whites and prosperous Chinese tradesmen, the cargo was generally sold at open auction. The choicest girls, selected for their youth and attractiveness, were auctioned off to men looking for a concubine and jobbers who resold to smaller, inland markets. Prices varied from girl to girl, but usually started with a minimum bid of $200 and climbed to $500 or higher. The refuse, those unsuitable for auction, were sold to waterfront brothelkeepers or put to work in the Chinatown cribs.

The virgin market, May Ling remarked, was conducted on a somewhat higher level. Procurers in China contracted for the girls at an early age, generally two through five. The parents then raised the girls, and the procurer meanwhile contracted to deliver virgins of a specified age group, and on a specified date, in San Francisco. Even now, her master held contracts on some four hundred virgins, ages two through sixteen, who were available for delivery on demand. Thus, there was always a plentiful stock to supply future markets.

Starbuck listened with only one ear. His attention

was fixed on the platform. Several men had stepped forward to probe and fondle a girl who looked to be no more than fourteen. She stood dull-eyed and submissive, abject in her nakedness. The auctioneer began the bidding at $200, and within minutes she was sold for $375. The man who bought her paid the auctioneer, and a bill of sale, with the girl's mark, was quickly produced. The document was legal and binding in American courts. There were quotas restricting Chinese immigration, but there were no laws forbidding the sale of Chinese girls into bondage. The young girl, now a legally bound slave, was swiftly dressed and hustled away by her new master.

"A fortunate girl," May Ling observed, noting his interest. "Had she not attracted a buyer, she might have joined those who work in the cribs."

"So young?" Starbuck said without thinking. "A girl that age in the cribs?"

"Oh, yes," May Ling replied, studying him with a half-smile. "But she would be much older tomorrow. The cribs age a girl quickly."

"How long do they last?"

"Four years, perhaps less," May Ling said in a low voice. "The work is hard, and men use them in cruel ways. Their minds go wrong, or they become diseased, and then they are no longer of value to their master."

Starbuck felt a sudden revulsion. "You mean they go crazy?"

"Some do." May Ling kept her tone casual. "For

most, it is the sailor's disease—the pox—that claims them."

"What happens then?"

"They are sent to the hospital."

"Hospital?" Starbuck said, looking at her. "To be cured?"

"No, to die." Her appraisal of him was deliberate, oddly watchful. "The crib masters have a secret place they call the hospital. When a girl outlives her usefulness, she is taken there and given a pallet. An attendant places beside her a cup of water and a cup of rice, and a small oil lamp. He informs her that she must die by the time the oil burns out. Later, when he returns, the girl is almost always dead— sometimes by starvation, usually by her own hand."

"Jesus Christ!" Starbuck scowled, shook his head. "Some hospital."

"Yes." An indirection came into May Ling's eyes. "The people of Little China call it 'the place of no return.' "

Too late, Starbuck sensed the trap. He wiped away the frown and quickly plastered a dopey smile across his face. Yet he wasn't at all sure he'd fooled May Ling. She'd brought him here, and purposely suckered him into a conversation about crib girls, all to get a reaction. That much was now abundantly clear, and he realized she was swifter than she appeared. No questions, no need to interrogate him. A night's lovemaking, and her innocent manner had effectively lowered his guard. Then she laid the bait and waited to see his reaction. A goddamned Oriental mousetrap! And he'd gone for the cheese.

"Well, now!" He gave her a lopsided grin. "Let's hope none of my little virgins ever needs a trip to the hospital."

"Would that bother you?"

"At a thousand bucks a head!" he roared. "You bet your sweet ass that'd bother me!"

She giggled softly. "Do you truly find it sweet?"

"Sweeter than sugar, and twice as nice!"

May Ling took his arm and they turned to leave the warehouse. On the street, Starbuck gave her a squeeze and made himself a promise. One more dip of the wick, then he'd ditch her fast.

And get the hell out of Chinatown.

CHAPTER 8

The miners came in forty-nine
The whores in fifty-one.
And when they got together
They produced the Native Son.

Nell Kimball scarcely heard the lyrics. She was seated in a curtained loge with Starbuck, whose attention was directed to the stage. Covertly, out of the corner of her eye, she was watching him with a bemused look. She thought him a most unlikely whoremaster.

Onstage, a buxom songbird was belting out the tune in a loud, brassy voice. A ballad of sorts, it traced the ancestry of Nob Hill swells to the mating of whores and miners who had settled San Francisco during the Gold Rush. There was an element of truth to the ditty, and it was a favorite with audiences on the Barbary Coast. Tonight, the crowd in the Bella Union was clapping and stamping their feet, and roaring approval as the lyrics became progressively vulgar.

Starbuck looked like a peacock in full plumage. He was tricked out in diamonds and a powder-blue suit, with a paisley four-in-hand tie and a gaudy lavender shirt. The getup fitted the image of a whoremonger with grand ideas, but Nell Kimball was having second thoughts. Even the gold tooth left her unconvinced. Her whore's intuition told her Harry Lovett was something more than he appeared.

Earlier, Denny O'Brien had ordered her to entertain him royally. At first, she'd been a bit miffed, her vanity wounded. Harry Lovett had spent the last two days in Chinatown—doubtless getting himself screwed silly by Fung's prized hussy—and that put her in the position of playing second fiddle. Around the Bella Union she got top billing, acting as O'Brien's strong right arm. She supervised all the show girls, occasionally wooing a high roller personally, and she wasn't accustomed to standing in line behind a sloe-eyed Chinese slut. Yet orders were orders, and she'd learned the hard way never to provoke O'Brien's temper. He considered Lovett topdrawer business, and it wouldn't do to let Fung outshine them in the entertainment department. However she managed it, Lovett was to be given ace-high treatment, and made to forget the China girl's bedroom artistry. All of which meant a long night in the saddle.

For Starbuck's part, he felt like he'd come home. Nell Kimball was his kind of woman. Unlike May

Ling's charade, there was no pretense about Nell, nothing phony. She was a saloon girl who had fought and clawed her way to the top of her profession. A tough cookie, honed by experience, she could handle a wise-ass chump or a mean-eyed drunk with equal ease. She looked to her own interests, always a step ahead of the competition, and God pity anybody who got in her way. Her counterpart was found in mining camps and cowtowns throughout the West, and she was the only kind of woman Starbuck fully understood. Moreover, he admired her for perhaps the best of reasons. Except that she wore bloomers, there wasn't a nickel's worth of difference between them. In all the things that counted, they were very much birds of a feather. Hard-headed realists, blooded but never whipped, survivors.

Then, too, Starbuck had to admit she was nothing shy in the looks department. She was compellingly attractive, tall and statuesque, with enormous hazel eyes and sumptuous figure. Her tawny hair was piled in coils and puffs atop her head, and she carried herself with assured poise. Her gaze was direct, filled with a certain bawdy wisdom, and she seemed to view the world with good-humored irony. He thought that was perhaps the one essential difference between them. He saw the world through the eyes of a confirmed cynic. She saw it through a prism that was still slightly rose-tinted, and he considered that a weakness.

By and by, perhaps later tonight, he fully intended to exploit that weakness. His visit to the slave-girl auction that morning, coupled with May Ling's boastful remarks about Fung, had merely strengthened his original assessment. Without an overlord to keep the peace, Chinatown and the Barbary Coast could not coexist. Denny O'Brien, given the scope of his ambition, could never resist a takeover attempt in Chinatown. Someone restrained him from doing so, and that someone was the man who cracked the whip in San Francisco. Unless he missed his guess, Starbuck thought it entirely likely that Nell Kimball knew the someone's name. A gentle touch, and his softsoap routine, might very well persuade her to talk. Contrary to what people thought, the way to a whore's heart was not between her legs. Affection and kindness were what turned the trick.

The chesty songbird ended her number and the curtain rang down to wild applause. Starbuck poured champagne and lifted his glass in a toast. The evening was far along, but he'd made no overtures, no suggestive remarks. He figured it was a new experience for Nell, and certain to pique her interest. He wasn't far short of the mark.

"So tell me," she said with a quizzical look. "Have yourself a good time in Chinktown, did you?"

"No complaints," Starbuck allowed. "Course, I'd have to say those Chinamen take a little getting used to."

"Yeah, that Fung's a real pistol, isn't he?"

"I suppose he's all right . . . for a Chinaman."

"On the Coast, we call him Fung Long Dong."

"Oh?" Starbuck saw a glint in her eye. "Why's that?"

"Because he's got a permanent hard-on." Nell laughed at her racy admission. "Screws anything that's not nailed down. Women, girls, even little boys, so I've heard."

Her laugh was infectious, and Starbuck grinned. "Wouldn't surprise me. After seeing that three-ring circus he runs—the dogs and his hatchet men—I'd believe anything."

"Forget the dogs, honeybun! You just stay clear of Wong Yee and Sing Dock."

"His hatchet men?" Starbuck asked. "What's the story on them?"

"All bad," Nell said quietly. "When they kill someone, they tidy up the corpse's clothes, comb his hair, and press a smile on his mouth. God knows what they do before they kill him. They're both as queer as a three-dollar bill."

"No accounting for taste," Starbuck said with a crooked smile. "I've always preferred the ladies, myself."

Nell gave him a cool look. "How'd you like May Ling? Not that anybody ever called the little tramp a lady."

Starbuck mugged, hands outstretched. "A gentleman never tells. You're right about one thing, though—she's no lady!"

Nell warmed to the remark. "Well, it just bears out what I've always said. Those China girls have got no class. You're lots better off here on the Coast."

"Now that you mention it," Starbuck said casually, "I got pretty much the same story in Chinatown. The way Fung talks, there's no love lost between him and Denny."

"I guess not!" Nell tossed her head. "Denny would cut that Chink's heart out and dance on his grave."

"What stops him?"

"I don't follow you."

"What stops him from walking in there and taking over Chinatown? Hell, Fung and his hatchet men wouldn't stand a chance! If I was Denny, I'd do it in a minute."

Nell blinked and looked away. "You'd have to ask Denny about that. I keep my nose where it belongs."

"I'll bet!" Starbuck ribbed her. "Strikes me, you pretty much know what's going on around the Bella Union."

"Maybe I do," Nell observed neutrally. "But smart girls learn not to talk out of school, and I sit right up at the head of the class."

Starbuck let it drop for the moment. "Well, you're the number-one girl around here. No question about that! Wish to hell I had someone like you to run my operation. It'd sure take a load off my mind."

"Since you brought it up," Nell said slowly, "I'm curious about something. Have you ever operated a whorehouse before?"

"Nope." Starbuck's mouth widened in a devil-may-care grin. "But I'm all set to give 'er one helluva try!"

"You've got brass." Nell cocked her head in a funny little smile. "A hundred virgins and four whorehouses! How in God's name do you figure to pull it off?"

"I pray a lot," Starbuck said, deadpan. "Course, I've got a way with the ladies. So that ought to smooth things considerable."

"Now you're bragging."

"Think so?" Starbuck gave her a rougish wink. "There's one way to find out."

Nell laughed a low, throaty laugh. "Sounds like you're getting fresh, Mr. Lovett."

"The idea crossed my mind."

"Then I suppose we'll have to find out . . . won't we?"

Starbuck put his arm around her, and she scooted closer on the divan. The curtain rose and a line of can-can dancers went prancing across the stage. She let her hand slip down over his thigh, and gave him a playful squeeze.

Late that night, Nell suggested they retire to her room. The Bella Union was still going strong, the barroom and the theater packed with a raucous crowd. Onstage a team of acrobats was performing to assorted hoots and jeers. The audience seemed unimpressed by gymnastic feats of daring.

Denny O'Brien and High Spade McQueen were

standing near the end of the bar. The action was
heavy at the gaming tables, and they appeared deep
in conversation. Starbuck yelled and waved, attract-
ing their attention as Nell tugged him toward the
stairs. McQueen barely glanced around, but O'Brien
smiled knowingly and gave him the thumbs-up sign.
Starbuck responded with a jack-o'-lantern grin, and
rolled his eyes at Nell. He looked like a randy drunk,
immensely pleased with his prospects for the night.

There was little need for pretense. His head
buzzed from the effects of too much champagne, and
he was in a very mellow mood. Several bottles of
bubbly had been consumed during the evening, and
Nell, who was no slouch herself, had matched him
glass for glass. She was bright-eyed and giggly, and
led him up the staircase with a slight list to her step.
Yet, despite his muzzy look, he was reasonably sober. He kept a grin glued on his face, but reminded
himself that the night's work had really just begun.
He still had to sound Nell out, gull her into revealing
a name. And it had to be accomplished without
arousing suspicion. Wondering about the best approach, he waved one last time to O'Brien, then
trailed Nell up the stairs. The sway of her hips and
the glow of the champagne brought him to what
seemed a logical compromise. He thought perhaps
their talk might wait until after she'd shown him how
it was done on the Barbary Coast.

The rooms on the second floor of the Bella Union
were reserved for the showgirls. Most of their tricks,
ten dollars for five minutes' rutting, were turned on

the sofas in the theater boxes. A big spender, who wanted the full treatment, was brought upstairs. There, for the right price, he got to take his time. Fifty dollars bought him an hour, and a hundred purchased the whole night. The girls were versatile, willing to satisfy even the most exotic request, and the johns always got their money's worth. No one left the second floor of the Bella Union wanting more.

The third floor was occupied exclusively by the house staff. Denny O'Brien's suite consisted of a sitting room, bedroom, and private bath. Across the hall, High Spade McQueen's quarters were comparable, though somewhat smaller. Other staff members, who included the stage manager and the house manager, were assigned somewhat less spacious accommodations. Nell occupied a corner room at the end of the hall. The view overlooked the alley.

Upon entering, Starbuck was pleasantly surprised. The atmosphere was considerably more homey than he'd expected. A tall wardrobe, with a full-length mirror, was flanked by a bureau and washstand. Opposite was a grouping of two chairs and a table, upon which stood a gilt clock and a collection of porcelain figurines. The windows were draped, a hooked rug covered the floor, and a large brass bed occupied the far corner. Quite clearly, Nell had gone to great lengths to create a warm and comfortable refuge for herself. The room seemed somehow out of place in the Bella Union.

After locking the door, she turned to Starbuck.

Her hands went behind his neck, pulling his head down. Her kiss was fierce and passionate, demanding. She pressed herself against him, and he could feel her breasts and the pressure of her thighs on his loins. He stroked her back and fondled the soft curve of her buttocks, and she uttered a low moan. They parted and, in the umber glow of a lamp, hurriedly began undressing.

Her body was sculptured: high, full breasts, a stemlike waist, and long, shapely legs. She stood before him a moment, her clothes heaped at her feet. Then his arms encircled her, and she clung naked to his hard-muscled frame. Her hand went to his manhood, swollen and pulsating, and she grasped it eagerly. He kissed her lips, then the nape of her neck, felt the nipple of her breast grow erect under his touch. They caressed, played a game of tease-and-tantalize, until they were aroused and aching and the excitement became unbearable. At last, slipping out of his embrace, she pulled him down on the bed.

The hard questing part of him found her. She was ready for him, moist and yielding, and she took him deep within the core of herself. His hands clutched her flanks and they came together in an agonized clash. Her legs spidered around him, and she jolted upward, timing herself to his thrust. She clamped him viselike, her hips moving in a circle, and exhaled a hoarse gasp. He arched his back and drove himself to the molten center, probing deeper and deeper. She screamed and her nails pierced his back like talons.

Time lost meaning, and they crossed the threshold together.

A long while later Starbuck lay staring at the ceiling. Nell was snuggled close, her head nestled in the hollow of his shoulder. He felt her breath eddy through the matted curls on his chest, and sensed she was on the verge of sleep. Champagne and the afterglow of their lovemaking had left her sated, drifting lightly on a quenched flame. He thought there would never be a better time to pop the question. Yet, even with her defenses lowered, he cautioned himself to proceed slowly. He put his lips to her ear and gently stroked her hair.

"Wanna hear a secret?"

"Umm. I like secrets."

Starbuck's voice was warm and husky. "May Ling couldn't hold a candle to you. Strictly no contest, and that's a mortal fact."

"Omigod!" Nell hugged him tightly. "That's the sweetest thing anyone ever said to me in my whole life."

"I meant every word of it—cross my heart."

"Does that mean you'll stay out of Chinatown?"

"Would that make you happy?"

"Would it ever!" Nell's eyes suddenly shone, and she laughed. "Why, it would make that little pigeon-toed bitch turn pea-green with envy!"

"Consider it done," Starbuck said with a beguiling grin. "Chinatown's seen the last of Harry Lovett."

"You won't regret it." Nell squirmed around and

kissed him soundly. "I'll keep you so worn out you won't have strength enough to eat."

"Hell, why not!" Starbuck chuckled and settled back on the pillow, watching her a moment. "Now that I've told you my secret, you tell me yours."

"Ask away." Nell gave him a sassy, nose-wrinkling smile. "I've already shown you most of my secrets, anyway."

"Well—" Starbuck hesitated, his features sober. "I was wondering why you're afraid of Denny O'Brien."

"Denny?" Surprise washed over Nell's face. "What gave you the idea I'm afraid of Denny?"

"Aren't you?"

"Not on your tintype! Denny's not nearly as tough as he puts on. Besides, if he ever tried any rough stuff with me, he knows I'd take a hike. And p.d.q. too!"

"You could've fooled me."

"Honeybunch, you just lost me. Fooled you when?"

"Earlier tonight," Starbuck replied, "when I asked you why Denny hasn't taken over Chinatown. You clammed up tighter than a drum."

"So what?"

"So I'd say you're scared of him. Damn good and scared!"

"No—" Nell's voice skipped a beat. "Not Denny."

"Who, then?"

"The blind . . ."

Her words trailed away, and she stiffened in his arms. Starbuck studied her with open curiosity. "Go ahead, finish it. The blind————?"

There was an awkward pause. "Harry, take some good advice. While you're in Frisco, don't ask too many questions. What you don't know can't hurt you."

"That bad, huh?"

"You just take my word for it . . . okay?"

"Hell, forget I asked!" Starbuck laughed jovially. "No skin off my nose."

"And let's keep it that way." Nell burrowed deeper into the hollow of his shoulder. "I like your nose just the way it is."

Starbuck dropped it there. He knew he'd learned all he would for one night, and there was no need to push it further. He pulled her to him in a tight embrace, saying no more. Yet the words stuck in his mind, and he found himself genuinely baffled. He lay very still, silently repeating something that seemed to make no sense.

The blind . . .

CHAPTER 9

"Tell me about Mr. Lovett."

"I do not trust him, master."

"Please explain."

May Ling was seated across the table from Fung Jing Toy. A hatchet man had escorted her into his chambers only moments ago. Earlier that afternoon, when the one named Harry Lovett had departed her lodgings, she knew she would be summoned to the house on Washington Street. She had spent the balance of the afternoon in deep reflection, artfully phrasing the report she would deliver to her master. Now, under Fung's benign gaze, she began what seemed to her a perilous journey. She dared not to be wrong.

"I believe he is an imposter." Her voice was soft and troubled. "One who pretends to be what he is not."

Fung stared at her in a mild abstracted way. "Did he abuse you?"

"No, master," May Ling said quickly. "He was very gentle for a *fan kwei*."

"How did he differ from other white men I have sent to you?"

"He was not impatient or crude. Nor was he cruel in his demands. We joined three times during the night, and each time he took me without harshness. Today, when we returned from the auction, we joined once again. He was even more considerate . . . gentle."

Fung weighed her words a moment. The white devils, even the wealthy ones, were renowned for their coarse sexual habits and their lack of sophistication in bed. Yet, just as there were brutal Chinese, so might there be gentle white men. To think in absolutes was to cloud one's judgment.

"So then," he said quietly. "Your suspicion was aroused because he did not treat you in the manner practiced by white men?"

"I thought it strange, master. You told me his plan was to open several brothels, and such men are known for their barbaric customs. He was not what I expected."

"Very well," Fung nodded. "Mr. Lovett apparently has attributes uncommon to brothelkeepers. Is there more?"

"Yes, master," May Ling noted seriously. "His behavior at the auction was most revealing."

"You followed my instructions?"

"Oh yes! As you ordered, I asked no questions and gave him no reason for alarm. When I suggested attending the auction, he was very excited, very curious. He believed it was something I had thought of only then. A small inspiration to make his tour of Little China more enjoyable."

"What happened then?"

"At the auction, I observed him closely. His curiosity quickly turned to an attitude of disapproval. He held his tongue, but it was there to see, nonetheless. He frowned, and suddenly became very thoughtful."

"Perhaps he is a thoughtful man."

"Perhaps," May Ling said tactfully. "Quite, soon, however, a circumstance arose which allowed me to test him. I led him into a discussion of slave girls who are unsuitable for auction. His questions enabled me to speak of conditions in the cribs . . . and the hospital."

"Ah!" A pinpoint of light glittered in Fung's eyes. "You trapped him!"

"I merely deceived him, master. He betrayed himself."

"In what way?"

"He was shocked," May Ling remarked. "When I explained how the crib girls end their days, his expression was one of loathing. The very idea of the hospital was abhorrent to him."

"He told you that?"

"Not in words," May Ling said, her eyes downcast. "I sensed it, master. His reaction was that of a white devil missionary. He felt sadness and compassion for the crib girls."

"We were informed that this is his first venture as a brothelkeeper. According to O'Brien, he was what the whites call a con man. Perhaps he has not yet acquired the dispassionate nature necessary to such work."

"Certain things cannot be hidden, master. Whatever his designs are, the man named Lovett is not what he claims. He is an imposter."

"You speak now of intuition, things you divine rather than fact itself. Is it not so?"

"A woman knows," May Ling said, looking directly at him. "How she knows cannot be explained, but that makes it no less real. This man is dangerous, and I fear he will bring evil to your house. I must say what I believe to be true, master."

For a protracted interval, Fung was silent. He steepled his fingers together, considering both the girl and her statement. She was young, but wise beyond her years. Several times in the past he had used her to gain insight into men who sought to do business with him. Her intuition was a mystic thing, and a force not to be regarded lightly. Then, too, everything she'd told him merely served to reinforce his own sense of disquiet. Something about Lovett bothered him, and it was for that reason he had arranged the liaison with May Ling. He examined the alternatives, and quickly decided to heed her warning. The sale of a hundred virgins was, after all, a thing of no great consequence.

"I have learned," he said at length, "that Mr. Lovett will sleep with O'Brien's whore tonight."

"Nothing escapes you, master."

"Quite so," Fung agreed loftily. "I have eyes everywhere, even in the Bella Union."

"Will the Kimball woman also attempt deception?"

"No," Fung said without inflection. "O'Brien is blinded by greed. He suspects nothing."

"A shame," May Ling commented slyly. "But then, no *fan kwei* could be expected to have your wisdom and foresight."

A wintry smile lighted Fung's eyes. "You have performed the task well, and I am pleased."

"I live only to serve you, master."

"Leave me now. Other matters require my attention."

May Ling obediently rose, placed her hands together, and dipped low in a bow. She stepped backward to the door, then turned and walked past the dogs. Fung snapped his fingers, and one of the hatchet men appeared in the doorway. He took pen and paper off the table, and laboriously scrawled a note in English. Then he folded it and looked up at the waiting hatchet man.

"You will deliver this message to the blind white devil."

The Snug Café was located on O'Farrell Street, in the heart of the Uptown Tenderloin. Shortly before midnight, a closed carriage rolled to a halt in the alleyway behind the café. Wong Yee and Sing Dock stepped out of the carriage and inspected the alley in both directions. There was no one in sight.

The hatchet men assisted Fung down from the carriage. He walked directly to the back door of the café and knocked. He was expected, and the door swung open almost instantly. Knuckles Jackson, a pugnosed bruiser who served as bouncer, waved him through and closed the door. Wong Yee and Sing Dock exchanged a look. Only here would the master dispense with their services and enter unguarded. Neither of them thought the order odd, for only here was he safe without them. Still, it did nothing to lessen their concern.

Inside, Knuckles Jackson led Fung through a storage room and up a flight of stairs. There he stopped and rapped twice on a door. A muffled voice responded and he ushered Fung into a lavishly appointed office. The furniture was black walnut, intricately carved, and upholstered in plush velvet. Logs crackled in a black marble fireplace, and a crystal lamp bathed the room in dim light. Beyond the fireplace, cloaked in shadow, stood a massive walnut desk.

The man seated behind the desk was in his early fifties. He wore a frock coat and striped trousers, and a black cravat with a pearl stickpin. His features were lean and angular, and his gray hair was complimented by a neatly trimmed mustache. His eyes were all but invisible behind dark tinted glasses. He gestured toward a chair, and smiled.

"Do come in, Fung. Have a seat."

"Thank you, Mr. Buckley." Fung took the chair,

folding his hands in his lap. "It was kind of you to see me on such short notice."

"Not at all." Buckley dismissed Knuckles Jackson with a nod, and waited until the door closed. "Now, what can I do for you? I daresay it's nothing inconsequential at this late hour."

"That is so." Fung's tone was curiously deferential. "A problem has arisen, and I felt it should be brought to your attention immediately."

"Well, well, that does sound serious. Suppose you tell me about it."

"I regret to say it involves Denny O'Brien."

"Oh?" The smile faded and a shadow of irritation crossed Buckley's features. "I trust you and Denny aren't at one another's throats again?"

"I have not overstepped my boundaries. To my knowledge, neither has O'Brien. As you directed, we have worked together in a spirit of cooperation."

"And now?"

"There is no dispute with regard to territory. O'Brien confines himself to the Barbary Coast, and I do the same in Chinatown. In that respect, we have both honored your wishes."

"Diplomacy has its place, but let's dispense with it for the moment, shall we? Please come to the point."

"Yes, of course," Fung said promptly. "O'Brien sent a man to me three days ago on a business matter. I now have reason—"

"A white man?"

"Indeed, so," Fung said with no trace of resentment. "A white man by the name of Harry Lovett, who purports to be a whoremaster from Colorado."

"Very well. Please go on."

"I now have reason to believe Lovett is not what he claims."

"Not a whoremaster?"

"Precisely."

"What is he, then?"

"I have no idea." Fung offered an elaborate shrug. "Because the situation is confused, I thought it wise to seek your counsel."

Buckley sighed, tilting back in his chair. "In the interest of time, why not start at the beginning? And please, Fung, spare me the details. Stick to essentials, the bare bones."

The reproach was delivered in a condescending tone. Fung, who suddenly felt very Oriental and very much out of his element, evidenced no offense. Instead, he launched into a straightforward account of the past three days. He outlined O'Brien's role as intermediary, and went on to describe his meeting with Lovett. He dwelled at length on the matter of a hundred virgins, and Lovett's unusually quick acceptance of the asking price. With a certain flair for intrigue, he then recounted May Ling's role in the affair, and the sequence of events leading to the slave-girl auction. He concluded with a summation of May Ling's misgivings, adding that he, too, shared her doubts. There he paused and awaited Buckley's reaction.

"Are you telling me you're relying solely on this

girl's intuition . . . her feelings about Lovett?"

"To a large extent," Fung admitted. "She has great insight into men, and her perceptions have never failed me before."

Buckley's look was colored by skepticism. "A bit like reading tea leaves, isn't it? You really have nothing concrete to support your view."

"I am satisfied." Fung's features grew overcast. "I no longer wish to do business with this man Lovett."

"What harm could come of it? We have the fix in with immigration, so he's obviously not a government agent. I fail to see how he poses a threat."

"A threat assumes many guises. I have no way of knowing who Lovett may or may not be. On the other hand, I do know the value of caution. I would prefer to cancel the arrangement without delay."

Buckley appeared to lose interest. "Do as you please. Simply inform Lovett the deal's off."

"There are other considerations," Fung said in a musing voice. "O'Brien has quite probably charged Lovett a middleman's fee. That places me in an awkward position."

"Exactly what is it you're asking?"

"I wish you to intercede on my behalf. O'Brien will accept your judgment, and the matter will end there."

"I dislike getting involved in these petty squabbles. Good God, you and Denny are grown men! Work it out for yourselves."

Fung gave him a straight, hard look. "As you are aware, O'Brien bears me personal ill will, and he also covets Chinatown. Were I to withdraw from this arrangement—thereby causing him financial loss—he might easily use it as a pretext to start trouble. Without your intercession, our spirit of harmony may very well be jeopardized. I urge you to reconsider."

"In short," Buckley said with heavy sarcasm, "you want me to pull your chestnuts out of the fire?"

"I bow to your wisdom at all times. As you have so often reminded me—you are the boss."

Buckley gave the matter some thought. "Very well," he said finally, "I'll look into it. I want you to understand something, though. When you make your problems my problems, I begin wondering if maybe I don't need myself a new boy in Chinatown. You might reflect on that before you come begging favors again."

"I most humbly apologize." Fung rose and bowed slightly from the waist. "I wish only to maintain the peace and prosperity we enjoy under your guidance."

"Good night, Fung. I'll let you know what happens."

Buckley sat perfectly still until the door closed. Then he removed his glasses and massaged his eyes. He was tired and his head ached, and at times like tonight, he felt very much like a rooster atop a dung heap. The footing somehow never seemed all that firm. Nor had he yet accustomed himself to the smell.

*　　*　　*

Denny O'Brien was summoned late the next morning. The Snug Café wasn't yet open for business, but he, too, entered through the alley door. Upstairs, he kept his greeting short and polite, and dropped into a chair before the desk. Buckley went straight to the point.

"Fung paid me a visit last night. He's jumpy about a deal you arranged with some fellow named Lovett."

"What d'you mean?" O'Brien said with an annoyed squint. "What's there to be jumpy about?"

"He wants out," Buckley said flatly. "He seems to think your friend Lovett isn't on the up and up."

"That's crazy!" O'Brien burst out. "Harry Lovett's as square as they come!"

"What makes you think so?"

"Mattie Silks herself sent him to see me. She's the biggest madam in Denver, and anyone she recommends is ace-high in my book."

Buckley looked somber. "Have you checked him out? Wired Mattie Silks or some of our friends in Denver?"

"No." O'Brien shook his head in exasperation. "Why would I check him out? Jesus H. Christ, the man's loaded! He's ready to hand Fung a hundred thousand—for virgins, no less!"

"And I take it you've cut yourself in for a piece of the action?"

"Why not?" O'Brien bridled. "I made the introduction, didn't I?"

"Perhaps that's the problem." Buckley's tone was

severe. "I got the distinct impression Fung suspects you slipped a ringer in on him. He's convinced Lovett is a setup of some sort."

"Goddamn him!" O'Brien roared vindictively. "That slant-eyed little son-of-a-bitch never stops! He won't be satisfied till I'm six feet under and turned into worm meat."

"Have you given him reason?"

"Hell, no! You laid out the rules and I've stayed on my side of the street. Chinatown don't mean beans to me."

"Then why would he turn leery so quickly? From what he told me, it sounds like a fairly routine deal."

"It's spite, plain and simple." O'Brien face congealed into a scowl. "He's willing to queer the deal just to give everybody a laugh at my expense. That makes him look like a big man to all his Chink pals."

"I think not." Buckley's headshake was slow and emphatic. "His concern was genuine. He believes there's something fishy, and he would sooner be safe than sorry."

"By Jesus!" O'Brien said stubbornly. "I won't hold still for it. I stood to make a cool ten thousand on this deal, and I mean to have it."

"You're wrong." Buckley's voice was suddenly edged. "You'll do exactly what I tell you to do, Denny. I won't allow you or anyone else to upset my applecart. Do I make myself clear?"

"I hear you," O'Brien said grudgingly. "But it goes down hard, you taking that slope-head's side against me."

"Wrong again," Buckley replied with weary tolerance. "I haven't ruled one way or the other, not yet."

"I don't get you."

"It occurs to me that Mr. Lovett and I should have a talk. You bring him around late this evening. I'll make my judgment then, and it won't have anything to do with you or Fung. All very impartial, based strictly on my impression of Lovett."

"Little risky, isn't it?" O'Brien looked worried. "He's no dummy, and you're not exactly somebody he'd forget real quick."

Buckley's laugh was strange and somehow cryptic. "Our talk might prove risky for Mr. Lovett. Only time and the tea leaves will tell."

O'Brien felt a tingle along his backbone. He'd heard that laugh before, and he knew precisely what it meant. Tonight there would be no quibbling, no questions left unanswered. Nor would there be anything remotely resembling a second chance.

Harry Lovett was a dead man unless he passed muster.

CHAPTER 10

It was half-past eight when Starbuck arrived at the Bella Union. He reeked of rosewood lotion and was attired in yet another of his spiffy outfits. He walked through the barroom and paused in the doorway of the theater. Thumbs hooked in his vest, he slowly scanned the crowd.

His appointment with Nell was for somewhere around nine. Their plans, with one exception, were much the same as last night. A theater box was reserved, chilled champagne was on order, and the first part of their evening would be devoted to the early show. Afterward, a late supper would be served in the privacy of Nell's room. The balance of the night, something of a return engagement, would be spent in bed. There would be lovemaking and talk, lots of talk. Tonight, he expected to learn considerably more about San Francisco's underworld. Perhaps all he needed to know.

Standing in the doorway, he thought it strange

that Nell was nowhere in sight. He glanced at the curtained box and saw that it was empty. Then, checking his watch, it occurred to him that she might still be in her room. He was about to turn when High Spade McQueen laid a hand on his shoulder. He looked around.

"The boss wants to see you." McQueen jerked his chin toward the staircase. "Now."

"Why sure thing, High Spade. Lead the way."

Something in McQueen's attitude alerted him. When they reached the staircase, any lingering doubt was dispelled. McQueen casually lagged behind and followed him, rather than leading him up the stairs. He knew then he was in trouble. He warned himself to go slow and keep a sharp lookout.

On the balcony, McQueen opened the office door and motioned him through. Denny O'Brien was seated behind the desk, his expression grim. Starbuck heard the door close, and realized he was sandwiched between them. With a jaunty air, he flipped O'Brien a salute and approached the desk.

"Evening, Denny," he said with a jocular smile. "How's tricks?"

O'Brien's hand appeared from beneath the desk, holding a pistol. "Don't make any sudden moves."

"Judas Priest!" Starbuck croaked. "What the hell's the idea?"

"Shut your trap." O'Brien looked past him. "Mac, pat him down."

McQueen expertly went over him. The Colt Lightning was discovered almost immediately, and removed from its shoulder holster. His arms were checked for a sleeve gun; then his waistband and all his pockets were thoroughly searched. He waited, certain the hideout gun in his boot top was next; but his legs weren't touched. Finally, McQueen shoved him into a chair and looked across at O'Brien.

"He's clean."

"You're sure he hasn't got a hideout?"

"One peashooter." McQueen palmed the Colt and stuck it inside his belt. "That's it, boss."

O'Brien laid his pistol on the desk. Then, with a venomous glare, his gaze shifted to Starbuck. "I oughta bust your goddamn skull wide open."

"For Chrissake!" Starbuck said, squirming around in his chair. "What's the matter? What'd I do?"

"I'll ask the questions!" O'Brien's first slammed onto the desk. "You just gimme some straight answers, or else I'll let Mac and his sailor pals feed you to the sharks."

"Anything at all, Denny. Go ahead, ask away."

"How come you told me you're in thick with the sporting crowd in Denver?"

"I never said that," Starbuck corrected him. "I told you I mostly worked the mining camps. All I said about Denver was that me and Mattie Silks are on good terms."

"You're a liar!" O'Brien shouted. "I wired Mattie and she said she never heard of you."

"That's a crock," Starbuck said stoutly. "No way on God's green earth Mattie wouldn't vouch for me."

He saw he'd guessed right. O'Brien's eyes gave him away, and he quickly backed off from the bluff. "All right, so I wired her and just haven't got the answer yet. It amounts to the same thing. If she don't give you a clean bill of health, you'll get deep-sixed so fast you won't know what hit you."

"Denny, I'll give you odds on what her wire says."

"Don't get too cocky," O'Brien warned him. "You've still got your balls in a nutcracker."

"What's that supposed to mean?"

"Suppose you tell me about your talk with Fung."

"Fung?" Starbuck looked bewildered. "Hell, there wasn't much talk to it. He set a price, and we dickered for a while, then I finally agreed. That's the way we left it."

"You had a deal, then? You're sure of that?"

"I'm plumb sure. No two ways about it."

"When did he say he'd make delivery?"

"Well . . ." Starbuck stopped, thoughtful a moment. "He didn't say, not exactly. He allowed it would take a while to get that many virgins together, and told me he'd be in touch."

"How long? A week, two weeks?"

"He never spelled it out, and I never asked. I'd already agreed to pay top dollar, so I figured he'd hop right to it."

"Didn't it ever occur to you that you might be getting the runaround?"

"Why would he do a thing like that?"

"Forget it," O'Brien muttered. "What did he ask you about me?"

"Nothing." Starbuck shrugged, shook his head. "Near as I recollect, your name wasn't even mentioned."

O'Brien gave him a swift, intense look. "Think back on it, real hard. Maybe he asked you how long we've known each other? Whether or not we've done business before? Anything along that line?"

"Not a word," Starbuck said without hesitation. "Course, he seemed to know all about me and what it was I wanted. I just naturally assumed you'd managed to fill him in before I got there."

"You assumed right." O'Brien mulled it over briefly, then glanced up. "What about the girl, May Ling? She mention me, try to draw you out somehow?"

"Same story," Starbuck observed. "She never said boo about anything except Chinatown and the slave-girl trade."

"Yeah, that's right. She took you to the auction, didn't she? Cooked you a Chink meal and screwed your ears off—and never asked one question about me! Is that what you're saying?"

"That's the works, Denny. Start to finish."

O'Brien's voice suddenly turned querulous. "You stupid son-of-a-bitch! Do you think I'm gonna sit here and let you con me like some snot-nosed hayseed?"

"Con you?" Starbuck was genuinely surprised. "I'm telling it to you straight. Honest to Christ!"

"Bullshit!" O'Brien glowered back at him. "I happen to know you asked Nell how come I never tried to take over Chinatown."

"So?"

"So where'd you dream up that idea? I'll tell you where! Fung and that little Chinee bitch put the bee in your ear. The whole time you were with 'em, they pumped you dry about me, didn't they?"

"No, goddamnit, they didn't!" Starbuck sounded indignant. "I told it to you just the way it happened."

"Then why'd you ask Nell what you did?"

"Because any fool could see you and Fung hate each other's guts. Nobody has to say anything! It's plain as a diamond in a goat's ass."

"And you figured it out all by yourself?"

"Hell, yes!" Starbuck blustered. "Fung and his hatchet men wouldn't be any match for you and your boys. That's plain to see, too. I guess it just got my curiosity working overtime."

"Curiosity about what?"

"Well, I don't mean to insult you, Denny. But, Jesus Christ, nobody's got your arms tied, have they? The way it looks to me, you could've gobbled up Chinatown anytime you took a notion. It's like I told Nell—if it was me, there wouldn't be no way I could resist giving it a try."

O'Brien's silence was all the answer Starbuck needed. He sensed Nell had lied. She hadn't told O'Brien about his greater curiosity, the vague questions he'd asked about an underworld kingpin. Nor had she mentioned her own slip of the tongue, her unfinished statement that ended abruptly with "the blind." Quite clearly, she had lied to protect him. Whether she realized it or not, she had nudged herself a step closer to his side of the line. He now had something approaching an ally in the enemy camp. A little softsoap, with a dash of blackmail added, would soon bring her around.

O'Brien, who seemed to have recovered his humor, finally broke the silence. "Harry, I'll have to hand it to you. You're a pretty smooth article."

"Why, thank you, Denny. I'm sort of sweet on you, too."

"Don't misunderstand me," O'Brien countered. "You're not out of the woods yet."

"Oh, how so?"

"Well, as it happens, we've got a helluva problem with Fung. He wants to back out on the deal. Somehow or other, he's turned leery toward you."

"Why?" Starbuck demanded. "What's his reason?"

"I'm not altogether sure," O'Brien said, frowning. "From what I gather, he's got it in his head you're working with me—a swindle of some sort—or else you're a government agent."

"He's nuts!" Starbuck scoffed. "I don't work for you or anyone else. And that goddamned sure includes the government!"

"All the same, that's what we're up against."

"Then we'll just wait till you get Mattie's wire. Once you show him that, he'll know I'm on the level and we're back in business."

"Harry, if it was up to me, I wouldn't hesitate a minute. But it's out of my hands now."

Starbuck's pulse quickened. "I don't get your meaning."

"You've got an appointment." O'Brien rose and stuffed his pistol in the waistband of his trousers. "Tonight you're to talk with the big man himself, Mr. Frisco."

"Mr. Frisco?"

"Let's get a move on. You're expected, and I wouldn't care to keep him waiting."

With O'Brien in the lead, and McQueen bringing up the rear, they went through the door and crossed the balcony. On the way down the stairs, Starbuck was acutely aware that his gun had not been returned. He also understood, though it was left unspoken, that he had passed only Denny O'Brien's test.

Mr. Frisco, and a sterner test, was yet to come.

A gentle rain was falling as the carriage turned off O'Farrell Street. Starbuck wasn't at all surprised that their destination was located in the Uptown Tenderloin. His theory regarding the boss of San Francisco's underworld was now confirmed.

All the way uptown he had tried in vain to learn the identity of Mr. Frisco. His questions finally provoked Denny O'Brien, and he was told to drop the subject. Still, with or without a name, it was clear O'Brien and Fung answered to one man. A man who rubbed elbows with the city's social elite, the rich and the powerful. A mastermind who had created a brilliant cover, disassociating himself completely from Chinatown and the Barbary Coast. And therefore a man who was exceedingly dangerous.

The thought was foremost in Starbuck's mind as the carriage rolled to a halt in the alleyway. He knew the next few minutes would determine whether he lived or died. Mr. Frisco had gone to great lengths to conceal his identity. Yet he apparently had no qualms about exposing himself to a Colorado whoremaster. The conclusion was obvious, and the hazard involved was beyond question. Unless Mr. Frisco got all the right answers, the end result was chillingly simple to predict. One whoremaster, more or less, would never be missed.

The alley door opened and Knuckles Jackson waved them inside. Starbuck was treated to yet another search, but took scant comfort from the fact that his hideout gun once again went undetected. McQueen and Jackson, who belonged to the same brotherhood of gorillas, remained on guard in the storeroom. O'Brien escorted him up the stairs, which meant he was covered front and rear. The chances of shooting his way out weren't even worth calculating. His wits were now his only hope for survival.

The light in the office was dim, and the man behind the desk sat immobile. Starbuck had the fleeting impression of a store-window dummy propped up in a chair. Then O'Brien closed the door, removing his hat, and walked forward. Starbuck followed suit, quickly inspecting the office. The door to the store-room stairs was the only exit.

"Here he is," O'Brien said, halting in front of the desk. "Harry Lovett."

"Thank you, Denny." Buckley made a small gesture of dismissal. "Wait downstairs. I'll call if I need you."

O'Brien seemed on the verge of questioning the order. Then he bobbed his head, turning away, and crossed the office. A moment later the door closed. Starbuck grinned and stuck out his hand.

"Pleased to meet you, Mr. Frisco."

Starbuck was rocked by a sudden jolt of aware-ness. His arm extended, leaning over the desk, he got his first good look at the man. The face was a living waxwork, and behind the dark tinted glasses, the eyes were marble-like. He had the eerie sensation of gazing into the eyes of a stuffed animal, glassy and unmoving. Nell's word's flitted through his head, and abruptly it all made sense. The blind man! She'd almost blurted it out, and now he saw it for himself. The boss of San Francisco's underworld was *blind*. His mouth popped open and he slowly withdrew his hand. He stood there, too stunned to speak.

"Have a seat, Mr. Lovett." Buckley motioned him to a chair. "I presume it was Denny who referred to me as Mr. Frisco?"

"Yeah." Starbuck took a seat, rapidly collected his wits. "He said it was all the name I needed to know."

"By no means," Buckley said with a frosty smile. "My name is Buckley. Christopher Buckley."

"Well, Mr. Buckley, maybe you can explain something to me. What's all this strongarm business about? I came out here to buy myself some whores, and now I've got people sticking guns in my face."

"I'm afraid Denny overreacts at times. You see, Mr. Lovett, we have a difference of opinion with respect to the girls you wish to purchase. I've been asked to arbitrate the matter."

"You're talking about Fung trying to welch on our deal?"

"Exactly." Buckley inclined his head in a faint nod. "In Fung's words, you are not what you represent yourself to be, Mr. Lovett."

"So Denny told me." Starbuck switched to a light and mocking tone. "Dumb goddamn Chinaman! Somebody ought to tell him he's got his head screwed on backward."

"Perhaps you wouldn't mind answering a question?"

"Fire away," Starbuck said cheerfully. "I've got no secrets."

"Are you familiar with Lou Blomger?"

"Why, hell, yes! Everybody in Denver knows Lou Blomger. You name it, he runs it! The rackets, politics—the whole ball of wax."

"I wired him this morning." Buckley indicated a telegram lying open on the desk. "If you care to read his reply, he says in no uncertain terms he never heard of Harry Lovett."

"What's that prove?" Starbuck protested. "Blomger's out of my league. I work the mining camps, not Denver. He wouldn't know me from Adam's off ox."

"Come now, Mr. Lovett. A man with your connections—Mattie Silks, no less—and Blomger never heard of you. I find that difficult to believe."

Starbuck took a chance. "Tell you what, Mr. Buckley. You're so fond of sending wires, send one to Bailey Youngston in Leadville. He owns the Texas House Saloon and half the town to boot. Ask him if I didn't knock down the biggest score of my life, not two months ago, sitting right in his joint. Hell, for the right price, he'll even tell you the sucker's name!"

There was a long silence. "Very well, Mr. Lovett," Buckley said at length. "I will defer my decision for the moment—but only on three conditions. One, we will await replies from Mattie Silks and your friend, Youngston. Next, as a gesture of good faith, you will deposit one hundred thousand dollars in the bank of my choice by closing time tomorrow. Will that present any problem?"

"No problem at all," Starbuck assured him earnestly. "I came prepared to pay in cash, so you just name your bank and I'll be there johnny-on-the-spot."

"Fine," Buckley said with dungeon calm. "I feel quite certain that will go a long way toward dispelling Fung's apprehension."

"You said there were three conditions?"

"Indeed, I did." A cold smile touched the corner of Buckley's mouth. "Until the matter is resolved to my satisfaction, you will make no attempt to leave San Francisco. Need I elaborate on that condition further?"

"No, sir, no need. I get your drift completely."

Starbuck knew he'd been given a reprieve, nothing more. Bailey Youngston was the owner of the Texas House Saloon, but nobody in Leadville had ever heard of Harry Lovett. Youngston might answer a wire from a stranger, and he might not. That was a toss-up, and could go either way. The money, on the other hand, was a surefire certainty. And tomorrow at closing time was less than twenty-four hours away.

All of a sudden Starbuck felt like a juggler with one too many balls in the air. Yet there was no question which one he had to grab first, and fastest.

He wondered where the hell he could lay his hands on $100,000!

CHAPTER 11

Nell was waiting in the theater box. The Bella Union was already packed, but she easily spotted them as they moved through the crowd in the barroom. O'Brien paused near the staircase, talking with Starbuck a moment. Then, accompanied by High Spade McQueen, he mounted the stairs and disappeared into his office.

Starbuck looked toward the box and saw her. Doffing his hat, he waved, smiling broadly. She waved back, watching as he crossed the theater and went up the short flight of stairs leading to the loge. Earlier, one of the bartenders had told her he'd left the Bella Union with O'Brien and McQueen. She had no idea where they had gone or why. Nor was she about to ask. Their business dealings were none of her concern, and she preferred to keep it that way. Experience had taught her that inquisitive women often learned too much for their own good. In her view, she was paid to entertain, not ask questions.

"Sorry I'm late."

Entering the box, Starbuck tossed his hat on the sofa and took a chair beside her. Nell gave him a dazzling smile, and leaned forward to kiss him lightly on the mouth.

"No need to apologize, lover. You're here now, and that's what counts."

"We still set to have supper in your room?"

"Of course." She removed a bottle of champagne from an ice bucket and filled two glasses. "What's an hour more or less? The night's young."

"That's my girl!" Starbuck winked and lifted his glass in a toast. "Here's mud in your eye."

Nell laughed, clinking glasses. "Yours, too, honeybun."

Starbuck appraised her as she sipped champagne. He detected a false note in her voice and saw the guarded look in her eyes. He seriously doubted that O'Brien had confided in her, or told her that a meeting had been arranged with Buckley. Yet she was curious, and clearly biting her tongue not to ask questions. He thought to himself that it was a good sign. Her curiosity made her vulnerable.

Handled properly, tonight's development could accomplish two essential goals. She might easily be beguiled into revealing more about Buckley, and his place in the scheme of things. With time at a premium, any scrap of information was vital, and she represented the only dependable source. Further, the more she revealed, the simpler it would be to enlist her as an ally. By playing on her curiosity, and her fear of O'Brien, she might be forced into a conspiracy from which there was no return. A certain risk was attached, but he really had no choice. Tonight would determine whether or not he could trust her, and exactly how far she would go in the event push came to shove. All that remained was to sound her out.

Tossing off his champagne, he refilled their glasses. Then, a thumb hooked in his vest, he sat back and grinned expansively.

"So far it's been some night."

"Oh?"

"Yessir, it has for a fact. Denny introduced me to the big boy himself, in the flesh."

"The big boy?"

"The blind man." Starbuck watched her out of the corner of his eye. "Christopher Buckley."

Surprise washed over Nell's face. "Denny took you to see Buckley?"

"Sure did," Starbuck said carelessly. "Had ourselves a pretty nice chat, too."

Nell nodded, then smiled a little. "You're going up in the world. Not many people get to meet Mr. Buckley."

"You mean to say you've never met him?"

"Nooo," she said slowly. "He's out of my league."

"Then how'd you know he was blind?"

"Blind?"

"Yeah." Starbuck idly gestured with his champagne glass. "Last night you started to say something about the blind somebody or other, but you never finished it."

"I was talking out of turn. I didn't know Denny had arranged a meeting."

"Tell you the truth, I don't think Denny arranged anything."

Nell gave him a glance full of curiosity. "I'm not sure I understand."

"Well—" Starbuck took a sip of champagne, pondered a moment. "Unless I read it wrong, when Buckley say frog, Denny squats. Am I right or not?"

"You're close enough."

"Thought so." Starbuck bobbed his head sagely. "Buckley ordered him to bring me around all because of that damn fool Chinaman."

"Fung?"

"Nothing serious." Starbuck rocked his hand, fingers splayed. "Fung evidently got cold feet about our deal. Had some asinine notion that Denny and me were out to gaff him somehow."

Nell looked upset. "You mean Buckley thought you weren't on the level?"

"The way he put it, he'd been asked to arbitrate the matter. That's fancy lingo for saying it's up to him whether or not the deal goes through."

"What happened?"

"Won't know for a couple of days," Starbuck observed casually. "He wants to check out my references before he decides, and I told him that was fine by me. Harry Lovett's got nothing to hide."

"You're sure of that?" Nell asked anxiously.

"Buckley's one man you don't want for an enemy."

Starbuck uttered a low chuckle. "I got the same impression myself. Denny acted like he was in the presence of Jesus Christ and the Lord God Jehovah all rolled into one."

"You're getting warm, lover. So far as this town's concerned, anyway."

"Now that you mention it," Starbuck appeared thoughtful, "on the way uptown, Denny called him 'Mr. Frisco.' I reckon the name fits, or else Denny and Fung wouldn't report to him like good little soldiers."

"Denny told you that?"

"Told me what?"

"About reporting to Buckley?"

"Nope," Starbuck readily admitted. "But it's plain enough to see. Denny and Fung are like lieutenants; one runs the Coast and the other runs Chinatown. Buckley cracks the whip, and whatever hoop he holds up, that's the one they jump through."

"I wouldn't say that out loud too often if I were you."

"Why?" Starbuck looked at her directly. "It's the truth, isn't it?"

Nell averted her gaze. A troupe of acrobats went tumbling across the stage, and she watched them in silence for a time. Finally, with a furtive shrug, she spoke in a low voice.

"Harry, the truth can get you hurt. Take some good advice, and don't let anybody know you've figured out how things work in Frisco."

"Yeah, I suppose you're right."

"I know I'm right."

"All the same, there's one thing that damn sure doesn't figure."

"You'll ask anyway," Nell said reluctantly, "so go ahead."

"How the hell's a blind man put the fear of God in someone like Denny O'Brien?"

"I'll give you three guesses, and the first two don't count."

"You make it sound awful simple."

"Nothing simpler, if you have the stomach for it." Starbuck smiled. "How about a clue?"

"Oh, suppose we call it the second oldest profession in the world?"

The curtain at the door opened and O'Brien stepped into the box. He nodded to Nell, his mouth split in a wide smile. Then he moved around the sofa and genially clapped Starbuck on the shoulder.

"Enjoying the show?"

"Which one?"

"Which one?" O'Brien parroted, gesturing toward the stage. "I only see one."

"Oh, that?" Starbuck rolled his eyes at Nell. "Just between you and me, Denny, I'm waiting for the finale."

"Harry, you're a sport! Goddamn me if you aren't."

"Let's just say there are other things I prefer to acrobats."

"You'll be spending the night with us, then?"

Starback looked at him, unable to guess what might be going through his mind. The question was phrased in the manner of an invitation, but there was an undertone of command in O'Brien's voice. Whether the message was meant for Starbuck or Nell seemed a moot point. The owner of the Bella Union hadn't popped into the box to make small talk. He was there for a purpose.

"Nell's the one to ask." Starbuck let go a hoot of laughter. "I can go all night and then some, but a girl needs her beauty sleep."

"Don't worry about Nell," O'Brien advised with heavy good humor. "She's lots tougher than she looks."

"I'll let you know in the morning."

"You do that, Harry."

O'Brien grinned, as if at some private joke. Then he glanced at Nell and turned away. The curtain parted and they were once more alone in the box.

Starbuck poured champagne, seemingly unperturbed by the interruption. He noted that Nell's manner was pensive and oddly taut. Her gaze was fixed on the stage. He gave her leg a squeeze and chortled softly to himself.

"That Denny's a card, isn't he? Always funning around—"

"You lied to me!"

"Lied?" Starbuck feigned astonishment. "What the hell are you talking about?"

"Stop it!" Nell said in a shaky voice. "You're try-

ing to con me, and I don't appreciate it one damn
bit."

"You got a crystal ball, or did you figure that out
all by yourself?"

"I don't need a crystal ball. I know Denny like
the back of my hand, and he wasn't playing patty-
cake and roses. He came up here to give you a warning."

Starbuck smiled lamely and lifted his hands in a
shrug. "You've got me dead to rights. I needed help
and I wasn't exactly sure how to go about asking."

"What kind of help?"

"I'm caught in the middle," Starbuck lied,
straightfaced. "Denny and Fung are out to axe one
another, and they're using me as a stalking horse.
That's what brought Buckley into it. He doesn't want
any trouble, and he's willing to sacrifice me to keep
the peace."

Nell looked skeptical. "Is that the truth or some
more of your malarkey?"

"Buckley ordered me not to leave town, and
Denny just got through warning me to stick close to
the Bella Union. That pretty well tells the tale,
doesn't it?"

Starbuck was improvising now. By threading a
strand of truth into the web of fabrication, he hoped
to draw her over to his side. She was silent for a
time, her face blank, her eyes opaque. Then, finally,
she sighed and her expression softened.

"Okay, lover, I'm a sucker for a sob story and
you've got me hooked. How can I help?"

"First off," Starbuck said quickly, "show me how to slip out of here without being seen—maybe later, sometime after we've gone to your room. That way Denny will think I'm tucked in for the night."

"Are you planning to skip Frisco?"

"No," Starbuck said without guile. "Buckley ordered me to come up with the hundred thousand by tomorrow. I've got it stashed somewhere safe, and I want to deliver it on my own. That'll show good faith, and go a long way toward getting me out of the middle."

"All right," Nell agreed. "Denny had a dumbwaiter installed to bring meals up to the third floor. Once the kitchen closes, we'll use that to get you downstairs and then you can slip out the alley door. What's next?"

"I want the story on Buckley, the whole ball of wax. If he decides to play rough, I'll need something to trade, something he'd consider worth a standoff."

"Holy Hannah," Nell said with a theatrical shudder. "You ask a lot, don't you?"

"Only enough to keep me alive."

"Don't kid yourself." Nell looked at him with dulled eyes. "Buckley doesn't have to bargain with anybody. He has a dozen different ways to silence you, and all of them permanent."

"A man plays the cards he's dealt. It's that or run, and I've never been one to turn tail. Besides, I don't like the way Danny and Fung sandbagged me."

"What the hell? It's your funeral."

"Not yet." Starbuck grinned. "You just give me

the lowdown on Buckley, and I'll bluff him right out of his socks."

"There's not a lot to tell. I only know what I've heard when Denny goes on a toot and lets his tongue wag too much."

"How long has Buckley been top dog?"

"Long before my time. Twenty years, maybe more."

"Jesus," Starbuck marveled. "He must be tough. How'd he get his start?"

"The Tenderloin," Nell replied. "From what I gather, he killed the previous boss and just stepped into his shoes."

"You're saying a blind man was able to pull that off?"

"Well, he wasn't blind then. According to Denny, he was wounded in the shootout and lost his sight afterward. His men stuck by him and he branched out from there."

"Why would they stick by a blind man?"

"Because he's one brainy bastard! Even without eyes, he can outthink lugheads like Denny. On top of that, he's masterminded every crooked deal in this town. Nothing moves without his say-so."

"Are you talking about Chinatown and the Coast?"

"No." Nell slowly shook her head. "I'm talking about Frisco, from the bay to the Golden Gate."

"*Politics!*" Starbuck's eyes narrowed with sudden comprehension. "That's what you meant earlier, wasn't it? When you said something about the second oldest profession?"

Nell bobbed her head. "Buckley *is* the Democratic Party. That's why Denny calls him Mr. Frisco. His wardheelers deliver the votes and he owns city hall like he'd foreclosed on the mortgage."

"So it's not fear—personal fear—that keeps Denny and Fung in line. They toe the mark because he's the political kingfish. Is that it?"

"No question about it," Nell affirmed. "He hand-picked Denny to run the Coast, and the same with Fung in Chinatown. One word from him and they'd both be out on their ears. He made them and he can break them. It's just that simple."

"In other words," Starbuck mused thoughtfully, "Denny's plug-uglies and Fung's hatchet men couldn't save them no matter what."

"That's the setup," Nell remarked. "They've got the muscle, but Buckley's got the clout. He controls the mayor and the police department and every patronage job in the city. If he says Denny and Fung are out, then they're out. Period!"

Starbuck considered a moment. "How about payoffs? The take on the Coast alone must be worth a fortune. Is there a bagman—a go-between—or does Denny deal directly with Buckley?"

"Search me." Nell gave Starbuck a bemused look. "I only know what I hear, and nobody talks about payoffs. Even when he's drunk, Denny's not that thick."

"What about graft? Bribes? Anyone with Buckley's power has to knock down a mint with under-the-table loot."

"Oh, I imagine he robs the city like a bandit. But you couldn't prove it by me. I've never heard a rumor to that effect, much less read anything in the newspapers. He keeps a tight lid on the operation, real hush-hush. They way I get it, nobody but him knows the full score."

"How do you mean?"

"Well, it's like he wears two hats. One for politics and one for vice. He keeps them separate, never mixes one with the other. So nobody down here has any real pull with city hall or the police department. It all begins and ends with Buckley."

"Very cagey," Starbuck nodded. "One king with two kingdoms. Nobody trusts anyone else, so there's never a chance they'll join forces and kick him off the throne."

"I told you he's a brainy bastard."

"All the more reason for me to show up with the money tomorrow."

Nell smiled wanly. "You'd better think about tonight, lover. Otherwise, there won't be any tomorrow."

"As a matter of fact"—Starbuck leaned forward and poured the last of the champagne—"we're going to order another bottle of bubbly and pretend we're having ourselves a high old time. When we start up to your room, I want Denny to think we're sloshed to the gills. That way he won't get any funny notions and come tiptoeing around in the night."

"What about when we get to the room?"

"What about it?"

"Do we have to pretend then," Nell vamped him with a sultry look, "or can we play it for real?"

Starbuck laughed. "We'll play it any whichaway you like. How's that sound?"

"Love it!" Neil giggled and clapped her hands. "Simply love it, Mr. Lovett."

Starbuck wasn't sure whether she intended a pun. Nor was he curious enough to pursue it further. His thoughts turned instead to the dumbwaiter and the long night ahead.

Dawn suddenly seemed all too close for comfort.

CHAPTER 12

She had the gift of natural repose, not unlike a sleeping cat. She lay curled in the iron band of his arm, cloyed with the scent of love. Her breasts dipped and swelled with the rise and fall of his breathing.

Their lovemaking had been slow and tender. Tonight she had given herself completely, and he had brought her to full and wondrous climax. Her undulations timed to the questing thrust of his manhood, they joined in an explosive burst of sweet agony. In that final moment, her contractions had held him fast, draining him, and she discovered something she had known with no other man. She found enkindled need, and the stirring of emotion.

Now, awake and restive, Starbuck's thoughts centered on more practical matters. One step remained before they parted for the night. She had committed herself by talking openly and agreeing to assist in his escape from the Bella Union. Yet he distrusted any arrangement based solely on emotion; troublesome second thoughts might later cause her to regret the act. He felt the need to further guarantee her switch of allegiance from O'Brien. Loyalty, in his experience, was determined only in part by the degree of jeopardy one person was willing to risk for another. The greater part of loyalty was anchored to self-interest, and he saw that as an essential element yet to be realized. He wanted her obligated not to him but to herself. A commitment whereby she would lose greatly in the event she was tempted to backslide.

Starbuck patted her on the rump and gently disengaged from her close embrace. Then he stretched, yawning, and swung his legs over the side of the bed.

"Time to get a move on."

"I know, damnit." Nell sat up in bed, her breasts round and firm in the dim light. "Why is it the good things never last?"

Her words presented an opening, and Starbuck seized on the opportunity. "Funny you mentioned that. I've been lying there thinking the same thing myself."

"You have?"

"Well, not exactly the way you mean, but pretty close. I got to toying with an idea about the future."

"Whose future?"

"Yours and mine."

"Honestly?" Nell said on an indrawn breath. "You really mean it?"

"Honest Injun." Starbuck gathered his pants off a

nearby chair and began dressing. "Course, it all depends on how things turn out with Buckley."

"All what?"

"Nothing's certain, but let's play 'suppose' a minute. Suppose Buckley puts his stamp of approval on the deal. Suppose Denny and Fung salute and figure they'd be wiser to obey orders, and I end up with my hundred virgins. Suppose I take the girls back to Colorado and open a string of cathouses. In other words, suppose it all works out just the way I'd planned."

"I'll bite," Nell said, thoroughly mystified. "Suppose it does?"

"Then I'll need someone to run the operation for me. Someone like you."

"Me!" Nell squealed. "You're not serious?"

"The hell I'm not!" Starbuck began stuffing his shirt-tail into his pants, and gave her a dopey grin. "I've got big ideas and plenty of money, but I'm sort of shy on know-how. You said it yourself, when you asked me if I'd ever run a whorehouse. I guess that's what put the notion in my head."

"There's not all that much to it, not really."

"Say's you." Starbuck screwed up his face in a frown. "I don't know beans from buckshot about anything. One house would be headache enough for a tyro like me. But I aim to open four houses all at once! Think on that a minute."

"You're right," Nell conceded. "An operation that size could cause you some grief."

"Grief!" Starbuck snorted. "Christ, I'd be worse

off than a one-legged man in a kicking contest. Just for openers, I'd have to hire a madam for each house. Then I'd have to figure out a way to keep them honest and make goddamn sure their books are straight. Otherwise, they could skim off the cream and leave me wondering how I went broke so fast."

"Honey, I hate to be the one to tell you, but the madams aren't your real problem. It's the girls! When you put that many females under one roof, it turns into a slam-bang catfight, night and day. Once you lose control, the whole operation could go to hell in a handbasket."

"That's my point," Starbuck said forcefully. "I need someone to select the right madams and ride herd on all five houses. A supervisor or manager, someone who knows all the tricks of the trade. To my way of thinking, that someone is you."

"You really mean it, don't you?"

"Damn right!" Starbuck sensed it was time to dangle the carrot. "Matter of fact, I've already thought it out, and I'm willing to offer you ten percent right off the top. With four houses, I figure we'll rake in an easy million a year, maybe more. Your slice wouldn't exactly be termed chicken feed."

"Omigawd!" Nell whispered, awestruck. "A hundred thousand dollars! I'd be rich!"

"The sky's the limit," Starbuck observed grandly. "We'd make a helluva team, you and me. No telling where it would end."

Nell's head was buzzing. She suddenly saw an opportunity to put the Bella Union and the Barbary

Coast behind her. The manager of a Colorado whore-house empire was by no means a candidate for saint-hood. Still, it was the only profession she knew, and it was several rungs up the ladder from the life she'd led in Frisco. Moreover, it offered the chance for financial independence, wealth beyond anything she had ever imagined. Which meant never again having to spread her legs for whiskey-soaked highrollers and pot-gutted old men.

Then there was Harry Lovett. He evoked re-sponses in her that were all but forgotten. A sense of tenderness and affection, the deep-felt exhilaration of needing and being needed. On the surface he was glib and conniving, a grifter out to make his mark and devil take the hindmost. Yet there were quick-silver splinters of time in which she'd caught fleeting glimpses of the man beneath the rough exterior. A sensitive man with wit and understanding, even a trace of compassion. Knowing all that, she too won-dered where it might end. Other whores had married their way out of the houses, so the idea was by no means farfetched. Harry Lovett might very well be the man for her. A chance for a fresh start and a new life. Her last chance.

At length, dizzied by the thought, she realized he was waiting on an answer. Then, on the verge of replying, a shadow of anxiety clouded her features. She suddenly remembered who she was and where she was. The star whore of the Bella Union, and no less a prisoner than the slave girls of Chinatown. Denny O'Brien always collected on a debt, and she owed him . . . more than she cared to admit.

"I'm sorry, Harry." She smiled the saddest smile he'd ever seen, and shook her head. "It's a great idea, but it wouldn't work."

"Why the hell not?"

"Nobody quits Denny," she said simply. "It's a rule of the house, and he doesn't make exceptions. Especially in my case."

"Forget O'Brien," Starbuck countered. "Once Buckley gives the go-ahead, we're off and running."

"I don't understand."

"Nothing to it," Starbuck scoffed. "I'll tell Buckley that either you're included in the package or it queers the whole deal."

"Suppose he calls your bluff?"

"Not a chance in a thousand. Fung would go off like a skyrocket and accuse O'Brien of deliberately scuttling the deal. That'd give Buckley more troubles than he's got now. He just wouldn't stand for it."

"You sound awful sure of yourself."

"Why not?" Starbuck laughed. "Once I make up my mind to something, that's it! Either I get you in the bargain or the deal's off. I'll just buy myself some whores from somebody else."

"You'd do that for me?"

"Hide and watch. One way or another, you're on your way to Colorado."

Nell bounded out of bed and threw herself on him. She smothered him with kisses, her arms circled around his neck, and finally planted one soundly on his mouth. When he pried her loose, her face was lighted with an exhuberant childlike glow.

"I hope that doesn't wear off before we get to Colorado."

"Honeybun, you haven't seen anything yet. Wait till I really get warmed up!"

"Tell you what I do see." Starbuck looked her up and down. "You step out in the hall like that and we're liable to draw a crowd."

Nell laughed a bawdy little laugh. Then she turned, wigwagging her fanny, and jiggled to the wardrobe. She slipped into a housecoat and began buttoning it up. All the while, she was humming softly under her breath.

Watching her, Starbuck wasn't proud of himself. Exactly as he'd planned, he had spoon-fed her a fairy tale and she had swallowed it whole. She was now in his camp, and there was virtually no chance she would betray him to O'Brien. Yet, however much her loyalty was tested, she would come out on the short end of the stick. Her days on the Barbary Coast were numbered, and from tonight onward the future itself would prove highly uncertain. Not for the first time, it occurred to him that the detective business was a dirty game. He felt somehow soiled by what he'd done. All the more so because he'd done it before and would very likely do it again.

"I'm ready anytime you are, lover."

Starbuck nodded, watching her a moment longer. "Any idea what you'll tell O'Brien in the morning?"

"Why, I'll just bat my baby-blues and tell him

you slipped out while I was asleep. He'll never know the difference."

Starbuck smiled. "You know something? You would've made a helluva con man."

"Honey, a whore spends her whole life on the con."

She laughed softly and led the way to the door. After a quick peek outside, she signaled the all-clear. Then they stepped into the hall and walked toward the dumbwaiter.

A light fog hung over the city like gossamer curtains. Starbuck stopped at the entrance to the alleyway and checked the street in both directions. The hour was late, and he saw no one but a gang of drunken sailors weaving toward the waterfront. He crossed the street and strode off in the direction of the Palace Hotel.

The fog was an unexpected ally. Streetlamps, shrouded in a fuzzy glow, were visible half a block away. But the lampposts themselves were hidden by the swirling gray mist. He thought it unlikely that anyone could trail him in such weather. Still, all things considered, too much vigilance was better than too little. At the corner of Sutter and Montgomery, he stepped quickly into the darkened doorway of an office building. Waiting several moments, he listened intently, alert for the sound of footsteps. He heard nothing, and there were no signs of movement near the intersection. Presently, satisfied he wasn't being followed, he left the doorway and turned the corner. He reversed directions and disappeared into the fog. He walked swiftly toward Nob Hill.

Some ten minutes later, a bleary-eyed servant admitted him to the mansion of Charles Crocker. He was ushered into the study and asked to wait. Embers still simmered in the fireplace, and he soon rekindled a cheery blaze. Standing with his back to the fire, he warmed himself, slowly inspecting the room. The wooden panels were polished walnut, and one entire wall was bookshelves, stuffed from floor to ceiling with tomes bound in Moroccan leather. The books appeared untouched by human hands, and, quite probably, unread. He was examining a framed Audubon etching when the study door opened.

Charles Crocker marched into the room and slammed the door with a resounding thud. His eyes were gummed with sleep and he looked even fatter attired in a nightshirt and woolen robe. His expression was one of acute annoyance.

"What the hell do you mean coming here at this hour? Don't you realize it's after four o'clock?"

Starbuck returned his stare with sardonic amusement. "Crooks don't keep civilized hours. I operate on their timetable these days."

"Well, it better be important." Crocker flopped down in an overstuffed armchair. "I'm not accustomed to being awakened in the middle of the night."

"It's important." Starbuck took a chair across from him, lit a cigar. "Are you familiar with a man named Christopher Buckley?"

Crocker gave him a look of walleyed amazement.

"Whether I am or not has no bearing on our business. Why do you ask?"

"Because he's the man behind your train robbers."

"You're out of your mind!"

"Think so?" Starbuck blew a plume of smoke into the air. "Suppose I fill you in on the last few days. Then you can decide for yourself."

Crocker groaned and slumped deeper into his chair. Starbuck briefly outlined everything he'd uncovered since their last meeting. He established the link between the train robbers and Denny O'Brien, then went on to describe the deal he'd struck with Fung Jing Toy. From there, he recounted the conversation with Buckley and the gist of the problems entailed. He omitted few details, and firmly demonstrated the chain of command in San Francisco's underworld. His report ended with a summary of his arrangement with Buckley. He stressed the time element and the need for speed.

"So that's it," he concluded. "To pull it off, I'll have to produce the hundred thousand no later than noon today."

A thick silence settled over the room. Crocker, obviously disgruntled, gazed at Starbuck for a long, speculative moment. Then he shook his head in stern disapproval.

"I'm afraid you've overstepped the bounds of your assignment. I retained you to catch a band of train robbers, not organize a civic crusade. Your zeal is to be commended, Mr. Starbuck. But my only interest is in halting the robberies, nothing more."

"Why settle for half a loaf?" Starbuck gave him a hard, wise look. "We can capture Red Ned Adair, then offer him immunity to turn state's evidence against O'Brien. After that, we take it step by step, playing them off one against the other. When we're through, we'll have Buckley and most of his stooges behind bars. It's a perfect setup, made to order."

"No, thank you," Crocker said with an unpleasant grunt. "Your instructions are to eliminate Adair and his gang of robbers. The assignment begins and ends there. Do I make myself clear?"

All at once the truth came home to Starbuck. A practicing cynic, and something of an iconoclast, he had always viewed the world as a place of dupes and rogues. The dupes, in the natural course of things, were preyed upon by the rogues. Yet, in his absorption with the case, he'd forgotten that Charles Crocker, one of the great robber barons of the era, was essentially a rogue. Since rogues seldom locked horns with other rogues, Crocker quite naturally had no interest in exposing Christopher Buckley. The premise gained even more credence when politics were involved. A can of worms, once opened, might lead anywhere. Perhaps to the Central Pacific, and Charles Crocker himself.

"Here's the deal," Starbuck said stonily. "You have the money delivered to my hotel room before noon. I'll follow the plan I've just laid out and push it to the limit." He paused, took a long draw on his cigar. "Now, maybe you don't like the idea, but you'd like the alternative even less. Turn me down and I'll take the story to the newspapers. I've got a hunch your name would end up in big, bold head-lines."

"Confound you!" Crocker's eyes were angry, re-proachful. "I won't be dictated to, and I damn well won't allow you to bullyrag me. Take heed, Mr. Starbuck!"

"Save your breath," Starbuck said with a clenched smile. "When I accepted the assignment, I told you how I work. I don't take orders and I don't quit till the job's done. Buckley's a spoiler, the worst kind, and I figure he deserves to get axed. One way or another, I aim to see that it happens."

Crocker's features colored dark with blood. He rose and moved to the fireplace. Hands clasped be-hind his back, he stood for a long time staring into the flames. At last, he took a deep breath, blew it out heavily. When he turned around, his face was pale and there was a look of resignation in his eyes.

"Very well," he murmured in assent. "I'll go along with your request. But I warn you, Mr. Star-buck. Under no circumstances is my name to be con-nected with Christopher Buckley! Defy me on that and I will personally hound you out of the detective business."

"Why, hell's fire!" Starbuck laughed, a sudden harsh sound in the still room. "You just leave it to me, Mr. Crocker. I'll make you a hero! Goddamn if I won't."

"Yes, I agree." Crocker nodded gravely. "You are truly damned if you don't, Mr. Starbuck."

"Aren't we all?" Starbuck said with a cynical grin. "Have a seat, and let me tell you what I've got in mind."

Crocker walked to his chair and sat down. His expression was solemn and his mood attentive. Starbuck waited a moment, puffing quietly on his cigar. Then, with obvious relish, he began talking.

The first step, he explained, was the capture of Red Ned Adair.

CHAPTER 13

Shortly before dawn, two days later, Starbuck left the Palace Hotel by a side entrance. Once outside, he crossed the street and ducked into an alleyway. He waited several moments, until he was certain he wasn't being tailed. Then he turned and walked swiftly toward the Central Pacific train yard.

All the preparations necessary to his plan had been completed. Yesterday, at the stroke of noon, a package had been delivered to his hotel room. Inside were several packets of bills, large-denomination notes totaling $100,000, and a terse message from Charles Crocker. According to instructions, Crocker had quietly issued two orders. The first concerned today's morning train to Los Angeles: there were to be no extra guards on the express car. Crocker had announced the measure as a new gambit to deceive the robbers into believing there was nothing of value in today's shipment. At the same time, he directed that a major transfer from the San Francisco mint be put aboard the train. Starbuck had every confidence that the gang's inside man—the Judas—would leak word of this unusual operation. Red Ned Adair was virtually certain to rob the morning southbound.

Crocker's second order had been carried out in absolute secrecy. A trusted aide, less than an hour ago, had awakened Captain Tom Kelly, Chief of Security for the Central Pacific. The aide, under firm instructions never to leave Kelly's side, had then accompanied the security chief while he routed seven express guards from their beds. The men were quickly collected in the chill predawn darkness and bundled aboard waiting carriages. Once assembled, they were driven to a warehouse on the edge of the Central Pacific train yard. There, they were issued rifles and sidearms, then told to wait. Kelly's instructions, delivered by the aide, were specific and purposely vague. A man named Starbuck would arrive at the warehouse shortly before sunrise. All details regarding the mission would be explained at that time. Kelly was to follow his orders explicitly and without question.

Hurrying toward the train yard, Starbuck was satisfied that everything was now in place. Yesterday afternoon, following a meeting with Buckley, he had deposited the $100,000 in a bank selected by the political kingpin. The ploy, much as he'd expected, bought him time and got Denny O'Brien out of his hair. Within the hour, the second phase of his plan would swing into operation. Accompanied by the security force, he would travel southward from the city. Not long after their departure, the morning train, with an unguarded express car, would roll toward Los Angeles. The bait was laid and the trap would be sprung somewhere around noontime. All that remained was to ambush Red Ned Adair.

A few minutes before dawn, Starbuck stepped through the door of the warehouse. A group of men, jammed together in a stench of sweating bodies, were gathered around a potbellied stove. Their faces were grim, and most of them, still half-asleep, were holding steaming mugs of coffee. Conversation stopped, replaced by watchful silence, as he closed the door and moved forward. The only sound was a coffeepot, hissing and rattling on top the stove.

Starbuck, approaching closer, sensed the tension. Yet nothing in his tone or manner revealed the slightest trace of concern. He spoke with authority, iron sureness.

"Captain Kelly?"

"That's me."

A man of formidable size, tall and massively built, separated from the group. His hands were large and gnarled, and his voice was a stilled rumble. There was a heavy-lidded, lizard-like alertness to his eyes.

"I'm Luke Starbuck."

Kelly accepted his handshake, frowning. "Pleased to meet you."

"Has anyone left this room since you were brought here?"

"No," Kelly acknowledged stiffly. "We've not

been here more than a few minutes ourselves."

"Good," Starbuck nodded. "Ask your men to finish their coffee and get ready to go."

"Go where?" Kelly raised an uncertain eyebrow. "I was given to understand you'd fill us in on the particulars."

"I will," Starbuck said evenly, "when the time's right."

Kelly's eyes became veiled. "Well, now, maybe you wouldn't mind explaining what all the mystery's about. We're more than a little curious, as you might well appreciate."

"Sorry," Starbuck said with an odd smile. "Where we're going—and what we've been assigned to do— will have to wait till we get there."

"Is that so?" Kelly demanded churlishly. "Then maybe you could at least tell us why we were rousted out in the middle of the night? Without so much as a by-your-leave!"

Starbuck gave him a swift, appraising glance. "Captain Kelly, you've got your orders and I've got mine. Suppose we let it go at that and get on with the job?"

"By the sweet Jesus!" Kelly said loudly. "I'm responsible for these men, and I'll not take them off to God knows where until I've had an explanation."

"For the moment, you've had all the explanation you need. We're on official business, and at the proper time, I'll lay it out for you in black and white. That's twice I've said it, so don't make me repeat myself again."

"Oh, repeat yourself, is it?" Kelly said with a sudden glare. "Well, mister-whoever-the-hell-you-are, I don't know you from Paddy's pig! You could talk yourself blue in the face and I'll not move from this spot unless I hear the reason why."

A vague disquiet settled over Starbuck. Something told him there was more to Kelly's objections than met the eye. Aside from resentment, which was natural enough at being reduced to second-in-command, there was some darker element just below the surface. The man was too antagonistic, too intractable, far more so than the situation dictated. Yet Starbuck hadn't the time nor the inclination to pursue it further. Sunrise was the deadline for their departure, and faint shafts of light were already streaming through the windows. He decided to force the issue.

"Captain Kelly," he said flatly, "the only thing you need to know is that I speak for Charles Crocker. Your instructions were to follow my orders to the letter. If that puts your nose out of joint, that's your problem. Take it up with Crocker when we get back."

"Instructions!" Kelly roared. "I've had no instructions, except from Crocker's flunky. Considering your high-handed manner, that won't do. Not for Tom Kelly, it won't!"

"Like it or lump it," Starbuck said roughly. "You're under my orders, and that's that."

"Says you." Kelly's nostrils flared. "I'll just have myself a talk with Crocker and see who's giving the orders around here. I've a strong notion there's a nigger-in-the-woodpile somewhere."

Starbuck fixed him with a pale stare. "I can't allow that."

"Blood of Christ!" Kelly said furiously. "I wasn't asking your permission. You can go or stay as you please! I mean to have a word with Charlie Crocker."

"No." Starbuck's face took on a hard cast. "You're not going anywhere except where I tell you to go."

"Out of my way!"

Kelly brushed past him and started toward the door. Starbuck struck out in a shadowy movement. He buried his fist in the big man's kidney, and Kelly's mouth opened in a great whoosh of breath. Shifting slightly, Starbuck spun him around and exploded two splintering punches flush on the jaw. Kelly went down like a pole-axed steer. He lay still a moment, then groaned and rolled heavily to his knees. He tried to rise, but his face twisted in a grimace of pain and he remained kneeling. Starbuck, scarcely winded, stood over him.

"Enough?"

"Enough," Kelly bobbed his head. "I think you busted something inside."

"You'll live."

There was a gruff buzz from the other men, and Starbuck turned. His brow seamed, and he eyed them with a steady, uncompromising gaze. When he spoke, his voice was scratchy, abrasive.

"Only one man gives the orders, and that's me. Anybody sees it otherwise, now's the time to step forward."

No one stepped forward. He waited several moments, then turned once more to face Kelly. The big man climbed slowly to his feet, and stood with a hand clutched tightly to his kidney. Starbuck gestured toward the door.

"I want everybody outside and in those carriages . . . now."

Kelly looked dazed, punchy. He stared down at the floor, tightlipped, his teeth locked against the pain. At length, he drew a deep breath and glanced up at his men.

"Let's go," he rasped hoarsely. "Everybody in the carriages."

Starbuck led the way through the door. Outside, he split the men into two groups, indicating Kelly was to ride in the lead carriage. When everyone was settled, he climbed aboard and took a seat beside the security chief. He ordered the driver to head south, and as they rolled out of the train yard the sky lightened into perfect cloudless blue. He glanced back and a slow smile creased his mouth.

The morning train stood chuffing smoke outside the terminal.

A mile or so north of the farmhouse Starbuck ordered the carriages off the road. Several hundred yards to the east, the wooded creek meandered southward. Following his directions, the carriages were driven across a grassy field and halted beneath the trees.

There he left Kelly and the men, and struck off on foot downcreek. His recollection of the gang's hideout was fairly accurate. Still, some time had passed since he'd trailed Adair and the band of robbers to the farmhouse. Leaving nothing to chance, he thought it wiser to personally scout the terrain. Today there was no margin for error.

Some while later he spotted the farmhouse through the trees. Quiet as a drifting hawk, he approached to within fifty yards, then went belly down on the ground. He crawled forward and stopped under the shelterbelt of woods. Hidden by shadow, he removed his hat and slowly scanned the layout.

Off to one side of the house, the woman was hanging a wash on a clothesline. Her husband was puttering around in a shed near the barn. The corral stood empty and the barn doors were closed. All of which confirmed his judgment about Red Ned Adair. The gang had ridden out earlier on the saddlehorses, leaving their carriages concealed in the barn. The holdup, in all likelihood, had already occurred. Without extra guards, the Central Pacific southbound was a pushover, and the express-car messenger would have offered only token resistance. Even now, the robbers were probably following the same twisting route back to the farmhouse.

Starbuck turned and studied the high ground across the creek. From the top of the knoll, he recalled, there was a clear view of the farmhouse and

the barn and the fields beyond. Outlaws were crea-
tures of habit, and he thought it reasonable to assume
they would again approach the hideout by way of
the wooded knoll. The time to strike was when they
dismounted outside the corral. Flushed with success,
saddlebags stuffed with loot, their defenses would be
at a low ebb. Further, with the barn doors closed,
they would be caught in the open with nowhere to
run. All that, combined with the element of surprise,
should turn the trick very nicely. Barring mishap, the
robbers would never know what hit them.

Worming back to the creek, Starbuck rose and
took off at a dogtrot upstream. Several minutes later
he reached the carriages and found the men sprawled
on the ground, smoking and talking quietly amongst
themselves. Kelly stood off to one side, propped
against the base of a tree. His expression was sullen
and withdrawn.

The men scrambled to their feet as Starbuck
halted near the lead carriage. He signaled them to
gather around and waited while Kelly ambled over
to join the group. Then he went straight to the point.

"You're all aware of the train holdups that have
taken place over the past year. I was hired by the
Central Pacific to catch the robbers, and I've located
their hideout. It's a farmhouse, about a mile downstream, on the west side of the creek. Today, we're
going to lay an ambush and put an end to those
holdups."

A murmur of excitement swept over the men.
Starbuck hesitated a moment, then silenced them

with upraised palms. "Here's the way it'll work. Once we get downstream, I'll assign you to positions and point out the best fields of fire. Then we wait till the gang rides in and dismounts at the corral. That's when we hit 'em."

"A question." Kelly nailed him with a corrosive stare. "Who's their leader, and how many are there in the gang?"

"Glad you asked," Starbuck remarked. "Altogether, there'll be seven men. The leader's a gent by the name of Red Ned Adair. He's easy to spot because he's a carrot-head, bright red hair." He paused, glancing around the group. "Adair is not—I repeat—he is not to be killed. I want him taken alive."

"Are you saying," Kelly asked bluntly, "that you want the others killed?"

"When you shoot a man," Starbuck replied calmly, "I've always found it's best to kill him. Otherwise, you're liable to make him mad and then he'll kill you."

Kelly gave him a long, searching stare. "What about this fellow Adair? He'll more than likely be shooting back at us. Are you saying we're not to return his fire?"

"Nobody," Starbuck underscored the word with heavy emphasis, "will fire at Adair but me. I'll either cripple him or keep him pinned down till the fight's over. So if you catch red hair in your sights, shift to another target. That's a direct order."

Kelly offered an elaborate shrug and said no more. The other men obediently bobbed their heads in affirmation. When there were no further questions, Starbuck dropped to one knee on the ground. He took a twig and sketched a crude map in the dirt.

"Here's the lay of the land. We'll go downstream and then . . ."

A brassy noonday sun stood high overhead. Squatted behind a tree, Starbuck watched as Red Ned Adair led his gang down the knoll and forded the creek. The robbers were laughing and exchanging wise-cracks, clearly in high spirits. The holdup, quite ob-viously, had come off without a hitch.

Standing, Starbuck quickly surveyed the wooded terrain. Kelly and four men were posted across the stream, on the forward slope of the knoll. Concealed by undergrowth, they were all but invisible beneath the dim shadows of the trees. The three remaining guards were flanked directly to his right, spread out along the west bank of the creek. He had assigned himself the point position, nearest the farmhouse. His shot would be the signal to open fire.

Easing around, he took a quick peek from behind the tree. The gang was aproaching the corral, and the farmer walked forward to greet them. The woman, standing at the corner of the house, looked on in silence. He thumbed the hammer on his carbine and wedged the butt into the hollow of his shoulder. He centered the sights on Red Ned Adair.

A shot cracked and bark exploded beside his head.

Cursing savagely, he crouched and swung around

as the gunfire became general. His gaze went across the creek and he saw Kelly jacking another shell into his own carbine. Without thought, operating on sheer instinct, he caught the security chief's chest in his sights and levered three quick shots. The slugs jolted Kelly backward a step at a time. The last one slammed into his brisket, splattering bone and gore, and he dropped the carbine. His hands splayed and clawed at empty air, then his legs buckled. He hit the ground and went tumbling head over heels down the knoll.

Starbuck whirled even before the body rolled to a halt. All around him the guards' rifles continued to bark, laying down a heavy volume of fire. He stepped around the tree and saw that Red Ned Adair and three of the gang were still mounted. Their horses were spooked, pitching and rearing in wild gyrations. Yet their sixguns were out, and while their aim was none too good, they were blazing away at the treeline. A quick glance confirmed that the farmer and the other robbers were down, either dead or dying.

All in an instant, Starbuck realized his only chance was to drop Adair's horse. He stepped clear of the trees, looking for an opening, and advanced toward the corral. Behind him, a staccato volley of gunfire broke loose, and the last three gang members pitched from their saddles. He saw Adair look in his direction and sensed he'd been recognized. A split-second later the outlaw leader fired, and a slug snarled past overhead. Then, before he could align his sights, Adair got control of his horse and took off down the road at a gallop. He let go a snap shot, but knew he'd missed even as he pulled the trigger. Horse and rider vanished in the next moment, blocked from view by the house.

Starbuck sprinted toward the corral. The gunfire abruptly ceased and an eerie silence descended over the farm. From behind, he heard the guards shouting to one another and vaguely noted the sound of running footsteps. The outlaws' bodies, grotesque in death, littered the ground closer to the barn. He charged past them, only to spot Adair far in the distance. He swore, skidding to a stop, and flung the carbine in the dirt. Then, almost a reflex action, he turned and caught up the reins of a loose horse. He stepped into the saddle as the guards approached and slowed to a walk. His finger stabbed out at the man in the lead.

"You!" he ordered. "Arrest the woman in the house and charge her with accessory to robbery. Then take Kelly's body to Charles Crocker. Deliver it personally! Tell him it's a present from me."

The guard gawked at him. "A present?"

"You heard right," Starbuck growled. "A present named Judas."

"What about you, Mr. Starbuck? What'll I tell him about you?"

"Tell him to look for me when he sees me."

Starbuck reined sharply around and gigged the horse in the ribs. Some distance away he saw a plume of dust drifting upward against the muslin-blue sky. He rode toward San Francisco.

CHAPTER 14

Late that afternoon, Denny O'Brien arrived at the Snug Café. After pounding on the alley door, he was admitted by a startled Chinese dishwasher. Knuckles Jackson, who doubled as one of Buckley's bodyguards, was hurriedly summoned from the front of the café.

O'Brien, whose manner was agitated and somewhat irrational, demanded to see Buckley. His appearance at the café during the daytime was unprecedented, and led to a heated argument. At last, albeit reluctantly, Jackson left him in the storeroom and went upstairs. Several moments passed; then the door opened and Jackson gave him a look reserved for fools and harebrained Irishmen.

Buckley was seated behind the desk. His composure was monumental, and his expression betrayed no hint of aggravation. Yet, when he spoke, his tone was clipped and stiff, angry.

"You were told never to come here in daylight."

"I'm sorry, but I had no choice."

"On the contrary, only an imbecile fails to exercise choice. Your presence indicates that you deliberately *chose* to ignore my wishes."

"For Chrissake, nobody saw me!"

"You miss the point," Buckley said with sudden wrath. "I will not allow anyone to override my orders." He took out a pocket watch, opened the lid, and deftly fingered the exposed hands. "Five-o-seven! Which means it will be dark in less than two hours. I presume that never occurred to you?"

"What I have to say wouldn't wait."

"Indeed?" Buckley returned the watch to his vest pocket. "Has the Bella Union burned down, or is it some lesser calamity?"

"Lots worse." O'Brien dropped into a chair before the desk. "We've got trouble! A shitpot full of trouble."

"Perhaps you could be a bit more specific?"

"It's Harry Lovett," O'Brien said, clearing his throat. "I just found out the son-of-a-bitch is a Pinkerton."

Buckley received the news with surpassing calmness. "What leads you to believe so?"

"Him and a squad of railroad bulls jumped Ned Adair and his boys this morning. Suckered them into a trap and blasted the whole gang straight to hell."

"Does that include Adair?"

"No," O'Brien said quickly. "Ned fought his way

clear. It was nip and tuck, but he came through without a scratch."

"A pity," Buckley observed dryly. "Exactly what happened?"

"Ned and his boys robbed the morning train to Los Angeles. His inside man at Central Pacific—the chief security bull—told him there wouldn't be any guards on the express car. Sure enough, there weren't, and the holdup went off slick as a whistle."

"No guards," Buckley mused to himself. "Offhand, I'd think that would have alerted Adair. It seems patently obvious."

O'Brien spread his hands in a gesture of bafflement. "None of it makes any sense. Kelly—that's the security bull—hadn't never tipped him wrong before. But goddamn if Kelly don't show up at the farmhourse—"

"Farmhouse?"

"Yeah, a farmhouse south of town. Ned used it as a cover whenever he pulled a holdup."

"Go on."

"Well, like I said, Kelly was there. Ned says he fired the first shot, evidently at someone in his own party. Then all of a sudden, Kelly goes down and the next thing you know, Lovett pops out from behind a tree. Ned thinks Kelly tried to get Lovett, and instead, Lovett got him."

"Brilliant." Buckley invested the word with scorn. "Did Adair deduce all that by himself?"

"Ned's no dimwit," O'Brien said defensively. "The way it looks, Kelly got himself boxed in and couldn't get word to Ned. Then he tried to turn it around at the last minute, and ended up dead."

"Greater love hath no man," Buckley added with satiric mockery. "Perhaps we could move on to the part about Lovett."

O'Brien hunched forward in his chair. "Ned spotted him the second he stepped out of the trees. Lovett was trying to draw a bead on him, but Ned winged a shot and took off. All his men were down, so it would've been suicide to stick around any longer."

"He's quite certain it was Lovett? In the heat of the moment, he couldn't have been mistaken?"

"No mistake," O'Brien said dourly. "It was Lovett, all right. Ned swears to it."

Buckley considered the thought. "Then we can surmise that Lovett had already identified Adair as the gang leader. Working backward, we can assume that Adair led him to you, and quite recently too. That would explain Lovett's little charade over the past week."

O'Brien looked blank. "What's a charade?"

"A deception," Buckley replied with cold hauteur. "One specifically engineered and acted out for gullible louts like yourself. It would appear our Mr. Lovett is an undercover operative for the Central Pacific."

"That's what I said!" O'Brien blurted out. "The bastard's a Pinkerton!"

"Perhaps." Buckley examined the notion a moment. "Whether he is or isn't seems a moot question at this point. What concerns me most is that you and your merry band of train robbers led him directly to me."

"The hell it did!" O'Brien denied hotly. "It was Fung! Except for him, you wouldn't have never heard of Lovett."

"You have a short memory." Buckley's voice dropped. "Fung was suspicious of him from the start. You also forget that I've warned you repeatedly about train holdups. I believe my comment was to the effect that the return in no way justified the risk."

"What's train holdups got to do with Fung?"

"Everything," Buckley said gruffly. "All of it involves greed, your greed. I gave you the Barbary Coast, but you weren't satisfied with that. You had to have something extra, smalltime side deals. Train robbery was one, and introducing Lovett to Fung was another. So you see, it's all of a piece, Denny. Bluntly put, you're too greedy for your own good . . . or mine."

"Wait a minute!" O'Brien objected. "You're not blaming me for this Lovett thing, are you? Jesus Christ, how was I to know he's a Pinkerton?"

"Again, the point eludes you." Buckley dismissed it with a brusque gesture. "Let's press on, shall we? At the moment we have a larger problem, and unless I'm mistaken, it has little to do with today's train robbery."

"Oh?" O'Brien appeared thoroughly confounded. "What problem's that?"

"Harry Lovett," Buckley told him. "If his primary target was Adair, then why did he concoct such an elaborate cover story? Why get involved with you or Fung? Why risk a hundred thousand dollars merely to gain my confidence?" He paused, reflective. "Something of an enigma, isn't it?"

"I give up," O'Brien said, attentive now. "Why?"

"Because Adair was only a means to an end. On balance, that seems the only logical conclusion. Lovett was after bigger game from the very start. Whether or not he suspected it would bring him to my door, we'll probably never know. What matters is that it did, and he capitalized on it quite cleverly. Quite cleverly, indeed."

"You think he's after you?"

"I think that's precisely what he's after."

"So what do we do now?"

"A good question."

Buckley placed his elbows on the arms of his chair, steepled his fingers. His eyes, shaded by the tinted glasses, appeared metallic, glittering yet dead. O'Brien had the strange sensation that behind those eyes was something inhuman, even demonic. An elemental force that fed itself on hate and power, and the bones of anyone who stood in its way. One thought led to another, and he dimly pondered where that left him. Then, suddenly, Buckley's voice jarred him back to the present.

"I'm afraid I have some bad news for you, Denny."

"What kind of bad news?"

"Ned Adair is expendable," Buckley said with

chilling simplicity. "I want you to get rid of him . . . today."

"Kill him?" O'Brien gave him a murky look. "What the hell for?"

"For the best of reasons." Buckley permitted himself a grim smile. "Without Adair there's no link to you, and therefore no link to me. Lovett will be left with nothing but allegations. And as we all know, allegations aren't worth a dime a dozen."

O'Brien massaged his nose, thinking. He knew, though the message was left unstated, that Ned Adair was not the subject at issue. His own knowledge of Frisco's underworld, and how the operation was structured, posed a far graver threat to Buckley. One false step and he himself would end up at the bottom of the bay. Yet, like many Irishmen, he was cursed with an obdurate nature and a volatile temper. He also possessed loyalty to those he considered friends; betrayal for the sake of expediency was to him the greatest blasphemy. His code had little to do with common standards of decency, but it was nonetheless the code by which he lived. He never welched on a deal or gaffed a friend—and he never betrayed a trust.

"I won't do it," he said stoutly. "Ned's been with me since the old days, and I've no better friend in the world. I'd sooner kill my own mother."

"An admirable sentiment," Buckley said with wintry malice. "However, in this case, we have to concern ourselves with the practical solution. If Adair were caught, and persuaded to talk, then your arrest would be a virtual certainty." He stopped, slowly shook his head. "You know I can't allow that to happen, don't you, Denny?"

"Ned won't talk," O'Brien protested. "He'd go to the gallows before he opened his mouth. As for me, I've never ratted in my life, and I've no intention to start now."

"Indeed?" Buckley's tone was icy. "Then let me put it to you this way, Denny. Are you willing to risk your neck to save Adair?"

"Look here," O'Brien said stubbornly. "Why kill Ned when there's a better way? I'll put him on a ship tonight and send him off to China. Christ, he'd be gone two years, maybe more! By then, this whole thing will've blown over and be long forgotten."

Buckley immediately thought of Fung. Once in China, Adair could be dispatched by Fung's associates with Oriental efficiency and a minimum of fuss. For the moment it would salve O'Brien's rebellious mood; later, if necessary, Fung would be delighted to dispatch the Irishman, as well. Overall, it seemed the perfect solution to an unwieldy problem.

"Very well," he conceded with a show of tolerance. "We'll strike a compromise. You put Adair aboard the first clipper bound for China. Not tomorrow or the next day, but tonight! Any delay in shipping him out and all bets are off. Fair enough?"

"Plenty fair," O'Brien agreed. "I'll handle it myself so there won't be any slipups. Before midnight, Ned will kiss Frisco goodbye, and that's a promise."

"Don't fail me," Buckley reminded him. "Otherwise, I'll be forced to call your marker. Adair or you, that's the proposition. Understood?"

"Understood," O'Brien said in a resigned voice. "One way or another, I'll have him on his way with the evening tide."

"I'm sure you will, Denny."

O'Brien looked into the dead eyes and an involuntary chill touched his backbone. Unless he delivered on the promise, there was no doubt the marker would be called. Either Ned Adair vanished tonight or his own life was forfeit. There was no third choice.

Nell sensed trouble when O'Brien hurried through the door of the Bella Union. He looked not just angry, but somehow shaken, unnerved. A moment later intuition turned to certainty. He brushed past High Spade McQueen without a word and rushed up the stairs. Something was seriously wrong, and the source of the problem was hardly in question. Somehow it involved Red Ned Adair.

Earlier that afternoon, on her way downstairs, she'd seen Ned Adair enter O'Brien's suite. Covered with sweat and grime, he had left the impression that the Devil himself was on his heels. Before she reached the stairwell, O'Brien had erupted in a burst of profanity. The sound of his curses carried clearly along the hall, and she'd thought at the time that Adair had finally pulled one boner too many. Then, dismissing it from mind, she had gone on about her business.

Now, watching O'Brien take the stairs two at a time, she was struck by a wayward thought. She wondered if it somehow involved Harry Lovett. He hadn't put in an appearance last night, and she'd heard nothing from him today. That seemed to her very strange, out of character. Knowing she expected him, he was too considerate not to have sent a message. Unless he was unable to send a message!

Stranger still was the fact that Ned Adair hadn't set foot out of O'Brien's suite since arriving. Try as she might, she couldn't imagine a connection between Adair and Harry Lovett. Yet she was no great believer in coincidence. Adair was hiding from something or somebody, and whatever he'd done, it had thrown O'Brien into a towering rage. Added to Harry Lovett's curious disappearance, it seemed altogether too timely for mere coincidence. She suddenly decided to do a little eavesdropping.

A glance toward the barroom confirmed that McQueen's attention was diverted elsewhere. She casually mounted the stairs and made her way to the third floor. As she passed O'Brien's suite, which was next to her own room, she heard loud voices from inside. Quietly, she entered her room and went directly to the washstand. Long ago, she had discovered that the wall separating her quarters from O'Brien's was wafer-thin clapboard. Further, she'd found that a girl could easily get an earful, and learn all sorts of secrets. All it required was a water glass.

She placed the open end of the glass flush against the wall. Then she pressed her right ear tightly to the bottom of the glass, and stuck her finger in her left ear. The effect was not unlike that produced by a megaphone. Sounds were amplified, and voices carried with remarkable clarity. She listened closely, and the wall seemed to evaporate. An argument was raging, and in her mind's eye, it was not difficult to imagine their faces.

"I won't go! I don't give a shit what Buckley says. I won't go, and that's that!"

Ned Adair stopped pacing, suddenly turned and glared at O'Brien. Dull despair was etched on his features, and dark bruised-looking rings circled his eyes. He sat down heavily on a sofa, his face doughy and stunned. His stomach rolled, and an unmanning sense of nausea seized him. He shook his head wildly.

"Mexico, maybe." He passed a hand across his eyes and swallowed hard. "But I'll be goddamned if I'll go to China. Not me!"

"You're damned if you don't." O'Brien's voice was firm. "Unless you sail tonight, you're a dead man. No two ways about it, Ned."

"I'll take my chances," Adair said morosely. "All I need's a fast horse and an hour's head start. Buckley wouldn't never find me! Not in a million years."

"No soap," O'Brien informed him. "I gave my word to Buckley. You take off running and it's my neck that'll get chopped. I'd have to stop you—and I would."

Adair's jaw fell open, as though hinged. "Jesus,

Mary and Joseph! Are you saying you'd kill me, Denny?"

O'Brien shrugged. "I'm saying I won't die for you. Now that you've brought the Pinkertons down on us, there's no way around it. You either sail for China or you get deep-sixed."

"You—" Adair stammered. "You're blaming me? It was you that opened the door to Lovett and took him under wing. I had nothing to do with it. Nothing!"

"No more of your guff!" O'Brien suddenly bellowed. "You're the one that robbed the train, and you're the one that led Lovett straight to the Bella Union. And to me, too! So dry up and take your medicine like a man. That's my final word on it, Ned."

Adair blinked several times. Under O'Brien's ugly stare, all his courage abruptly deserted him. He gloomily bowed his head and nodded. "Have it your way, Denny. I'd sooner sail the China Sea the rest of my life than have you down on me."

"That's the spirit!" O'Brien laughed heartily. "We'll sneak you down to Mother Bronson's joint after dark, and she'll arrange passage on the finest clipper in port. Hell, it'll be like an ocean voyage, Ned! You'll have yourself a grand time."

Adair mumbled an inaudible reply. His eyes, oddly vacant, were fixed on the floor.

On the other side of the wall, Nell numbly lowered the water glass. She paled and her cheek muscles grew taut, and her face was no longer a pleasant sight. She felt swept up in a nightmare, the floodgates of fear suddenly opened and swirling madly about her. She crossed the room in a daze and sat down on the edge of the bed. Her ears rang with the words and she choked off a cry. She couldn't believe it, wouldn't believe it.

Harry Lovett a Pinkerton? Adair and O'Brien—even the blind man!—panicked by the dapper grifter who had shared her bed. The same devil-may-care jokester who had offered her a job and promised her a new life and sworn to take her away from the Barbary Coast. It wasn't true, none of it. For if it was, then he had lied to her, used her. She couldn't credit that, not from Harry Lovett.

Her head pulsated like a huge festering wound. She heard again the words of Denny O'Brien and she reasoned muzzily that it was a mistake. Some monstrous and terrifying mistake. She wondered what to do, and even as she asked herself the question, she knew she would do nothing. A girl had to live, and only a fool took sides when men drew the line.

She would wait and see, and do what she'd always done. She would go with the winner.

CHAPTER 15

Nell looked wretched when she opened the door. Ugly lines strained her face and her features were smudged downward. She stared at him with a mixture of dismay and surprise, momentarily dumbstruck.

With a last glance along the hall, Starbuck stepped into her room and closed the door. He twisted the key, locking the door, then turned toward her. As though expecting applause, he doffed his hat and flashed his gold tooth in a wide grin. Her face blanched, eyes round as saucers.

"How did you get in here?"

Starbuck chuckled. "I bribed the cook to send me up in the dumbwaiter."

"The cook!" she repeated sharply. "Are you crazy?"

"Like a fox," Starbuck said with a jocular wink. "I told him we had a little hanky-panky going on the side. He took to the idea right away, even wished me luck. I got the feeling he's one of your secret admirers."

"You fool!" Her voice rose suddenly. "He'll report it to McQueen. He's probably on his way out front right now."

"No chance," Starbuck assured her. "I slipped him a hundred, and told him there'd be another hundred when I come back down."

"What's to stop him from squealing to McQueen, then? Or weren't you worried about what happens to me when you leave?"

"Don't trouble yourself," Starbuck said lightly. "Silence goes to the highest bidder. I'll give him an extra hundred just to make sure he stays bought."

Nell regarded him with an odd steadfast look. "The way you bought me?"

"Bought you?" Starbuck saw anger, resentment and a trace of fear in her eyes. "I don't get your meaning."

"The hell you don't!" she said furiously. "You're a lowdown rotten bastard, Harry Lovett! You promised me the moon and I went for it like a schoolgirl with a case of the vapors."

"What in Christ's name are you talking about?"

"You're a Pinkerton!" she said loudly, staring at him through a prism of tears. "A lying, good-for-nothing snake in the grass! I know the whole story, so don't try to deny it."

"A Pinkerton?" Starbuck was genuinely astounded. "Where the deuce did you get an idea like that?"

"From Denny." She sniffed and dabbed at the tears. "I overheard him talking to Ned Adair. I know you're after Ned for robbing trains and I know—"

"Slow down," Starbuck broke in quickly. "Ned Adair's here? He's somewhere in the Bella Union?"

She motioned toward the window. "You're too late," she said, indicating the deepening indigo of nightfall. "Denny took him—got him out of here— right after it turned dark."

"You started to say O'Brien took him somewhere, didn't you?"

She tossed her head. "Wouldn't you like to know?"

"I have to know," Starbuck said urgently. "It's important, Nell. So damned important you wouldn't believe it."

"Tough tit, hotshot!" She made an agitated gesture with both hands. "I don't talk to Pinkertons."

"I'm not a Pinkerton," Starbuck said with a lame smile. "O'Brien was close, but I've never had anything to do with the Pinkertons. I work on my own."

"Your own?" she murmured uneasily. "Are you trying to tell me you're not a detective?"

"No," Starbuck confessed. "I'm a detective, but I run my own operation. I don't work for any of the big agencies."

"What's the difference?" Nell gave a dark, empty look. "You still conned me and fed me that line of hooey about Colorado."

"I'm not proud of it," Starbuck admitted. "I had a job to do and I went about it the best way I knew how. Maybe I conned you, but it wasn't like I had any real choice. It stuck in my craw the whole time."

"Go crap in your hat, buster! You wanted information, and you pumped me till the well ran dry. You got me hooked with your sweet talk and all the rest of that nonsense, and it never meant a thing to you. Nothing!"

"That's not true." Starbuck studied her downcast face. "The only lies I told you had to do with the job. Everything else was on the square." He lifted her chin, looked directly into her eyes. "The other part—what you're talking about—wasn't any lie. I meant every word of it."

"Honest to God?" She drew a deep, unsteady breath. "You're not just saying that? You really mean it?"

"Straight gospel," Starbuck said earnestly. "When I leave Frisco, you're going with me. You're through with O'Brien and the Barbary Coast and all the rest. That's a solid-gold promise."

Nell stared at him in an intense, haggard way. She was filled with conflicting emotions, and terrified that she might once again be played for a fool. Her lips trembled and she tried to smile, a tortured smile. There was a hungry, questing quality in her eyes, and she searched his face uncertainly. She wanted desperately to believe.

Then, suddenly, she stood within the circle of his arms. She shuddered convulsively against him and pressed her cheek to his chest. Her voice was muffled, almost a plea.

"I'm with you, lover. Where do we go from here?"

Starbuck took her shoulders and held her at arm's length. "You know I've got to get O'Brien and Adair, don't you?" She nodded dumbly, and he went on. "Then I want you to tell me where they've gone. Unless I'm wrong, time's running out fast."

"Once you've caught them, is it over? Will we be able to leave then, Harry?"

"You just pack your duds and wait for me. We're as good as on our way."

Nell briefly recounted everything she'd heard through the wall. Listening to her, Starbuck could generally reconstruct the sequence of events since Adair's escape at the farmhouse. It was no great surprise that everyone involved, Buckley included, now knew he was a detective. Yet one aspect of the situation left him troubled. Buckley's insistence that Adair depart San Francisco—or be killed—was ominous. The blind man quite obviously understood that the trail led to the Snug Café, and had taken measures to sever the link. Which meant there wasn't a moment to spare.

"That's all," Nell concluded. "Denny browbeat Ned into it, and I heard them leave a few minutes after it got dark."

"You mentioned Mother Bronson's joint. Who's she?"

"A witch who runs a dive on the waterfront. She shanghais sailors and sells them to captains of outbound ships. I guess Denny figured she would know which clippers are sailing tonight."

"Would O'Brien hang around until Adair ships out?"

"Probably," Nell said hesitantly. "From what I overheard, he wouldn't take any chances. Ned wasn't too keen on the idea."

"Then I reckon I'd better head for Mother Bronson's."

"Be careful," Nell cautioned. "She's tougher than most men on the Coast. And that includes Denny O'Brien."

"I'll watch myself."

Starbuck walked to the door and turned the key. With his hand on the knob, he stopped and looked around. "You be ready when I get back. Things are liable to happen fast when the fur starts to fly."

"I'll be waiting," she replied with a sudden sad grin. "I've no place to go without you, lover."

The door opened and closed, and he was gone.

A misty rain was falling, and the night was ripe with the smell of the sea. The streetlights were dim silvery globes, their lamps casting flickering shadows on the wet streets. Sailors, stumping along with the bowlegged gait peculiar to seamen, clogged the waterfront.

Starbuck walked toward Battery Point. Out in the bay, anchored away from the wharves, were hundreds of ships. Their silhouettes were fuzzy through the mist and fog, but the ghostly assemblage indicated Frisco's importance as one of the world's major ports. The lanterns of small boats bobbed like fireflies on the rolling water. Known locally as Whitehall boats, the craft ferried sailors ashore for a fee. From there, once his foot touched dry land, the seaman ventured forth at his own peril.

Oceangoing ships, not to mention the men who sailed them, were a complete mystery to Starbuck. Yet the waterfront itself was infamous, with a reputation for danger and foul play known even to landlubbers. The Barbary Coast was rough and sordid, but altogether tame compared to the waterfront. Starbuck had few illusions about the hazards that lay ahead.

All along the wharves was a seedy collection of gaming dives, whorehouses, and busthead saloons. Vice was the stock in trade, and after months at sea, the sailors were victims of their own shipboard fantasies. On reaching port, Jack Tar set off in search of women, alcohol, and gambling. The wilder the women, the better, and even popskull whiskey was none too potent for a sailor with a thirst. Whether able seaman or galley cook, he had money and was eager to blow it on a non-stop, night-and-day spree. Waiting to accommodate him was an assortment of vultures in human form.

Those who operated the waterfront dives were specialists who dealt in live bodies. Their ostensible aim was to provide the seafearer with diverse forms of entertainment. Their principal business, however, was the traffic in shanghaied sailors. The seaman's origin, whether Scandinavian or German, French or British, was of no consequence. The first step was to fleece the sailor of his wages, either at the gaming tables or at the hands of blowsy whores. Then, once he was penniless, the bartender slipped him a drink drugged with sulphate of morphine. Afterward, the warm body was delivered to a ship captain who paid cash on the spot. The sailor awoke to find himself on a voyage that lasted two to four years. Though the practice was widespread, few seamen made any effort to avoid the waterfront. The danger of being shanghaied was considered one of the lesser hazards of shore leave in Frisco.

The Whale, a sleazy dive operated by Mother Bronson, was located at Battery Point. Crude even by Frisco standards, it was a saloon with girls for rent by the trick or by the hour. The ramshackle building squatted directly on the wharf, with water lapping at the pilings below. By rowboat, the trip from The Whale to a waiting clipper was only a matter of minutes. For the shanghaied seaman, it was also a one-way trip. The next port of call was generally halfway around the world.

Starbuck drew stares the moment he stepped through the door. The patrons of The Whale were rough-garbed sailors, rank with the smell of sweat and cheap whiskey. While few of them spoke the same language, they were all dressed similarly and appeared stamped from the same mold. By contrast, Starbuck looked like a peacock among a flock of guinea fowl. His powder-blue suit and pearl-gray fedora left a buzz of conversation in his wake.

Walking to the bar, he ordered whiskey and took his time lighting a cigar. He ignored the stares and the muttered comments, idly inspecting the room. Several house girls were working the crowd, but they held his interest only briefly. On the way to the waterfront, he had formulated a loose, though somewhat credible, cover story. With a glib line of patter, and a little name dropping, he hoped to bluff his way past Mother Bronson. From there, depending on how the dice fell, he would attempt to take O'Brien and Adair without bloodshed. One elbow hooked over the bar, he sipped his drink and waited.

Presently, the door to a back room swung open. The woman who emerged was tall, with shoulders as wide as a man's, and had the stern look of a grenadier. Her hair was pulled back in a severe bun, and her drab dress somehow accentuated the massive bulk of her figure. A lead-loaded blackjack was wedged into the belt cinched around her waist. She looked entirely capable of felling man or beast with one blow.

Plowing through the crowd, she moved directly to the bar and stopped beside Starbuck. She sized him up, her beady eyes noting every detail of his gaudy attire. At last, with her hands on her hips, she rocked her head from side to side.

"Little out of your element, ain't you, sport?"

"You Mother Bronson?"

"That's the name." She gave a tight, mirthless smile. "Who's asking?"

"Johnny One-Spot." Starbuck thought the name had a certain ring. "I've got a message for Denny O'Brien."

"Oh, do you?" Her smirk widened into a smug grin. "And what makes you think you'd find him in a dump like this?"

"High Spade McQueen sent me." Starbuck knocked back his whiskey and wiped his mouth. "He said to tell you the plan's been changed. I'm to explain to O'Brien himself, and no one else."

"Are you, now?" She signaled the barkeep. "Have another drink, sport. We'll talk about it some and see where that takes us."

"What's to talk about?"

The barkeep brought another glass and the bottle. His hand passed over Starbuck's glass, deftly opening and closing, as he poured for Mother Bronson. Then he filled Starbuck's glass and casually walked away.

"Well, Johnny One-Spot"—she lifted her glass— "here's mud in your eye."

She tossed down her drink and Starbuck followed suit. He puffed importantly on his cigar and looked impatient. "I haven't got all night. You gonna take me to Mr. O'Brien or not?"

There was the merest beat of hesitation. Then her smile broadened. "Tell you the truth, you haven't got hardly any time at all, sport."

"What the hell's that supposed to mean?"

"Ask me again when you wake up."

"When I—?"

Starbuck's eyes glazed and the cigar dropped from his mouth. He slumped against the bar, then staggered sideways, and his knees suddenly turned rubbery. He pitched face down on the floor.

Mother Bronson stooped, rolling him over, and took one of his legs under each arm. Effortlessly, she dragged him toward the rear of the saloon. One of her girls rushed to open the door and she disappeared into the back room. There, waiting silently, were Denny O'Brien and Ned Adair. She let go his legs and turned to O'Brien.

"Well, dearie, there's your man. Colder'n a mackerel!"

"No," O'Brien said, staring down a moment. "I think he's Ned's man. Call it a going-away present."

"Present!" Adair repeated with a quizzical look. "You want me to take him with me?"

"Only partway." O'Brien smiled evilly. "Feed him to the sharks once you get out to sea."

Mother Bronson threw back her head and roared with laughter.

Starbuck awoke to a curious yawing motion. His vision was blurred and his head felt as though it had been cleaved down the middle. Several moments elapsed before his eyes cleared and he was able to collect himself. Sitting up, he gazed around and slowly realized he was in a cargo hold. Then, with sudden clarity, it struck him.

He was on a ship! A clipper ship bound for the Orient!

His last recollection was of Mother Bronson. Everything afterward was a blank, but not too difficult to piece together. He'd walked into a trap, with Denny O'Brien very likely watching from the back room. Then, like a prize sucker, he'd never given it a second thought when Mother Bronson called for another round of drinks. Yet he hadn't been shanghaied. Nothing so simple would satisfy O'Brien. The orders, without doubt, were to kill him and dump his body at sea.

He cursed himself for a fool. Standing, his hand went to the shoulder holster and found it empty. He lifted his pants leg and discovered they'd missed the hideout gun in his boot top. The stubby Colt was a last-ditch weapon, but deadly at short ranges. The thought occurred that it was his one hope for deliverance, and he reminded himself to make every shot count. He cocked the hammer and moved toward a ladder at the rear of the hold.

On deck, he saw that he was amidships. The rain had stopped, and stars were visible through occasional gaps in the clouds. Off the port side, far in the distance, he spotted a flashing light and the broken outline of a land mass. He realized with a start that the clipper was approaching the Golden Gate. Only minutes separated the ship from the open sea.

Crouching down, he scuttled toward the railing on the port side. Then, growing closer, he heard voices from the quarterdeck. The shadowed figures of two men appeared out of the dark. One, wearing a billed cap, was clearly a ship's officer. The other, who paused at the stairway, was Red Ned Adair. Starbuck froze, watching them intently.

"You're the captain," Adair remarked testily. "But the sooner we toss him overboard, the better I'll like it."

"I've no quarrel with that, Mr. Adair. As I told you, after we've cleared land's end, you can do as you please."

Adair grunted and started down the stairway leading to the main deck. Then, squinting hard, he suddenly saw Starbuck crouched low in the dark. His jaw popped open in a startled cry.

"Lovett—!"

The captain and Ned Adair went for their guns in the same motion. Starbuck leveled his arm and the snubby Colt spat three times. The slugs stitched an oval pattern in Adair's chest, and he tumbled down the stairway. A bullet tugged at the sleeve of Starbuck's jacket, and he saw the captain staring at him over the sights of a bulldog revolver. His arm moved and the Colt recoiled twice in quick succession. One slug punched into the captain's stomach, the other ripped through his throat and tore out the back of his skull. The impact flung him backward and he dropped raglike on the quarterdeck.

The helmsman shouted, and the thud of footsteps from below decks galvanized Starbuck to action. Working frantically, he stuffed the Colt in the waistband of his trousers and jerked off his boots. Then, in two swift strides, he crossed the deck and dove headlong over the railing. The shock of the icy water struck him like a blow, and a moment later he knifed cleanly to the surface. Bobbing about in the waves, he somehow got his bearings, and saw the flash of a beacon far astern.

A wayward thought seized him, and he vaguely wondered if sharks attacked in the dark. Then, with a stoic sense of fatalism, he dismissed it from mind. He turned into the tide and swam toward the distant light.

CHAPTER 16

The sky was like tarnished pewter, heavy with clouds. False dawn left the alleyway obscured in gloom, and a murky stillness hung over the street. Starbuck checked behind him, then rounded the corner of the Bella Union and halted at the kitchen door. He took out a pocketknife and began working on the lock.

His nerves were gritty and raw, and his head pounded with a dull, grinding weariness. The long swim, some four miles through bone-chilling seas, had sapped his strength to the very marrow. He'd come ashore at Point Lobos, and from there made his way to the Cliff House, a fashionable restaurant on the oceanfront. The manager, shaken by the sight of a waterlogged apparition, had loaned him a driver and carriage, and sent him off wrapped in a woolly blanket. Warm at last, he'd stretched out on the seat and slept during the ride back to the city. When the driver let him off at the hotel, he had felt somewhat

restored, though still a bit unsteady on his feet. A
hot bath and a change of clothes had improved his
spirits, if not the lingering sense of exhaustion. Then,
on the point of leaving the room, he'd suddenly remembered an old friend, packed away in his suitcase. He walked out of the hotel with the Colt .45
jammed in a crossdraw holster.

Now, probing at the lock, his one concern was
Nell. He could only surmise that she was still in her
room, waiting for him to return. She was level-
headed, no stranger to tight situations, and he
thought it unlikely she would have betrayed herself
to O'Brien. It was reasonable to assume she had
worked her normal shift, and resisted the temptation
to ask questions. Yet, given the circumstances, the
night would have proved an ordeal. Her position was
untenable, hinging on a slip of the tongue, and by
now the pressure would have taken its toll. She
wouldn't be safe until he had her clear of the Bella
Union, and out of harm's way. Only then would he
turn his attention to Denny O'Brien.

The tumbler in the lock abruptly clicked and he
eased through the door. He moved across the empty
kitchen, with scarcely a glance at the dumbwaiter.
He was cautious, but not overly concerned. With
sunrise still an hour away, not even the swampers
would have begun work. He followed a passageway
toward the front of the building, and emerged
through a door near the end of the bar. There he
stopped, senses alert, listening.

The barroom was still as a graveyard. He waited

several moments, one ear cocked to any noise, then walked to the staircase. On the second floor he paused again, but saw no one and heard nothing. Another flight up, he flattened against the wall and edged one step at a time onto the third-floor landing. After a while, he proceeded gingerly along the hall. He ghosted past McQueen's room, and then, opposite the door to O'Brien's suite, he suddenly went stock-still. From inside, he heard the low drone of voices. Insofar as he could determine, there were only two men, quite probably O'Brien and McQueen. He briefly considered busting through the door and taking them prisoner. On second thought, however, he rejected the idea. Any commotion would arouse others, and make it impossible for him to spirit Nell out of the Bella Union. Her safety, for the moment, took priority over all else. Besides, O'Brien believed he was dead, snugly tucked away in some shark's belly. Time enough to disabuse him of that notion later in the day. All the time in the world, once Nell was out of danger.

On tiptoe, alert to creaky floorboards, he made his way to the end of the hall. He paused in front of Nell's room, debating whether to rap softly, then decided to try the doorknob. It turned, and he swiftly ducked inside, closing the door behind him. The latch clicked and in the same instant his guts turned to stone.

Nell lay sprawled on the floor. Her arms were akimbo, her hair loose and fanned darkly across her face. The bodice of her dress was torn, exposing her breasts, and her skirt was hitched up over her legs. She seemed too still, deathly still.

Starbuck scooped her up in his arms and carried her to the bed. Only then, with streamers of light flooding through the window, was her condition aparent. She had been beaten, expertly and brutally, with methodical savagery. Her nose was broken, her lips puffy and discolored, and her left eye was swollen shut. As he lowered her onto the bed, she groaned and her good eye slowly rolled open. Her mouth ticced upward in a ghastly smile.

"Harry."

"Don't try to talk."

"You came back for me."

"Told you I would." Starbuck forced himself to smile, leaning closer. "Now, you rest easy and let me have a look at you."

He gently brushed the hair out of her face. Unwitingly, moved by some urge to touch her, he placed his hand on her waist. She recoiled, and a sharp spasm of pain distorted her features. Her mouth opened in a wheezing moan and frothy red bubbles leaked down over her chin. She gasped, laboring desperately to get her breath.

Starbuck knew then her condition was beyond hope. Her rib cage was shattered, and the bloody froth told the tale. One lung, perhaps both, had been punctured. From the punishment she'd absorbed, blows that hard, it seemed entirely likely her insides were torn apart. A veteran of death and dying, he recognized all the signs. The life force was quickly draining out of her, and she hadn't one chance in a thousand. Which was one step removed from zero.

"Nell," Starbuck said softly. "Can you hear me?"

Her eye fluttered open. The agonized look subsided, and she struggled to bring him into focus. Her head moved in a slight nod.

"Was it O'Brien? Did he do this to you?"

"No." Her voice was weak. "He sicced McQueen on me."

"Why?"

"He knew I was"—she grimaced, caught her breath—"only one who could've told you . . . Mother Bronson's."

"He let McQueen work you over because of that?"

"Doesn't matter." She blinked, her eye suddenly brighter. "I waited, and you're here now."

"I'm sorry," Starbuck said hollowly. "I got back as fast as I could."

"Harry, do something for me?"

"Anything," Starbuck told her. "You name it, and it's yours."

"Don't leave me here."

"I won't."

"Take me with you—to Colorado—the way we . . ."

Her voice trailed off and her mouth parted in a shuddering sigh. Then her eye rolled back in her head, and she stopped breathing. She died within the space of a heartbeat.

Starbuck tenderly closed her eye and sat for a

long while holding her hand. Finally, prying her fingers loose, he stood and squared himself up. He realized he'd wanted to tell her his real name, and felt some loss that there had been no time. A slow sense of rage, fueled by his own shame, settled over him. His mouth hardened, and the rage turned to quiet steel fury. He pulled the Colt and walked quickly to the door. Without looking back, he stepped into the hall.

The murmur of voices was still audible from O'Brien's suite. Starbuck quietly tested the doorknob, then braced himself and swung the door wide. He barged into the sitting room, the Colt extended and cocked, and kicked the door shut. O'Brien was seated in an armchair, and McQueen was lounged back on a nearby sofa. A bottle, almost three-quarters empty, and a couple of glasses stood on a table between them. O'Brien's face went chalky.

"Lovett!"

"Just call me Lazarus." Starbuck's eyes were cold, impassive. "Only your boys never quite put me down for the count."

"What—" O'Brien faltered, staring at him with open disbelief. "How'd you get away from Adair?"

"Simple," Starbuck said lazily. "I killed him."

McQueen slowly rose to his feet. His jacket was splattered with flecks of blood, and the knuckles on his right hand were skinned raw. Starbuck wagged the barrel of the Colt in his direction.

"Don't get sudden."

"What the hell; you got the drop on me."

"All the same," Starbuck said shortly, "any funny moves and you'd better take a deep breath. It'll have to last a long time."

"You talk big with a gun in your hand."

"Give me an excuse and I'll fix it so you won't have to listen anymore."

"Hold off, Mac!" O'Brien interjected quickly. "He's got nothing on us."

"Think not?" Starbuck eyed him keenly. "Let's just say I've got all I need and then some."

O'Brien laughed. "With Adair dead, your case is out the window. There's no way you can tie me to those train holdups."

"I had something better in mind."

"Yeah, like what?"

Starbuck's gaze bored into him. "For openers, we'll take a walk down to your office. Then you're going to show me the ledgers you've got locked in your safe."

"Ledgers?" O'Brien went white around the mouth. "You're off your rocker! Those are my books for the Bella Union. The house accounts."

"No," Starbuck said with wry contempt. "I'd lay odds one of them is your insurance policy against Buckley. You're too slick not to keep a record of the payoffs."

"In a pig's ass!" O'Brien fixed him with a baleful look. "Even if there were payoffs, why would I keep a record?"

"A little something in reserve, something to hold over Buckley's head. The way he operates, you know you'd need it sooner or later. I figure you've got enough to convict him a dozen times over."

O'Brien peered at him, one eye sharp and gleaming. "What's your game, Lovett? Pinkertons don't get involved with political shenanigans. Maybe you're looking for a payoff yourself."

A ferocious grin suddenly lit Starbuck's face. "You'd be surprised about us Pinkertons. There's a payoff, all right, but it's not exactly what you had in mind."

"What d' you mean?"

"A rough guess would be twenty years. You and Buckley ought to make perfect cellmates. Two peas in a pod."

"Guess again!" O'Brien eyes glazed with rage. "You've got bats in the belfry if you think I'm gonna hand over those ledgers. I'll see you in hell first!"

"Don't take it so hard," Starbuck taunted. "There's lots of things worse than twenty years."

"How about me?" McQueen gave him a humorless yellow-toothed smile. "You gonna send me to the rockpile, too?"

"Nope." Starbuck's faded blue eyes narrowed. "You're something special, McQueen. You've got a date with the hangman."

"Hangman!" A sourly amused look came over McQueen's face. "Who the hell am I supposed to've murdered?"

"Nell," Starbuck said quietly. "She died a couple of minutes ago."

McQueen scowled with stuffed-animal ferocity.

He read the expression in Starbuck's eyes, and saw revealed there a cold, implacable truth. He would never live to reach the police station, much less a trial by jury. He had already been judged and sentenced. And before him stood a self-appointed executioner.

O'Brien suddenly rose from his chair. The movement momentarily distracted Starbuck, and McQueen took the only chance open to him. With an unintelligible oath, his hand snaked inside his coat and reappeared with a Sharps derringer. An instant before he could bring the gun to bear, Starbuck fired. The first round, a hurried snap-shot, caught him in the shoulder. Knocked off balance, he slammed backward and sat down heavily on the sofa. The second slug drilled through his sternum and the third struck him squarely in the heart. He sat bolt upright a moment, then the light flickered and died in his eyes. The derringer slipped from his grasp and he slumped dead on the sofa.

Starbuck crossed the room in two swift strides. He patted O'Brien down, relieving him of a belly gun, and tossed it on the chair. Then, in a quick, savage gesture, he motioned with the Colt.

"Let's get that safe open. Any tricks—anyone tries to stop us—and you'll wind up on the meatwagon. Savvy?"

O'Brien nodded sullenly. "No tricks."

"You lead the way."

Several minutes later they emerged from the Bella Union. O'Brien had the ledgers under his arm and the snout of a Colt pressed against his spine. Starbuck flagged a hansom cab and shoved him inside. After a word with the driver, Starbuck stepped into the cab and seated himself. He kept the pistol trained on O'Brien's stomach.

"What now?" O'Brien asked as the cab pulled away from the curb. "Where're you taking me?"

Starbuck's expression was sphinxlike. "You'll see when we get there."

"What's the harm in telling me? It's the police station, isn't it? You're gonna have them lock me up."

"You'd like that, wouldn't you? By suppertime, Buckley would have you sprung and on the next clipper to China."

O'Brien's jaw muscles worked. "What d'you want, Lovett? You've got the goddamned ledgers. Isn't that enough?"

"Not near enough," Starbuck said levelly. "We're headed for a warehouse, down at the train yard. We'll have it all to ourselves, just you and me. One way or another, I figure today's your day to turn songbird."

"Songbird?" A vein in O'Brien's temple stood out like twisted cord. "You want me to rat on Buckley?"

"That's the idea," Starbuck said, motioning with the Colt. "Those ledgers are only part of the story. Your testimony ought to cap it off real nice."

"It'll never happen! Denny O'Brien don't rat on nobody!"

"Wanna bet?" Starbuck regarded him evenly. "You'll talk . . . or else."

"Or else what?" O'Brien demanded. "You're not fooling anyone, Lovett. I'm no good to you dead, and we both know it."

"It's the other way round." Starbuck gave him a strange, crooked smile. "Unless you talk, you're no good to me alive. Think of it a while, and you'll see what I mean."

O'Brien saw a catlike eagerness in his eyes. Suddenly, as though his ears had come unplugged, the Barbary Coast boss got the message. Harry Lovett wanted to kill him, and would, given the slightest pretext. Which mean that his life, from that moment forward, had only one measure of value. So long as he testified, he would be allowed to go on breathing. His decision, considering the alternative, was really quite simple.

He decided to sing like a golden-throated canary.

Early that evening Starbuck walked from the train terminal and hailed a cab. Thus far, all the pieces had fallen into place, and he thought it might be wiser to quit while he was ahead. Yet one step remained, and he was determined to try. He ordered the driver to take him to Chinatown.

His day had been hectic, but rewarding. Denny O'Brien, under questioning, had proved himself a veritable gold mine of information. Once he began talking, it became apparent he had something bordering on total recall. He revealed names and dates and places, and, in most instances, tied them to events that established an unassailable time frame. Those slight lapses of memory he suffered were easily brought to light by the ledgers. There, too, the evidence was overwhelming. With meticulous care, he had entered every payoff, noting the date and the amount, along with the percentage of gross take from various Barbary Coast operations. The entries, itemized in O'Brien's laborious scrawl, covered prostitution and gambling as well as the all-pervasive protection racket. The ledgers substantiated that Christopher Buckley had shared in the proceeds to the tune of more than $1,000,000.

Late that afternoon, after taking a deposition from O'Brien, Starbuck had at last notified Charles Crocker. Shortly thereafter, a squad of Central Pacific security guards reported to the warehouse. O'Brien was sequestered in a windowless room, and men were posted both inside and outside the building. Their orders were direct and without equivocation. Anyone who attempted forcible entry to the warehouse was to be shot on the spot. When Starbuck departed the warehouse, he'd had no qualms about O'Brien's safety. Nor any concern that his songbird would try to fly away.

On the Street of a Thousand Lanterns, a crowd was gathered outside Fung Jing Toy's house. A policeman was posted at the door, and a paddy wagon stood at curbside. Starbuck paid the hansom driver, then eased through the throng of Chinese who stared silently, almost expectantly, at the front door. He approached the policeman and nodded amiably.

"What's all the commotion?"

"Oh, would you believe it?" the officer replied in a thick brogue. "The big Chink himself has done been murdered."

"Fung Jing Toy?"

"Aye, the very one," the officer observed solemnly. "God rest his heathen soul."

The door opened, and a murmur swept through the crowd. Several policemen, formed in a protective wedge, escorted two Chinese down the steps and hustled them into the paddy wagon. Starbuck instantly recognized the men, Wong Yee and Sing Dock. The last time he'd seen them they were guarding the entrance to Fung's underground chamber.

"Are those the killers?"

"Caught red-handed," the officer affirmed. "And them the Chink's own *boo how doy*. Cut him to ribbons with their hatchets, they did. Terrible sight. Terrible."

Starbuck turned and walked away. Somehow he wasn't surprised by Fung Jing Toy's death. Some dark complex of gut instinct and premonition had warned him that Buckley would move swiftly. With Denny O'Brien in custody, Mr. Frisco couldn't risk the possibility of still another turncoat. All the more imperative, Fung represented a corroborative witness, the one man who could substantiate O'Brien's testimony. Buckley, expedient to the end, had simply ordered the Chinaman's assassination.

Yet Starbuck was surprised by the choice of assassins. Wong Yee and Sing Dock were clearly the tools of Christopher Buckley. Their loyalty to a white-devil overlord, rather than Fung, confirmed Buckley's absolute domination of the Chinatown tongs. Still, while a key witness had been silenced, the blind man had no reason for celebration. He was, ironically enough, very much in the dark.

The ledgers were the one element Buckley couldn't have foreseen, and never suspected. A mute form of corroboration that spoke louder than words.

Mr. Frisco was shortly due the shock of his life.

CHAPTER 17

"Perhaps you could elaborate, Mr. Starbuck."

"Well, in a manner of speaking, you might liken it to the links in a chain. Adair led me to O'Brien, who in turn led me to Fung. From there, things led straight to Buckley. He was the last link in the chain."

"You refer to Christopher A. Buckley, proprietor of the Snug Café. Is that correct?"

"Correct."

"Now, you used the analogy—links in a chain. Would you consider it valid to broaden the analogy, and call it a chain of command?"

"Yes, I would," Starbuck agreed. "It was organized along military lines. Fung and O'Brien were like field commanders, with their own sector of operations. They were free to run things to suit themselves, but they were responsible for their actions. In other words, they reported to a higher authority."

"So Fung controlled Chinatown and O'Brien

controlled the Barbary Coast. They operated independently on day-to-day matters, but they were answerable for the overall results in their sectors. Is that essentially correct?"

"Yes."

"Would you consider it a fair statement to characterize Christopher Buckley as their commander-in-chief?"

"I would," Starbuck acknowledged. "He appointed them, and he could strip them of command any time he took a notion. His orders were the last word."

"By that, you mean there was no appeal?"

"None whatever. He was the last link in the chain, and his word was final. It all stopped there."

The Grand Jury room, located in the Hall of Justice, went silent. The jurors were attentive, listening raptly, their eyes fixed on Starbuck. They gazed at him with the look of circus spectators watching a tiger eat its keeper. From the news stories, they knew he had killed three men during the course of his assignment in San Francisco. Hushed and eager, they waited to hear more.

Edgar Caldwell, the district attorney, paused for dramatic effect. He adjusted his spectacles, and stood for a moment consulting his notes. An ambitious man, he was commonly thought to be a force in county politics. Yet his conduct of the hearing indicated he was putting distance between himself and Buckley's local machine. He was seeking an indictment, but on the man rather than the Democratic

Party. At length, he turned back to the witness chair.

"Mr. Starbuck, a minute ago you testified that—and I quote—things led straight to Buckley. What did you mean by 'things'?"

Starbuck wormed around in his chair. With a straight face, he briefly recounted his cover story, and the offer to buy one hundred Chinese slave girls. Then he told of Fung's suspicions, which led ultimately to the meeting with Buckley. He concluded with a short synopsis of the meeting, and Buckley's open admission of power.

"Let's be clear on that point," Caldwell insisted. "Buckley stated that he'd been asked to arbitrate the matter?"

"Yes."

"Then he went on to state that he would approve the deal—the sale of a hundred Chinese virgins—if your references were in order. Isn't that correct?"

"So far as it goes," Starbuck amended. "I also had to show good faith by putting up a hundred thousand in cash."

"Which you obtained from your employer, Charles Crocker?"

"That's right."

"To recap, Mr. Starbuck." Caldwell struck an elegant pose for the jurors. "Buckley dictated the terms necessary to consummate the deal, and he then imposed those terms on both Fung and O'Brien. Is that your testimony?"

"Yes, it is."

"Have you any direct knowledge of why Fung and

O'Brien would comply with his demands?"

"I do," Starbuck nodded. "O'Brien called him Mr. Frisco. He stated that Buckley could approve or disapprove the deal, and everybody would just have to live with the decision. The question at issue—and Buckley confirmed this in our meeting—was how to conclude the deal and still keep peace between Fung and O'Brien."

"If I may paraphrase," Caldwell said, one eye on the jurors. "Buckley would hand down his edict, and his henchmen, Fung and O'Brien, would have no choice but to obey. A fair summation of the facts?"

"In a nutshell, that's the way it worked."

"Very well, Mr. Starbuck. Suppose we move on. In previous testimony, one Dennis O'Brien identified a certain set of ledgers. He stated that one ledger in particular dealt with payoffs to Buckley, as regards criminal activities on the Barbary Coast. Are you familiar with the ledgers in question?"

"I personally observed O'Brien take those ledgers from his office safe in the Bella Union."

"So the ledgers were intact—all entries previously recorded—at that time?"

"Yes."

"Did O'Brien voluntarily surrender the ledgers?"

"No." Starbuck smiled. "I forced him to open the safe at gunpoint."

"Please describe the events that transpired immediately thereafter."

"I took O'Brien to a warehouse . . ."

Starbuck's testimony consumed the better part of

an hour. When he was finished, Caldwell excused him from the witness chair and thanked him profusely. The jurors sat spellbound as he walked from the room. Their expressions indicated they believed the man, and the story he'd told.

Outside, moving along the corridor, he felt an enormous sense of relief. Three weeks had elapsed since the capture of Denny O'Brien and the death of Fung Jing Toy. In that time, waiting for a grand jury to be empaneled, he had worked closely with the district attorney. His continued presence had also worked as an influence on O'Brien. The Barbary Coast boss had cooperated fully, and turned state's evidence in exchange for a reduced sentence. A convincing witness, he had testified earlier in the day. And along with his ledgers, he'd apparently made an impression on the jurors.

There now seemed little doubt as to the outcome. An indictment would be forthcoming, and Buckley would stand trial on charges ranging from criminal conspiracy to accessory to murder. Conviction would very likely put him behind bars for the rest of his life.

For Starbuck, it was the end to a long and trying period. He had enjoyed the chase, and felt great personal accomplishment at having brought Mr. Frisco to bay. Still, there were bad memories as well, and a change of scenery seemed very much in order. His thoughts turned to Denver.

Then, rounding the corner into the lobby, he abruptly stopped. Christopher Buckley, being led by another man, appeared through the front entrance and walked toward him. He recalled Buckley was scheduled to testify before the grand jury, and briefly considered not speaking. But upon second thought, he changed his mind. A last word with the blind man seemed a fitting end to the case.

"Afternoon, Mr. Buckley."

"Good afternoon." Buckley halted, his expression quizzical. "I'm afraid you have the advantage of me."

"Luke Starbuck," Starbuck replied with a ghost of a grin. "Otherwise known as Harry Lovett."

"Of course!" Buckley said, smiling faintly. "How could I ever forget that voice?"

"Yeah, I reckon a voice is pretty hard to disguise."

"Well, that's past us now, Mr. Starbuck. I understand you've even dispensed with your gold tooth."

"Oh?" Starbuck asked pleasantly. "Keeping tabs on me, are you?"

Buckley's smile turned cryptic. "You remember my associate, Knuckles Jackson? He keeps me up to date on the latest newspaper accounts of your activities. All the more so since you've become such a celebrity."

Starbuck and Jackson traded nods. A large man, Jackson had a square and pugnacious face, with cold gun-metal eyes. For a moment, Starbuck couldn't place him. Then, suddenly, he recalled the night O'Brien and McQueen had escorted him to the Snug Café. Jackson was the resident gorilla who guarded the alley door. His presence here today spoke for itself. He was apparently trusted to act as Buckley's seeing-eye dog and chief bodyguard.

"Funny thing," Starbuck said, glancing back at Buckley. "All this hoopla about me doesn't amount to a hill of beans. I've got an idea you're the one they'll remember."

"On the contrary!" Buckley's tone was lordly, somehow patronizing. "You shouldn't be so modest, Mr. Starbuck. The public loves to be titillated, and you've certainly shown them the seamier side of San Francisco. Small wonder it's captured their imagination."

"Here today, gone tomorrow," Starbuck said lightly. "People forget real quick."

"True," Buckley said with an indulgent smile. "Fame rides a fleet horse. Nonetheless, you're to be congratulated on a splendid job. You have a few peers in your particular line of work."

Starbuck tried to divine his mood. For a man facing prison, he was altogether too congenial, and far too unconcerned. His excessively reasonable tone somehow rang false. Then, too, there was something strange about his expression. Behind the tinted glasses, the dead eyes seemed oddly mocking, alight with laughter. The effect was unsettling, vaguely unnatural.

"I admire the way you're taking it all in stride, Mr. Buckley."

"Why not?" Buckley spread his hands in a bland gesture. "Life is very much like a melodrama, Mr.

Starbuck. Look closely and you'll find that pathos and farce always merge in the end. What appears to be reality is often little more than illusion."

"I wouldn't know about that," Starbuck remarked. "Course, just from the sound of it, I get the feeling you're not losing any sleep over this grand jury business."

"You tell me," Buckley said almost idly. "Should I be losing sleep?"

"You're on your way to testify, aren't you?"

"Indeed I am."

"Then I reckon you'll be able to answer the question yourself. There's no illusion so far as the jurors are concerned. It's all hard fact."

"So I hear," Buckley said, not without bitterness. "O'Brien and his ledgers apparently make for a convincing tale."

Starbuck regarded his somberly. "You must have inside sources. Those ledgers were a pretty well-kept secret."

"People talk," Buckley replied absently. "A secret ceases to be a secret once it's known by a second party. But, of course, that's hardly news to a man in your profession."

"No, I guess not." Starbuck nodded, acknowledging the truth of the statement. "Leastways, I never had any trouble getting people to talk about you."

Buckley smiled humorlessly. "Come now, Mr. Starbuck. Denny O'Brien talked because you put a gun to his head. Except for that, you would never have gotten past the stage of speculation and conjecture."

"Maybe so," Starbuck admitted. "The way it worked out, we'll never know. He talked, and that's all that counts."

"Ah, yes," Buckley commented loftily. "The hard facts you spoke of a moment ago."

"Hard facts," Starbuck said slowly, emphatically, "and all down in black and white."

"You believe they'll indict me, then?"

"Let's just say I'd lay odds on it."

"A sporting man to the end, hmm?"

"No, I only bet on sure things."

"Touché," Buckley said equably. "And what of you, Mr. Starbuck. Where to now that your terrible swift sword has done its work?"

"Another town, another job," Starbuck countered easily. "There's so many crooks around, it keeps a fellow in my line pretty much on the go."

"Indeed?" Buckley paused as though weighing his words. "Another town, another job sounds imminently practical, Mr. Starbuck. Allow me to wish you good hunting . . . elsewhere."

"Some men might take that as a threat."

"Perhaps." Buckley smiled without warmth. "I'm sure you'll take it in the spirit in which it was intended, Mr. Starbuck."

Starbuck laughed and gave him an offhand salute. With a nod to Knuckles Jackson, he walked to the front entrance and pushed through the door. Outside, he found the way barred by a gang of reporters and several newspaper cameramen. For all the publicity surrounding the case, he had thus far avoided both interviews and photographs. Today, with the grand jury in session, the press cast aside any pretense of civility. Camera powder flashed and reporters swarmed forward, peppering him with questions.

"What's the latest, Mr. Starbuck?"

"No comment."

"Will they indict Buckley?"

"Your guess is as good as mine."

"C'mon, be a sport. Give us the lowdown!"

"I only know what I read in the papers."

"Can we quote you on that?"

"Suit yourself."

"Have a heart, Mr. Starbuck! We're only trying to do our job!"

"No comment."

To a chorus of groans and invidious remarks, Starbuck brushed past them. He hurried down the steps and walked toward Kearny Street. A moment later he disappeared around the corner.

Early the next morning Starbuck was ushered into Charles Crocker's office. The railroad tycoon greeted him with an ebullient smile and a bear-trap handshake. Once they were seated, Crocker tossed a newspaper across the desk.

"Have you seen that?"

"Yeah, I read it at breakfast."

Starbuck's photo stared back at him from the front page. Emblazoned across the top was a bold headline, which in itself told the story. The grand jury had indicted Christopher Buckley on all counts.

"You did it!" Crocker boomed out jovially. "By Christ, you said you would—and you did!"

"I got lucky."

"Luck, hell!" Crocker beamed. "Nobody gets his picture on every front page in town because he's lucky. You pulled off a feat of detection that's unrivaled. You're the toast of San Francisco!"

"So I read."

The irony of the moment wasn't lost on Starbuck. Crocker, not quite a month ago, had strenuously opposed the plan to expose Buckley. Yet now, basking in the reflected glory, he was something of a hero himself. His statements to the newspapers implied that the Central Pacific Railroad was in large measure responsible for Buckley's downfall. The idea struck Starbuck as amusing. All the more so since Crocker was now portraying himself as a paragon of civic virtue. He thought it a strange and unlikely role for a robber baron.

"Yessir," Crocker said with vinegary satisfaction, "you nailed Chris Buckley to the cross, and we all owe you a vote of thanks. San Francisco won't ever be the same again!"

Starbuck shrugged off the compliment. "I just did my job."

"Your job and then some!" Crocker said, jubilant. "You called Buckley and his crowd spoilers, and you were right. I'll have to admit I wasn't sold on the idea, not at first. But you turned me around, Luke.

You made me see the light!" His voice rose triumphantly. "This is a proud day for the Central Pacific. A proud day!"

"Speaking of trains," Starbuck said wryly, "I've got to get a move on. I aim to catch the eastbound out of Oakland this evening."

"Eastbound?" Crocker suddenly looked perplexed. "Where are you going?"

"Denver," Starbuck said with a tired smile. "That's my headquarters, and I've got business to look after."

Crocker pursed his lips, solemn. "The Central Pacific needs a new chief of security. Any chance you would consider it assuming I made it worth your while, stock options and that sort of thing?"

"Thanks all the same." Starbuck shook his head. "I appreciate the offer, but I'm not what you'd call a team man. I work best alone."

"I suspected as much," Crocker said with exaggerated gravity. "You will return for Buckley's trial, won't you? I understand it's been set for the spring court docket."

"Wouldn't miss it for the world."

"I should hope not!" Crocker frowned uncertainly. "O'Brien alone will never convict him. Your testimony is vital."

"I'll be here," Starbuck assured him. "You've got my word on it."

Crocker took a bank draft from inside a folder on his desk. "I intended to give you this, anyway. A bonus, so to speak." He leaned forward, extending the draft. "Perhaps it will also ensure your return for the trial."

Starbuck accepted the draft, studying it a moment. Then he looked up with some surprise. "Ten thousand is mighty generous. I would've settled for what you owed me and no bones either way."

"You earned it." Crocker laughed a short, mirthless laugh. "Ten dead men at a thousand dollars a head seems to me a rare bargain."

"Eleven." Starbuck gave him a lopsided grin. "Course, the farmer didn't rightly count. He just got in the way of a stray bullet."

"Nonetheless, he was a member of the gang. It appears I owe you another thousand, Luke."

"I'll collect when I see you in the spring."

"Done!" Crocker trumpeted. "Here's my hand on it!"

Starbuck rose and shook hands. Then, after a parting word, he walked from the office. On his way to the elevator, he stuck the bank draft in his wallet and chuckled softly to himself. A thousand dollars a head was no bargain. He'd killed men for lots less, simply because they needed killing.

And in the end, someone had to kill them.

CHAPTER 18

There was a slight chill in the air and fog obscured the waterfront. Farther away, beyond the city, a wintry sunset slowly settled into the ocean.

Starbuck stood on the fantail of the ferry. His eyes were fixed upon distance, faraway and clouded. A roll-your-own was stuck in the corner of his mouth, and he smoked without haste. San Francisco, quickly falling astern, was lost within some deeper reflection. His thoughts were on men, and events.

On the whole, he felt he'd done a creditable job. The band of train robbers and their leader had been exterminated. Fung Jing Toy was dead, leaving Chinatown in turmoil. O'Brien, who most assuredly deserved killing, would nonetheless emerge from prison an old and withered shadow of the man who had once ruled the Barbary Coast. Christopher Buckley would be convicted and die an inmate, blind and ultimately enfeebled, in some dank prison cell. So what began as a routine assignment had ended with the downfall of Frisco's underworld hierarchy. A certain pride in a job well done was by no means out of order.

Yet, with some cynicism, Starbuck saw the darker side as well. In his view, there was no logical progression in human affairs. There were merely tides of change borne on violence and an endless upheaval of political structures. The winners hung the losers—or carted them off to prison—and things went on much as they always had and always would. The evils of man, corruption and greed, were the single constant. And in one of the stranger quirks of life, a man bursting with virtue was often less esteemed than the spoilers. The voters, for all their sanctimonious tommyrot, understood greed and willfully sought those pleasures that were considered wicked and depraved. A reformer, therefore, lasted only a short while. The spoilers went on forever.

Viewed from that perspective, the only change wrought would be a change in names and faces. A new political kingpin would step into the void and quickly replace Buckley. Another thug would batter his fellow thugs into submission, and emerge the czar of the Barbary Coast. The tong wars of Chinatown would produce yet another vice lord, and the market in Oriental slave girls would continue to flourish. A whole new cast of characters would rise to ascendancy in Frisco's underworld. And soon, from the waterfront to the Uptown Tenderloin, it would return to business as usual.

Still, all things considered, those were problems

San Francisco would have to solve for itself. Starbuck saw his own role clearly, and moral judgments, while an engaging exercise, were not his bailiwick. He was a detective, not a civic crusader. He'd been hired to rout a gang of train robbers, and Red Ned Adair was dead.

Case closed.

From one standpoint, however, the case would never be closed. Over breakfast that morning, while reading the *Examiner*, he'd realized how fully the Frisco job had altered his own future. His testimony before the grand jury, and the attendant publicity, had resulted in his photo being splashed across the front pages of newspapers throughout the West. His anonymity, always an edge in past cases, was gone forever. Once a face in the crowd, he would now be known and recognized wherever he traveled. Coupled with his reputation, that loss of anonymity might shorten his life span considerably.

The upshot seemed equally clear to Starbuck. Now, more than ever, he must become a master of disguise. A man of a thousand faces, none of them his own. An undercover operative in every sense of the word. In short, a detective and a chameleon, all rolled into one.

Unbidden, the memory of Nell popped into his head. Since the night of her death, she had never been far from his thoughts. Not that he wanted to remember, or made any conscious effort to do so. Quite the contrary, the hurt and the shame were emotions yet to be reconciled. Whenever possible, he nudged all thought of her to some dark corner of his mind. Yet, despite his attempts to forget, she was always there. A vision too easily summoned, and a reminder of things lost forever.

With the clarity of hindsight, he understood he'd overplayed his hand. That night, when he'd left her alone at the Bella Union, he was supremely confident. No doubt existed that he would shortly capture Ned Adair and return to spirit her away from the Barbary Coast. He was cocky, altogether too sure of himself, and in his blind rush to get the job done, he had sadly underestimated Denny O'Brien. In effect, he had gambled Nell's life on the assumption he could outsmart a pack of cutthroats and thieves who were already wise to his game. And he'd lost.

That was the part he couldn't forget. To risk his own life was one thing. He was, after all, being paid to accept whatever risk the job entailed. To risk Nell's life was another matter entirely. Her only stake in the game was a fabrication of lies and promises. In the end, of course, he would never have welched completely on their arrangement. He fully intended to take her away from the Barbary Coast and somehow relocate her in Colorado. Perhaps set her up in a respectable business of some sort, or at the very least secure her a job a cut above the Bella Union. Yet the fairy tale about his whorehouse empire, and their partnership in the enterprise, was unadulterated poppycock. However good his intentions, he had gulled her with a pipe dream that resulted in her death.

Looking back, he saw now that he'd made a fatal error in judgment. He should have gotten her out of the Bella Union, and once she was safe—only when she was safe—should he have gone off in search of Ned Adair. At the moment, time had seemed imperative, and unwittingly or not, he had elected to jeopardize her rather than jeopardize the mission. In retrospect, it was an unconscionable decision, all the worse because he'd compounded poor judgment with dumb planning. But then, as the old-timers were fond of saying, hindsight was no better than hind tit.

The memory of Nell would never leave him. Nor would he ever wholly absolve himself of her death. With time, he might learn to live with it. One day, perhaps, he might even find justification for the act. Her death, in the larger sense, had brought about the downfall of Frisco's underworld leaders. But that, too, was more excuse than vindication, and in no way would it mitigate what he'd done. The thought of Nell Kimball would remain a burden, and one he deserved. By all rights, she belonged with him now, on her way to Colorado. He wouldn't forget why he stood alone . . . and curiously lonely.

"Hullo, Starbuck."

Knuckles Jackson halted beside him at the railing. Starbuck was instantly alert. A sudden chill settled over him, and it left a residue of uneasiness. His muscles tensed, every nerve stretched tight, yet his expression revealed nothing. He took a drag on his cigarette and tossed it over the side. Then he fixed Jackson with a stony stare.

"Let me guess," he said evenly. "You've got business in Oakland, and you just happened to board the same ferry."

"Not exactly." Jackson's mouth zigzagged in a gash-like smile. "I've got business, but not in Oakland. It's with you."

"I'm listening."

Jackson returned his gaze steadily. "Yesterday, when you had that little talk with Mr. Buckley, he was tryin' to be reasonable about things. He wanted me to make sure you got the message."

"What message was that?"

"He don't want you to show up for the trial."

Starbuck's eyes narrowed. "Guess I had wax in my ears yesterday. You're saying that without me, there's no one left but O'Brien. So you somehow manage to kill him, and when I fail to testify, there goes the prosecution's case. All charges dismissed and Buckley walks away with a clean bill of health."

Jackson gave him a wide, peg-toothed grin. "You're pretty swift. I wasn't too sure m'self, but the boss said you'd see the light. He figured a word to the wise and you wouldn't come anywhere near that trial."

"And if I do?"

"Too bad."

"Too bad if I show up?"

"No." Jackson touched the brim of his hat. "Too bad you asked the wrong question."

Out of the corner of his eye, Starbuck caught a glint of metal on the upper deck. In that split second, he realized Jackson had a confederate. The signal, touching his hat, was prearranged. A signal to end it there.

All in a motion, Starbuck pulled the Colt and dropped to one knee. A slug thunked into the wooden railing, followed an instant later by a loud report. He saw a man on the upper deck, squinting at him down the barrel of a revolver. Thumbing the hammer, he extended the Colt to arm's length and let go two rapid shots. The man stiffened, and a pair of bright red dots, centered chest high, appeared on his coat front. He stumbled, arms flapping like a scarecrow, and his legs suddenly collapsed beneath him. The gun went skittering from his hand and he keeled over backward, spread-eagled on the deck.

Starbuck twisted around. The hammer was cocked and his finger tightened on the trigger, then he stopped. Knuckles Jackson stood frozen at the rail, his hands empty and very prudently held in plain sight. His look was one of disbelief, and outright terror. The look of a vicious dog suddenly cornered by a boar grizzly.

Climbing to his feet, Starbuck's expression turned immobile and dark. His eyes flashed with a cold glitter as he took a step closer. A grim line of rage, naked and revealed, tugged at his mouth.

"You sorry sonovabitch! I ought to kill you."

"Nothin' personal," Jackson croaked. "I was just followin' orders."

"Then here's an order for you. Buckley's so keen on messages, I want you to carry one back to him."

Jackson swallowed hard. "Yeah?"

"Tell him for me that I'll see him at the trial."

"I sure will, them very words."

"One more thing," Starbuck said softly. "Tell him if anything happens to Denny O'Brien, I will personally stop his clock, tick-tock and all. You got it?"

"I got it."

"Then start swimming."

"Swimming?" Jackson's face went ashen. "What d'you mean?"

"You heard me." Starbuck commanded. "Hit the water and make like a duck."

"Jeezus Christ!" Jackson bawled. "You ain't serious! I'd drown before I got halfway to shore."

"I'm dead serious." Starbuck wiggled the Colt with a menacing gesture. "You can haul ass over the side or die where you're standing. Only make up your mind *muy* goddamn *pronto!* I'm through talking."

Jackson opted for the water. He gingerly climbed over the railing and hung there a moment, staring down with a look of queasy horror. Then he leaped, his hat drifting lazily in the air, and hit the ferry's wake with a leaden splash. An instant later he surfaced, spewing water, and bobbed about like a cork in a stormy sea. Arms flailing, he finally got himself oriented with the distant shore. He struck off at a slow crawl toward the city by the bay.

Starbuck grinned, watching from the fantail a long while. Then, not at all displeased with the outcome, he shoved the Colt in its holster and strode off in the direction of the passenger cabin. His step was jaunty, and he was quietly humming a Frisco ditty to himself.

> The next time I saw darlin' Nell
> She was gussied up for a spree.
> She had a pistol strapped 'round herself
> And a banjo draped acrost her knee!

The Warlords

The Warlords

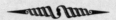

MATT BRAUN

St. Martin's Paperbacks

This is a work of fiction. All of the characters, organizations, and events portrayed in this novel are either products of the author's imagination or are used fictitiously.

THE SPOILERS / THE WARLORDS

The Spoilers copyright © 1981 by Matt Braun.
The Warlords copyright © 2003 by Winchester Productions, Ltd.

For information address St. Martin's Press, 175 Fifth Avenue, New York, NY 10010.

ISBN: 978-1-250-30856-6

Our books may be purchased in bulk for promotional, educational, or business use. Please contact your local bookseller or the Macmillan Corporate and Premium Sales Department at 1-800-221-7945, ext. 5442, or by e-mail at MacmillanSpecialMarkets@macmillan.com.

Printed in the United States of America

The Spoilers St. Martin's Paperbacks edition / November 2002
The Warlords St. Martin's Paperbacks edition / July 2003

St. Martin's Paperbacks are published by St. Martin's Press, 175 Fifth Avenue, New York, NY 10010.

10 9 8 7 6 5 4 3 2 1

To
Bettiane
THE BRIGHTEST STAR IN MY CONSTELLATION

Author's Note

THE WARLORDS is based on a true story.

In the summer of 1915, bands of Mexican revolutionaries raided across the Rio Grande into Texas. Known as the Army of Liberation, the rebels destroyed property, burned railroad bridges, and killed civilians and army troops with a savagery born of racial hatred. Thousands of people fled the border in terror.

There were rumors that Germany was behind the raids. In Europe, Germany was at war with England, France and Russia, jointly known as the Allies. Speculation in Washington was that Germany, in an effort to prevent the United States from joining the Allies, had hatched a plot to bring war to the Rio Grande. The rumors, despite credible evidence of a conspiracy, were never acknowledged by the United States government.

President Woodrow Wilson ordered the U.S. Bureau of Investigation into action. A Special Agent was dispatched to the Rio Grande, his assignment to uncover the truth about German involvement with the Army of Liberation. His investigation, conducted with the aid of the Texas Rangers and the army, revealed a complex of racial tension, international intrigue, and barbarity at its worst. The border, that summer of 1915, ran red with blood.

THE WARLORDS is fiction based on fact. Literary license had been taken with time and place, and certain historical characters central to the story. Yet the events depicted, particularly the savagery on the Rio Grande, adhere closely to the truth. THE WARLORDS actually happened.

Chapter One

Berlin was at its most pleasant in early spring. The snows of winter were gone and a riotous profusion of flowers lined the paths of the Rosengarten. Strollers paused to stare at the imposing marble statue of Empress Auguste Viktoria.

Not far away the bridle paths of the Tiergarten wound through stately copses of oak and hemlock. Officers of the German General Staff were out for their morning ride, cantering past with the rhythmic click of shod hooves on packed earth. The silver spikes on the crown of their helmets glinted beneath a warm May sun.

North of the Tiergarten was the stone monolith that served as headquarters for the General Staff. The building occupied a square block on the Bendlerstrasse, broad marble steps fronting the busy thoroughfare. Guards posted at the doors stood resplendent in blue uniforms trimmed with gold, rifles grounded by their jackboots. Their eyes were fixed straight ahead.

Colonel Franz von Kleist hurried up the steps. The breast of his tunic was bedecked with an array of medals, among them the Iron Cross with clusters. The guards snapped to attention, their rifles at present arms, and he returned their salute as he pushed through the doors. A wide rotunda, flanked on either side by sweeping staircases, swirled with officers and enlisted men. Germany was at war and everyone seemed in a rush.

On the second floor, von Kleist moved along a corridor

toward the center of the building. He was posted to the Abwehr, the German secret intelligence service, and he'd been summoned to a meeting at Wehrmacht headquarters. He entered a large anteroom, where the adjutant, a young major, quickly ushered him through a set of floor-to-ceiling double doors. The inner office was lavishly appointed, with thick carpeting, lush leather furniture, and a massive walnut desk. The Imperial flag hung draped from a standard anchored to the floor.

The officer behind the desk was Field Marshal Heinrich von Luettwitz. A portly man with a leonine shock of gray hair, he was Chief of Staff of the Oberkommando der Wehrmacht, the Supreme Command of the German Imperial Armed Forces. Another man, leaner and with a hint of arrogance in his attitude, rose from one of the leather chairs. He was General Alexis Baron von Fritsch, chief of the Abwehr. Von Kleist was directly under his command.

"There you are, Franz," he said, motioning to a chair. "We were just talking about you."

Von Kleist marched to the desk. He clicked his heels, nodding first to von Luettwitz, then to von Fritsch. "Field Marshal. Herr General," he said, rigid at attention. "How may I be of service?"

"Sit down, Colonel," von Luettwitz ordered. "We have asked you here to discuss a rather delicate matter."

"And one of the utmost secrecy," von Fritsch added. "Nothing discussed here today will go outside this room."

"Yes, sir." Von Kleist removed his helmet and seated himself. "I understand."

Von Leuttwitz and von Fritsch were of the aristocracy east of the Elbe River, the very core of German military power. Their titles had been bestowed on their forebears centuries ago by Frederick the Great, the ancient King of Prussia. Von Kleist was himself Prussian, descended from generations of military leaders who had served the Reich from the Napoleonic Wars to the present day. They served now at the pleasure of Kaiser Wilhelm II, Emperor of Germany.

"We are concerned," Field Marshal von Luettwitz said, "that the United States might be drawn into the war. The sinking of the *Lusitania* was an unfortunate incident."

General von Fritsch nodded. "One we may regret beyond anything we might have imagined."

Three days ago, on May 7, 1915, the *Lusitania* had been sunk by a German submarine off the coast of Ireland. The British liner, torpedoed amidships, went down with over a thousand passengers aboard, almost two hundred of whom were Americans. The incident had created a fury of outrage in the United States, and raised the specter of America entering the war. Great Britain and France were urging President Woodrow Wilson to mobilize his army.

"Let us be realists," von Luettwitz said gruffly. "Nothing is as we planned on the Western Front. A stalemate does not win a war."

"All too true," von Fritsch agreed. "The industrial might of the United States could easily tip the balance. We cannot afford such a risk."

Von Luettwitz sighed heavily. "Everything seemed so simple a year ago. I tell you frankly, gentlemen, I thought the Continent would be ours by now."

Colonel von Kleist shared the opinion. Looking back, he had fully expected the German army to rout the Allied forces. The World War, for all practical purposes, began with the assassination of Archduke Ferdinand of Austria-Hungary by a Serbian nationalist in June 1914. On July 28, after failed peace negotiations, Austria-Hungary declared war on Serbia.

Germany, which was aligned with Austria-Hungary and the Ottoman Empire, declared war on Britain and France on August 3. The following day, Britain, France and

Russia, universally known as the Allies, declared war on Germany. On the morning of August 4, Germany invaded Belgium, and shortly afterward swept into France. The British Expeditionary Force sailed for the Continent.

By the spring of 1915, the armies of Europe were mired down in static warfare. On the Western Front, a line of trenches 475 miles long ran from neutral Switzerland to the North Sea. On the Eastern Front, the Tsar's forces had been pushed back beyond Poland, but the Russian army was by no means defeated. The bloodletting on both fronts was staggering, with nearly a million men killed and wounded in just nine months. The year ahead would almost certainly separate victor from vanquished.

"In any event," von Luettwitz said at length, "the Kaiser is adamant on one point. America must not be drawn into the war."

General von Fritsch steepled his fingers. "That is why we asked you here today," he said, nodding to von Kleist. "The Abwehr has been assigned the mission of resolving the situation. You will be placed in command of a special operation."

"Herr General!" von Kleist sat straighter, his eyes suddenly alert. "I am a soldier and I live to serve the Reich. What is it you wish me to do?"

"Something rather extraordinary," the Field Marshal interjected with ominous calm. "The Kaiser has ordered that we start a war between Mexico and the United States."

Von Kleist's expression betrayed nothing. He was a tall, saturnine man, quick and intelligent, with the effortless confidence of those rarely afflicted by doubt. Three years ago, at age thirty, he had been selected for the War Academy, a school for officers destined to attain the highest rank. After graduation, he had been posted to the Abwehr, and promoted twice since the war began. He was the youngest colonel on the General Staff.

"I am honored by such an assignment," he said now. "How do you wish me to proceed?"

"With dispatch," von Luettwitz told him. "Our objective is to shift the focus of America to its own national security. A war with Mexico should do quite nicely."

Von Fritsch permitted himself a wry smile. "There is nothing that so commands attention as a threat to one's sovereignty. The United States must be made to look inward—and away from Europe."

"And the resources, Herr General?" von Kleist asked. "How are we to fund this war?"

"You will have unlimited resources at your disposal. The Kaiser had ordered the Reich treasury to provide whatever funds are necessary."

"So there you have it," Field Marshal von Luettwitz said. "Devise a plan of action and prepare it for our review. Shall we say in three days?"

"*Jawohl!*" von Kleist snapped to attention. "We will bring *Götterdämmerung* to America."

General von Fritsch smiled. "Precisely."

The train ground to a halt before the Madrid station house. Colonel Franz von Kleist and Captain Otto Mueller, dressed in civilian clothes, stepped off the lead passenger coach onto the platform. They were met by the cultural attaché of the German Embassy, who arranged for a porter to collect their luggage. A car was waiting at curbside outside the depot.

The date was May 20, six days after von Kleist's plan had been approved by the General Staff. He and Mueller had traveled incognito, under forged passports, by ship to Lisbon and then by train into Spain. Arrangements with the German Embassy had been made by Abwehr cryptographers through encoded telegram. No one in Madrid knew the nature of their mission.

Otto Mueller was one of the wiliest intelligence officers in the Abwehr. He was twenty-seven, of average height and build, his guile belied by eyes as light as cornflowers. Until recently he had operated a network of undercover agents behind French lines on the Western Front. The intelligence gathered had been invaluable to the war effort, and he'd been awarded the Iron Cross. Von Kleist had personally selected him to spearhead the military campaign in Mexico.

The embassy attaché, who doubled as the local Abwehr agent, was all too aware of von Kleist's identity. In an effort to make conversation, he elaborated on points of interest as they drove. Madrid was the capital of Spain, a center of commerce and industry situated along the banks of the Manzanares River. They passed the royal palace, located on the site of an ancient Moorish fortress, which had fallen to Castilian conquerors in 1083. Farther along, on Paseodel Prado, they went by the Prado Museum, which housed priceless masterpieces of Spanish, Flemish and Venetian art.

King Alfonso XIII, the current ruler of Spain, had elected to maintain neutrality for his country during the war. Major cities, such as Madrid and Barcelona, Spain's principal port on the Balearic Sea, quickly became hotbeds of intrigue and espionage for intelligence agents throughout Europe. The embassy aide remarked that foreign agents from England and France were particularly active, enlisting local operatives to conduct surveillance and gather information. Madrid was, for all practical purposes, a city of spies.

At the embassy, von Kleist paid a courtesy call on the Ambassador, Ludwig Brudermann. A man of circumspection, the Ambassador made small talk and evidenced no interest in the presence of an Abwehr official. Afterward, von Kleist and Mueller retired to their rooms, refreshing themselves from the long train journey. Early that evening, with the embassy attaché as their guide, they motored off toward the center of the city. The attaché purposely took a circuitous route, turning and doubling back on narrow, cobblestone streets. Von Kleist finally satisfied himself that they were not being followed.

Shortly before eight o'clock they drove toward the western district of the city. A few minutes later they passed Ciudad Universitaria and turned into one of the more exclusive residential enclaves of Madrid. On a hillside cul-de-sac, the attaché pulled into the courtyard of a large, two-story home, clearly influenced by traditional Spanish architecture. The attaché remained in the car, and von Kleist and Mueller were met at the door by a manservant who bowed them into a tiled vestibule. Their appointment, arranged through the embassy, was with Victoriano Huerta.

The manservant ushered them into a library paneled in dark walnut. The slate-tiled floor was almost hidden by a buttery Andalusian rug and oil paintings in gilt frames decorated the walls. Huerta rose from a tall wingback chair and walked forward to greet them with an outstretched hand. He was a man of blunt edges, with dark features, a full mustache, and quick, penetrating eyes. He spoke no German, and they spoke no Spanish, so they resorted to a language all three of them detested. They conversed in English.

"General Huerta," von Kleist said, clasping his hand. "We appreciate you meeting with us in private."

"A pleasure, Colonel," Huerta replied with cautious warmth. "Welcome to my home."

"Allow me to introduce my colleague, Captain Otto Mueller."

Mueller clicked his heels, exchanging a handshake, and

Huerta motioned them to chairs. Once they were seated, the manservant served brandy from a crystal decanter on a marble-topped sideboard, and then left the room. When the door closed, Huerta lifted his glass in a polite toast. His eyes were inquisitive, and guarded.

"I confess you have me intrigued," he said. "Ambassador Brudermann was somewhat vague about the purpose of your visit."

"One soldier to another—?" von Kleist hesitated.

"Of course," Huerta said. "There is no need for ceremony among men-at-arms. Please speak frankly."

"General, our purpose is at once simple and complex. We wish to return you to power in Mexico."

"At the very least, such a venture would be ambitious to the extreme. I often fear for my life here in Spain."

Mexico was in the midst of bloody revolution. Porfirio Diaz came to power in 1876, establishing himself as dictator, and ruled for almost a quarter century. Francisco Madero, nobleman and idealist, organized a revolt and ousted Diaz in 1910. Madero's military leaders were Victoriano Huerta, Emiliano Zapata, and former bandit Doroteo Arango, otherwise known as Pancho Villa. Huerta then organized a coup d'état, assassinating Madero, and seized power in 1913.

Venustiano Carranza, governor of the state of Coahuila, immediately enlisted the support of Zapata and Villa, and waged war on Huerta. After a year of civil strife, Huerta fled Mexico in 1914 and took refuge in Spain. Carranza deferred national elections, assuming dictatorial powers, and quickly found himself at war with Villa and Zapata. The Mexican Revolution, now in its fifth year, continued unabated in pitched battles across a ravaged land. Villa and Zapata were more determined than ever to bring freedom to their countrymen.

Huerta had been in exile almost a year. To return to

his native land, and exact retribution on his enemies, was his most fervent dream. He looked at von Kleist.

"Why would Germany be interested in my future? I assume there is advantage to be gained in some manner."

"A strategic advantage," von Kleist admitted. "The Kaiser prefers that America not become involved in a European war. Our goal is to keep President Wilson preoccupied with matters at home."

"I see," Huerta said thoughtfully. "How does that involve my return to Mexico?"

"We wish to create a diversion along the border of Mexico and the United States. One that will turn the eyes of America toward the Rio Grande River—rather than Europe."

"How do you propose to create this diversion?"

"Through your influence," von Kleist said with a cordial smile. "We understand you still have loyalists in Mexico, officers and men who served under your command. We would ask them to provoke an incident of sufficient magnitude to unsettle security on the border."

Huerta held his gaze. "Colonel, an incident of such magnitude could result in more than a diversion. Mexico hardly needs a war with the United States."

Von Kleist was a shrewd manipulator of men and events, and he possessed a marvelous talent for duplicity. In large degree, he believed every lie he told. He spread his hands in a bland gesture.

"General, you have my oath as an officer and a gentleman that we intend nothing so drastic as a war. A series of raids across the border—let us say, guerrilla raids— should suffice to preoccupy the Americans."

There was a moment of weighing and deliberation. Huerta accepted no man's word, but he fed on his own ambition. He finally nodded in agreement.

"If I assist you—" he paused to underscore the

thought—"how does that further my cause?"

"Quite easily," von Kleist said with bogus conviction. "The raids I speak of will destabilize the situation for Venustiano Carranza. The opportunity then exists for you to unite your forces and at last become the savior of Mexico." He shrugged, as though the point was obvious. "Divide and conquer, the oldest of military maxims."

"You neglected to mention Villa and Zapata."

"What are they without the leadership of Carranza? They are peasants leading a rabble army."

"Yes, you are right!" Huerta barked with a quick triumphant nod. "Divide and conquer even as they fight among themselves. I will return stronger than ever."

"General, I truly believe it was ordained, your destiny."

Von Kleist went on to explain salient details of the operation. Captain Otto Mueller would travel to Mexico and organize Huerta's loyalists into a cohesive force. Germany would underwrite all costs of the border raids, and supply the rebels with arms and munitions. The end result would be an army of liberation, awaiting Huerta's return.

"To our success!" Huerta said, raising his brandy glass in a toast. "You are indeed a man of vision, Colonel. I salute you."

Von Kleist tipped his glass with a modest smile, inwardly delighted by his performance. He employed his limited Spanish to seal their pact.

"Viva Mexico!"

Chapter Two

The cherry trees were in blossom. A sea of pink and white encircled the Tidal Basin, the bloom of the trees in bright contrast to the stark lines of the Washington Monument and the Jefferson Memorial. The delicate scent drifted like perfume on a light breeze.

The blossoming of the trees marked the rite of spring in Washington, D.C. Three years ago, Japan had made a gift of over a thousand trees, an expression of international unity with America. The trees, which were the double-flowering Kwansan variety, had involved a ceremonial planting by the then First Lady, Mrs. William Howard Taft, and the Viscountess Chinda of Japan. Cherry blossom time in the nation's capital had quickly become one of the most anticipated events of the year.

Secretary of State Robert Lansing stared out a window of the White House. His mood was somber, and his thoughts were a world away from the colorful spectacle of cherry trees. He was a fleshy man, bald and beefy, with a widow's peak of black hair that gave him a satanic look. He had been selected by President Woodrow Wilson to shepherd the country through a dark period in foreign affairs. Today, he felt less like a statesman than a general assessing enemy troop emplacements.

Only that morning, in the Oval Office, he had briefed the president on the latest German mischief. He genuinely believed that Kaiser Wilhelm would resort to any trickery, diplomatic or otherwise, to keep the United States out of the war. The meeting in Spain between Victoriano Huerta and Colonel Franz von Kleist led him to conclude that an incident of some sort was being planned along the Mexican border. He had expressed that belief to the president.

Woodrow Wilson was a scholar and an idealist. But he was a man of soaring intellect, ever alert to the folly and misadventures of jingoistic leaders. He dreaded the thought of America being drawn into what he privately called the "European squabble." He abhorred even more the thought of American boys dying on the fields of France to undo the age-old rivalry of emperors and kings. He was determined it would not happen.

Lansing was of an equal mind. Yet the sinking of the *Lusitania* had sparked renewed debate in Congress for intervention. On general principle, he despised politicians and their quickness to pander to public anger and fears. He nonetheless recognized that congressional leaders, given sufficient provocation, could force Woodrow Wilson to alter his stance on war. And the telegram on his desk gave him even greater pause, for Europe was an ocean away, perhaps the lesser threat to national security. War, like lager or schnapps, could also be imported to American soil.

The door to his office opened. Forrest Holbrook, the Director of the U.S. Bureau of Investigation, entered with his customary brisk pace. He was in his early forties, the elder son of a patrician New England family, a Yankee to the core. A slender stalk of a man, light touches of gray in his hair gave him a distinguished appearance. His easy smile and pleasant manner disguised a will of steel.

"Good morning, Forrest," Lansing said, exchanging a handshake. "Thank you for coming right along."

"Not at all," Holbrook said genially. "Your message sounded somewhat urgent."

Lansing motioned to a chair, then seated himself behind his desk. "We may have a problem with the Germans," he said, holding out the telegram. "Read this and see what you think. It came in overnight."

The telegram was from MI-6, the British intelligence agency. Encrypted in London, it was dated May 26 and had been decoded into plaintext. The message related that an MI-6 agent stationed in Madrid had reported a meeting between Victoriano Huerta, deposed president of Mexico, and Colonel Franz von Kleist. The MI-6 agent had identified von Kleist as an officer in the German Abwehr, under the direct command of General Alexis Baron von Fritsch. The meeting had taken place on the evening of May 20.

"Certainly took their time," Holbrook said, dropping the telegram on the desk. "I have a feeling the Prime Minister signed off on this before it was sent."

"No question of it," Lansing agreed. "Six days from Madrid to London to Washington indicates discussion at the highest level. The Brits would move heaven and hell to drag us into the war."

"Do you think that's the purpose of the message?"

"Anything the Brits send us has only one purpose. But I believe there is far more to it than that. Far more."

"I suspect you're right, Mr. Secretary. What interest would the Germans have in the Mexican Revolution?"

"Unless I'm wrong," Lansing said, "their only interest would be to foment problems between Mexico and the United States. Unlike Great Britain, the Krauts desperately want to keep us out of the war."

Holbrook nodded. "Our best intelligence says that Huerta still has a loyal following. I presume he could instigate raids across the border and stir up considerable trouble. But that begs the question of why he would act as stalking-horse for the Germans."

"I've given that a good deal of thought. Suppose the Germans have struck a deal to return him to power, somehow ousting Carranza in the process. Carry it a step further and suppose his part of the bargain is to unite the various factions—Villa and Zapata—and turn their revolutionary anger toward America. What would that accomplish?"

"Our military would be engaged on the border rather than in Europe. But does anyone, even Huerta, believe he could win such a war?"

"Huerta was disgraced," Lansing said in a reflective tone. "Humiliated in battle, driven from his homeland, forced into exile. The Germans could probably make him believe anything—if it restored his honor."

"Still seems a bit farfetched," Holbrook commented. "Villa and Zapata were largely responsible for Huerta's defeat. Why would they join him in any venture?"

"Forrest, I'm simply speculating on possibilities. All we know for certain is that the Germans are courting Huerta, and to no good end. We must assume they intend us harm in one fashion or another."

"Given sufficient funds, perhaps Huerta could resurrect himself and his cause. Germany might feel any scheme, however outlandish, is worth underwriting."

"I am reminded of the old Roman proverb," Lansing said. *"Si vis pacem, para bellum."*

Holbrook cocked his head. "If you want peace, prepare for war. Do I have it correct?"

"Exactly so, and it behooves us to ensure peace. Hostility with Mexico would not be in our best interests."

"What is it you wish me to do, Mr. Secretary?"

"Open an investigation." Lansing's eyes burned with intensity. "Determine what Huerta and the Germans are planning that would result in conflict of any nature. We can't be caught napping on this one."

"No fear of that," Holbrook said confidently. "I have just the man for the job."

"Get him on it, then, the sooner the better. President

Wilson has authorized whatever resources you feel are necessary to the task."

"And if we uncover a plot in the making?"

Secretary of State Robert Lansing smiled. "We will foreclose on their options. Quickly and expeditiously. Do you take my meaning?"

Holbrook understood perfectly.

Lafayette Square was located directly across from the White House. Originally part of a tree-shaded park, the seven-acre plot for the square was dedicated to General Marquis Gilbert de Lafayette in 1824. A statue of the French general commemorated his service to the colonies during the American Revolution.

Frank Gordon cut through the square. His meeting at the Treasury Department had been interrupted by a call from the Director, and as he walked along in the forenoon sunlight, he caught the scent of cherry blossoms from the Tidal Basin. He crossed 17th Street to the Executive Office Building.

Gordon was tall, with the lithe build of an athlete, his chestnut hair set off by a square jaw and eyes the color of water on stone. He'd begun his career in law enforcement in the Virginia State Patrol, and his natural skills as an investigator led to headlines in several sensational cases. Three years ago, he had been recruited into the U.S. Bureau of Investigation, rapidly advancing to the rank of Special Agent. He was tough and resourceful, tenacious as a bulldog when working a case.

The Director's office was located on the second floor of the Executive Office Building. Holbrook, who was a prominent Boston lawyer, had been chosen to head the Bureau when it was created as a division of the Department of Justice in 1908. The Bureau was mandated to investigate the violation of federal laws, as well as foreign intrusion in U.S. territories. In seven years, Holbrook had increased the force to over three hundred agents and established field offices in major cities. He served as the chief law enforcement official in America.

A secretary escorted Gordon into Holbrook's office. The Director was seated behind his desk, puffing on a briar pipe, his features momentarily wreathed in smoke. J. Edgar Hoover, his assistant and general liaison with the field force, was perched on a chair as though awaiting orders. Hoover was short and pudgy, with the face of a gargoyle and the fussy manner of a schoolmarm. Gordon thought he was the quintessential bureaucrat, loyal to no one but himself.

"Come in, Frank," Holbrook said. "Edgar and I have just been chatting about your new assignment. Have a seat."

Gordon took a chair. "I'd welcome a new assignment, Chief. I've done about all I can with the counterfeit boys over at Treasury."

"Not much as investigators, are they?"

"The way they operate, it's a wonder the country's not flooded with funny money. They're more clerks than cops."

"Treasury will struggle along somehow." Holbrook paused, waved his pipe. "Tell me, Frank, what do you know of the Mexican Revolution?"

"Just what I read in the newspapers," Gordon replied. "Seems like there's a new dictator every week or so. They've been fighting forever."

"Five years, to be precise," Hoover interjected. "But only three dictators, if you include Diaz. Francisco Madero, had he lived, would have brought democracy to Mexico."

Holbrook was often amused by Hoover's pedantic nuggets of information. Today, he chose to ignore the interruption. He looked at Gordon. "Are you familiar with the name Victoriano Huerta?"

"Yes, sir, that rings a bell," Gordon said. "Wasn't he one of the dictators who got the boot?"

"Yes, and in a manner of speaking, Huerta's your next assignment."

Holbrook went on to detail the events of the past week. He first explained the Abwehr, and then elaborated on Colonel Franz von Kleist's position with the German Intelligence Service. From there, he reviewed Britain's MI-6 report on von Kleist's meeting with Huerta. He concluded with Secretary of State Lansing's speculation about a conspiracy to incite hostilities with Mexico.

"Of course, it's all conjecture at this point. President Wilson has nonetheless ordered a thorough investigation of the situation. We must determine if Huerta is actually in league with the Germans."

Gordon considered a moment. "The British report places Huerta in Madrid. Do you think there's any chance he'll try to enter Mexico?"

"Not right away," Holbrook said. "His life would be forfeit if he were caught. Carranza would have him executed on the spot."

"So how would he put an operation together?"

"Huerta has a network of loyalists in Mexico, especially in the northern states along the Rio Grande. Assuming there is a conspiracy, I suspect he'll work through them for the immediate future. He wouldn't return until the operation is up and running."

Gordon rubbed the bridge of his nose. "Knowing the Germans, I doubt they'd trust a bunch of Mexicans to pull this off. Wouldn't they have someone on the ground to oversee things?"

"Quite likely," Holbrook acknowledged. "If they are indeed funding the operation, they'll want to orchestrate it every step of the way. Probably from their consulate in Matamoras."

"Why Matamoras?"

"Because it's directly across the Rio Grande from Brownsville. The area is highly populated, and it's always been a tinderbox for hostilities between Mexicans and Texans. The Germans couldn't ask for a better place to start a jolly little war."

"Just so, Mr. Director," Hoover said in a portentous voice. "Historically speaking, the area has an abysmal record for racial tension. Texans, in the main, look upon Mexicans as a lesser species."

"Sounds like the place to start," Gordon said. "Does the Bureau have any contacts in Matamoras?"

"Nothing official," Holbrook noted. "However, I put Edgar on it and he's opened a few doors. Tell him, Edgar."

Hoover preened. "I've exchanged wires with the governor's office in Austin. You will be met upon arrival by a ranking Texas Ranger. One who speaks Spanish, I might add."

"Good thing," Gordon said with a trace of irony. "I barely manage in English."

The attempt at levity went past Hoover. "In addition," he said, "I have wired General James Parker, who commands Fort Brown at Brownsville. He will provide whatever assistance you require."

"Appreciate it, Edgar," Gordon said. "I'll take all the help I can get. Thanks for paving the way."

"Also—" Hoover consulted his notepad. "You are booked on the Southern Limited, which departs at six-o-five tomorrow morning. You will change trains in Atlanta, Dallas and Austin."

"Thanks again," Gordon said in a jocular tone. "Gives me time to kiss my girl good-bye."

"Which one?" Holbrook asked with a wry smile. "I thought you were playing the field these days."

Holbrook was married to a Boston matron who had

given him four children and a substantial mortgage. He took vicarious pleasure in Gordon's romantic escapades, which were the talk of the Bureau. Hoover, although single, frowned on office gossip.

Gordon grinned. "Chief, I just haven't found the right girl. Keeps me busy looking."

"No doubt." Holbrook puffed a thick wad of smoke from his pipe, his expression abruptly serious. "Our concern about Huerta and the Germans may come to nothing. But if our worst fears are realized, always remember you speak for the President of the United States. Allow no one to impede your investigation."

"I won't forget," Gordon said soberly. "Anyone gets in my way will wish he hadn't."

"And, Frank."

"Yes, sir?"

"Be careful down there. Texas is still something of the Wild West."

"Don't worry about me, Chief. I'm a little wild myself."

J. Edgar Hoover thought it was misplaced bravado. Forrest Holbrook thought it was typical of the man.

Gordon would leave his mark on the Rio Grande.

Chapter Three

The earth shimmered under a blazing noonday sun. A ray of light suddenly splintered away and became a glistening span of feathers. Then it emerged in a slow glide, dropping below the blinding haze, and took the shape of a hawk. Sweeping the sky in lazy circles, it caught an updraft and again disappeared into the sun.

Gordon thought it was the most desolate land he'd ever seen. He was seated by a window in the rear coach, looking out as the train rattled southward. The countryside was studded with thorned brush, palmetto, and dense thickets of chaparral. There were occasional rolling prairies of grass that seemed to stretch endlessly to the horizon.

The trip, with layovers in Atlanta and Dallas, had consumed the better part of six days. As the train slowed, the engineer setting the brakes, Gordon marked the date at June 2. The outskirts of Brownsville, dotted with sunbaked adobe structures, slowly gave way to modern frame and brick buildings. He collected his suitcase from the overhead rack as the train ground to a halt before the depot.

The heat struck him like an open furnace when he stepped onto the platform. Beads of sweat popped out on his forehead and he wondered how hot it got in full summer. He looked around for anyone wearing a badge and saw a man standing in the shade from the overhang of the depot. The man was neatly dressed, wore boots and a wide-brimmed Stetson, and carried a Colt Peacemaker holstered on his right hip. He ambled forward.

"Special Agent Gordon," he said, hand outthrust. "I'm Sergeant Hoyt Maddox, Texas Rangers."

"Glad to meet you." Gordon retrieved his hand from the other man's crushing grip. "How'd you spot me?"

"One lawdog always knows another. Besides, you're not exactly dressed for the Rio Grande valley. You look a little boiled."

"Does it always get this hot here?"

"Today's one of our cool spells," Maddox said with a crooked grin. "Couldn't be more'n ninety, in the shade."

"Ninety," Gordon repeated, his shirt collar already wilted. "Are you stationed in Brownsville, Sergeant?"

"No, they sent me down from headquarters at Austin. I'm sort of the chief trouble-shooter for unusual jobs."

Gordon could believe it. Maddox was built like a great bear, all muscle and sinew, thick through the shoulders with sandy hair and a brushy mustache. His craggy features and gray, deep-set eyes gave the impression of rocklike strength.

The pistol he wore was the weapon of Old West lawmen, a single-action Colt .45 with a 5½ inch barrel. Gordon watched as he pulled out the makings, sprinkled tobacco in a creased paper, and rolled himself a smoke. A flick of his thumbnail struck a match and he lit the cigarette. He looked up as he snuffed the match.

"Got us rooms at the hotel," he said. "We'll drop off your bag and go on to Fort Brown. General Parker's expectin' us *muy pronto*."

Gordon nodded as they walked around the depot. "How much have you been told about the assignment?"

"Damn little, and I gotta admit I'm getting curiouser and curiouser. What's the straight dope?"

"No need to go through it twice. Let's wait until we see the general."

"Guess I can hold off till then."

Brownsville was a thriving community with a population of ten thousand people. The county seat of Cameron County, it was located on the banks of the Rio Grande, some twenty miles from the Gulf of Mexico. Elizabeth Street, the town's main thoroughfare, was paved with creosoted wooden blocks embedded in the ground. An electric streetcar trundled back and forth through the business district.

The Miller Hotel occupied a corner at Twelfth Street. After dropping off his suitcase, Gordon and Maddox proceeded east on Elizabeth. The fragrance of blooming bougainvilleas hung in the still air, and farther along, flocks of green parrots sat perched in willow trees. Fort Brown was situated at the end of the street, and in the distance, on a dusty field, a polo match was underway. The field was lined with sweltering spectators.

A brick wall separated the garrison from the town. The fort housed the 12th Cavalry Regiment, and fell under the broader command of General Frederick Funston, headquartered in San Antonio. Funston had fewer than twenty thousand troops to secure a 1,745-mile border running from the Gulf of Mexico to the Arizona-California line. Fort Brown, with two thousand men, was responsible for the border from the Gulf to the town of Del Rio, some four hundred miles upriver. Scattered outposts were stretched thin along the winding Rio Grande.

The garrison headquarters was located on the north side of the parade ground. Gordon and Maddox entered the orderly room, where they were expected, and the Sergeant Major showed them into the commander's office. General James Parker was in his late forties, a rawboned man with ruddy features and a grenadier mustache. The office, like the man, was utilitarian, the sole decorations the national flag and the regimental standard. Maddox quickly performed the introductions.

Parker motioned them to chairs before his desk. "Welcome to Fort Brown," he said, nodding to Gordon. "It's not every day we have someone operating under orders from the president. I must confess I'm somewhat mystified."

"Secrecy seems to be the byword," Gordon said, shaking his head. "I thought you would have received a communiqué of some sort from Washington."

"Nothing of any substance. Simply a directive to provide whatever assistance you may require."

"Same here," Maddox observed. "The governor told me to put myself at your disposal."

"Well, then—" Parker paused, staring across the desk. "Perhaps you could enlighten us, Mr. Gordon. What's all the mystery about?"

Gordon briefed them on the situation. He reviewed the Madrid meeting between Colonel Franz von Kleist and Victoriano Huerta, as reported by British Intelligence. Then he stressed the gravity of the German Abwehr sending von Kleist, perhaps its top agent, to meet with Huerta. The only reasonable conclusion was that a conspiracy had been set in motion against the United States.

"I've been sent here," Gordon said, "to stop it before it starts."

Parker regarded him thoughtfully. "The Germans are capable of any underhanded scheme to preclude our joining forces with the Allies. I nonetheless find it difficult to comprehend that Huerta could mount an offensive campaign of any significance."

"Same goes for me," Maddox said in a steady voice. "Huerta would be a damn fool to come back to Mexico. He barely got out alive the first time."

Gordon's eyes were pale and direct. "Secretary of State

Lansing believes a conspiracy of this sort could very well succeed. His view is that the racial tensions here might enable Huerta to start a border war."

Parker and Maddox exchanged a guarded look. The animosity on the border went back to 1836, when Texas declared independence from Mexico. Nine years later, when Texas was annexed into the Union, the United States humbled Mexico in a brief, bloody conflict. After the Mexican War, the signing of the Treaty of Guadalupe Hidalgo led Mexicans in Texas to believe their land had been stolen. In 1879, when the Supreme Court ruled in favor of Anglos in a land dispute, the flames of racial hatred were fanned even higher. Over the next quarter century there were countless clashes along the border, some bloodier than others. The antagonism between Texans and Mexicans was hardly less in 1915 than it had been in 1836.

General James Parker grew silent, staring at a shaft of sunlight filtering through the window. His expression was abstracted, a long pause of inner deliberation. Finally he glanced up at Gordon.

"We like to think we have things under control," he said. "To be frank, we do well to stop the Mexican Revolution from spilling over onto American soil. Hardly a day goes by when we don't skirmish with gun traffickers smuggling weapons into Mexico."

"Works the other way 'round, too," Maddox grudgingly admitted. "We've got two companies of Rangers on the border 'cause Mexicans cross the river and steal livestock damn near every night. Their revolution uses up lots of horses."

Gordon massaged his jaw. "All of that makes it easier for Huerta and the Germans to pit Mexicans against Texans. And a war on Texas would quickly escalate into a war *with* America. Maybe it's just that simple."

"How can we assist you?" Parker asked.

"I need to develop a spy network in Matamoras. Preferably Mexicans we can trust."

"Good as done," Maddox said with a laugh. "The Rangers couldn't operate without informants. We keep 'em on a regular payroll."

Gordon was reminded that espionage was often a matter of contacts, rather than an intellectual exercise. He thought Sergeant Hoyt Maddox was his man.

The *Isabella* docked in New York on June 10. A luxury liner, operating with Spanish registry, the ship sailed under a neutral flag and plied the Atlantic without fear of German submarines. The crossing from Lisbon, Portugal, had been uneventful.

Victoriano Huerta came down the gangway with his bodyguard. He was met by Enrique Terrazas, a loyalist who lived in Texas and acted as liaison with a clandestine network of loyalists in Mexico. After clearing customs, the men took a taxi uptown, where Huerta was booked into a suite at the Waldorf-Astoria. He regaled Terrazas with the latest news of his alliance with the Germans.

Shortly afterward, Colonel Franz von Kleist walked down the gangway. He was dressed in civilian clothes and carried a passport without reference to his military status. On the crossing from Lisbon, he and Huerta had refined their plan for organizing the loyalists in Mexico. Their discussions were made all the more cordial by virtue of a hundred thousand dollars having been transferred to Huerta's bank account in New York. To avoid detection, they had disembarked the ship separately and henceforth would meet only as the mission required, and in secret. They would not be seen together until Huerta returned to Mexico to personally take command of loyalist forces.

Von Kleist cleared customs as would any other

German national. Outside the terminal, with a porter carting his luggage, he was met by an attaché from the German Embassy. A motorcar waited at curbside, and after the luggage was stored, they were driven to the embassy in midtown Manhattan, on East Forty-Fifth Street. Ambassador Kurt Rintelen greeted von Kleist with all the courtesy due a high-ranked member of the Abwehr. They retired to Rintelen's spacious office for a private meeting.

"How was your journey?" Rintelen asked after they were seated. "Pleasant, I trust."

Von Kleist gestured aimlessly. "Calm seas, excellent food, and interesting shipboard acquaintances. What more could one ask?"

"What more, indeed." Rintelen hesitated, his gaze inquisitive. "The foreign office informed me by courier of your mission. I was instructed that all matters are to be considered top secret."

"Such an operation requires nothing less, Herr Ambassador. Only those with a need to know are to be informed."

"I understand you were traveling with Huerta."

"All quite discreet," von Kleist said. "*El Supremo*, as he thinks of himself, has grand visions. A return to the throne, in a manner of speaking."

"Of course," Rintelen observed. "Through intermediaries, we have arranged for Flores and Mendoza to meet with you at three this afternoon. May I ask you a question, Colonel?"

"Certainly."

"Flores and Mendoza act as arms merchants for Pancho Villa here in the United States. Do you propose to create an alliance between Villa and Huerta?"

"Hardly," von Kleist said with a smug look. "The Kaiser agrees that a candle must sometimes be burned from both ends. I am empowered to offer Villa the same arrangement we have with Huerta."

"*Mein Gott!*" Rintelen said, clearly shocked. "You intend to play one against the other? Do I understand correctly?"

"I intend to play both for the Fatherland, Herr Ambassador. There are no certainties in a military operation of this magnitude. We double our chances by engaging both Huerta and Villa."

Kurt Rintelen thought it was diabolical, somehow beneath a Prussian Officer. But he was a diplomat, serving at the whim of Kaiser Wilhelm, and hardly in a position to pass judgment. He managed a tactful smile.

"Machiavelli would have approved the tactic, Colonel. You have a gift for subterfuge."

"I accept that as a compliment, Herr Ambassador. Let us hope I play the game as well as Machiavelli."

Shortly before three o'clock Alberto Flores and Felix Mendoza arrived at the embassy. They had fought beside Villa in the Revolution until he decided their talents would serve him better elsewhere. For the last year, working through a front company, they had been purchasing guns and munitions from American manufacturers for shipment to remote towns along the Rio Grande. The arms were then smuggled across the river to Villa's troops.

Von Kleist received them in a lavishly furnished conference room. A manservant wheeled in a cart of coffee and rich German pastries, and von Kleist proceeded to charm them with praise for the military genius of their leader. Once the preliminaries were out of the way, he went straight to the point. He offered them the exact proposal he had presented to Huerta in Madrid.

The Mexicans exchanged a veiled glance, the coffee and pastries forgotten. Mendoza finally cleared his throat. "Señor, pardon our ignorance," he said. "We are simple men who work to free our country of tyrants. Are you offering us aid in the fight against Carranza—" he paused, his eyes dark with suspicion—"or are you suggesting we make war on the United States?"

"One step at a time," von Kleist said amiably. "Carranza must be overthrown and General Villa could more quickly achieve that end with our financial assistance. Do you agree?"

"*Sí,* señor," Mendoza conceded. "Our army has more men than rifles. The *Revolución* desperately needs arms."

"And once you have them, General Villa will rightfully occupy the Palace in Mexico City. Is it not so?"

"Yes, it is so," Flores interjected. "But how does this involve the United States?"

"Permit me to explain," von Kleist said smoothly. "We do not ask General Villa to declare war on the United States. We ask only that his forces conduct raids across the Rio Grande. If he wishes, the raids could be disguised as the work of bandits."

Flores studied him. "And your purpose is to distract the American military from the European war. Nothing more?"

"Exactly."

"You spoke of funds," Mendoza said. "What amount of assistance would your government provide?"

"Three hundred thousand dollars," von Kleist said, drawing out the words. "Fifty thousand immediately, and fifty thousand a month for five months. We trust General Villa to honor the agreement."

Mendoza and Flores were visibly impressed. After a moment, Mendoza nodded. "We will communicate your proposal to General Villa. Are we to contact you here or elsewhere, señor?"

"You may contact me here for the immediate future."

Von Kleist felt confident the offer would be accepted. Villa was a brigand and pirate long before he had become a revolutionary general. His greed would almost certainly sway his decision, and along with Huerta's loyalists, the border would run red with blood. In the end, the United States would declare war on Mexico.

Flores and Mendoza emerged from the embassy a few minutes before four o'clock. Steve Willard, an agent for the Bureau of Investigation, watched the Mexicans from a doorway of a building near the corner. His partner had tailed Huerta from the docks, and he had followed von Kleist. He thought their surveillance would send shock waves through Washington.

MI-6, the British intelligence agency, had advised the U.S. State Department that Huerta and von Kleist had sailed aboard the *Isabella*. The information was yet further verification of a conspiracy, and Director Holbrook had ordered the Bureau office in New York to conduct around-the-clock surveillance. The first day's results were more than anyone might have imagined.

Flores and Mendoza were known to the Bureau as arms merchants for Pancho Villa. Steve Willard was an agent, rather than a Bureau analyst, but it seemed to him that two and two equaled four. The Germans were already involved in some clandestine operation with Victoriano Huerta. There was little doubt in Willard's mind that they were now plotting with Villa along similar lines. Perhaps a devious scheme for Huerta and Villa to join forces.

He hurried off to draft his report to Director Holbrook.

Chapter Four

Matamoras was on a level plain bordering the Rio Grande. Fields and orchards ripe with produce surrounded a town of nearly seven thousand people. Yet its prosperity was attributable only in part to the land and local agriculture.

Even in a time of revolution Matamoras remained a town of merchants, the trade center for northern Mexico. New Orleans forwarding houses filtered their goods through its waterfront to the mines and haciendas and countless villages scattered throughout the interior. In return, wool and hides from outlying ranchos were trailed to the border; copper and gold were transported from distant mines by railroad. The wealth of an area larger than Texas itself was funneled through the town for shipment to the broader marketplace in New Orleans.

The International Bridge, spanning the Rio Grande and connecting Matamoras to Brownsville, had been built in 1910. A mile or so from the bridge was the town's main plaza, a sprawling square with shops and vendors, the municipal hall, and a stately cathedral crowned with a bell tower. The town had fallen to various revolutionary factions over the past five years, but commerce and trade went on uninterrupted, regardless of who occupied the dictator's throne in Mexico City. The latest *El Presidente* was Venustiano Carranza and Matamoras continued to thrive, attending to business, ever a town of merchants.

The German Consulate was located on Calle Morelos, a block east of the main plaza. A large two-story stone and masonry building, the consulate served northern Mexico under the auspices of the German Embassy in Mexico City. Erwin Reinhardt, the Consular in Matamoras, was a weedy man with pince-nez glasses and precise hand gestures. His studious expression was like that of a cat chewing wax, for yesterday, with the arrival of the new attaché, his life of uncomplicated routine and leisurely pursuits had been altered forever. He was seated in his office with Captain Otto Mueller.

Mueller, attired in civilian clothes, was ostensibly posted as the new agricultural attaché. He had arrived late yesterday, June 14, the sole passenger on a tramp steamer from Lisbon. He carried papers from the German General Staff which effectively placed Reinhardt and the Consulate staff under his command. Reinhardt, purposely kept in the dark, had previously been ordered by encrypted cablegram to arrange a meeting with two of Huerta's loyalists. Until last night, when Mueller briefed him, Reinhardt hadn't realized that he was host to an espionage operation. He was still in a state of shock.

A decorated officer, and a member of the dreaded Abwehr, Mueller found it vaguely amusing. He was a handsome man, tall and clean-shaven with short-trimmed blond hair and an air of bluff assurance. Yet he had cultivated a deliberate manner, with a stolid expression that shielded every emotion and left others to wonder what he was thinking. Erwin Reinhardt was wondering that very thing when an aide knocked on the door and stepped inside. The aide avoided eye contact with Mueller and looked at Reinhardt.

"Your guests have arrived, Herr Consular."

"Yes, yes," Reinhardt said with an agitated little wave. "Show them in, Hans."

Augustin Garza came through the door, followed by Basilio Ramos. Reinhardt, who was fluent in Spanish, introduced himself and then Mueller. He asked the men to be seated, inquiring if they spoke English, almost apologetic that Mueller was not conversant in their native language. Garza replied in English.

"There is no need for formality," he said. "We received a letter from General Huerta on the day your message arrived. He is now in New York and has instructed that we cooperate fully. How may we assist you?"

Mueller abruptly took charge. "I am an officer of the German General Staff. I had the privilege of meeting General Huerta in Madrid. Did his letter explain the mission we are here to discuss?"

"No, it did not," Garza said. "Secrecy is required in case our enemies intercept our mail. The general simply ordered that we cooperate in whatever is asked."

"And are you prepared to follow those orders?"

"We are soldiers," Garza said stiffly. "Do not concern yourself about our ability to follow orders."

Mueller actually wasn't concerned. In Madrid, Huerta had briefed him about the men here today. Garza was the former commander of a cavalry squadron during the Huerta regime. His face looked as though it had been hewn from rough walnut, with an angular nose, a shaggy mustache, and cold brooding eyes. He was a serious man, deadly when aroused.

Ramos was smaller, with gold-capped teeth, his wizened face the shade of old leather. His hair was shiny with pomade and, above a curled mustache, his black eyes sparkled with cunning. He had served as the adjutant of Garza's cavalry squadron, and was always to be found in the thick of the fighting. His ferocity in battle was legend.

Garza and Ramos had been captured when Carranza's

Constitutionalist forces overran the border in 1914. Yet in Matamoras, the town of merchants, anything was for sale, and a substantial bribe secured their pardon from the local *comandante*. Exile being the wiser option, they crossed the river and settled in the small Texas community of San Diego, where most of the inhabitants were of Mexican origin and bitterly resentful of Anglos. Garza and Ramos were welcomed, even idolized, for their hatred of Texans was equaled only by their love of Mexico.

"General Huerta," Mueller said in a measured tone, "has authorized the raising of a new army in his name. The German government will provide the necessary funds for arms and munitions."

Garza fixed him with a speculative gaze. "What interest does Germany have in our revolution?"

"We do not want the United States involved in the European war. Our mission is to draw their military forces to the border."

"And how do we accomplish that?"

"By killing Texans," Mueller said with a tight smile. "The more the better—and soon."

"*Madre de Dios!*" Garza's eyes took on a cold, tinsel glitter. "I like the idea of killing Texans."

"*Si, mi Coronel,*" Ramos said with a guttural accent. "We have long wanted the blood of the *gringos. Verdad?*"

Garza nodded slowly, deliberately, silent a moment. His gaze was still fixed on Mueller. "I understand your purpose in killing Texans. How does it help our revolution?"

"General Huerta needs an army," Mueller said matter-of-factly. "You will recruit it for him in the name of a war on Texans. Then, at the opportune moment, General Huerta will return—" he paused with a baroque sweep of his arms—"and you will lead your forces in the overthrow of Carranza. Your revolution will at last be won."

"*Mil Cristos*," Garza said, his mouth set in an ugly grin. "You are a clever one, my friend. Very clever."

"General Huerta and my superiors devised the strategy. Like you, I am a soldier who follows orders."

"How do we go forward? What is it you wish me to do?"

"Draft a plan of action," Mueller said urgently. "Determine how you will recruit a force of men. Decide how quickly you can strike."

Garza's thoughts leaped ahead. The Rio Grande valley was largely populated by Mexicans and *Tejanos*, people of Mexican ancestry. With the coming of the railroad in 1904, thousands of white settlers were drawn to the border, and the economic lifeblood of the valley changed from ranching to farming. Developers bought grazeland cheaply and re-sold it dearly as farmland to settlers.

In ten years, hundreds of thousands of acres were ir-rigated to grow cotton, corn, and sugarcane. The farmers drained the stream flow of the Rio Grande valley, seventy percent of the water having originated from tributaries in Mexico. The economic division widened the ethnic division, and racial tensions grew progressively worse on both sides of the river. Anglo settlers saw Mexicans and *Tejanos* as racial inferiors, nothing more than common laborers. Peons.

Garza knew where he would recruit his army. "I will sound a call to arms," he said, evangelical fire burning in his eyes. "When do you wish to see my plan?"

"In two days," Mueller said. "We must move with dis-patch."

"*Sin falta*." Garza grinned ferociously. "Consider it done."

Otto Mueller thought he'd never seen a man more eager to kill.

Early that evening, Sergeant Hoyt Maddox and Captain Bob Ransom entered the Miller Hotel. They checked in the dining room for Gordon and then took the stairs to the second floor. Maddox rapped on the door of a room overlooking Elizabeth Street.

Gordon opened the door and motioned them inside. The room was spacious, with a comfortable bed, a wardrobe and dresser, and a private bathroom. A listless breeze ruffled the window curtains.

"Glad we found you," Maddox said. "We went by the post, but you'd already left. Had your supper?"

"Ate downstairs," Gordon said. "Why, what's up?"

"The captain's boys just gave us an earful."

Captain R.L. "Bob" Ransom was commander of Ranger Company A. His unit, along with Company B, commanded by Captain Jack Fox, patrolled the border upriver to the town of Del Rio. Company A was responsible for the lower Rio Grande, and Ransom was headquartered in Brownsville. His informants had been poking around Matamoras for the last ten days.

Ransom was a thickset, hardfaced man in his late thirties with dark hair and a wiry mustache. His eyes were curiously impersonal, not so much cold as stoic, somehow detached. Gordon had bided his time day by day, his patience growing thin, waiting for Ransom's informants to uncover a lead. He found the Ranger captain abrasive, a little too impressed with himself.

"Goddamn greasers," Ransom said brusquely. "Always *mañana* even when you tell 'em to get a rush on. Feel like kickin' their butts half the time."

"I understand," Gordon said. "What do you have?"

"For openers, a new Kraut popped up at the German Consulate yesterday. My boys heard he's an attaché, but he's got a military look. Hair's cropped short, marches around like he's got a board up his ass, regular little soldier. His name's Otto Mueller."

Gordon nodded. "We thought the Germans might send a military advisor. What else?"

"Starts to get interestin'," Ransom said with a dark smile. "This afternoon two Mexicans, Augustin Garza and Basilio Ramos, paid a call on the German Consulate. We know these jaybirds from way back and then some. They commanded a cavalry outfit for Huerta."

"Offhand, I'd have to say it's more than coincidence. We have to assume they were there to meet with Mueller."

"That'd damn sure be my guess. Where do we go from here?"

"I'll have to think about it," Gordon said. "Good job all around, Captain. I appreciate your help."

Ransom understood he'd been dismissed. "Don't mention it," he said, glancing at Maddox. "Let's get ourselves some supper."

"Thanks all the same, Cap'n," Maddox begged off. "Maybe I'll catch up with you later."

"Suit yourself."

Ransom abruptly turned and went out. When the door closed, Maddox looked at Gordon. "You treated him pretty short after he'd done you a favor. Any special reason?"

The two men had spent a great deal of time together over the last ten days. They were now on a first-name basis, and a measure of trust had formed from what seemed a joint mission, their personal mission. Gordon regarded him with a level gaze.

"Hoyt, like it or not, some things don't go any further than you, me, and General Parker. Are we agreed on that?"

"Yeah, I suppose," Maddox said hesitantly. "What're we talkin' about, just exactly?"

Gordon handed him an envelope. The letter had been delivered only that afternoon by a Bureau courier to Fort Brown. Director Holbrook, in terse language, related the arrival of Huerta and Colonel von Kleist in New York. He went on to recount the meeting between von Kleist and Villa supporters, and his concern that Huerta and Villa might join forces. He closed by urging Gordon to redouble his efforts.

"Never happen," Maddox said, handing back the letter. "Villa would shoot Huerta on sight. Ol' Pancho's not one to forgive and forget."

"Never say never," Gordon told him. "But even if you're right, Villa's still been added to the mix. The Germans are playing every angle."

"So what's that got to do with cutting Ransom off at the knees?"

"Captain Ransom will be told what he needs to know. Having to rely on his informants, I've felt things slipping out of my hands. We need our own agents in Matamoras."

"Yeah, maybe so," Maddox conceded. "You talkin' about Mexican agents?"

"Yes, I am," Gordon said. "Three, maybe four people who have no love for Huerta. Do you think you could find that many? I'll see to it they're paid well."

"Frank, I'll sure as hell try. So far, you've only mentioned Huerta. What about Villa?"

"Well, like they say, a bird in the hand. We've got what sounds like a German army officer working with Huerta's loyalists. Let's stick with them for the moment."

Maddox suddenly chuckled. "Cap'n Ransom's gonna be some pissed off. He's been the big dog hereabouts."

"A big dog, and if I read him right, a big talker. We can't afford to compromise the mission."

"You won't get no argument out of me."

Gordon went on with his plans for Matamoras.

Augustin Garza and Basilio Ramos returned to the German Consulate the following morning. The date was Wednesday, June 16, and Garza marked it as a turning point in the struggle for liberty. He carried with him a blueprint for the overthrow of Anglo rule in Texas and beyond.

They were shown into the consular's office. After the amenities, Reinhardt excused himself and left the room. There was a clear sense that he'd been ordered to busy himself elsewhere. Otto Mueller, though cordial, wasted no time on ceremony. He went directly to the point.

"Have you devised a plan of action, Herr Garza?"

"Yes, we have," Garza said with some pride. "We call it the Plan of San Diego."

"To what does the name refer?"

"The town in south Texas where Basilio and I have lived for the past year. By giving it this name, it will appear the revolt originated in Texas."

"Revolt." Mueller repeated it, clearly pleased by the choice of words. "How will this revolt be organized?"

Garza spread a sheaf of handwritten papers on the desk. The Plan of San Diego was drafted in Spanish, but he interpreted for Mueller's benefit, explaining the points in English. The plan was subtitled "Manifesto to the Oppressed People of America" and called for the emancipation of people of all races in the United States. The opening verbiage condemned the exploitation of land by whites and damned their racist attitude toward people of color.

The cornerstone of the plan was an armed uprising against the government of the United States. Equality and independence was the clarion call, and people of color would reclaim from whites the lands comprising Texas,

New Mexico, Arizona, Colorado, and California. The army of liberation would be restricted to Mexicans, Negroes, and American Indians, with the covenant that all ancestral lands would be returned to the Indians. To cleanse any vestige of racial bigotry, every male Anglo over the age of sixteen would be put to death.

Power under the plan was vested in a Supreme Revolutionary Congress. Initially, the rebellion would be governed by a Provisional Directorate, which designated Garza as Chief of the Armed Forces, and alluded in vague terms to the support of Mexicans and *Tejanos* throughout Texas. Elections would be held as the revolt spread, and every racial group would have equal representation in the Supreme Revolutionary Congress. The Congress, if it chose to do so, could unite with Mexico for added protection against the United States.

Garza went on to explain that the rebellion would be widely publicized, particularly among Mexicans and *Tejanos*. There were over two hundred Spanish-language newspapers in the Southwest, and their editors would each receive a printed copy of the Plan of San Diego. A full-page advertisement would be run in *Regeneración*, the largest of the lot and anarchist in tone, published by the Magon brothers in California. The emphasis would be on solidarity and social revolution, vindication of the exploited masses against their Anglo oppressors. In South Texas alone, there were over a hundred *Regeneración* clubs, each of them filled with partisans awaiting a call to action.

Mueller was stunned by the enormity of the plan. He had expected something smaller in scope, guerrilla raids across the border, the devastation and pillaging of Texan ranches and farms. For a long moment, he sat staring at the sheaf of papers as though he might find revealed there the answer to life's mystery. He finally looked up at Garza.

"I tell you frankly, I am most impressed by the military

foresight of your plan. You must hate the Texans even more than I suspected."

"Far more, *señor*," Garza said with a quick swipe at his mustache. "All Mexicans live to avenge their ancestors. Dead *gringos* are merely a start."

"Do you actually intend to kill all Texans over sixteen?"

"Killing *gringos* will swell our ranks as much as reclaiming land stolen from our people."

"And the Negroes, the Indian tribes? Will they too unite under your banner?"

"Who cares?" Ramos cut in, voice crackling. "Our banner will draw all Mexicans—even the worst enemies of the *Revolución*!—to join in the fight for justice. We will have three men for every rifle you supply."

"That is good," Mueller said with a vigorous nod. "General Huerta has already received the initial funding. His man Enrique Terrazas will contact you soon about smuggling arms across the river. Now, so that I understand fully, how will you proceed?"

"We will start by forming juntas across northern Mexico and southern Texas."

"What are juntas?"

"A cadre of loyalists," Garza informed him. "General Huerta's followers and revolutionaries who lost faith awaiting a strong leader. They will recruit men by the hundreds to our cause."

"Good, good," Mueller replied succinctly. "How quickly can you conduct the first raid?"

Garza regarded him with an odd, steadfast look. "A series of raids will take place on the Fourth of July, what the *Americanos* call Independence Day. The irony of it will be lost on no one. Don't you agree, *señor*?"

Mueller understood they were talking about nothing less than the conquest of Texas. He thought it was the de-

lusion of a madman and a zealot, but it would unquestion-
ably achieve the goal. The military power of the United
States would shortly be drawn to the border, and he might
yet provoke a war. He smiled at Garza and Ramos, as
though struck by the wonder of it all.

"Brilliant!" he announced with genuine warmth. "The
Fourth of July."

Chapter Five

H *ola*, Aniceto."

Pizana smiled. "Augustin, *mi compadre*."

"*Cómo está*, Luis?"

"*Bueno*," Vasquez said. "And you?"

"*Vivo graciadios*," Garza replied. "I think I will live another day."

"*Que tal*," Pizana said with a laugh. "You will live forever."

"God willing."

The three men seated themselves on the porch of Pizana's home. Garza's horse, and the dun gelding belonging to Vasquez, were tied to a hitch rack in the yard. A warm afternoon sun drifted westward as Pizana's wife brought them bottles of cerveza, the native beer. Vasquez lifted his bottle with a broad smile.

"*Salud*."

"*Salud*," Garza echoed. "To victory!"

Aniceto Pizana was a stocky man in his early forties. A *Tejano*, he owned a small ranch on the Arroyo Colorado river, outside the town of Rio Hondo. Luis Vasquez, also a *Tejano*, was tall, with fiery eyes and a black mustache. Industrious, if not prosperous, he leased grazeland from an Anglo rancher and ran a few cows. They were to be the first recruits in the Plan of San Diego.

Garza believed the key to any military campaign was quick and decisive action. Last night, after the meeting concluded with Otto Mueller, he had assigned Ramos to begin recruiting in the town of McAllen. They reclaimed their horses from a stable in Matamoras and separated once they crossed the International Bridge. Ramos rode west along the river, and Garza continued on through the darkened streets of Brownsville. His destination was the town of Rio Hondo, some twenty miles north of the border.

San Diego, the town for which he'd named the revolutionary plan, was another hundred miles to the north. There was no question in his mind that he could raise dozens of *soldados* in a *Tejano* community where he had lived for the last year. But he recognized the need for junta leaders closer to the border, men who could recruit loyal fighters and conduct raids along the river. The initial strikes against Texas would require field commanders who were familiar with the lower Rio Grande valley.

Aniceto Pizana and Luis Vasquez were names that immediately came to mind. The area around Rio Hondo was yet another *Tejano* stronghold, with fully two-thirds of the inhabitants of Mexican heritage. *Regeneración*, the anarchist newspaper, was widely followed by the people, for it expressed the outrage everyone shared about injustice at the hands of Texans. Men of stature, such as Pizana and Vasquez, had formed *grupos*, active discussion groups, to debate the economic discrimination against Mexicans and *Tejanos*. Vasquez was particularly outspoken about direct action to overthrow the yoke of oppression.

"I am here," Garza said now, "to tell you of a new movement for justice. A plan to avenge all we have suffered at the hands of the *gringos*."

"*Ah, chihuahua!*" Vasquez said in a loud, vindictive voice. "I thirst for vengeance more than beer. Are you serious?"

"*Si*," Garza said. "Very serious."

Pizana's brow puckered in a frown. "How would you do this thing, Augustin?"

"We will bring the *Revolución* to Texas!"

Garza rapidly explained the Plan of San Diego. He omitted any mention of German involvement, but he stressed the coalition of Mexicans, Negroes, and various Indian tribes. He spoke of the power of such a coalition, and how an uprising throughout the southwest would drive the Americans from the lands of the native people. His words brimmed with the conviction of a prophet.

"We will sweep the land," he assured them earnestly. "You two will be foremost among my field commanders, *guerreros* in the fight for liberty. We will reclaim the honor of our ancestors."

"*Sangre de Cristo*!" Vasquez barked. "How I have waited for someone to lead us against the accursed Texans. I am your man!"

"Augustin, I ask you," Pizana ventured carefully. "Do you truly intend to kill *gringos* just sixteen—children?"

"I do," Garza said, a cold venom in his stare. "The American *presidente* must realize he will lose a generation unless he concedes victory. We will spare no Texan, young or old."

Pizana passed a hand across his eyes. "Then I cannot follow you, however just the cause. I have children of my own, two *niños*." He paused, his voice clogged with apprehension. "The *gringos* would surely kill them in retaliation."

"You are certain of this?"

"Never more certain of anything."

"You understand what will happen if you betray our cause? If you speak of it even to your *mujer* in the privacy of your bed?"

"*Si*," Pizana said woodenly. "You would kill me."

"And your children," Garza said with chilling calm. "I will not stomach a traitor."

"*Yo entiendo*," Pizana said softly. "I understand."

Garza turned. "And what of you, Luis? Are you still game for the fight?"

"On my oath!" Vasquez squared himself up stiffly. "I will move my wife and children across the river by this time tomorrow. I told you, *mi jefe*, I am your man."

"Your name will bring glory to our people."

Garza was disappointed about losing Pizana. But he was pleased with the spirit shown by Vasquez, and felt confident he'd found a daring field commander. One who would not flinch however repugnant the order. A man, in fact, very much like himself. One who would relish the killing of gringos.

McAllen was located some fifty miles upriver. The town was the county seat of Hidalgo County, with a population of six thousand, and situated roughly eight miles north of the Rio Grande. The prosperity of the town was tied directly to farms and ranches that dotted the countryside.

A large Mexican community lived on the south side of town. Crops and cattle required cheap labor, and over the years increasing numbers of Mexicans had migrated north of the border. Some families were fifth or sixth generation on Texas soil, and thought of themselves as *Tejanos*. Anglo residents, for the most part, still thought of them as Mexicans.

Basilio Ramos rode into town late that afternoon. His job was to recruit a junta leader, someone who commanded respect throughout Hidalgo County. The obvious candidate, selected by Garza, was a local merchant who had previously supported the Huerta regime. Andres Villarreal owned a mercantile store on the south side of town, and was widely regarded within the Mexican community. He was a fifth-generation *Tejano* who fervently decried the racial discrimination suffered by his people.

Villarreal was a portly man with the sharp eyes of a merchant. He received Ramos in a small office at the back of his store, inquiring politely as to the purpose of the visit. Ramos, who was neither articulate nor subtle, often became frustrated if pressed to string together complicated thoughts. He carried with him a duplicate set of papers detailing specifics on the Plan of San Diego, and he spread them across Villarreal's desk. He referred to the papers like a schoolmaster consulting lecture notes.

"There you have it," Ramos said when he finished. "Colonel Garza personally commissions you as the district junta leader. We will drive the *gringos* from Texas."

"Yes, I see," Villarreal said, squinting with concentration. "Tell me, what part does General Huerta play in this scheme?"

"None."

Ramos was under orders to lie about Huerta, as well as the Germans. Garza was determined to bring the various political factions together, all in the name of racial justice. No mention was to be made of Huerta for the moment.

"We fight for all Mexicans," Ramos went on in a strident voice. "Once we have won, we will redistribute the land to the people. Equality for all!"

"There would certainly be land enough for all. Especially if you kill all the *gringos*."

"Only the men, *señor*. We do not make war on women and children."

Villarreal was silent a moment. He knew Ramos and Garza from the old days, and he'd always considered them competent military leaders. But the plan before him now was insane, the work of a lunatic, dangerous to the extreme.

He thought it would result in Anglos reckoning a bloodbath on Mexicans and *Tejanos*.

"A suggestion," Villarreal said tactfully. "Allow me to bring a few men of influence into our discussion. I think we need consensus on so important a matter."

Ramos hesitated. "How long will it take?"

"An hour, certainly no more. There is a *cantina* down the street where you could have a drink. Their food is good as well."

"*Hecho!*" Ramos said, gathering his papers from the desk. "I have been riding since last night. I could use a drink."

"Have one for me," Villarreal said pleasantly. "I will arrange the meeting as quickly as possible."

"*Bueno.*"

Ramos walked from the office. Villarreal waited a moment, then moved through the store and cautiously peeked out the front door. A half-block downstreet, he saw Ramos turn into the saloon. Quickly, with no explanation, he ordered a clerk to watch the store. He hurried off uptown, toward the courthouse.

Not quite an hour later, Ramos returned to the store. He was comfortably full, having downed two beers along with a plate of *carne asado*, *frijoles*, and fresh-baked *tortillas*. As he came through the door, he saw Villarreal at the rear, near the office, bobbing his head in a frantic motion. A man, hidden at the side of the door, stepped into view.

"Hands up!" he ordered, looking over the sights of a pistol. "Don't try nothin' dumb."

"*Que pasa?*" Ramos glanced around, saw the glint of a badge. "Who are you?"

"Name's Ledbetter," the man said. "Sheriff of Hidalgo County."

"I have done nothing—"

Ledbetter poked him in the ribs with the pistol. When he raised his arms, the sheriff removed a gun from his waistband and the packet of papers from inside his jacket. The pistol jabbed him in the back.

"You're under arrest," Ledbetter said. "Conspiracy to commit murder."

Ramos glowered at Villarreal. "*Hijo de puta!*" he shouted. "You are *muerto. Muerto!*"

"No," Ledbetter said in a gruff voice. "You're not gonna kill nobody, Peppy. Let's go."

He marched Ramos toward the county jail.

A freight train pulled into McAllen shortly after midnight. Gordon and Maddox, neither of them carrying luggage, stepped off the platform of the caboose. Sheriff Horace Ledbetter was waiting outside the depot.

After a round of introductions, they turned uptown. Ledbetter, who was fluent in Spanish, had translated the papers taken off Ramos. Late that afternoon, he had wired Ranger headquarters in Brownsville, stating he'd arrested a Mexican who was plotting insurrection. Gordon and Maddox had caught the last train out of town.

On the way to the courthouse, Ledbetter shook his head. "Damnedest thing I ever come across," he said. "Some jaybird name of Augustin Garza put it together with this here Ramos. Looks like they figgered to declare war on Texas."

"We know the names," Maddox observed. "Has Ramos said anything?"

"Not a peep," Ledbetter replied. "But wait'll you get a look at them papers I took off him. Bastards was plannin' to kill every man Texan over sixteen."

"Lucky you caught him," Gordon said. "We didn't know they'd crossed the border."

"Lucky we've got some good Meskins like Andres Villarreal. 'Cept for him, you still wouldn't've known."

The jail was in the basement of the courthouse. Ledbetter introduced them to the jailor and then showed them the papers found on Ramos. Gordon stood at Maddox's shoulder while the Ranger translated, and read aloud, the Plan of San Diego. The magnitude of the conspiracy was far greater than they expected, sufficient to put the United States on war alert. Perhaps sufficient to start a war.

So far, though, there was no hard evidence to implicate the Germans. By mutual agreement, Gordon and Maddox had already decided not to mention the Germans unless the situation left them no choice. The mere rumor of German involvement would attract unwanted attention from the press, and almost certainly cause panic along the border. The less said the better.

"Definitely a federal violation," Gordon remarked when Maddox finished reading. "I forget the statute under the Criminal Code, but it covers insurrection. Or a conspiracy to incite insurrection."

Maddox snorted. "Yeah, I'd say they was tryin' to incite."

"Do you think the Indians would join in an uprising of this sort?"

"Tend to doubt it. The army whipped the tribes damn bad when they drove 'em onto reservations. I'd bet the Apache wouldn't even fight. And they're the toughest of the lot."

"What about Negroes?"

"Well, the jigs might be something else. There's some that'd probably go along."

Gordon inwardly flinched at the racial slur. From what he'd seen, all Texans, including Maddox, were prejudiced to some degree. The order of prejudice seemed to be Mexicans, Indians, and at the bottom of the heap, Negroes. He wondered where Orientals fit into the scheme of things.

"Let's have a talk with Ramos."

Sheriff Ledbetter walked them back to the cell block. There was a dungeon atmosphere to the place, with dank walls and bare light bulbs hanging from the ceiling. He unlocked the door to a barred cell and swung it open. Ramos was seated on a bunk with no blankets and a dirty mattress.

"Don't let him fool you," Ledbetter said. "He talks American real good."

Gordon and Maddox entered the cell. "Señor Ramos," Gordon said, "I'm with the U.S. Bureau of Investigation and this is Sergeant Maddox of the Texas Rangers. We'd like to ask you some questions."

Ramos refused to look at them. "Help yourself by helping us," Gordon said reasonably. "You're going to prison for a long time unless you agree to provide information. Where can we locate Augustin Garza?"

There was a long beat of silence. "Let's try again," Gordon said. "Tell us about Otto Mueller."

Ramos blinked, clearly caught off guard. But he recovered quickly, his surprised expression turning to a blank look. He stared at the opposite wall of the cell.

Maddox stepped forward. "You listen to me, you goddamn pepper-gut. We mean to have some answers. *Comprende?*"

Ramos smiled. "*Chinga tu madre.*"

Maddox hit him. The blow was a short, chopping right that broke his nose and split his lip in an ugly smear of blood. Ramos toppled off the bunk onto the floor, out cold.

"Damn, Hoyt," Gordon cursed softly. "Why'd you do that?"

Maddox grunted. "The sorry sonovabitch insulted my mother. What'd you expect me to do?"

"Well, he's no good to us unconscious."

"You don't understand these people, Frank. Ramos thinks he's a bad *hombre*, and the only way we'll get anything out of him is to beat it out of him. That's the way it works with Mexicans."

The Rangers had a reputation for brutal treatment of prisoners. The brutality was a carryover from old days, when Rangers were the first line of defense against marauding Comanches and Mexican *bandidos*. In many instances, the prisoner was shot "while trying to escape," or simply hanged from the nearest tree. Gordon wanted no part of it.

"Here's the way I work," he said to Maddox. "We'll take him back to Brownsville and prefer charges in federal court. Maybe he'll open up once he's facing trial."

"Fat chance," Maddox muttered. "You're just whistlin' in the dark."

Sheriff Ledbetter cleared his throat. "You gents got my curiosity whetted. Who's this Otto Mueller you asked about?"

"Nobody special." Maddox fobbed him off with a weary shrug. "Just a trick question."

Gordon silently wished they'd caught Otto Mueller rather than Basilio Ramos. He was already mentally composing his report to Director Holbrook, and he could imagine the reaction in Washington. Hardly what anyone expected of the Germans.

A corkscrew twist called the Plan of San Diego.

Chapter Six

Gordon and Maddox, with Ramos in manacles, arrived in Brownsville late the next morning. From the train station, they went directly to the county jail, which also served as the lockup for federal prisoners. Ramos was detained in a maximum security cell.

Outside the courthouse, Gordon and Maddox separated. They were agreed that it was now imperative to enlist undercover agents for surveillance work in Matamoras. Maddox had leads on people who had formerly worked for the Rangers, but he hadn't yet made contact. He went off to talk with them.

Gordon hurried on to Fort Brown. There, he met with General Parker and related all they'd uncovered through the capture of Basilio Ramos. When he went over the papers dealing with the Plan of San Diego, Parker's features darkened. The general seemed particularly alarmed about the edict for the execution of male Texans.

"We cannot allow that to happen," he said with a troubled frown. "Here on the border, Texans dying at the hands of Mexicans would lead to a race war. God only knows where it would end."

"General, I couldn't agree more," Gordon said. "Hoyt Maddox is out right now trying to arrange Mexican undercover operatives for Matamoras. I hope to have something in place by this evening."

"Do you have any idea of the Germans' timetable on

this madness? Should I order more patrols along the river?"

"From what we know, Ramos and this fellow Garza have just started recruiting leaders at the local level. I think it will be a while before they raise a fighting force of any significance."

"I pray you're correct," Parker said. "In any event, keep me appraised of what you uncover in Matamoras. Any warning at all will allow me to react accordingly."

"I'll be in touch the moment I know something."

Gordon used the regimental adjutant's office to draft his report to Director Holbrook. The date was Friday, June 18, and he felt he at last had something of consequence to report. When he finished the draft, the adjutant gave it to a cryptographer for encoding, the message to be sent by priority telegraph. Director Holbrook would receive it sometime that afternoon.

From the garrison, Gordon walked to the hotel. In his room, he took a steamy bath, then stropped his straight razor and shaved a two-day growth of stubble. He changed into one of the lightweight tropical worsted suits he had bought shortly after his arrival in Brownsville. Since yesterday, he'd begun carrying his personal sidearm, a Colt Model 1911 automatic in .45 caliber. The pistol was snugged tight in a cross-draw holster cinched to his belt.

Maddox found him in the hotel dining room, finishing a late lunch. The dining room was almost empty, and after Maddox ordered coffee, he briefed Gordon on the arrangements for Matamoras. The key operative was Hector Martinez, a Mexican national who at various times had been a gunrunner for Villa and an informant for the Rangers. Martinez supported Villa and Zapata, and loathed both Huerta and Carranza. His political ideology, and his mercenary nature, made him the perfect undercover operative.

Martinez's sister, Guadalupe Palaez, would act as the conduit for intelligence information. Her husband, a Villa *soldado*, had been killed when Carranza's forces overran Matamoras last year. To protect her three-year-old son, Antonio, she had crossed the border and now lived in Brownsville. The third operative was Manuel Vargas, the younger cousin of Martinez and Guadalupe. The entire family opposed anyone who threatened Mexico, or the welfare of *Tejanos* in Texas. They had agreed to work for a flat rate of three hundred dollars a month.

"We could do lots worse," Maddox concluded. "They're family, so they won't sell one another out. And they got real hot when I told 'em about the Germans. Saw right away it'd only hurt Mexico in the end."

"It sounds good," Gordon said, thoughtful a moment. "Are you sure we can trust them?"

"Dead certain," Maddox said flatly. "They try to double-cross us and I'll kill 'em. I made that clear before I explained the job."

"I'd say that's as good a basis for trust as any. When can I meet them?"

"We're set for eight tonight. Ought to be dark by the time we get to Mextown."

The southwest corner of Brownsville was known to Anglos as Mextown. There, near the river, Mexicans and *Tejanos* lived in a warren of adobe homes and unpaved streets. Guadalupe Palaez's house was a four-room adobe, located hardly a stone's throw from the banks of the Rio Grande. She greeted them at the door that evening, and Gordon could scarcely contain a look of surprise. She was in her early twenties, with lovely oval features, an olive complexion, and dark, lustrous hair. Her loose-fitting dress did nothing to hide her sumptuous figure.

Hector Martinez was stoutly built, alert and observant, with a sweeping handlebar mustache. The cousin, Manuel Vargas, was shorter and clean-shaven, with a quick smile and a deferential manner. There was no sign of Guadalupe's son, and Gordon assumed she had already put the boy to bed. After everyone was introduced, they took seats around a small dining table lit by a kerosene lamp. Maddox, to set the right tone, once again explained that Gordon was in charge of the operation.

"We have much to discuss," Gordon said, nodding around the table. "Sergeant Maddox tells me you speak English."

"Oh, yes," Martinez said with an affable smile. "Here or across the river, ever'body talk a little *inglés*. Just don't use the big words, *por favor*."

"All right, no big words."

Gordon briefed them on what was needed. He wanted one of the men to maintain a watch on the German consulate at all times. The movements of Otto Mueller, as well as Augustin Garza, were of particular interest. The other man would have the more dangerous assignment, infiltrating the inner ranks of Garza's rebel organization. To ensure the security of the operation, all routine matters would be channeled through Guadalupe. They would meet only when the men had something imperative to report.

"*Bueno*," Martinez said when he finished. "Manuel will watch the Germans like a hawk. His is a face even the ugly *chicas* don't remember. Me, I will find a way to get close to this Garza."

"Garza is no fool," Gordon said seriously. "You will have to be sly—uh, clever—to deceive him."

"*Aiiii caramba!*" Martinez spread his hands with a toothy grin. "I am clever like the fox, *señor*. You will see."

Gordon thought there was a fine line between confidence and overconfidence. He started to say something more, then decided to let it go. Hector Martinez looked like he had nerve enough for a dozen men.

Soon enough, they would find out if he was clever as well.

• • •

Garza crossed the International Bridge shortly after eight o'clock. Matamoras was quiet and dark except for the main plaza, where bars and nightspots attracted a crowd every evening. His mind was elsewhere and he ignored the people, the melodic strain of guitars.

On Calle Guerrero, he left his horse stabled at a livery. Then he recrossed the plaza and walked east to the German Consulate. His knock was answered by a servant, who recognized him from his previous visits. He was shown to an office along the central corridor.

Otto Mueller was seated at a desk. He was writing in his daily log, portions of which would later be transcribed into codetext and forwarded to Colonel von Kleist at the embassy in New York. He looked up at the interruption.

"Herr Garza," he said, rising from his chair. "I hadn't expected you back so soon."

"I have things to report," Garza said. "I thought it best that you hear it in person."

"*Ja*, your reports should always be in person. Please have a chair."

Garza seated himself before the desk. "I regret to say—" he made a sharp, angry gesture—"Ramos has been captured by the Texas Rangers. They have him locked in the jail in Brownsville."

"*Gott im Himmel!*" Mueller looked thunderstruck. "How could such a thing happen?"

"Ramos was betrayed by one of our countrymen in the town of McAllen. I received the news when I returned to Brownsville this afternoon."

"Will Ramos betray you?"

"There is nothing to tell," Garza said without expression. "He was carrying papers complete with details about the Plan of San Diego. The Rangers know everything."

"Not everything," Mueller reminded him. "Do you think Ramos will betray me—and Germany?"

"You and your superiors have nothing to fear. Basilio Ramos is a soldier, and he knows his duty. Even under threat of death, he will never talk."

"Let us hope you are correct. But in any event, they now know your name. You were listed in those papers as the military commander."

"I am not concerned," Garza said. "Once we begin operations, my name would have become known. What does concern me is that we have lost the element of surprise."

"Do not be discouraged," Mueller said expansively. "Karl von Clausewitz, the father of all German strategy, postulated that surprise is but one of many variables in battle. Leadership, in his words, overshadows all else."

"Revolution breeds its own leaders."

"Even so, how will you replace Ramos?"

"Consider it done," Garza said. "I have recruited a man who will become my new second-in-command. His name is Luis Vasquez and he burns with a hatred of *gringos*. He will serve us well."

Mueller looked at him. "I am pleased you have found a good man. But we will need many leaders for what lies ahead."

"How do you think I heard of Ramos' capture? I enlisted two such men only this afternoon."

Garza went on to explain. That afternoon he had called on Miguel Barragan, a Huerta loyalist and former cavalryman who had taken refuge in Brownsville. He had secured not only Barragan, but also Barragan's son-in-law, Juan Cross, a man of mixed blood, Negro and Mexican. Cross was widely respected throughout the Negro community in the Rio Grande valley.

"Barragan is a veteran fighter," Garza continued, "and Cross will be a great value in recruiting Negroes to our cause. It is important for people to see that we welcome all men of color to the rebellion."

"Yes, of course," Mueller said with an indulgent air. "But we both know that Negroes and Indians will be of secondary importance. Mexicans will comprise the bulk of our army."

"I have never said otherwise."

"So where are they? You tell me of Vasquez and Barragan—and what was the name?—Cross. We require not three men but thousands!"

"I am not a magician," Garza said curtly. "We have accomplished a great deal in two days. The army you speak of will take time."

"Time is a commodity in short supply. The German Reich provides the arms and you are to provide the men. General Huerta assured us this would be done."

"And it will be done."

"When?"

"I expect to have at least a hundred men by the end of the month."

"A hundred!" Mueller repeated harshly. "We were told there are thousands of Huerta loyalists. Where are they?"

Garza bristled, his eyes dark as slate. "You do not understand my people, *señor*. They must see a thing happen before they believe it is possible. On July fourth, they will believe *gringos* can be killed."

"Yes, but how many will you kill? You say you will have only a hundred men."

"How could I give you a number? We will kill all we can find."

Mueller sighed heavily. He had expected Garza to mobilize a minimum of a thousand men in the remaining two weeks of June. Whether or not Huerta had misled them about the number of loyalist forces in Mexico was a moot point. Colonel von Kleist had charged him—Otto Mueller—

with the mission of bringing death and chaos to the Rio Grande border. He dared not fail.

"Let me be frank," he said bluntly. "General Huerta will not continue to receive our support unless there is decisive action. Sufficient to draw the attention of America to the border."

"I understand," Garza said. "What do you suggest?"

"On July fourth, I think it would be wise to disrupt communications and destroy transport. Telephone and telegraph lines, railroad bridges, and, of course, a great number of civilian casualties. Actions that will cause the U.S. military to be placed on alert!"

"I see no problem with what you ask."

"Good," Mueller said. "How soon can you prepare a formal plan of attack?"

"Do you mean specific targets?"

"Targets. Time of attack. Line of march. A plan, Herr Garza."

Garza thought the German approach to war was too rigid, almost a scholarly exercise. His time of attack would be in the dark of night. His targets would be those that offered light resistance and weak defenses. His line of march would be across the river. He could have presented Mueller with a plan tonight; yet he cautioned himself not to offend or antagonize. He nodded with what he hoped was a sage look.

"I will have a formal plan for you on Monday."

"Excellent," Mueller said importantly. "We will make a good German of you yet, eh, Herr Garza?"

Garza didn't trust himself to reply.

The Bezar Hotel overlooked the main plaza. The accommodations were the finest in Matamoras, and the guest list included businessmen, government officials from Mexico

City, and world travelers. There was an air of faded opulence that appealed to a highbred clientele.

Mueller was having a late supper in the nightclub, where people of culture and taste gathered for an evening's entertainment. He had moved into the hotel after two nights at the consulate, and a numbing antipathy for the tiresome manner of Consular Erwin Reinhardt. The company to be found at the hotel was, by comparison, almost cosmopolitan.

There was, in addition, Maria Dominguez. She was the star attraction of the nightclub, a singer of sultry voice, warm sensuality, and revealing gowns. She was tall, with rounded breasts, lissome legs, and hair dark as a raven's wing. Her mouth was at times pouty and suggestive, and her teasing eyes forever held the promise of wanton abandon. Mueller thought she was the loveliest woman he'd ever seen.

For the past two nights, he had sent boxes of roses to her dressing room. Included with the flowers was a personal note, elegantly phrased, inviting her to join him for champagne. She acknowledged neither the note nor the roses, but tonight, accompanied by guitars and a violin, she watched him as she sang a torchy ballad. Mueller couldn't understand the lyrics, but somehow knew she was singing words of love, raw with emotion. He sensed, perhaps more hope than truth, that she was singing to him.

After the show, she disappeared backstage. Mueller chided himself for thinking he'd impressed her with roses and flattering notes. He was no ladies' man, though he had occasionally enjoyed an affair with women attracted by his rugged good looks and stolid manner. His mistress was the army, the soldier's life, and he again admonished himself for believing he might win the attention of a Latin beauty. Then, magically, she was standing beside his table.

"*Buenas noches,*" she said in a husky voice. "May I join you?"

"Yes, of course," Mueller stumbled to his feet and held her chair. "I had lost hope you would accept my invitation."

"How could I ignore a man who sends me roses? You are very thoughtful."

"Please consider it a token of my admiration. A beautiful woman deserves no less."

"How gallant." She gave him a bright, theatrical smile. "Are you in Matamoras on business?"

Mueller shrugged. "Only in a manner of speaking. I am the agricultural attaché at the German Consulate."

"Ummm, that sounds so very exciting. And your lovely note was signed Otto Mueller. May I call you Otto?"

"Yes, by all means, please do."

A waiter, unbidden, appeared with a bottle of chilled champagne and fluted glasses. He poured, nodding to Mueller with a conspiratorial look, and whisked away from the table. Maria Dominguez lifted her glass, tiny bubbles popping over the rim, and leaned closer. Her eyes were mischievous, merrily wicked.

"I think we will be friends . . . Otto."

Mueller felt dizzy. "Nothing would please me more. Nothing."

"Oh, never fear, you will be pleased. I promise."

Her throaty laughter left him intoxicated.

Chapter Seven

Thousands of handbills were circulated throughout the Rio Grande valley over the weekend. The language was inflammatory and the content was a strident call to arms. The heading was in bold print.

LOS MEXICANOS EN TEXAS

There followed a litany of racial and economic discrimination by Texans against Mexicans and *Tejanos*. In a fiery diatribe, the people were reminded that Texans had denied them and their children an education, and deliberately reduced them to poverty. The purpose, which was appallingly successful, was to force them to work at menial jobs for slave wages. Their average pay was but ten cents an hour.

The Plan of San Diego was outlined in brief statements that would strike home with all people of Mexican heritage. The points stressed were the liberation of Texas from gringos, the transformation of *Nuevo Texas* into an independent republic, and distribution of the land to the people in equal shares. The execution of all male gringos over the age of sixteen was presented as simple justice for generations of tyrants.

The handbill exhorted all Mexicans and *Tejanos* to heed the call for independence and join the rebellion in the fight for freedom. Augustin Garza was identified as Chief

Military Commander of the Army of Liberation.

On Monday afternoon Hector Martinez crossed the International Bridge to Matamoras. In his pocket was a copy of the handbill, the ink smudged in places, clearly a rush job. He assumed it had been hastily printed over the weekend and thought it was a crafty move on the part of Garza and the Germans. With the capture of Basilio Ramos, the authorities were alerted to the Plan of San Diego and there was no longer any need for secrecy. The recruitment of men for the Army of Liberation could now be done openly.

Martinez had been searching for a way to approach Garza. Since Friday evening, after the meeting with Gordon and Maddox, he'd discarded various ploys for how he could have learned of Garza and the Plan of San Diego. None of the ideas was really plausible, and all of them, subjected to scrutiny, would probably have gotten him killed. By circulating the handbill along the river, Garza had solved the problem for him. He could simply answer the call for volunteers.

There were dozens of small, working-class *cantinas* in Matamoras. The saloons radiated outward from the main plaza and was frequented by laborers and the unemployed, men who would openly endorse a rebellion against *gringos*. Martinez began on the plaza, pulling out the handbill and questioning bartenders as to where he might find Augustin Garza. Everyone had seen the handbill, but no one knew where Garza made his headquarters. Several men, some drunker than others, loudly announced their willingness to join the rebellion.

Undeterred, Martinez slowly worked his way onto streets bordering the plaza. Finally, in a *cantina* on Calle Morelos, a block east of the German Consulate, the bartender acknowledged he'd come to the right place. He was told to wait, and after ordering a beer, he took a seat at a table toward the rear. The bartender's son was sent off as a messenger and a short while later a large man with a curly mustache entered the door. He walked directly to the table.

"*Buenas tardes*," he said. "You are asking for Colonel Augustin Garza?"

"*Si*." Martinez stared back at him with round, guileless eyes. "Who are you?"

"I am Capitán Luis Vasquez, executive officer to Colonel Garza."

"*Valgame Dios*!" Martinez jumped to his feet, waving the handbill. "I am here to join the rebellion, *mi capitán*."

"Not so loud, *hombre*." Vasquez motioned him to be seated, than took a chair. "What is your name?"

"Hector Martinez."

"Where do you live?"

"Brownsville for now," Martinez said, flapping his arms. "I am *Tejano* and have suffered much at the hands of Texans. I take work wherever I can find it to earn my bread."

The lie was impossible to disprove, for itinerant *Tejanos* wandered the border searching for odd jobs. "So." Vasquez watched him intently. "You are willing to kill *gringos*?"

"*Si, mi capitán*!" Martinez said with a big loopy smile. "I wish to be a *soldado* in your army."

Vasquez was impressed by the man's personable manner. He was impressed as well that Martinez had shown the initiative to cross the border and volunteer for service. Miguel Barragan was actively recruiting in Brownsville, but someone was needed to spread the word in outlying areas. He nodded, the decision made.

"I like your spirit, Martinez. At the moment, however, we have great need of someone who can carry our message and recruit soldiers. I think you are the man for the job."

"No disrespect intended, *mi capitán*, but I am here to fight for liberty."

"And you will," Vasquez said. "I hereby appoint you a sergeant in the Army of Liberation. You will recruit men for our cause, and at the proper time—you will lead them into battle."

"*Sargento!*" Martinez marveled. "I never expected such a thing. *Caramba!*"

"Your assignment will be to travel the border, convince men in distant *pueblos* to join our cause. This is an important responsibility, *comprende*?"

"*Yo entiendo, mi capitán.*"

"*Bueno.*" Vasquez rose from his chair. "I will take you now to meet our leader, Colonel Garza. He is a great man."

Martinez beamed. "I am honored by your consideration, *mi capitán.*"

The headquarters for the Army of Liberation was an adobe house, rented only yesterday, around the corner on Calle 5. Martinez noted that it was within a block of the German Consulate, the proximity a telling point in itself. His introduction to Garza was perfunctory, and brief.

On the way back to the bridge, Martinez committed everything he'd learned to memory. Yet the thing he remembered most was that Garza's gaze was so empty of emotion that both eyes seemed to be made of glass. He thought he had known many dangerous men in his time on the border, but none more dangerous than the one he'd met today. He warned himself to caution, and vigilance.

His first misstep with Augustin Garza would be his last.

Manuel Vargas waited until the next day to begin the surveillance operation. Martinez had briefed him on the meetings with Garza and Vasquez, and given him physical descriptions of both men. He felt confident he would recognize them on sight.

On Tuesday morning, Vargas crossed the bridge into Matamoras. He had given a good deal of thought to his disguise, fully aware that he must blend in with the surroundings, become all but invisible. The masquerade he adopted was that of a scruffy street vendor, for the main plaza was crawling with vendors of every description. His final concern was a disguise that would allow him the mobility to go anywhere.

A southerly breeze chased puffy white clouds through the sky as a forenoon sun rose steadily higher. The plaza was crowded with shoppers and ringed with open-air stalls, magnified by wagons and carts and men on horseback into an unrelenting din of noise. Vargas moved through the crowds with a shallow wooden tray held in his hands and supported by a leather strap around his neck. The tray contained plugs of tobacco, loose cigarettes, and thick, black cigars which sold for a peso apiece. He was lost among the throngs of people milling about the vast square.

The south side of the plaza opened onto Calle Morelos. Vargas positioned himself at the southeast corner, near a vendor with gaudy ribbons and cheap cotton handkerchiefs. From there, he had an unimpeded view of the entrance to the German Consulate. Farther along, he saw a man sweeping the sidewalk outside the *cantina* where Martinez had been enlisted by Luis Vasquez. Martinez had told him it appeared to be the local hangout for men sympathetic to a rebellion in Texas. He thought he might wander down there later in the afternoon.

Shortly before eleven o'clock, he saw two men turn the corner from Calle 5 onto Calle Morelos. As they approached closer, he identified them as Vasquez and Augustin Garza. He watched as they rapped the door-knocker at the German Consulate and were admitted by a servant. For the next hour, he did a brisk business with men who stopped to buy cigarettes and plug tobacco on their way to the plaza. He wasn't surprised that he sold only two of the ropey black cigars. Not many men would surrender a peso for a smoke.

The bells in the cathedral tower tolled the hour at noon. A few minutes later, Garza and Vasquez emerged from the consulate in the company of a well-dressed man with hair the color of wheat. As they approached the corner, Vargas mentally reviewed the description he'd been given by Frank Gordon, and identified the man as Otto Mueller, thought to be a German military officer. The three men walked past Vargas, engaged in conversation, and he realized they were speaking English. They rounded the corner onto the plaza.

Vargas waited to a count of ten, then followed at a discreet distance. Up ahead, he saw the men turn into a fashionable sidewalk café, one patronized by the more affluent people of Matamoras. A waiter came forward, inspecting Garza and Vasquez like soiled linen, but then, with a sharp word from Mueller, he seated them at a table near the sidewalk. When the menus arrived, it appeared Garza was translating from Spanish to English for Mueller's benefit. Mueller insisted on ordering a bottle of wine with their meal.

The crowds became heavier at noontime, and Vargas slowly worked his way closer to the café. Finally, as though he'd found a good spot to hawk his wares, he positioned himself on the sidewalk with his back to the table. The three men were the only ones conversing in English, and Vargas found it simple to distinguish their voices from other patrons seated nearby. Garza and Vasquez were clearly deferential to the German, and a celebration of some sort was under way. Mueller was playing the role of genial host.

"I am quite pleased," he said in a convivial tone. "Your progress to date is excellent, commendable, in fact. Everything appears to be on schedule."

"Nothing will delay us," Garza said, nodding vigorously. "Our plan is sound, and more men rally to our cause every day. We will be ready."

Mueller chuckled softly. "Those handbills were a masterpiece. I wish I could say it was my idea."

"There is credit enough for all," Garza said smoothly. "Your contribution is essential to what we will achieve."

"You are too kind, Herr Garza."

The conversation was cryptic in nature. The men seemed aware they were in a public place, and none of them made direct reference to the Plan of San Diego. Yet it was apparent to Vargas that something decisive was about to happen, and soon. Otto Mueller reinforced the thought when he raised his wine glass in a toast.

"To your great success, gentlemen. *Salud*!"

The sky was clear and black as velvet, bursting with stars. Along the river, fireflies blinked in wayward flight and lamps lighting the windows of houses were already being turned down. A dog barked somewhere in the distance.

Gordon and Maddox moved through the darkened streets not long after eight o'clock. Late that afternoon an envelope had been left with the desk clerk at the hotel. The note inside was from Guadalupe Palaez, inviting Gordon to her house sometime after dark. The purpose of the note required no explanation.

Nor was it necessary to elaborate on the "after dark" remark. The streets in the Mexican district of Brownsville were virtually deserted an hour or so after suppertime. The people who lived there worked twelve-hour days, usually jobs of strenuous labor, and they retired early. Darkness reduced the risk that *gringos* would be seen entering the house.

Guadalupe opened the door at their knock. She quickly closed it as they moved inside, and for a moment she was standing close beside Gordon. In the amber glow of the lamp, her features were an odd mixture of poise and vulnerability, innocence and earthy wisdom. He was intensely aware of her smell, like a damp, sweet orange.

"Please, come in," she said, stepping past him with a winsome smile. "Hector and Manuel are waiting."

Martinez and Vargas were seated at the small dining table. Guadalupe's son, Antonio, was on the floor, playing with a carved wooden pony on wheels. He was a chubby, brown-faced cherub, and when she scooped him up and carried him to the bedroom, he squealed with laughter. Gordon and Maddox took chairs at the table.

"*Buenas noches*," Martinez greeted them. "Manuel and I have been busy across the river. We have much to report."

Gordon nodded. "Have you located Garza?"

"Oh, yes," Martinez said with a jokester's smile. "I am now a sergeant in the Army of Liberation."

Maddox rolled himself a cigarette as they listened. Martinez related how he had found Luis Vasquez, a name unknown to any of them until now. He went on to say he'd been enlisted as a recruiter, promoted to Sergeant, and introduced to Garza, all within the space of an hour. Guadalupe returned from the bedroom as he finished his report. She seated herself beside Gordon.

Vargas then recounted his experiences as a street vendor. He told them about Garza and Vasquez visiting the consulate, and later, how he'd eavesdropped on their conversation with the German, Otto Mueller. After their meal, the three men had parted outside the consulate, and late that afternoon, he had trailed Mueller to the Bezar Hotel, where he tried to sell him a cigar. A casual conversation with the doorman revealed that Mueller was a guest at the hotel.

"That's mighty fine work," Maddox said, exhaling the words in a stream of smoke. "Sounds like something's liable to pop pretty quick."

"I think you are right, *señor*," Vargas said. "Their manner at the café was like that of a *celebración*. Garza assured the German there will be no delays."

Gordon thoughtfully scratched his jaw. "I'd say they've set a date for a military action of some sort. The question is, when?"

"And where?" Maddox added, stubbing out his cigarette in an ashtray. "We've got a lot of border to cover. They could hit and be gone before we know it."

"We really don't have a clue." Gordon paused, then looked at Martinez. "Hector, you've apparently gained the confidence of this Vasquez. Could you get him to talk about what they're planning?"

"I can try," Martinez said. "But what excuse do I have for being in Matamoras? They expect me to be over here recruiting men."

"Use that as your excuse," Gordon said, suddenly seized by the idea. "Tell them the men you've spoken with want to know when they will be issued weapons. When they will be asked to assemble, and where." He forced a rueful smile. "When they can begin killing *gringos*."

Martinez cocked an eyebrow. "You know, Vasquez might believe every word of it. You are a truly gifted liar, *señor*."

Gordon laughed. "Forget the compliments and get me the information." He turned to Vargas. "Manuel, you stick with Mueller everywhere he goes. His actions might somehow tip their hand."

"I am as his shadow," Vargas mugged, hands outstretched. "Whatever he does, I will see it."

The meeting finally broke up when they had exhausted all their ideas for gathering intelligence. Guadalupe walked Gordon and Maddox to the door and held it open as they started outside. Gordon hesitated, not certain why, and looked into her eyes. A smile tugged at the corner of his mouth.

"Thank you for your note," he said, wondering if he sounded as awkward as he felt. "I look forward to the next one."

"Yes, and soon," she said with a vibrant smile. "I am sure of it, *señor*."

Maddox was waiting for him on the street. They turned back toward the center of town and walked along in silence for a time. Finally, Maddox exhaled a sharp, whistling breath. He shook his head.

"I hope to Christ Martinez comes through with the where and when. We're gonna be up shit creek if he don't."

"Hoyt, you took the words right out of my mouth."

"Goddamn Germans," Maddox cursed, his features troubled. "I just expect we ought to have a talk with General Parker. Don't you think?"

"First thing tomorrow," Gordon said. "We'll ask him to beef up patrols along the river. Way things look, we're running out of time."

"Only one trouble."

"What's that?"

"It's a mighty long river."

They walked off into the darkness.

Chapter Eight

The moon hung like a white lantern in an indigo sky. The land was lighted by a luminous, silvery glow so bright that trees and bushes stood out in stark relief. The steel rails of the railroad tracks glittered onward into the night.

Augustin Garza was mounted on a sorrel gelding. Behind him, formed in columns of twos, rode fourteen men, most of them *Tejanos*. The men were armed with Winchester repeating rifles, smuggled into Texas with funds supplied by the Germans. Directly ahead, ghostly in the moonlight, lay the town of Harlingen.

The date was July 4, and the Army of Liberation was on the move. Garza thought of it as the vanguard of the army to come, for scarcely more than forty men had been recruited into the ranks. Over the past two weeks he had deceived Otto Mueller, inflating the numbers actually enlisted, still confident of the future. Tonight's raids would rally men by the thousands.

Garza had split his force into four parties. He would lead one group against the farm town of Harlingen, some thirty miles northwest of Brownsville. Luis Vasquez, with twelve men, would raid an Anglo ranch ten miles farther north, outside the town of Sebastian. Miguel Barragan and Juan Cross, leading smaller groups, were assigned to dynamite the railroad bridges near Raymondville and Russelltown.

The raids were designed to prove that all *gringos* were

vulnerable to attack. Civilians would be executed, law officers would be killed, and railway transportation, essential to the economy of the lower Rio Grande valley, would be disrupted with the destruction of two major railroad bridges. Mexicans and *Tejanos* would awaken to the reality of the Plan of San Diego. Nothing in the Anglo world was immune to devastation.

Harlingen was the second-largest town in Cameron County. By now, three hours short of midnight, the fireworks and festivities of Independence Day were concluded and the townspeople had retired to their homes. But law enforcement officers, rather than ordinary civilians, were Garza's target tonight. Because of Harlingen's size, two deputy sheriffs were stationed there on a full-time basis. They were to be sacrificed in the name of liberation.

Garza brought his men into town through a shadowed alleyway. The main street was deserted, illuminated by the moon and electric lampposts on each corner. The raiders dismounted in the alley behind the small office maintained by the sheriff's department. To discourage townspeople who might be awakened by gunfire, nine men were posted on the street. Two men were left to hold the horses, and the other three followed Garza. He led them toward the office door.

Hank McGivern and Tom Harney were preparing to close the office for the night. What with the Fourth of July celebration, complete with a parade and fireworks and several drunks, their day had lasted well into the evening. Their only prisoner was a *Tejano*, arrested for starting a fight during the parade, and locked now in the tiny cell at the rear of the room. A fistfight was hardly a crime, and they were both agreed that a night in jail was punishment enough. He would be released in the morning.

Garza walked through the door with a drawn pistol. Crowding close behind him were the three raiders, their lever-action Winchesters covering the deputies. McGivern and Harney were taken unawares, dumbfounded by the sight of four armed Mexicans, and stared at them in a moment of baffled silence. Harney was the first to recover his wits.

"What the hell's this?"

"Justice," Garza said in a hard voice. "I am Colonel Augustin Garza, commander of the Army of Liberation. You have been sentenced to death."

"I don't care who you are," Harney snapped. "Put them guns away or you're gonna get yourself in a shitpot full of trouble. *Comprende*?"

Garza shot him. The slug struck Harney over his shirt pocket and he staggered, crashing sideways into a desk. His legs collapsed beneath him and he slumped to the floor. McGivern backed away, his eyes wild.

"Now hold on a goldurn—"

The three men with Garza opened fire. The crack of their Winchesters rattled off the office walls like the boom of a kettledrum. McGivern went down, his shirt pocked with bright red dots, his eyes rolled back in his head. A puddle of blood slowly spread across the floor.

"*Yanqui bastardos.*" Garza stared at the bodies a moment, then looked at the man in the cell. "Who are you?"

"Adolfo Munoz."

"Why are you in jail?"

"I fought a man," Munoz said haltingly, unnerved by the killings. "He called me names and I knocked him down until he could no longer stand."

"Good for you."

Garza took a ring of keys off a wall peg. He unlocked the cell door and motioned Munoz outside. "I am releasing you, but on a condition, *hombre*."

"Anything, *mi jefe*."

"Tell our people what you have seen here tonight.

Spread the message that we will drive the *gringos* from the land. Call on all men to join in our fight for liberty."

"I will tell them, *mi jefe*. I swear it."

"*Vaya con Dios*."

Munoz bobbed his head, stepping around the bodies, and hurried out the door. Garza collected a straw broom from where it stood propped in a corner and dipped it in the puddle of blood. Then, wielding the broom like a large paintbrush, he stroked bold letters across the wall. The message, dripping scarlet streaks, was left for all to read.

VIVA LIBERTAD!

The ranch compound was situated on the dogleg bend of a creek four miles west of Sebastian. A two-story frame house overlooked the creek, and off to the side was a bunkhouse and an equipment shed. Thirty horses stood hip-shot in a large corral.

Vasquez reined his horse to a halt on the south bank of the creek. His men were bunched loosely behind him as he sat staring at the compound, which was bathed in moonlight. The ranch was owned by Earl Stovall, and Vasquez had once worked for him as a *vaquero*. There was nothing random about the selection of the ranch for tonight's raid.

On Vasquez's signal, the raiders forded the creek. All of them were armed with Winchesters, and after hitching their horses outside the corral, they set about their assigned tasks. Half the men burst into the bunkhouse, where they rousted out five *Tejano* cowhands at gunpoint. The other men stormed the main house.

Earl Stovall, barefoot and still in his nightshirt, was brought outside. Behind him was his wife Mary, his eighteen-year-old son Dave and two girls, ages twelve and fourteen. The raiders roughly shoved them forward, the girls crying, clutching at their mother, shivering in their nightgowns. The family and the *vaqueros* were herded together where Vasquez waited by a tall oak tree in the front yard. Stovall peered at him uncertainly in the dappled moonlight.

"Vasquez?" he said tentatively. "Aren't you Luis Vasquez?"

"Meester Stovall," Vasquez said with heavy sarcasm. "You remember me, huh? Been a long time."

Stovall was a stern man, not above striking his *vaqueros* with anything handy when they were slow to respond. Three years ago, after an argument, he had whipped Vasquez with a quirt and thrown him off the ranch. He squinted querulously now, confused and angry.

"What's the idea of forcin' your way into my home?"

"Show a little respect," Vasquez said, mocking him. "I am a *capitán* in the Army of Liberation. You have heard of us, eh?"

Stovall had seen the handbills flooding the border. Until now, he'd thought the Plan of San Diego was the work of some haywire Mexican. "I won't have my family manhandled this way, Vasquez. What d'ya want here?"

"Oh, that is very simple, Meester Stovall. I have come here to kill you."

Vasquez rapped out a command. Four of his men quickly bound the hands of Stovall and his son with lengths of rawhide. Hemp ropes were tossed over a stout limb of the live oak as the rancher and the boy were prodded forward. Mary Stovall watched in horror, hugging her daughters, as nooses were slipped around the necks of her husband and son. Vasquez looked at Stovall with an evil grin.

"Do you have any last words, *amigo*?"

"No," Stovall said in a hollow voice. "Just don't hurt my wife and the girls."

"We do not harm women and children."

On his signal, Stovall and the boy were jerked off the ground. The ropes were snubbed around the base of the tree as they thrashed and kicked, their pale, bare legs flailing in the moonlight. Mary Stovall screamed hysterically as their faces turned purple, then dusky black, and their tongues, thick with spittle, lolled out of their mouths. Three long minutes passed while they strangled to death.

Vasquez made an impassioned speech to Stovall's *vaqueros*. His words seemed punctuated by the uncontrollable sobs of the woman and her daughters as they stared at the bodies dangling from the tree. He spoke of independence, a Texas free of *gringos*, and distribution of the land to the people. He urged the *vaqueros* to join the Army of Liberation, and while one readily volunteered, the others kept their eyes averted. He cursed them for cowards.

All the time he spoke, his men were busy torching the house inside and out, then the bunkhouse and the equipment shed. Within minutes, the buildings were roaring with flame, the moonlit skies brightened a rosy vermilion by the inferno. The remuda of ranch horses was released from the corral, walleyed with fright, as mounted men hazed them away from the burning compound. Over it all, the keening wail of Mary Stovall was like an animal in pain.

Vasquez turned to look at his handiwork, his teeth flashing white in the crackling flames. He reined his horse around, motioning to his men as they drove the remuda across the creek. His voice split the night in a shout of triumph.

"*Vamanos, muchachos!*"

They rode south from the carnage.

The moon floated westward in a cloudless sky. There was a bluish haze around its rim, and it cast a spectral light across the land. A warm breeze rustled the leaves of cottonwoods along the river.

The convoy was led by a Model-T Ford. Trailing behind was a Reo Touring sedan, followed by an open-bed Model-T pickup truck. Gordon and Maddox were in the lead car, with Captain Bob Ransom at the wheel. The twenty Rangers of Company A were loaded in the truck and the Reo sedan.

"Not far now," Ransom said over the wind whipping around the Model-T. "We're getting close to Los Indios."

Maddox peered ahead. "How much farther to Bud Grant's ranch?"

"Couple of miles past Los Indios."

"Never thought to ask," Maddox said, looking at Gordon. "You ever rode a horse before?"

"Don't worry about me," Gordon said. "I rode a horse to school every day when I was a kid. There weren't any cars back then."

"Where was this?"

"On a farm in Virginia."

"A farm?" Maddox sounded surprised. "I figured you for a city boy."

Gordon smiled. "Only since I got to Washington."

A few minutes later, the convoy sped through Los Indios. The town was dark for the hour was late, already past one in the morning. They were some twenty miles west of Brownsville, roughly following the course of the Rio Grande. Not quite ten miles west of Los Indios was Santa Maria, and between the towns was a ford in the river used by Mexican *bandidos* for generations. Captain Bob Ransom was convinced they would intercept the raiders at the ford.

Around eleven o'clock the town marshal in Sebastian had telephoned Ransom. The fire from the Stovall place had drawn neighboring ranchers to the scene of the raid. One of them rode into town, just four miles away, and notified the marshal of the hanging of Earl Stovall and his son. *Vaqueros* at the ranch reported that the leader of the raid was Luis Vasquez, who had identified himself as a captain in the Army of Liberation. Vasquez and thirteen men had driven a herd of horses south from the ranch.

Only minutes later, the Rangers had been notified of the execution of two deputy sheriffs in Harlingen. There were reports as well about the demolition of railroad bridges outside the towns of Raymondville and Russelltown. No one had seen the raiders in any of these incidents, and there was little chance of tracking them on horseback in the dark. Vasquez and his band were a different matter entirely, encumbered as they were by the stolen livestock. They were almost certainly driving the horses toward the border.

Ransom had immediately called Maddox and Gordon at the hotel. The significance of the raids occurring on the Fourth of July was lost on no one, and the executions, particularly the young Stovall boy, ratcheted their anger even higher. A long-time veteran of the border, Ransom drew a direct line on a map from Sebastian to the river crossing, and predicted the raiders were headed for the ford. Within a half hour, the automobiles were commandeered from local businessmen and the Rangers were ready to move out. The final step was put in place with a telephone call to the town marshal in Los Indios. Horses would be waiting for the Rangers at the ranch of Bud Grant.

The convoy, with twenty-three men jammed in the vehicles, was little short of a rolling arsenal. The Rangers were armed with pistols and lever-action carbines, the Winchester Model 94 in .30-.30 caliber. Maddox, who preferred a shotgun for night work, had raided the armory at Ranger headquarters. In addition to their pistols, he and Gordon carried the Winchester Model 97 12-gauge loaded with double-ought buckshot. The Model 97 was a pump-action shotgun, with six rounds in the tube and one in the chamber. Maddox joked that it would have saved Custer at Little Big Horn.

The vehicles pulled into the headquarters of Bud Grant's ranch shortly before two in the morning. Grant, like most ranchers, was on cordial terms with the Rangers, for they were his first line of defense against Mexican horse thieves. After being alerted by the marshal of Los Indios, he had rousted out his wrangler and several cowhands and put them to work by moonlight. There were now twenty-three horses, saddled and waiting, tied to the rails of a large corral. Ten minutes after arriving, the Rangers, formed in columns of twos, rode off upriver.

Captain Ransom, with Gordon and Maddox at the front of the column, set a fast pace. They were figuring time and distance, and despite their best efforts, they knew they might be too late. The Stovall ranch, where father and son had been hanged, was some thirty miles north of the border. The raiders had a head start of four hours or more, and in bright moonlight, the stolen horses could be pushed along at a rate of seven to eight miles an hour. The timing would be tight, and it was entirely possible Vasquez and his men had already crossed the river into Mexico. The variables were simply too many to calculate.

The ford was three miles west of the Grant ranch. A break in the trees on the north bank led down a slight incline to the Rio Grande. The rippling current of the river sparkled with moonbeams, and the shoreline was flooded with silvery light. As the Rangers approached the ford, horsemen suddenly appeared in the break between trees and drove a herd of horses, lathered with sweat, into the water. Captain Ransom, without an instant's hesitation, whipped his arm overhead and signaled his men to spread out. The Rangers fanned off to either side, forming a line to the front, and pulled their carbines from saddle scabbards. They brought their horses to a halt.

The raiders were caught in the middle of the ford. On Ransom's command, the Rangers opened fire, the crack of their carbines rending the night air. Three of the raiders were blown out of their saddles, and the others, taken completely unawares, reacted on sheer reflex. A few turned to fight, while the larger group, following the stampeded horses, spurred their mounts for the opposite shore. Gordon and Maddox cut loose with their shotguns, a hail of buckshot blasting two raiders off their horses. The Rangers fired another volley in a staccato roar.

Then, suddenly, the night went still. Eight raiders floated downstream, shot to ribbons, and six horses were dead or wounded. One Ranger was shot through the hand, the forestock of his carbine splintered, but the others emerged unscathed from the fight. Ransom ordered his men to collect the bodies of the dead raiders before they were lost to the river. There was no question of pursuing the raiders who had fled, for the Rio Grande was the international boundary. The Rangers were prohibited by treaty from entering Mexico.

Gordon and Maddox watched in silence while Rangers dragged bodies from the river. "Wonder if we got lucky," Maddox finally said. "I'd dance on his grave if we killed Luis Vasquez."

"How would we know?" Gordon said. "Neither one of us has ever seen him."

"Guess you've got a point."

Maddox noticed the strange look on Gordon's face as the bodies were pulled from the water. His curiosity got the better of him. "You don't mind my askin'—" he paused, rolling a cigarette. "You ever killed a man before?"

"No," Gordon said quietly. "That was my first one."

"Well, you did good. Some men tend to hesitate their first time out."

Maddox traced his family roots to the Texas Revolution, the war of independence with Mexico. His ancestors had served in the Texas Rangers from the time it was organized in 1835, and the number of Comanche warriors and Mexican *bandidos* they had killed was legion. He seldom spoke of the seven men he had killed.

"Hoyt, it's not a good feeling," Gordon said, staring at the body of a dead raider. "I'd just as soon it hadn't happened."

Maddox grunted. "Tonight won't be the last time, pardner. We're not anywhere near done with these sonsabitches. Not yet."

Neither of them said anything more, for they both knew it was true. The Army of Liberation had only just started its war.

Chapter Nine

Three days later Gordon and Maddox concluded a meeting with General James Parker. They emerged from the headquarters at Fort Brown and crossed the parade ground to the front gate. The sun went down along the western reaches of the river in a splash of molten gold.

The swiftness of events seemed to Gordon a promising sign for the future. On July 5, he had reported by plaintext telegraph to Director Holbrook with details of the raids. The same day, Texas Governor James Ferguson appealed to President Wilson for assistance in quelling the depredations. Newspaper headlines from coast to coast bannered the crisis on the border.

The response from Washington was immediate, and severe. Today, July 7, General Parker had been advised that an additional two thousand troops were being posted to the lower Rio Grande valley. President Wilson, in a terse statement to the press, announced that marauding bands would henceforth be treated "as belligerents entering American territory for unlawful acts." The army was ordered to apprehend the marauders, by whatever means necessary.

Hoyt Maddox reported that the state of Texas was no less vigilant. Governor Ferguson had detached two more Ranger units to the border, Company C under Captain John Sanders, and Company D, commanded by Captain Clell Morris. The barbarity of the July 4 raids was such that an outcry of rage spread from every corner of the Lone Star state. The governor, according to Maddox, had let it be known among the Ranger captains that summary justice was acceptable. In the future, they would take no prisoners.

Gordon thought of it as an eye-for-an-eye mandate. He had been mulling it over as they passed through the front gate and turned onto Elizabeth Street. He cast a troubled, sideways glance at Maddox.

"Will Ransom and the other captains take the governor at his word? Just kill their prisoners out of hand?"

"Oh hell, yes," Maddox said without hesitation. "We're fixin' to see open season on Mexicans."

"Whatever name you put to it, it's still murder. Lawmen are supposed to uphold the law."

"Well, Frank, you have to understand how things are. Most folks figure it's a waste of time to give a Mexican a trial and then wait around to hang him. Especially when he kills people in cold blood."

"That doesn't excuse it," Gordon countered. "The Rangers might as well be vigilantes."

Maddox shrugged. "I'm not trying to excuse it or defend it. I'm just tellin' you the way things are."

"Tit for tat isn't justice. Garza will use that to incite even more Mexicans to rebellion."

"Yeah, I reckon he will, and it'll likely work, too. There's not a helluva lot of justice on either side of the river."

The point was difficult to argue. In the past five years, thousands of people had fled the bloodletting of the Mexican Revolution and crossed the Rio Grande. On the north side of the river, they found an age-old prejudice by Anglos that made them ready recruits for Augustin Garza's Army of Liberation. *Tejanos*, their kinsmen by heritage, had long since learned a harsh lesson for those who sought freedom. Injustice was a way of life along the border.

Gordon and Maddox planned to take their supper in

the dining room at the hotel. As they approached the entrance, they saw Manuel Vargas cross the intersection of Elizabeth and Twelfth. He strolled past them at a leisurely pace and rolled his eyes with an almost imperceptible nod toward the southwest corner of town. A moment later, he disappeared around the corner of the hotel.

"Something's up," Maddox said as they entered the hotel. "Wonder what's happened now."

"Any news is bad news," Gordon replied. "Looks like we'll have a late night."

By eight o'clock, darkness had fallen over Brownsville. Gordon and Maddox, after a hasty supper, made their way through the narrow streets of the Mexican district. Guadalupe answered their knock and held the door as they moved inside the house. She smiled warmly at Gordon.

"*Buenas noches.*"

"Good evening," Gordon said, struck again by her radiant beauty. "We came as soon as we could."

Martinez and Vargas were seated at the small dining table. The wick on the lamp was turned low, and as they rose to exchange greetings, the look on Martinez's face was unusually sober. Everyone took chairs, and Guadalupe again seated herself beside Gordon. Maddox arched an eyebrow in question.

"We're all ears," he said. "What's the latest from Matamoras?"

"Garza is a happy man," Martinez said with a tight smile. "The raids have brought him much fame."

Gordon looked at him with a measured stare. "Does he say anything about his plans?"

"*Si*, but only in general terms. He brags that the war of liberation will deliver Texas into the hands of the people."

"Nothing more specific?"

Martinez spread his hands. "More men have volunteered since the raids. I even recruited a few myself in the last couple days. Otherwise Garza would grow suspicious."

"You still have his trust, then?"

"So far."

"How many men have volunteered?"

"That's a strange thing," Martinez said. "Luis Vasquez tells me maybe thirty or forty. But Garza keeps talking about invading Texas in force. How can you invade with so few men?"

Maddox chortled sharply. "They didn't do all that bad the Fourth of July. Scared the blue-billy-hell out of everybody in two counties."

"*Si*, but that was not an invasion, eh?"

"You're getting at something else, aren't you?" Gordon cut in. "That's why you called us here tonight."

"A very odd thing happened this afternoon."

"Odd in what way?"

Martinez nodded to Vargas. "Tell them, Manuel."

"I stay close to Garza," Vargas said. "A street *vendedor* can go anywhere and nobody pays attention. I followed him to the train station."

"The train station?" Gordon repeated. "Was he meeting someone?"

"No, he was carrying a valise. He boarded the overnight train to the interior."

"Where does this train go?"

"West to Reynosa, then south to many places along the railway line. It stops in Monterrey and returns the next day to Matamoras."

"That's odd all right," Gordon said in a musing tone. "Why would he leave if he's planning this big invasion?"

"Maybe it's a recruiting trip," Maddox suggested. "Reynosa's a good-size town, and it's smack-dab on the border."

"How far west?"

"Fifty miles or so."

"Too far," Gordon said with conviction. "If it's a recruiting trip, why wouldn't he send Vasquez? A commander planning an invasion sticks close to headquarters."

"*Verdad*!" Martinez leaned forward, intensely earnest now. "I asked myself the same question, *señor*. Why would he leave Matamoras at such a time?"

"Has there been any hint of a date for the invasion?"

"*Nada*."

"So where's he gone?" Maddox said. "It's got to be Reynosa or Monterrey. Any place else on that rail line is nothin' but a wide spot in nowhere."

Gordon frowned, shook his head. "Hoyt, it's not so much where he's gone. It's more a matter of *why* he's gone."

"Yeah, I'd buy that. Got any ideas?"

"I couldn't even make an intelligent guess."

"Look on the bright side," Maddox said. "Long as he's gone, there won't be any raids. Maybe we caught ourselves a breather."

"Maybe," Gordon said tentatively. "Or maybe it's the lull before the storm."

There was a prolonged moment of silence. No one said anything, but they were all thinking along the same lines. A certainty that went beyond words.

Augustin Garza, wherever he'd gone, would return.

Garza stepped off the train in Monterrey early the next morning. Juan Caballo, shoulders squared and eyes alert, waited on the platform. He moved forward with an outstretched hand.

"*Buenos dias, mi coronel*," he said. "Did you have a pleasant journey?"

"Not too bad," Garza said, accepting his handshake. "Is everything in order?"

"Rodriguez knows of your arrival, and Señor Hinojosa awaits you at the ranch. Just as you directed, *mi coronel*."

"*Bueno*."

Garza led the way through the station house. For the past three weeks, he had been corresponding with Hilario Hinojosa, who owned a ranch outside Monterrey. His letters were hand-delivered by a railroad conductor, adequately bribed to ensure discretion. Hinojosa's replies returned to Matamoras in the same manner.

Monterrey was situated along the banks of the Rio Santa Catarina. The city was surrounded by the peaks of the Sierra Madre Oriental and sprawled across a wide flood plain. A major industrial center, with a population of eighty thousand, the capital of the state of Nuevo León was second only to Mexico City. The Rio Grande was roughly a hundred miles to the north.

Outside the depot, Caballo had horses waiting. He and Garza mounted and rode through the Plaza Zaragoza, where a cathedral with a baroque façade was flanked by twin towers. They turned west on Padre Mier Avenue and proceeded to El Obispado, a massive domed structure which once housed a bishop of the church. Only last year, during campaigns across northern Mexico, Pancho Villa had made it his headquarters. The building now housed the offices of bureaucrats in Carranza's Constitutionalist government.

The office of Lieutenant Colonel Maurillio Rodriguez was located on the second floor. Rodriguez was in charge of the railroad-dispatching center for Monterrey, and controlled train transport throughout northern Mexico. He was short and heavyset, with a pencil mustache and pock-marked features. He greeted Garza with reserve.

"Your representative told me little," he said, motioning

to Caballo. "What is this matter of great importance you wish to discuss?"

Garza smiled. "I am here to make you a rich man, *Coronel*."

"How rich?"

"Ten thousand American now and ten thousand when our business is finished."

Bribery was a way of life in Mexico. The pay of army officers was paltry, and men who sought high office were inevitably corrupted by the system. Graft, if not openly condoned, was an accepted form of commerce.

Rodriguez tweaked his mustache. "What is it you wish for such generosity?"

"Trains," Garza said simply. "Sufficient transport for a thousand men on three, perhaps four, separate dates. All within the matter of a week."

"I have heard of you, Augustin Garza. Your Army of Liberation appears to have grown quite rapidly."

"Men of good faith embrace the opportunity to drive the *gringos* from Texas."

"You were a Huerta loyalist," Rodriguez said without expression. "President Carranza would have me shot for assisting you."

"Who will tell him?" Garza said, dismissing the notion. "Twenty thousand American dollars is worth such a minor risk. *Es verdad?*"

"When do you need these trains?"

"A month from now, perhaps a little more."

"Then let us say I am agreeable to your offer. If, of course, you are prepared to make payment."

Garza had carried a small valise from the train station. Two days ago he had finally revealed the full extent of his plan to Otto Mueller, and the German had readily supplied the necessary funds. He opened the valise now and placed a thick packet of American bills on the desk. Rodriguez nodded with a satisfied smile.

"I like a man who settles matters promptly. Give me a few days' notice before you need the trains."

"A pleasure doing business with you, *Coronel*. I will keep you advised."

"Just between us, I wouldn't mind killing a few *gringos* myself. *Buena suerte* on your Texas adventure."

"*Gracias*."

Some two hours later Garza and Caballo crossed a stream twelve miles south of Monterrey. A bright forenoon sun hovered over limestone mountains towering almost ten thousand feet in a cloudless sky. Las Espinas, a rancho of nearly twenty thousand hectares, lay in a spacious valley encircled by the mountains. The main *hacienda* was an adobe structure, two stories high, with wings extending north and south. Guards with Winchester rifles stood posted at the entrance.

Hilario Hinojosa welcomed them at the door. He was tall, with a beak of a nose, and a curled mustache that swept to his jawline. The former commander of Huerta's forces in Nuevo León, he had accepted amnesty from Venustiano Carranza and retired to a ranch owned by his family for generations. But he considered the amnesty merely a means of living to fight another day. His allegiance to Huerta had never faltered.

Hinojosa greeted Garza with a rough *abrazo*, the back-slapping hug of men who had shared the fortunes of war. Caballo, Hinojosa's adjutant of many years, was dismissed with an unceremonious wave. After the door closed, Hinojosa led Garza to a shady veranda in the north wing, which offered a spectacular view of the mountains. A servant brought cool drinks, *aguas frescas* with lime.

"So," Hinojosa said, tipping his glass in salute. "Your

raids on the *Norte Americanos* were a success. A good first step, eh?"

"One of many steps," Garza replied. "We have much left to accomplish."

"Do you trust the Germans?"

"No farther than I can spit. They care nothing for General Huerta, but we will use them to our own ends. A war with America will rid us of Carranza."

"And once he's gone," Hinojosa said, grinning broadly, "the general will return to reunite our country. Villa and Zapata will be as ashes in the wind."

Garza laughed. "You should see this strutting martinet I've written about, Otto Mueller. He thinks I am a simpleton, easily deceived. The fool!"

"Deception is a two-edged sword. Has he provided the funds we need?"

"*Dios mio*! The look on his face when I finally told him of our training camp here. He practically kissed me."

Garza opened the small valise at his feet. He held it out for inspection, stacks of cash glinting in the sunlight. "A hundred thousand American," he said with a sly smile. "We will drain the Germans as we would a milch cow."

Hinojosa's grin widened. "That will buy many *soldados*, my friend. Life is cheap these days."

The Mexican Revolution had impoverished tens of thousands of people. A man felt fortunate to find manual labor for five centavos an hour, and happily worked eighty hours a week. Monterrey's proximity to the border, where Texans earned as much in a day, merely fueled the fires of hatred. Hungry men would willingly fight, and die, to feed their children.

Garza closed the valise. "How many have you recruited so far?"

"Four hundred and nineteen," Hinojosa said, gesturing to the mountains. "They are camped up there, well-hidden and unseen. Caballo trains them in small units."

"We must have three or four thousand for our invasion of Texas. The Germans will provide ample funds to arm them."

"Do not concern yourself, Augustin. Now that we have the resources, I will raise our army."

"How soon?"

"A month, God willing," Hinojosa said. "Certainly by September."

"No later," Garza said firmly. "I cannot keep the Germans content with these small raids. They demand a respectable war."

"And we will give it to them, old friend."

"*Si*, I know you will not disappoint me."

"Fortune and death march to the same drummer."

Garza smiled. "Or the Army of Liberation."

They clinked their glasses in a toast to fortune. And death to the *gringos*.

Chapter Ten

Stars were sprinkled like diamond dust through a pitch-black sky. The road was faintly visible in the starlight, a narrow ribbon winding through thickets of mesquite and chaparral. The only sound was the muted thud of hoofbeats.

Luis Vasquez rode at the head of the column. Behind him were twenty men, a mix of *Tejano* and Mexican, all armed with pistols and rifles. They were approaching Rio Hondo, a town some twenty miles north of Brownsville. Their target tonight was a ranch on the Arroyo Colorado River.

Garza was still in Monterrey. Three days ago, when he'd departed Matamoras, he had left Vasquez in command and ordered raids to be conducted on July 10. Less than a week had passed since their previous raids, but he reasoned that the Rangers and the army would grow weary of constant vigilance. He felt the *gringos* needed a reminder that the Army of Liberation might strike anywhere, anytime.

Three raids were being staged tonight. Miguel Barragan, the junta leader in Brownsville, would attack the ranch of Bud Grant, outside the town of Los Indios. Grant was to be punished, hopefully killed, for providing the Rangers with horses the night of the July 4 raids. Juan Cross, Barragan's son-in-law, would assault a ranch farther upriver on the Rio Grande, west of Santa Maria. A warning would go out that those who assisted the Rangers would pay a heavy toll.

Vasquez planned to strike the ranch of Joe Scrivner. His purpose was as much his own as it was military, yet another personal score to be settled. Scrivner was the rancher from whom he'd leased grazeland along the Arroyo Colorado. When he was recruited by Garza, and moved his family to Matamoras, Scrivner had declared him in violation of their agreement for not making the July lease payment. Before he could arrange to sell his small herd, Scrivner had gotten a court order for forfeiture of the cows as recompense for a broken lease. He meant to exact from Scrivner a judgment of his own.

The ranch of Aniceto Pizana, the *Tejano* who had declined to join the Army of Liberation, was also on the Arroyo Colorado. Vasquez had briefly toyed with the idea of first calling on Pizana and enlisting him in the raid on Scrivner. Yet he recalled the day Pizana had refused Garza's offer as a junta leader, pleading the Anglos would kill his sons in retaliation. Pizana was an old and trusted friend, a man with an abiding hatred of *gringos*, but Vasquez knew his courage was weakened by fear for his children. He decided to leave Aniceto Pizana in peace.

A mile or so from Scrivner's ranch, the clatter of an automobile sounded on the road ahead. Headlamps suddenly flashed as a Model-T Ford rounded a curve and caught the horsemen in a glare of light. The driver frantically beeped his horn and the riders reined their startled horses into the brush. Vasquez cursed as two of the raiders opened fire with pistols, drilling holes through the rear fenders of the car. Then, as suddenly as it appeared, the Model-T was gone even as gunshots echoed through the still night air. The horsemen regrouped on the road.

"*Imbecils!*" Vasquez roared, gesturing wildly with his arm. "Scrivner will hear the gunfire. *Andale*! *Andale*!"

The raiders strung out behind as he whipped his horse into a gallop. A few minutes later they thundered into the ranch compound, expecting to be met by armed resistance. Instead, they found the main house dark and silent, and Scrivner's *vaqueros* milling around outside the bunkhouse. Vasquez reined his horse to a skidding halt, vaulting out of the saddle, and led several raiders into the main house. They discovered rumpled bed clothing, still warm to the touch, and signs of people overturning kitchen furniture as they hastily ran from the house. The backdoor stood wide open.

Vasquez was in a rage. He knew that Scrivner and his family, alerted by the gunshots, had escaped into the mesquite thickets not far from the rear of the house. In the darkness, with nothing more than faint starlight, a search of the dense thickets would be futile. He had fully intended to hang Scrivner and the rancher's two oldest sons, one seventeen and the other eighteen. But now, with the family hiding somewhere in acres of thorny mesquite, his long ride from the border had been for nothing. He felt like shooting somebody.

The raiders were ordered to torch every building in the compound. Scrivner's *vaqueros* were marched to the riverbank, where Vasquez waited in a mounting fury. He gave an impassioned speech about liberty and ridding Texas of *gringos*, and called on them to join in the rebellion. As flames consumed the main house and the outbuildings, they kept their eyes fixed on the ground, and not one stepped forward. He was tempted to shoot them all, but reason prevailed over anger. He cursed them for cowards and stalked away.

Luis Vasquez was a man who learned from his mistakes. On the last raid, he had stolen the horse herd, which slowed his retreat to the Rio Grande. The result was an ambush by the Rangers at the river crossing, and eight men killed. Tonight, wiser for the experience, he had the horse herd released from the corral and choused into the brush.

The compound was a blazing inferno as he led his men toward the border.

He swore he would one day return to kill Joe Scrivner.

Gordon and Maddox again rode with Captain Ransom. To the rear, in a convoy of commandeered automobiles, were the Rangers of Company A. Their destination, along rutted country roads, was Rio Hondo.

The first call had come in a few minutes before ten o'clock. A man who identified himself as Charles Winsfield reported twenty or thirty armed men on horseback. All of them were Mexican, he said, and they had fired on his car as he was leaving the ranch of his brother-in-law, Joe Scrivner. Without stopping, he'd driven to his home in Rio Hondo and called the Rangers. He was desperate with fear for his sister and her family.

Immediately afterward, calls had come in from the town marshals in Los Indios and Santa Maria. They reported attacks by Mexicans on two ranchers, with homes burned and five people killed. The raiders had retreated across the Rio Grande into Mexico, which eliminated any chance of catching them. Army patrols were already active in the area, and Ranger Company B was dispatched to investigate. Bud Grant, the rancher who had previously assisted the Rangers, was reported to have survived the attack.

Gordon had decided to investigate the incident outside Rio Hondo. The likelihood of intercepting the raiders was remote, but he nonetheless felt it might uncover new leads. He and Maddox, with Bob Ransom and Company A, commandeered cars from local businessmen and headed north. To cover any contingency, the Ranger companies under Captain Sanders and Captain Morris remained in Brownsville, held in reserve. Their concern was that more raids might occur before the night ended.

"Goddamn greasers," Ransom swore as they rattled along a dirt road. "Hit and run, and skip back across the border. Haven't got the guts to stand and fight."

"Always been that way," Maddox said. "They've been raidin' across the river since God was a pup. Nothing's changed."

"I wouldn't be so sure," Gordon said. "Garza's off to who knows where and they're still pulling raids. What's that tell you?"

"Well, maybe they're a little better organized. Garza probably left Vasquez in charge."

"Hoyt, I'd say they're a whole lot better organized."

The cars halted in the yard of Scrivner's ranch shortly before midnight. Every building in the compound had been consumed by flame, reduced to smoldering rubble. Scrivner and his wife, with their three children, stood in their night-clothes, silhouetted against the glow of embers. They were talking with a man dressed in shirt and trousers and a battered Stetson, a pistol strapped on his hip. He walked forward, a badge glinting on his chest.

"Glad you fellers got here," he said. "I'm Sam Burnett, town marshal of Rio Hondo. These folks have been hit hard."

"Captain Ransom, Texas Rangers," Ransom said. "This here's Sergeant Maddox and Special Agent Gordon. Anybody killed?"

"Wonder they wasn't," Burnett said. "Mr. Scrivner and his family lit out for the mesquite thickets. Stayed hid till it was over."

"Anybody identify the raiders?"

"Some of the *vaqueros* said the leader was Luis Vasquez. He used to run a few cows down the river a ways. Leased the land from Mr. Scrivner."

"Damn right, it's Vasquez!" Scrivner said in a loud voice. "I took his cows when he welched on the lease. Dirty bastard come back and burnt me out."

"Sorry about your loss, Mr. Scrivner." Gordon moved forward, nodding to the rancher. "We've identified Vasquez as an officer in this rebel movement, the Army of Liberation. Do you know of anyone he might have recruited from Rio Hondo?"

Scrivner scowled. "Him and Aniceto Pizana was thick as fleas. Wouldn't surprise me if they wasn't still in cahoots."

"Who's Aniceto Pizana?"

"Got a little cow outfit up the road about five miles. All the greasers hereabouts think he walks on water."

"Why is that?"

" 'Cause he don't like anybody that ain't Mex'can."

Scrivner was quick to elaborate. Pizana, he told them, was a strong advocate of *Regeneración*, the anarchist newspaper distributed from California. *Regeneración* denounced democracy as tyranny disguised, and called for abolishing private property rights to distribute the land equally to all people. Pizana had formed *grupos*, or discussion groups, among local Mexicans to preach the message of *Regeneración*. His scorn for *gringos* was known to everyone in Rio Hondo.

"The man's a rabble-rouser," Scrivner went on. "Wouldn't surprise me but what him and Vasquez are in this together. They're two of a kind."

Gordon took Maddox and Ransom aside. "What do you think?" he asked them. "Maybe we should pay this Pizana a visit."

"Bet your boots, we should," Ransom growled. "I'd lay odds he's mixed up with these raids."

"Let's not jump too quick," Maddox cautioned. "For all we know, Vasquez and his boys are over there right now. We might get ourselves ambushed in the dark."

Gordon looked at him. "You're saying tomorrow morning would be better?"

"Long about first light ought to be just right."

They agreed to spend the night at Scrivner's razed compound.

The sky was dull as pewter, the horizon tinged with the rosy hue of sunrise. On either side of the road, the land was an almost impenetrable thicket of mesquite. There was an oppressive quiet to the dewy silence of dawn.

The men were forced to stay on the road. The mesquite was impassable, the road like a tunnel through a thorny maze. They were dismounted now, leading their horses, not far from Pizana's house. Ransom led a column of Rangers on one side of the road, and Maddox led another column on the opposite side.

Sam Burnett, the town marshal, had told them the thickets opened onto an expanse of grazeland. The house was situated along the Arroyo Colorado, with the rear of the building facing the river. The front porch was perhaps fifty yards from the wall of mesquite, and there was no cover, nowhere to hide, once the thickets ended. Burnett, who was in Ransom's column, thought Pizana had only one *vaquero* on the small ranch. Whether or not Vasquez and his raiders were there was anyone's guess.

Some distance from where the road opened onto rolling grazeland, two men were left to hold the horses. The others moved forward, wary and alert, until they were at the edge of the thickets. Ransom held up his arm, and they paused to scout the clearing to their direct front. The house was silent, no one in sight, and no sign of smoke from the kitchen chimney. In a corral off to one side, six horses stood hip shot and dozing in the silty light. A mix of relief and disappointment swept through the men. Vasquez and his raiders were not there.

Then, suddenly, the crack of a rifle split the stillness. Gordon, who was behind Maddox, felt a whistling *zzzzz* as a slug seared past his head. The Ranger next in line grunted, a rosette of blood splotching his chest, and toppled into the road. The front windows of the house, which were open, erupted with muzzle flashes as two riflemen blasted away in a drumming roar. A second Ranger crumpled to the ground, and the others went flat, hugging the earth. Slugs buzzed through the mesquite like lead hornets.

"Sonsabitches!" Maddox shouted. "They sold us out."

"Who?" Gordon yelled back.

"Scrivner's *vaqueros*," Maddox said as a bullet kicked dust in his face. "Bastards warned Pizana."

"Spread out!" Ransom bellowed furiously. "Get off into the brush. Give 'em hell!"

The Rangers wiggled into the mesquite on either side of the road. They snaked along on their bellies, snagged by sharp thorns, and finally managed to spread out on a rough line at the edge of the thicket. Within moments, a withering volley from their Winchesters rent the morning, interspersed by the booming whump of Gordon and Maddox's shotguns. The windows of the house were blown out, raining shards of glass, and the front wall was pocked with a latticework of bullet holes. The house seemed to shudder under the impact of the barrage.

The rifles in the house went silent. A child screamed, a squealing bleat of terror so shrill it overrode the din of gunfire from the thicket. An instant later, a woman appeared in one of the windows, slugs plucking at the sleeves of her dress. Her arms were flung out, her face ravaged with fear.

"*No mas!*" she wailed in a crazed voice. "*Madre de Cristo! No mas!*"

The Rangers lowered their weapons, staring at the tragic figure framed in the window. "Hold your fire!" Ransom ordered. "The fight's done over, boys. Let's take that house!"

The men warily stepped out of the thickets as the woman disappeared from the window. The screams of the child racketed across the clearing as they advanced on the house, cautiously moved onto the porch. Maddox burst through the front door, his shotgun leveled, Gordon and Ransom on his heels. A dead man lay sprawled in the front room, his shirt drenched in blood, one eye punched through the back of his head by a slug. A boy of fourteen or fifteen cowered in a corner, his tear-streaked features frozen in shock. The woman crouched on the floor, her arms clutching a boy nine or ten years old. His left leg was shattered below the kneecap, his eyes glazed with pain. He moaned in terror as the Rangers stormed through the house.

Gordon pulled out his handkerchief and applied a tourniquet to the boy's leg. The boy whimpered, tears pouring down his cheeks, and the woman looked at Gordon, her eyes steely with malice. "*Barbaro!*" she cursed him savagely. "*Hijo de puta gringa!*"

The ferocity of her hatred made Gordon back away. Maddox stopped beside him, gazing down at the boy. "Damn shame," he said bitterly. "The kid catches a slug meant for his old man. Pizana's gone."

"Gone?" Gordon repeated. "Gone where?"

"Looks like he skedaddled out the back door and hit the river. I doubt we'll find him."

"How do you know it was Pizana? Who's the dead man?"

"Hired help," Maddox observed. "Burnett says he's Pizana's *vaquero*. Got himself killed for nothing."

Gordon shook his head. "We had them outnumbered

ten to one. Why did they wait and fight? Why didn't they run?"

"Well, I reckon that's the way with fanatics. I found stacks of this stuff over in the corner."

Maddox held out a handbill for the Army of Liberation and a copy of the anarchist newspaper, *Regeneración*. The headline article on the front page of the newspaper was a diatribe directed to Mexican revolutionaries. He loosely translated the opening text of the article.

" 'Monopoly of the land by the few and exploitation of the poor by the rich are the misery of the working class. Better to die on your feet than to live on your knees.' "

"Strong stuff," Gordon said. "Pizana must be a true believer."

"Yeah, I suppose," Maddox agreed. " 'Course, he didn't stick around to die."

"Maybe he will next time."

"You figure there'll be a next time?"

"Wouldn't there be for you? If somebody shot your son?"

Maddox nodded. "You're startin' to think like a Mexican."

"Hoyt, I'd say it's about time."

Chapter Eleven

Gordon awoke late that afternoon. A warm breeze ruffled the curtains on the window, and he lay for a moment staring at the ceiling. Images of the disaster at Pizana's ranch played out in his mind, and he again heard the boy's terrified screams. He thought it was all such a waste.

The boy had been taken to a doctor in Rio Hondo. Gordon and the Rangers were finishing a late breakfast at a local café when Sam Burnett returned from the doctor's office. The boy's leg was mangled from the knee down, and the doctor saw no alternative but to amputate. None of the men felt any pride in the work they'd done that day.

The Rangers returned to Brownsville late in the morning. Gordon and Maddox walked to the hotel, where they separated and went to their rooms. Neither of them had slept in some thirty hours, and the stress of the gun battle, with two Rangers killed, left them spent. Still, even though he was exhausted, Gordon tossed and turned, tangled in the sheets, his sleep restless and fitful. He couldn't shake the thought of a young boy without a leg.

The sun was dipping westward when he finally rolled out of bed. He padded barefoot into the bathroom, his bloodshot eyes staring back at him in the mirror. After he shaved, he took a long, steamy bath, all the time wondering where things had gone wrong. The three raiding parties had eluded pursuit and left behind burned-out ranches and five killed. He told himself it wasn't the way to fight a war. Or win one, for that matter.

Once he was dressed, he considered having dinner with Maddox. Then he decided against it, not certain he wanted to rehash their abortive expedition to Rio Hondo. Downstairs, he ate a solitary meal in the dining room, his vigor somewhat restored by a blood-red steak and three cups of black coffee. As he ate, his mind moved to Hector Martinez and Manuel Vargas, and the latest from across the river. He hadn't heard if Garza had returned to Matamoras.

After dinner, it occurred to him that there was no need to wait to be contacted. He could call on Guadalupe, and even if Hector and Manuel weren't there, she could brief him on the latest news. Then, amused by the thought, he admitted to himself that he would be just as happy to find Guadalupe alone. She was pleasant, undeniably attractive, and he remembered she had always made it a point to sit beside him when he'd met with the men. The night suddenly looked brighter.

Gordon weighed taking Maddox along. He finally concluded there was no reason to take Maddox, particularly if Guadalupe was alone. If there was any news of immediate value, he could relay it later, and looking at it another way, three was a crowd. Never one to fool himself, he realized he was rationalizing, cutting Maddox out in the hope that the evening might turn into something more than shoptalk. He wasn't sure it would lead to anything but he'd always been an optimist about such matters. Nothing ventured, nothing gained.

Shortly after eight o'clock, he knocked on the door of the little house by the river. Guadalupe answered, her features pleasantly surprised when she saw him standing in the spill of light from the doorway. "*Buenas noches*," she said with an engaging smile. "I didn't know you were coming by."

"Neither did I," Gordon said awkwardly. "Guess it was a spur-of-the-moment thing. Thought there might be some news."

"Please, come inside."

She stepped back and he moved into the small parlor. Antonio, her son, was on the floor, playing with his wooden pony. He laughed, climbing unsteadily to his feet, and tottered toward Gordon. She scooped the boy up in her arms.

"We didn't expect you," she said. "Hector and Manuel were here for supper, but they have returned to Matamoras. They hoped to learn more tonight."

Antonio waggled his chubby fingers, his eyes fixed on Gordon. They stared at one another a moment, and Gordon's smile dissolved into a somber expression. "Sorry," he muttered. "You were saying they hoped to learn more—?"

"*Perdoname, por favor*," she broke in. "I was just putting the baby to bed. Won't you sit down?"

"Yes, thank you."

Gordon took a seat on a small horsehair sofa. She disappeared into the bedroom, and he heard the boy making happy, unintelligible noises. His gaze strayed around the parlor, furnished with the sofa, two carved wooden chairs, and a small shrine, with a statue of the Virgin Mary, along one wall. To the rear of the room, in the dining area, the lamp on the table was extinguished. He recalled that the house was always immaculately clean.

Guadalupe returned shortly. She seated herself in one of the chairs, studying his sober look a moment. "You appear troubled," she said, genuinely concerned. "Did Antonio upset you somehow?"

"No—" Gordon faltered, passed a hand across his eyes. "I was just reminded of another boy, an older boy. He lost his leg this morning."

"The boy in Rio Hondo?"

"Yes . . . how did you know that?"

"Everyone in town has heard of it," she said in a sad voice. "The Rangers talk, and soon it is known to all *Mejicanos*. You don't blame yourself, do you?"

"No." Gordon hesitated, shook his head. "Yes, maybe I do. I keep thinking I might have done something differently. Stopped it somehow."

"You must not blame yourself. I have seen men at their worst in the *Revolución*, and the death of a child is nothing to those who make war. That is why I brought Antonio to Texas."

"Sergeant Maddox told me your husband was killed in the fighting at Matamoras. I never had the chance to say I'm sorry for your loss."

"*Con el favor de Dios.*" She crossed herself, touching her hand to her lips. "If God wills it, we must accept and go on. I cannot live in the past with my grief. Nor should you regret what you cannot change."

"Yes, that's good advice," Gordon said. "Women are wiser than men."

"Now you flatter me."

"Flattery is easy where you are concerned."

"*Señor*—"

"I would be pleased if you call me Frank. May I call you Guadalupe?"

"*Si,*" she said with a shy smile. "You asked about Hector and Manuel. There is some news."

"Oh?" Gordon said. "Has Garza returned?"

"No, he has not. But Matamoras is a place of rumor, and few secrets. There is talk he has gone to Monterrey to raise his army."

"Are these rumors to be trusted?"

"Hector believes so." She paused, her features serious. "There is another strange thing."

"Strange in what way?"

"Everyone knows of the raids last night. Luis Vasquez has not returned to Matamoras. Hector thinks that is unusual, very unlike him. Vasquez is one to crow of his victories."

"Hector may be right," Gordon agreed. "Is there talk of where Vasquez has gone?"

"*Nada*," she said simply. "He had just disappeared . . . like Garza."

"I'd have to say that's bad news. A man should keep his enemies close."

"Yes, where they can be watched."

Gordon laughed. "You prove my point. You are indeed a wise woman."

"And you are a flatterer." Her eyes sparkled with suppressed mirth. "May I offer you a cup of coffee?"

"Only if you call me Frank."

"Now you tease."

"I was never more serious in my life . . . Guadalupe."

"I will think about that," she said with a vivacious smile. "The coffee will be ready in a moment."

"I have all night."

"Now you flatter yourself."

Gordon was glad he hadn't brought Maddox.

The sun was like a fiery ball lodged in the sky. Early morning was a busy time along Elizabeth Street, with merchants opening for the day and businessmen hurrying to their offices. A burly deliveryman carried a block of ice, hooked with steel tongs, into the soda fountain shop.

Gordon and Maddox walked east toward Fort Brown. The air was redolent with the fragrance of bougainvilleas, vibrant purple and red leaves surrounding the stalks. Flocks of green parrots, perched in willow trees, sat dozing in the steamy warmth of the morning. A listless southerly breeze drifted across the river.

Maddox had thus far stifled his curiosity about last night. Over breakfast, Gordon had briefed him on the latest intelligence from Martinez and Vargas. But something in his manner, perhaps his tone of voice, betrayed him when he mentioned having met with Guadalupe alone. Maddox, though he suspected more than he'd been told, was too much the gentleman to ask.

Fort Brown was bustling with activity. On the parade ground, tents had been pitched to house the added troops posted to the garrison. Cavalry patrols, returning from a night on the border, passed mounted details headed upriver for daytime reconnaissance. Outposts on the upper Rio Grande maintained around-the-clock patrols that linked with those from Fort Brown. The 12th Cavalry Regiment now had four thousand men guarding the border.

Sergeant Major O'Meara greeted Gordon and Maddox as they entered regimental headquarters. He rapped lightly at the post commander's office and announced them as they went through the door. General Parker was seated behind his desk, reading summaries of reports telegraphed from distant field units. His features were slack, rimmed with fatigue, and he nodded to them with a tight smile. He appeared to have aged in the past ten days.

"Good morning," he said, as they seated themselves. "Sergeant Maddox, please accept my regrets for the loss of your two Rangers. Unfortunate, very unfortunate."

"Yessir, it is," Maddox said solemnly. " 'Specially since we never got within a country mile of Luis Vasquez."

"I know exactly how you feel. None of my patrols so much as caught sight of the raiders. They slip back and forth across the river like phantoms."

"General, we're lucky we only lost seven, including the Rangers. It could've been lots worse."

"No doubt you're right," Parker conceded. "What about this Pizana fellow you tracked down? Do you think he's involved with the rebellion?"

"If he's not, he will be," Maddox said. "Anybody that kills two Rangers better hightail it into Mexico."

Gordon nodded. "We feel fairly certain he's one of Garza's men, at the very least a recruiter. We found Army of Liberation handbills in his home."

"Anything new on Garza?" Parker asked. "I assume your agents still have the German consulate under surveillance."

"That's why we're here," Gordon replied. "We received a report last night that Garza's thought to be in Monterrey. There's speculation that he went there to raise a substantial number of men."

"Makes sense," Maddox added. "Monterrey's always been a hotbed of revolutionaries. He'll find plenty of men willin' to join the cause. They'd jump at the chance to kill a few gringos."

Parker looked concerned. "When you say a 'substantial number of men,' what does that mean? Do you have any idea as to a number?"

"Nothing as yet," Gordon said. "Of course, there's all this talk of invading Texas. So I think Garza would try for five hundred, probably more."

"Wouldn't that please the Germans?" Parker said acidly. "A force of five hundred crossing the Rio Grande would give the Germans exactly what they want. Congress would almost certainly declare war on Mexico."

A moment of silence fell over the three men. The prospect of war with Mexico, until now an abstract concept, suddenly seemed all too real. The raids, even with the brutal deaths of innocent people, were incidents that would eventually result in the capture or killing of those responsible. But the idea of an organized military force crossing the border raised the specter of America waging war on Mexico for the second time in less than a century. No reasonable man savored the thought of nations brought to conflict on the battlefield.

"There's more," Gordon said at length. "Our agents report that Luis Vasquez hasn't returned to Matamoras. The logical assumption would be that he's joined Garza—probably in Monterrey."

"I'd lay money on it," Maddox said firmly. "For both of them to disappear means there's something big in the works. Mexicans like to sit around and hatch a plot that'll make 'em all heroes."

"A war council?" Parker ventured. "Perhaps there's someone in Monterrey—another Huerta loyalist—working with Garza to organize a military campaign. The conspiracy might be larger than we suspected."

"Only one trouble," Maddox said. "We won't know anything till they make a move. We're operatin' in the dark."

Parker considered a moment. "Would it be possible to send your agents to Monterrey? Or is that too risky?"

"Way too risky," Maddox observed. "Martinez would be recognized by Garza and Vasquez. Vargas would tip his hand the minute he started askin' questions in a strange town. Never work."

"Hoyt's right," Gordon said. "We have to wait until Garza or Vasquez comes back to Matamoras. Odds are they will, if for no other reason than Otto Mueller. He's their conduit to the Germans."

"That reminds me," Parker said, taking an envelope from his desk drawer. "A letter came for you from Washington. It was sent to my attention."

Gordon opened the envelope. The letter was from Forrest Holbrook, head of the U.S. Bureau of Investigation. He related that Victoriano Huerta and Colonel Franz von Kleist were still in New York City, and, according to surveillance agents, the men had twice met with the utmost secrecy. There had also been another meeting between von Kleist and Alberto Flores, the representative of Pancho Villa. The mood in Washington, Holbrook noted, was one of apprehension and a high state of alert. President Wilson had authorized whatever measures necessary to avert a war with Mexico.

When Gordon finished reading the letter, he passed it around first to General Parker and then to Maddox. Parker made no immediate comment, but Maddox wagged his head with a troubled frown. "These Germans are slick customers," he said. "Workin' both ends against the middle with Villa and Garza. There'd be hell to pay if those two ever got together."

"Small chance of that," Parker remarked. "Whatever the circumstance, Villa would never trust a Huerta loyalist. Besides, he's too busy trying to overthrow Carranza."

Gordon looked puzzled. "Something about that I still don't understand. Why does Carranza allow Garza and the Army of Liberation to operate so openly? I can't believe he'd risk war with the United States."

"Actually, two reasons," Parker said. "All of Carranza's military leaders are corrupt, willing to look the other way if the price is right. General Nafarrate, the commander of the Matamoras district, is an excellent example."

"You think Garza paid him off?"

"I wouldn't be at all surprised. Particularly with the Germans bankrolling the operation. Wouldn't you agree, Sergeant Maddox?"

"Yessir, I sure would," Maddox said. "Nafarrate's a bandit in a fancy uniform. He'd sell his own mother."

"I suppose money talks," Gordon noted, again glancing at Parker. "You said there were two reasons they overlook Garza's private war."

Parker smiled grimly. "Pancho Villa is something of a tactical genius. Nafarrate, and the commander in Monterrey, have their hands full keeping him at bay. They have neither the time nor the troops to police the border—and Garza."

"Even if it leads to war with the United States?"

"I seriously doubt they believe that will happen. To them, Garza is just another rabble-rouser in a land of rabble-rousers. One more fly in the ointment."

"So we won't get any help from the Mexican government? Garza is our problem."

"I would say that sums it up rather nicely."

Gordon, with no little irony, felt like a Gypsy with a crystal ball. The future was all too clear.

Chapter Twelve

Late that morning Augustin Garza stepped off the train in Reynosa. Despite the sweltering heat in the passenger coach, he wore a jacket to conceal the pistol stuck in the waistband of his trousers. The breeze from the river was a welcome relief.

Luis Vasquez waited on the platform outside the depot. He waved to Garza with a wide grin and moved through the crowd of passengers hurrying off the train from Monterrey. Garza pulled him into a backslapping *abrazo*.

"*Hola*, Luis," he said. "*Cómo esta usted?*"

"*Muy bueno*," Vasquez replied. "All is well in Monterrey?"

"*Si, muy bien*. Hinojosa has established an excellent training camp on his ranch. He feels confident we will have at least three thousand men by early September."

"That is truly good news, *mi coronel*. And what of transport for the troops?"

Garza laughed. "Carranza's army is led by corrupt patriots. Maurillio Rodriguez, who controls the railways in Monterrey, will provide the trains we need. His greed made him cooperative."

Vasquez had horses hitched outside the depot. They mounted and rode toward a broad plaza, which was a mile or so south of the Rio Grande. Reynosa was directly across the river from Hidalgo, Texas, and some fifty miles west of Matamoras. The town cathedral was built of quarried pink stone, with figures of the twelve apostles carved in baroque style on the façade. Crowds of people moved through the stalls of open-air vendors on the plaza.

"What of the raids?" Garza asked, as they approached the plaza. "Everything happened as we planned?"

"Just as you ordered," Vasquez said. "We burned down three ranches and killed five *gringos*. All of our men escaped without injury."

"So you were able to elude the army patrols?"

"These *Americano* soldiers are like blind men once the sun goes down. They are helpless in the dark."

"Let us hope it remains so on the night we invade Texas. Who is the *jefe* we talk with today? Remind me of his name."

"Benito Sarajevo."

Vasquez led the way across the plaza. They reined to a halt before the municipal building, opposite the cathedral, and left their horses hitched outside. Benito Sarajevo, the mayor of Reynosa, was short and slim, with spectacles perched on the end of his nose. He looked up from his desk as they came through the door of his cluttered office. He peered at them over his glasses.

"*Que quieres*?" he said waspishly. "What do you want? Can't you see I'm busy?"

Garza gave him a riveting look. "I am Colonel Augustin Garza, commander of the Army of Liberation. You have heard of me?"

"*Si*," Sarajevo said. "I have seen your handbills and know of your raids over the river. Why are you here?"

"We are building a camp outside town. There will be many men there, and you will hear of this. You may think it wise to inform the authorities."

"What is this camp for?"

"Do not concern yourself," Garza said. "Nor should you feel obligated to speak of it to anyone. *Comprende*?"

Sarajevo sat rigid and erect. "I do not take orders from you, *señor*. Get out!"

"Luis, explain it to him."

Vasquez pulled a pistol from beneath his jacket. He placed the muzzle between Sarajevo's eyes. "Your silence will buy your life, little man. Do I make myself clear?"

Sarajevo blinked behind his spectacles. "*Si*," he whispered in a shaky voice. "*Yo entiendo*."

"Think of it as a blessing," Garza said, motioning Vasquez aside. "We will bring business to your merchants, for supplies are needed and there are men to feed. Everyone prospers, *es verdad*?"

"True," Sarajevo agreed quickly. "Prosperity is a good thing."

"Tell the people of your village not to talk of our camp with outsiders. Anyone who speaks of our presence should do so with his rosary beads in hand. Do you take my meaning?"

"*Sin falta*," Sarajevo said, bobbing his head. "My people will cause you no problems, *señor*. I will see to it."

"I knew we could count on your cooperation. *Muchas gracias*."

Outside, Garza and Varquez rode south from the plaza. An hour or so later, they turned west along a rushing stream and soon came to a copse of trees bordered by broken limestone hills. Miguel Barragan and Juan Cross, along with the cadre of raiders, were clearing brush and constructing scattered fire pits for cooking. Everyone briefly stopped work while Garza moved among them, shaking hands and congratulating them on the recent raids. The men treated him with the respect reserved for a commander who led them into battle with no thought for his own safety.

Vasquez then took him on a walking tour of what was to be the staging area for the invasion of Texas. He explained that he had chosen the site for its proximity to the railway line, which was slightly more than two miles to the east. The trains from Monterrey could be stopped south of Reynosa, and the men marched to the bivouac encampment along the stream. There was ample water, graze beyond the hills for a horse herd, and the location was removed from farms and ranches in the countryside. All things considered, it was the best site he'd found to suit their needs.

"You have done well," Garza complimented him. "We will camp here for two days, three at the most. No longer than it takes to organize our brigade for the attack on Texas."

"We will need horses," Vasquez said. "How do we go about buying so many mounts without arousing suspicion?"

"I have arranged that with Hinojosa. The horses will be purchased from distant *rancheros* in Nuevo Leon and trailed here. We cannot have three or four thousand mounted men seen on the road from Monterrey."

"*Caramba*, that never occurred to me! Carranza's troops would believe Pancho Villa was again on the march. You think of everything, *mi coronel*."

"I try, Luis."

Late that afternoon, one of the men, a cook in his former life, prepared supper for the raiders. The meal was simple fare, suitable for cooking over an open fire, all of it purchased at the plaza in Reynosa. He served *tortillas, frijoles*, and *cabrito*, kid goat roasted on spits. The men devoured everything, hungry after a day of hard work in the blistering sun. Coffee, sweetened with lumps of brown sugar, was their dessert.

Dusk found them grouped around fires, seated on handwoven wool serapes that served as bedding during the night. Garza sat talking with his commanders, the men smoking and sipping coffee as darkness settled over the land. Barragan was in his early forties, a hard man who rarely smiled, and Cross, his mixed-blood son-in-law, looked more Negro than Mexican. Vasquez listened as Garza finished briefing the two men on the training camp outside Monterrey.

"We will have a brigade of cavalry," Garza said. "I plan to cross the river in early September, and we will destroy everything in our path. Thousands of *Tejanos* will join our ranks when our strength becomes known."

"And the *Americano* soldiers?" Barragan asked. "They have now been reinforced, and even more are stationed on the upper Rio Grande. How do we overcome their numbers?"

"We will hit and run, Miguel. Strike where they are weakest, and choose the time and place for battle. We will defeat them with the guerrilla tactics of light cavalry that lives off the land."

"I wish the attack was tomorrow, *mi coronel*."

"Tomorrow will come soon enough." Garza glanced across the fire at Cross. "Tell me, Juan, have you been talking with the Negro people? Will they join our cause when we invade Texas?"

"I am sure of it," Cross said earnestly. "Their hatred of *gringos* is no less than ours. They await only a signal that we will wage war in strength."

"Then we must give them hope in the days ahead. Until the brigade arrives, we will take the fight to our enemies. Even more raids than before!"

Garza told them how death would be visited on Texas.

Garza returned to Matamoras the next afternoon. As he stepped off the train, he marked the date at July 15. He felt he'd accomplished a great deal in the month since his first meeting with the Germans. Soon, he told himself, the Army of Liberation would truly be an army.

Outside the depot he brushed past a street vendor sell-ing cigars and cigarettes to people on the platform. The train station was busy, and one more vendor hawking wares failed to arouse his attention. He moved through the crowd, unaware that the vendor followed a short distance behind. He walked toward the plaza.

A short time later he approached the house on Calle 5. He thought of it as a headquarters more than a home, and he'd left one of his men to speak with those who inquired about the Army of Liberation. For now, though, he was intent on a shave and a change of clothes before he called on Otto Mueller at the consulate. He hurried through the door.

The front room served as the headquarters office, and his man was seated at a crude wooden desk. Another man rose from a chair along the wall and moved forward with a sad smile and an outstretched hand. Garza was at first surprised, then shocked, when he recognized the man as Aniceto Pizana. He thought his friend looked haggard, somehow aged.

"*Valgame Dios*!" he said, accepting the handshake. "I did not expect to see you here, Aniceto."

Pizana lifted his arms in a weary shrug. "Much has happened since we last met. I have come to join your fight for freedom."

"You are welcome, *compadre*, most welcome. But your eyes tell me things are not well. *Verdad*?"

"*Si, muy malo.*"

Pizana went on to relate details of the raid on his home. He explained how he'd been falsely accused by John Scrivner, a neighboring rancher, and the gun battle that followed with the Texas Rangers. His youngest son had been grievously wounded, losing a leg to a surgeon's knife, and he was waiting for the boy's recovery before moving his family to Mexico. He had escaped after his *vaquero* was killed and made his way across the border, hiding by day and traveling at night. He was here now to enlist in the struggle for liberation.

"I want to fight," he concluded, his eyes fierce with hate. "I will give my life to drive the *gringos* from Texas."

"*Dios no se acobarda,*" Garza said. "God does not flinch. Nor will we in our fight for liberty. We will avenge your son's loss."

"I serve at your command, *mi coronel*. How can I assist in the cause?"

"Aniceto, I hereby commission you a *capitán* in the Army of Liberation. You will lead a company of men in our war on the *yanqui imperialistas*."

Garza got him quartered in a bedroom at the rear of the house. While he was shaving and changing clothes, he briefed Pizana on the pact with the Germans, and how, very soon, a trained army would march on Texas. He explained that Luis Vasquez would return in a week or so, and they would then plan a series of raids across the river. He left Pizana reeling with the possibilities for revenge.

Shortly before three o'clock, Garza walked around the corner to the German Consulate. His mind was on more weighty matters, and he again failed to notice the street vendor who trailed him on the opposite side of Calle Morelos. A servant admitted him at the door of the consulate, and he followed the hall to Mueller's office. Mueller looked up from his desk with a sharp frown.

"Well, Herr Garza, you finally grace us with your presence. Where have you been for the last week?"

"Monterrey," Garza said, seating himself in a chair. "I told you of my trip before I left."

"Yes, but you said nothing of being gone so long. What have you to report?"

"The training camp outside Monterrey is now operational, and railroad transport has been arranged to the border. We will have a brigade of at least three thousand men by early September."

"*Mein Gott!*" Mueller barked. "September is six weeks away. We need action now!"

"There is a Mexican proverb," Garza said calmly. "*Un cabello hace sombra.* Even a hair casts a shadow."

"Do not try my patience with riddles. What is your point?"

"Today you see a shadow and tomorrow you will see an army."

"Indeed!" Mueller said with heavy sarcasm. "September is not tomorrow."

Garza ignored the gibe. "I have just come from Reynosa, where we are clearing a staging area for the attack. The brigade will be transported there by train—in September."

"Your army crawls like a centipede to war, Herr Garza. What are your plans in the meantime?"

"Vasquez and our men will return from Reynosa before too long. I intend to conduct more raids into Texas."

"You and your raids," Mueller said in a sour tone. "Germany expects more for its financial support."

Garza stared at him. "I will need arms and munitions for four thousand men. No later than one month from today."

"A moment ago you said three thousand men."

"The shadow of the hair grows larger, *señor.* We must plan for four thousand."

"Very well, you will have your arms."

"*Gracias.*"

The conversation ended on that note. When Garza was gone, Mueller began drafting a report to Colonel von Kleist. He labored to put the best face on the situation, all too aware that von Kleist would not be pleased by further delay. As he wrote, he silently cursed Garza and the plodding pace of the Army of Liberation. He thought it small wonder the Mexican Revolution dragged on endlessly.

Mueller finished the report late that afternoon. The envelope would be placed in a diplomatic pouch, and carried by courier on a train to the German embassy in New York. With the round-trip travel time, Mueller calculated he would not receive a reply for at least ten days. By then, he hoped he would have more promising news, though he couldn't imagine what it would be. September now seemed the earliest he could deliver a war.

The one consolation to the delay was Maria Dominguez. Every night, at the dinner club in the Bezar Hotel, he watched her performance. His customary table was now permanently reserved, and the staff in the club treated him with deferential respect. Few men, he often reflected, were so fortunate, or so envied. There were no secrets among the hotel staff, or the club's regular patrons. Everyone knew he was sleeping with the most beautiful woman in Matamoras.

The affair was not without its burdens. Mueller had gone from sending her roses to buying her expensive gifts, mainly clothes and jewelry. She never asked directly but rather dropped subtle hints that the price of her affection was an occasional visit to the more exclusive shops on the plaza. By now, Mueller was so infatuated by her charms that no cost seemed too great. He was slowly spending himself into poverty.

That night, in his hotel suite, he gave her a black pearl ring. Her eyes went round with delight, and she threw herself into his arms. She peppered his face with kisses.

"*Caro mio*," she said in a breathless voice. "You make me so happy."

Mueller no longer cared that the warmth of her affection was enhanced by presents. He pulled her closer in a tight embrace. "How happy are you?"

"You wicked man." She vamped him with a vixen's smile and led him toward the bedroom. "Come, let me show you."

Later, their ardor spent, she lay curled with her head on his chest. She was asleep, her breath even and soft, but Mueller stared at the ceiling fan swirling in lazy circles. He thought he'd never known a woman so passionate, so devoid of inhibition in bed. A welter of claw marks on his back bore testament to her fiery nature, and it passed through his mind that the pearl ring was a good investment. Something on account for the future.

He idly wondered if she would like Berlin.

Chapter Thirteen

The last rays of sunset faded on the horizon as dusk settled over Brownsville. The lamplights flickered on, casting a sallow glow all along Elizabeth Street. A streetcar pulled away from the corner, trundling west into deepening nightfall.

Gordon and Maddox entered the hotel. They had just come from yet another meeting at Fort Brown, and their mood was solemn. The date was August 2, and as General Parker had noted, they were in a state quite close to suspended animation. The last raids had occurred something more than three weeks ago.

The dining room was crowded for a Monday night. They took a table near the window and listlessly surveyed the menu. Maddox ordered meat loaf, and Gordon finally decided on veal cutlets smothered in cream gravy, a dish he'd never heard of before coming to Texas. He'd also developed a taste for sweetened iced tea.

Neither of them spoke after the waitress took their orders. Their glum manner was that of men assigned to fight a war only to discover that their enemy had withdrawn from the battlefield. Since July 11, when three ranchers had been burned out, the Army of Liberation had vanished without a trace. Everyone was at a loss as to the reason, and communiqués from Washington demanding an explanation merely aggravated the problem. There were no ready answers.

The waitress returned with their plates. Gordon never ceased to be surprised that he actually liked the cutlets, which were breaded and fried and then lathered with a thick gravy. Maddox, who consumed anything that wasn't still twitching, dug into his meat loaf with an appetite that belied his mood. They ate in silence, lost in their own thoughts, hardly aware of the conversation of diners at nearby tables. Finally, Maddox paused, a wad of mashed potatoes loaded onto his fork, and looked up. His eyes were marbled with disgust.

"This waitin's pure hell," he said. "I'd lots sooner be swappin' lead with the bastards."

Gordon nodded. "I feel the same way myself."

"Know what it reminds me of?"

"What's that?"

"The time the nigger soldiers shot up Brownsville."

Once again, Gordon was struck by the prejudice so prevalent among the Rangers. He never said anything, for he wasn't about to change views so deeply ingrained by racial tension on the border. Instead, he speared a chunk of veal and tried to appear interested.

"Are you talking about soldiers from Fort Brown?"

"You mean you never heard of that?"

"No, I can't say as I have."

"Well, pardner, it was one helluva mess."

Maddox warmed to the tale. On a moonless night in the summer of 1906, several Negro soldiers of the Twenty Fifth Infantry went on a rampage. The direct cause of the incident was racial tension between townspeople and black troops stationed at Fort Brown. The soldiers ran amuck along Elizabeth and Washington Streets, indiscriminately firing rifles into the homes of whites. Two townspeople were killed and five were wounded.

President Theodore Roosevelt ordered an investigation. The Texas Rangers, working with the army's Criminal Investigation Division, determined that Negro soldiers had indeed attacked white citizens of Brownsville. Yet the black troops closed ranks, and despite intense questioning refused to identify the soldiers responsible. Teddy Roosevelt had the entire company placed under arrest, and ordered their transfer to Fort Sam Houston in San Antonio. A month later all the soldiers in the unit were dishonorably discharged from the United States Army.

"Ask me, they got off light," Maddox concluded. "Should've hung some of the bastards."

Gordon looked confused. "What's that got to do with our situation?"

"Niggers and greasers, six of one and half a dozen of another. Anybody that kills white people ought to have his neck stretched."

Maddox went back to his meat loaf. Gordon was tempted to point out the difference between a handful of angry soldiers and revolutionaries backed by the German military. But he knew it would be a waste of breath, an argument of reason against intractable bias. He had other things on his mind.

Three weeks ago Manuel Vargas had reported Garza's return to Matamoras. Since then, Garza had frequently been seen entering the German Consulate, presumably for meetings with Otto Mueller. He had also been seen in the company of a man who was now quartered at the house on Calle 5. Vargas, through discreet inquiry at the nearby *cantina*, had been able to identify the man. His name was Aniceto Pizana.

Gordon was hardly surprised. He recalled the raid on Pizana's house, and the young boy, Pizana's son, who'd had his leg amputated. Clearly, in the aftermath of the raid, Pizana had made his way to Matamoras and joined the Army of Liberation. The fact that he was living at the headquarters on Calle 5, and often seen in the company of

Garza, led to an obvious and disturbing conclusion. Pizana was now one of the leaders in the rebel movement.

Last night, Vargas had reported the return of Luis Vasquez to Matamoras. Vasquez had been gone almost four weeks, and the purpose of his absence, or where he'd been, was still unknown. But his return, and Garza's frequent meetings with Mueller, seemed a signal that action of some sort was imminent. Gordon was reluctant to send Hector Martinez to Matamoras, for his appearance so soon after Vasquez's return might somehow seem suspect. Yet, given the circumstances, he saw it as an acceptable risk. Martinez was their only chance at gathering needed intelligence.

Maddox pushed away his plate. He rolled a cigarette and lit up in a haze of smoke. "I'm meeting Ransom and some of the boys for a drink. You're welcome to come along."

"Thanks all the same," Gordon said. "I believe I'll try to catch Martinez and send him across the river. We have to find out what Garza's planning."

"Yeah, we're sure as hell fumblin' around like blind men. You want me there?"

"No, go ahead and meet Ransom. I can explain what's needed to Hector."

Maddox exhaled a streamer of smoke. "Hector might not be around." He paused, his eyes glinting with sardonic amusement. " 'Course, his sister could always take the message."

Over the past several weeks Gordon had visited Guadalupe's house three or four times a week. On occasion, he asked Maddox along, more of a courtesy than a necessity. By now, Maddox treated his solitary visits to the house by the river as something of an unspoken joke between friends. They both knew he rarely went there to see Hector Martinez or Manuel Vargas.

Maddox went off to join his Ranger friends for a drink.

Gordon took the stairs to his room, where he changed to a fresh shirt, combed his hair, and splashed his jawline with bay rum. By eight o'clock, he was standing before the door of the house and Guadalupe answered his knock. When he stepped inside, she kissed him on the mouth and lightly caressed his face with her fingers. Her dark, flirtatious eyes shone with merriment.

"Hector and Manuel are not here. Are you disappointed?"

"No, not at all," Gordon said with a gravelly chuckle. "I have an assignment for Hector, but you can tell him. Actually, I came to see Antonio."

"Of course," she said, rolling her eyes with a delightful little laugh. "Why else would you be here?"

Antonio squealed when Gordon entered the parlor. They were by now fast friends and playmates, and Gordon lifted him high overhead and swung him around in fits of giggles. Then he got down on the floor with the boy, listening attentively as he jabbered away, proudly showing off his toys. Within the hour his energy flagged and he yawned, leaning against Gordon, his eyes sleepy. Guadalupe carried him off to bed.

When she returned, Gordon was seated on the sofa. She sat down beside him and quickly kissed him on the cheek. "*Querido mio*," she said in a soft, throaty voice. "You are a good man."

"Who, me?" Gordon asked with mock surprise. "What makes you say that?"

"Oh, my son is an excellent judge of men. Just like his mother."

She settled into his arms and he kissed her long and tenderly. The sofa was small but they managed to stretch out and lay close. She murmured an endearment and nibbled his ear.

He reminded himself to tell her what he needed from Hector. Later.

Early the next morning, the train from Washington to New York pulled into Grand Central Station. Colonel Franz von Kleist stepped off a passenger coach and hurried along the platform. He was carrying a small overnight bag.

Von Kleist had traveled to Washington yesterday for meetings with the German Ambassador to the United States. Communiqués from the German General Staff, invoking the displeasure of Emperor Kaiser Wilhelm, had expressed concern for the delays in Mexico. As he went up the stairs to the main terminal, von Kleist was still stinging from the reprimand he'd received in Washington. He had been forced to justify continued funding for the mission.

Grand Central Station was a masterwork of functional design. The beaux-arts architecture, a mass of brick and granite, was an airy colossus completed before the turn of the century. The central chamber rose nearly two hundred feet high, with vaulted arches above massive stained-glass windows. The marble floor was immense and the constellations of the zodiac, gold against blue on the ceiling, gave it a kaleidoscope effect. The impression was like that of a vast amphitheater reaching for the stars.

Von Kleist hardly noticed. His thoughts were on Captain Otto Mueller, and the scathing telegram he planned to have encoded and fired off to Matamoras. The German General Staff, when informed of Mueller's latest estimate for action, had responded with a deadline of September 15 for war on the Texas-Mexico border. The ambassador in Washington, the highest German official in the United States, had delivered the message in blunt terms. Von Kleist would be recalled to Berlin and retired in disgrace unless the mission was completed. The honorable thing, if that happened, would be to shoot himself.

Outside the terminal, von Kleist took a taxicab to the Waldorf-Astoria hotel. Before departing Washington, he had wired ahead and arranged a meeting with Victoriano Huerta. On the tenth floor a manservant admitted him to a suite lavishly appointed with Louis XIV furnishings and a sweeping view of the New York skyline. For a moment, upon entering the sitting room, he reflected that Huerta was living in grand style at the expense of the German war effort. Then, with a force of will, he focused on the immediate, if somewhat onerous, task.

Huerta greeted him warmly. "*Buenos dias*, my dear Colonel von Kleist. How good to see you again."

"*Generalissimo*," von Kleist said with a perfunctory handshake. "I have just come from the German Embassy in Washington. The news is not good."

"I regret to hear that, Colonel. Please, won't you have a seat."

A sofa and chairs were grouped by an ornate marble fireplace. After they were seated, von Kleist went straight to the point. "The situation in Mexico has become intolerable. Delay upon delay and no end to it. We cannot continue in this manner."

Huerta smiled indulgently. "I received a letter only yesterday from Augustin Garza. He assures me a major attack will take place by early September."

"Garza's assurances have little currency. Captain Mueller says he is a man of many excuses."

"On the contrary, Garza has a gift for organization and logistics. We will field a brigade of cavalry for the invasion of Texas."

"I will be frank," von Kleist said stolidly. "My superiors have established a deadline of September 15 for the attack. In the event it does not occur, all funding for your return to power will cease." He paused to underscore the words. "No excuse will be acceptable beyond that date."

"Have no fear," Huerta said without concern. "The campaign will begin well before your deadline. In fact, there will be simultaneous action on two fronts. I waited to advise you until my plans were complete."

Huerta quickly elaborated. Pascual Orozco, one of his former generals, was even now organizing loyalist forces who had found sanctuary around El Paso and southern New Mexico. Orozco, who had distinguished himself against Carranza's army, was a brilliant field commander. In 1914, when Huerta went into exile in Spain, Orozco had taken refuge in the Mexican district of El Paso. His loyalist force would be comprised of two thousand veteran soldiers, perhaps more.

"I will lead the attack myself," Huerta went on. "We will strike along the upper Rio Grande even as Garza invades southern Texas."

Von Kleist was momentarily taken aback. In all their planning sessions, Huerta had never once mentioned a military campaign on the upper Rio Grande. Yet it was clear that the Mexican was not only a conniving old fox, but a master strategist as well. A coordinated attack on two fronts would impress the German General Staff as nothing short of genius. He silently explored ways that he might take credit for the idea.

" 'Fortune is ally to the bold,' " he said. "Virgil wrote that when Rome ruled the world. I think it is a fitting motto for our enterprise."

"*Si*," Huerta said, nodding sagely. "One that will speed my rule of Mexico."

"Indeed so, *Generalissimo*. Once we divert America's attention from Europe, you will be free to engage Carranza's army. And need I say, Germany will underwrite your swift fight to victory."

"I envisioned nothing less, Colonel."

Von Kleist left the hotel with his spirits restored. On the way to the German Embassy, he began composing the communiqué he would dispatch to General Alexis Baron von Fritsch, in Berlin. He imagined a summary of the message channeled through the chain of command to Field Marshal Heinrich von Luettwitz, and then to Kaiser Wilhelm himself. Worded properly, the communiqué would bring praise from the Emperor for a strategic gambit he'd heard only ten minutes ago. The upshot might very well be a promotion, and the sound of it made his ears ring.

General Franz von Kleist. *General*!

Late that afternoon he met with Felix Mendoza. Pancho Villa's emissary frequently traveled east to purchase arms and munitions for the *Villistas'* interminable war with Carranza. Von Kleist, as promised in their initial meeting, was providing $50,000 a month in support, and had already rendered $100,000 in funds. The date was August 3, and Mendoza was there to collect the latest payment. His manner was almost obsequious.

"General Villa sends you his most cordial regards. He often says you are the savior of the *Revolución*."

"Hardly that," von Kleist said with feigned modesty. "Our agreement included a quid pro quo that has nothing to do with your revolution. I'm sure you recall the terms."

"*Si, mi coronel*," Mendoza replied. "You wish *Villistas* to raid across the Rio Grande—disguised as *bandidos*."

"How much have I provided General Villa to date?"

"Why, one hundred thousand American. Surely you remember the amount."

"And have I requested anything in return, so far?"

"No, *mi coronel*." Mendoza's eyes narrowed in a shrewd look. "But I think you are about to tell me something. Am I correct?"

Von Kleist consulted a calendar on the wall. Then he

placed an envelope stuffed with bank notes on his desk. "Fifty thousand for August," he said, "and another fifty thousand on September 1. Are you following me?"

"*Si.*"

"And I want General Villa to begin his raids on September 17. Agreed?"

"Does the date have particular significance?"

"Nothing that need concern you or General Villa."

Mendoza pocketed the envelope. "General Villa is a man of his word, *mi coronel*. I will convey your wishes."

"Excellent."

September 17 was an arbitrary date. Von Kleist thought it would coincide closely with the date of Garza's invasion of Texas and Huerta's campaign on the upper Rio Grande. Villa's raids, even if a few days late, would pour oil on an already incendiary situation. America would declare war on Mexico.

All the contingencies, von Kleist told himself, were covered. Huerta and Villa might join forces to oust Carranza, or the triumvirate might join to defend Mexico against America. Whatever the case, no matter who ruled Mexico, the end result would be the same. America would look to its own security, and away from Europe.

Von Kleist thought it had been a remarkable day. By the middle of September, he would have accomplished something few men aspired to, or envisioned possible. Something that would leave his mark for all time.

He would bring war to America.

Chapter Fourteen

A sickle moon hung lopsided in the sky. Low clouds scudded past on a warm breeze, at times obscuring the moon and leaving the earth dappled with light. Stars were scattered like chips of ice against dark muslin.

On the night of August 4, Luis Vasquez crossed the Rio Grande. He led twenty horsemen, a mix of Mexicans and *Tejanos*, all of them armed with pistols and carbines. Their objective was Santa Maria, a town two miles north of the river and some thirty miles west of Brownsville. The patchy glow of the moon lighted their way.

Other raids were also in progress. Miguel Barragan and a party of twenty men were assigned to destroy railroad bridges east and west of La Paloma. Juan Cross and his band would attack the village of Carricitos, and attempt to recruit many of the Negro farm workers who lived there. Aniceto Pizana led thirty men, the largest contingent, for he might have to fight his way back across the border. He was raiding a ranch outside Rio Hondo.

A scout awaited Vasquez on the north bank of the river. Army patrols were increasingly active along the border, and he'd sent a man ahead to assess the situation. The scout reported that a mounted patrol had passed by, moving upriver, not quite a half hour ago. The patrol was in squad strength, nine troopers, and all of them seemed asleep in the saddle. Lethargy and boredom were at work, for there had been no raids in over three weeks.

Santa Maria was on the railway line that served towns scattered along the border. There were farms and ranches throughout the countryside, and the town, though small, was a trade center for the area. The railroad depot was on the southern edge of the community, with a main street extending several blocks to the north. There were homes on the side streets to the east and west, and a grain elevator north of the business district. With midnight approaching, the town was dark.

The Merchants & Grangers Bank occupied the southeast corner of the main intersection. Part of Vasquez's assignment tonight was to rob the bank, which would further unsettle the economy and bring added hardship to Anglo farmers and ranchers. He posted men to watch the street while others tore down a hitching post and used it as a battering ram to force the door. One of his men, who had learned demolitions in the *Revolución*, planted sticks of dynamite around the steel door of the vault. He lit the fuse and they quickly retreated outside.

The explosion rocked the entire town. Dogs started howling and lights began flickering on in houses surrounding the business district. The interior of the bank was demolished and the vault door was blown across the room, collapsing part of the front wall. Vasquez and three men climbed through the rubble, looting the vault, and stuffed gunnysacks with stacks of cash. As they came out of the bank, townspeople appeared from the side streets, many carrying rifles and shotguns. The raiders opened fire, and one of the townsmen fell dead by a hardware store on the opposite corner.

Vasquez ordered his men to get mounted. The fighting became general as more and more townspeople appeared from the darkness, drawn by the explosion and the sound of gunfire. A shotgun boomed, and one of the raiders toppled out of the saddle, pitching backward onto the ground.

The others reined their horses around, spraying lead in every direction, and rode south. The townsmen took cover at the sides of buildings and in doorways, and the length of the business district suddenly became a gauntlet. Another raider threw up his arms at the crack of a rifle and tumbled off his horse.

Halfway down the street, Vasquez shouted a command. The bank was but part of the night's mission, the other part still to be completed. He needed to buy time and he ordered twelve men to fight a rearguard action. They obeyed without question, wheeling their horses around, and delivered a hammering volley upstreet. Nine townsmen were caught in the open, running toward the riders, and four of them slumped dead to the ground. The others scurried for cover, joining those who hadn't left the protection of the buildings. The raiders gave way slowly, losing another man in the exchange of gunfire. They retreated toward the train depot.

Vasquez waited with six men formed in a skirmish line. The depot was closed for the night, and his demolitions expert was hurriedly placing dynamite charges around the base of the building. As the rear guard fell back, the men on the skirmish line opened up with carbines in a rolling drumbeat of rapid fire. The townsmen ducked, holding their cover, slugs thunking into stores and shattering windowpanes all along the street. Then, in the midst of splitting gunfire, Vasquez's voice rose above the racket.

"*Vamonos!*" he shouted. "*Andale! Andale!*"

The raiders, all of them now mounted, followed him at a clattering gallop over the railroad tracks. An instant later the train depot seemed to lift off its foundation in a thunderous explosion, and then disintegrated within the vortex of a towering fireball. Debris and flaming timbers rained down out of the sky as the horsemen vanished into the night.

The people of Santa Maria slowly emerged from their hiding places. Five of their neighbors lay dead and their train station had been reduced to a smoking pyre. None of them doubted who was responsible. Nor were they unaware of what it meant.

The Army of Liberation was again on the march.

The embers of a cooking fire glowed under the pale sickle moon. Five tents stood pitched in the yard of what was once the Scrivner ranch compound. The house and the outbuildings were now piles of charred rubble.

Joe Scrivner and his two sons slept in one tent. His wife and daughter shared another, while a third served as a makeshift kitchen. The four *vaqueros* made do with the other two tents, which were pitched off near the corral. The family's tents were close to the cool waters of the Arroyo Colorado.

Scrivner crawled out of his tent somewhere around midnight. He was troubled by an overactive bladder and generally had to relieve himself two or three times a night. As he stood on the bank of the river, steamy piss splashing the rippling water, he looked at the ruins of his home in the sallow moonlight. Carpenters from Rio Hondo were finally to start rebuilding tomorrow, and he thought it was none too soon. He was tired of living in a tent.

A strange sound caught his attention. He shook his pud, lowering the front of his nightshirt, and turned back to the tents. For a moment, squinting in the faint moon glow, he was hardly able to credit his eyes. What appeared to be thirty or more horsemen sat their mounts before the dull embers of the cook fire. He was momentarily dumbstruck, overcome by an urge to jump in the river and swim away. Then he realized he couldn't desert his family.

"Who's there?" he said, walking forward. "What d'you want?"

One of the riders dismounted. "Don't you recognize an old friend, *hombre*? I have come back."

"Pizana?" Scrivner peered closer. "Aniceto Pizana?"

"*Si*, you do remember, eh? Luis Vasquez and I tossed a coin to see who would have the honor. I won."

"What're you talking about? Honor of what?"

"Why, the honor of holding court for your crimes. I am here for justice."

"What crimes?" Scrivner demanded. "Get the hell off my land."

" Oh, I think not," Pizana said with cheerful menace. "I am now a *capitán* in the Army of Liberation. You have much to answer for, *señor*."

Pizana rapped out a command. His men dismounted, some moving into the tents and others gathering armloads of firewood. Scrivner's wife, his two sons, and his daughter were roughly forced outside in their nightclothes. The four *vaqueros*, their faces taut with fear and wearing droopy long johns, were pushed off to one side. Within minutes, a roaring bonfire lighted the yard. Pizana motioned for silence.

"Señor Scrivner," he said impassively. "You are accused of betraying a peaceful man—that would be me—to the Texas Rangers. Do you admit your guilt?"

"Hell, no!" Scrivner flared. "I don't admit nothin'."

"Maybe you remember Jose Zamora? The *vaquero* who worked for you?"

"Zamora quit the night my place got burned down. What about him?"

"Jose ran all the way to my *ranchero* that night. He told me of your quick treachery, your hate. He warned me the Rangers were coming at dawn."

"Zamora's a liar," Scrivner said. "He always was."

Pizana looked at the *vaqueros*, who stood huddled in their long johns. "What do you say, *amigos*?" he asked. "Is Jose Zamora a liar?"

The *vaqueros* kept their heads bowed, their eyes on the ground. A turgid moment of silence slipped past, then Pizana turned back to Scrivner. "You are the liar," he said in a hard, cold voice. "Because of you, my son lost his leg, and my friend and *vaquero*, Esteban Ferrua, lost his life. I find you guilty of these crimes."

"You're *loco*," Scrivner growled. "You've got no right to judge me."

"No, don't you see, you are wrong, *hombre*. I have judged you."

Pizana nodded to his men. Several of the raiders grabbed Scrivner and his two sons and shoved them to the edge of the riverbank. Helen Scrivner screamed, and her daughter, who looked to be fourteen or fifteen, burst out in tears. Scrivner glowered at Pizana.

"Leave my boys be," he snapped. "They're no part of this."

"Yes, I'm afraid they are," Pizana said. "The Army of Liberation requires the execution of any Texan over the age of sixteen." He paused, glancing at the youngsters. "John is seventeen, as I recall, and Paul is eighteen."

"Merciful Jesus!" Helen Scrivner cried, struggling against the men who restrained her. "They're only boys! Children!"

"I have my orders, *señora*."

"You sorry sonovabitch!" Scrivner bellowed. "You'll roast in hell for this!"

"I think you are probably right, *hombre*."

Pizana ordered six of his men to form a firing squad. At his command, they raised their carbines, and when he dropped his arm, they fired. The impact of the slugs knocked Scrivner and his sons off their feet and they lurched backward over the riverbank into the water. The current caught them, their bodies bobbing on the surface, and swiftly carried them downstream. Helen Scrivner moaned like a terrified animal, and her daughter stood frozen in shock. The four *vaqueros* kept their eyes fixed on the ground.

The raiders mounted on Pizana's signal. They rode south from the bonfire and the tents and the eerie, shrieking wail of a woman gone mad. Pizana told himself it had been a dirty night's work, and one best quickly put behind. But he knew he would never outdistance a father's curse. A dead man's last words.

He would surely roast in hell.

Garza emerged from the house on Calle 5 around nine the following morning. His pace was brisk and his stride confident as he walked toward the corner. He was quite pleased with last night's raids.

Vasquez and Pizana had returned to the house only an hour before. Barragan and Cross, whose names were still unknown to the American authorities, had retired to their homes in Brownsville. The rest of the men had dispersed, ordered to resume their normal activities until the next call to action. German funds ensured that they were well paid and loyal, and Garza refused to think of them as mercenaries. They were, in his view, patriots all.

Over the past hour Vasquez and Pizana had briefed him on the raids. He was delighted that Vasquez had returned with more than $11,000 from the bank at Santa Maria. A war chest independent of German funds provided for unforeseen contingencies. Yet he was even more pleased with the report delivered by Pizana. Until a man proved himself in the field, there was always a niggling doubt as to his competence as a leader. The executions performed by Pizana—with a firing squad, no less!—had removed all doubt.

A few minutes after nine Garza entered the German Consulate. He resented having to report to Otto Mueller, even when the news he brought was of a positive nature. But the Germans were financing the Army of Liberation, and so far, with cash disbursements and war materials supplied, he estimated their expenditures at somewhere near a half-million dollars. To return General Huerta to power, someone had to pay the piper, and he'd been assigned the job. He cautioned himself, as he did with some frequency, not to offend Mueller.

Down the hall, he knocked lightly on the door and entered the office. Mueller always seemed to be writing communiqués, or consulting entries in ledgers, and Garza often wondered if the German compulsion for detail was hereditary or taught. Today was no exception, and Mueller looked up from a ledger filled with precise notations that would have done justice to a calligrapher. He set his pen aside.

"Herr Garza," he said with a humorless smile. "I trust your raids went well."

"Yes, very well," Garza said, taking a chair before the desk. "We destroyed railroad bridges, a railway station, and burned a number of buildings."

"And did you kill any Texans? All in the name of liberation, of course."

Garza occasionally wondered if Mueller had ever killed anyone. He knew the man was an officer in the German intelligence service, probably versed in espionage and clandestine activities. But there was a difference between directing an operation and actually killing a man face-to-face. Everyone in Matamoras knew Mueller was involved with the singer, Maria Dominguez, and that he lavished her with gifts. Garza amused himself with the thought that Mueller was a lady-killer.

"What is war without death?" he said rhetorically. "Our raids accounted for nine dead *gringos*."

"Nine," Mueller repeated dully. "Hardly a number to inspire rebellion among the masses. But then, we have had this discussion before, is it not so?"

"We have antagonized the Americans, just as you asked. The day our brigade invades Texas will be the spark that ignites rebellion. Thousands will rally to our cause."

"And you are still planning on early September, correct? No revised estimates?"

"I intend to attack no later than the second week in September."

"Not a moment too soon, Herr Garza." Mueller indicated a cablegram on his desk. "I received an overnight message from Berlin. Your arms will arrive in Bagdad on August 10."

The Mexican port of Bagdad was some thirty miles downriver. The port was on the coast, at the mouth of the Rio Grande, and served oceangoing freighters. Cargo was off-loaded and hauled by wagon to a nearby spur line of the railroad. From there, it was transported to Matamoras and other towns in the interior.

Mueller went on to explain that the shipment would include four thousand Mauser bolt-action rifles and three million rounds of ammunition. The consignment forms identified the cargo as agricultural equipment, and the final destination was Monterrey. Garza would be responsible for transporting the arms from Monterrey to the training camp in the mountains.

"Notify your man in Monterrey," Mueller concluded. "He can expect the shipment on August 12."

"We will be ready," Garza said. "With arms, our training can now be completed. The brigade will march on schedule."

"But that is still a month away. We must continue to pressure the Americans in the meantime."

"I plan to conduct a series of raids in the next month. Every dead *gringo* wins further converts to our cause."

Mueller was silent a moment. He stared off into the middle distance, his eyes thoughtful. At length, his gaze swung back to Garza.

"Terror," he said, biting down on the word. "We must strike terror in the hearts of the Americans. Do you agree?"

"Of course," Garza replied. "Fear paves the road for our invasion."

"Then forget these ranchers and farmers. You must kill a man of prominence, perhaps a public figure. Someone whose death will prove that all Americans are vulnerable."

"A leader of some sort."

"Precisely!"

Garza nodded to himself, his mouth suddenly set in an ugly grin. He knew just the man.

Chapter Fifteen

SANTA MARIA DEVASTATED
NINE KILLED BY REBELS

The banner headline dominated the front page of the *Brownsville Daily News*. A three-column article went on to relate the destruction of the Santa Maria railway station and the death of citizens who valiantly resisted the attack. There was a report as well of a rancher and his two sons, executed by firing squad outside the town of Rio Hondo. An editorial sidebar castigated the Texas Rangers and the army for their lack of response.

"Helluva note," Maddox grumped, dropping the paper on the table. "You'd think we're supposed to be everywhere at once."

"We are," Gordon said, spreading butter over a biscuit. "We were caught flat-footed on this one."

"Well, we've got Martinez and Vargas to thank for that. Those boys just flat let us down."

"Hector tried but they gave him the brush-off. Vasquez jumped on him for not bringing in more recruits."

"Still say we got the short end of the stick. Goddamn newspaper just needs somebody to blame."

They were in the hotel dining room. Last night, when the calls began coming in, Company C had been dispatched to Carricitos and Company D to La Paloma. Gordon and Maddox had joined Ransom and Company A in a flying motorcade to Santa Maria. None of the columns had arrived in time to get into action. The raiders had already retreated across the border.

Only an hour ago, upon their return to Brownsville, had they learned of the killings outside Rio Hondo. The wife of Joe Scrivner had identified Aniceto Pizana as the leader of the raiders who had executed her husband and two sons. The *Brownsville Daily News*, published only that morning, had collected as much information as they themselves had tracked down. Their late breakfast at the hotel hadn't done much to relieve their sense of frustration.

Maddox rolled himself a cigarette. "The only saving grace was them folks in Santa Maria." He popped a match on his thumbnail and lit up. "Least they killed three of the bastards—which is more'n we did."

"Lots more," Gordon agreed. "I've been thinking about Pizana."

"What about him?"

"How he murdered Scrivner and his sons with a firing squad. What kind of a man kills young boys?"

"You'll recollect Vasquez hung Earl Stovall and his boy. Given a choice, I'd sooner be shot."

"You know what I mean," Gordon said. "I'm talking about the cold-blooded nature it takes to do something like that."

"Well, pardner—" Maddox exhaled a wad of smoke— "revenge is a way of life on the Rio Grande. Vasquez had a score to settle with Stovall, and the same goes for Pizana and Scrivner." He flicked an ash off his cigarette. "All this horseshit about liberation just gives 'em an excuse."

"I'd like to treat them to some of their own justice."

"So far, we're a day late and a dollar short in that department."

The hotel desk clerk entered the dining room. He spotted them and hurried over to their table. "Mr. Gordon. Sergeant Maddox," he said importantly. "Somebody just called from General Parker's office. He'd like to see you as soon as possible."

"Thank you kindly," Maddox said. "We'll trot on over there *muy pronto*."

"You don't mind my asking—" the clerk hesitated, then pushed on. "All this stuff I've heard about the Army of Liberation and how they run around killing people. You think they're serious about driving white folks out of Texas?"

"That'll be the day!" Maddox snorted a puff of smoke like an angry dragon. "Montezuma and a goddamn army of peons couldn't take Texas. Don't worry yourself about it."

"Nosir, I won't," the clerk said, backing away. "Figured it was just a bunch of hogwash. Glad to hear you say so."

Gordon waited until the clerk was out of earshot. "You think it's hogwash?" he asked, watching Maddox. "Considering it's the Germans and not Montezuma?"

"Who the Christ knows?" Maddox said with a grim laugh. "I'm just a Texas Ranger."

The morning was overcast, a smell of rain in the air. The parrots on the walk to Fort Brown seemed huddled into themselves, perched almost motionless in the trees. Sergeant Major Daniel O'Meara was waiting in the orderly room, and looked as though he was grinding his teeth to contain his anger over last night's raids. He ushered them into the post commander's office.

General Parker was standing at a window, hands clasped behind his back. He turned as they entered the office. "Good morning, gentlemen," he said, his manner solemn. "Pardon the meeting on such short notice. I know you've been up all night."

"Quite all right, General," Gordon said. "We just got back to town an hour or so ago."

"Please, have a seat."

They took chairs before the desk and Parker remained standing. "I understand you were at Santa Maria," he said. "Is it as bad as I've been told?"

"Yessir, mighty bad," Maddox acknowledged. " 'Course, you have to hand it to the folks there. Way they fought back took some sand."

"Indeed." Parker paced to the tall chair behind his desk, and stopped. "I've exchanged wires this morning with General Funston, at departmental headquarters in San Antonio. He's posed a question I haven't yet answered. I'd like your opinion."

Gordon and Maddox waited, holding his gaze. Parker squared his shoulders. "Do you believe this so-called Army of Liberation will raise sufficient forces to threaten Texas? Not just raids, but a concerted military attack?"

"We honestly don't know," Gordon said. "Our best intelligence indicates Garza is trying to raise a substantial force in Monterrey. But we haven't yet determined if he was successful."

Maddox cleared his throat. "General, we'd be a damnsight better off assuming the worst. Like they say, better safe than sorry."

"I'd have to agree," Gordon added. "Garza meets daily, sometimes twice a day, with Otto Mueller. The Germans won't be satisfied with these guerrilla raids." He paused, his eyes narrowed. "In my opinion, they're planning a full-scale military action."

"I regret to say I concur." Parker nodded, as if weighing some inner decision. "I will so advise General Funston, and request an additional five hundred troops. We must be prepared for any eventuality."

"Way it looks to me," Maddox said, "Garza and the

Germans are still pulling things together. We're gonna see more of these raids before anything big happens."

Parker's features darkened. "I've written a directive to my field commanders. In the future, there will be no excuse for not interdicting the rebels." His jaws clenched, his mouth a tight line. "They must be stopped at the border."

"I'd vote for that," Maddox said with a tired smile. "Hate to admit the Rangers have only caught 'em once, and that was mostly luck. They're slippery devils."

"One more thing," Parker told them. "I've ordered five-man details to ride guard on the trains day and night. Perhaps we can put a halt to railroad bridges being destroyed."

The statement was met with uneasy silence. Neither Maddox nor Gordon believed army troopers riding trains would have any effect on bridges being blown. Their hunch, which would later prove to be correct, was that the railroads, through long-standing political connections, had brought pressure to bear on the army. Parker seemed unaware of the skepticism implicit in their silence.

"Mr. Gordon."

"General?"

"We are in desperate need of better intelligence. Would it be possible for your operatives in Matamoras to step up their efforts?"

"I'll certainly speak with them, General. Maybe we can come up with a new gambit."

Gordon thought generals casually sent men into harm's way. The perspective from behind a desk in Brownsville was different than that in Matamoras. Particularly for Martinez and Vargas.

Any added risk might very well endanger their lives.

The land shimmered under the radiance of a luminous half moon. From his front porch, Alfred Austin could look out over his cornfields, the tall stalks buttery in the golden light. He thought himself the luckiest of men.

In the house, he could hear his wife puttering around in the kitchen. Mary was still attractive, even after twenty-six years of marriage, and he felt blessed by their union. She was a marvelous cook, a woman of deep religious beliefs, and she'd given him a fine son. No man could ask for more.

Austin considered himself fortunate in many ways. His farm, a thousand acres of rich topsoil, was located outside Sebastian, some thirty miles northwest of Brownsville. He was a deacon in the First Methodist Church, a major shareholder in the local bank, and owned a mercantile store, which was managed by his son. People looked upon him as a leader in the community.

The door opened, and his son, Charles, stepped out onto the porch. Every evening, after supper, they generally retired to rockers on the porch and discussed events of the day. Austin's one disappointment in life was that Charles hadn't yet married and given him grandchildren. He'd married at nineteen, and felt that Charles, pushing twenty-five, was long overdue. He had hopes the boy would quit sowing wild oats, and settle down.

"I'm plumb stuffed," Charles said, dropping into a cane-bottomed rocker. "Ma's peach cobbler takes the blue ribbon."

Austin idly wondered if his wife's cooking was why the boy hadn't left the nest. He tamped the dottle in his pipe and fired up with a kitchen match. "What's the talk in town?" he said between puffs. "Heard anything more about them renegades?"

"Nothin' new," Charles allowed. "Looks like they got away clean, even the ones at Santa Maria. The army's about as much use as teats on a boar hog."

"Terrible thing," Austin said, snuffing the match. "Just

last night all them people was alive and well, and now they're dead. God works in mysterious ways."

"Dad, I don't know that it's got a lot to do with God. Not unless He's set a bunch of stinkin' Mexicans on the warpath."

"Well, the rascals better steer clear of our neck of the woods. They come nosin' around here and we'll give 'em a hot old time."

Austin was the leader of the Sebastian Law and Order League. He'd formed the group several years ago, to combat Mexican bandits who crossed the border to rustle livestock. The membership was comprised of farmers and ranchers, and they prided themselves on having summarily hanged every bandit they'd ever caught. Following the July 4 raids, and subsequent killings, Austin had urged the members to renewed vigilance. At every opportunity, he'd expressed his contempt for the Army of Liberation. He called them the "Child Killers."

Charles shared his father's views. But his principal interests were in running the store and chasing girls without promise of wedlock. He was perfectly content to live at home and add to his considerable girth on his mother's cooking. All this talk of Mexicans driving Texans from the land seemed to him preposterous, and he dreaded yet another lecture from his father on bandits posing as liberal idealists. He moved to change the subject.

"Drummer called on me today," he said. "His company's come out with the latest thing for women. They call 'em brassieres."

"Brassieres?" Austin echoed blankly. "What're they for?"

"Well, the idea come over from Europe. The name sounds sort of French, don't it? They're a little halter contraption that lifts up a woman's bosom."

"How's that again?"

"Don't you see, it's an improvement on a corset. Woman straps on this brassiere and it holds her bosoms nice and pert."

"No, by gum," Austin said indignantly. "We're not stockin' a thing like that in my store. Sounds downright sacrilegious."

"C'mon, Dad," Charles said. "We're livin' in the modern age. Time's change."

"Not while I'm—"

Austin stopped, sitting forward in his rocker, and peered out at the cornfield. A man stepped through the thicket of willowy stalks, followed by another and another, then thirty or more leading horses. As the men advanced across the moonlit yard, he saw that they were Mexican. He jumped to his feet.

"Don't do nothing foolish," the one in the lead yelled. "You try to run and I'll shoot you."

"Who are you?" Austin said in a stern voice. "What d'you riffraff want around here?"

"I am Captain Luis Vasquez, field commander of the Army of Liberation. We are here to deliver you from your evil ways."

"You'll play hell deliverin' me from anything. Get off my land!"

"No, I think not, *señor*."

Austin knew he was doomed. He considered trying a run for the house, and a gun, but realized he would never make it. Then his wife stepped through the door and moved onto the porch, stopping beside him. Her eyes squinched with concern.

"Alfred, who are these men?"

"You get on back in the house, Mary. I'll handle this."

"Your husband is right, *señora*," Vasquez said with a cruel chuckle. "What we do tonight is not for women."

Five minutes later the house went up in a blazing inferno. Mary Austin was left standing in the yard as her husband and son were marched out onto the road. Sebastian was only a mile north of the farm, and Vasquez fully intended to occupy the town. Last night, when he'd attacked Santa Maria, he hadn't been prepared for armed resistance by the townspeople. The oversight had cost him three men.

Tonight, he led a force of fifty raiders. Upon reaching Sebastian he split them, half on either side of the main street. His attack was orchestrated, carried out with quick precision, every man assigned a task. The windows of Austin's store were smashed and the building torched, billowing smoke and flame. Townspeople who ventured into the business district were driven back by volleys of gunfire from the raiders' rifles. Austin and his son, their arms bound, were positioned beneath a telephone pole.

Vasquez had been ordered to make a public example of Alfred Austin. The Sebastian Law and Order League was the largest citizens' organization in southern Texas, widely noted for its harsh treatment of Mexicans. A message was to be sent tonight, discouraging anyone who might have similar ideas. As nooses were slipped around the necks of Austin and his son, Vasquez halted in front of them. The ropes were tossed over the bars of the telephone pole, three men on each rope.

"Alfred Austin," Vasquez said in a loud voice, "the Army of Liberation has convicted you of crimes against the Mexican people. The sentence is death."

Austin glowered at him. "You're nothin' but a bunch of heathen murderers. I damn you and God will damn you."

"You can't do this!" Charles screamed frantically. "I haven't done anything wrong. I don't deserve to die!"

"You are your father's son," Vasquez said. "And you belong to his Law and Order League. You have convicted yourself."

"Please, God, don't let 'em do it! Please!"

"Charles, shut up," Austin told him. "Beggin' a greaser won't change anything. Get hold of yourself."

"*Atención!*" Vasquez ordered. "*Ahora, pronto!*"

The men on the ropes heaved at his command. The Austins, father and son, were hauled off the ground and pulled halfway up the telephone pole. Their legs flapped, desperately trying to gain a foothold in midair, their features dark and contorted as they strangled to death. When the men tied off the ropes at the base of the post, the bodies hung limp, necks crooked at a grotesque angle. The stench of voided bowels carried on a vagrant breeze.

Sporadic gunfire filled the night as townspeople began trading shots with the raiders. Vasquez swung into the saddle as his men raked the street with a withering volley, then another and another. He led them south from Sebastian, flames from the blazing store lighting the sky. His strident shout rose above the thud of hoofbeats.

"*Viva liberación! Viva independencia!*"

Chapter Sixteen

Ranger headquarters was in an annex at the rear of the courthouse. The room was small, with a desk and filing cabinets, and a rack of long-guns on the floor. A wall clock ticked on toward seven-thirty-eight.

The call had come in from Sebastian a few minutes after seven o'clock. According to the town marshal, Alfred and Charles Austin had been hanged, their store and farmhouse burned down. The Mexican raiders were last seen riding south out of town.

Gordon and Maddox had been summoned from the hotel. They were gathered around the desk with Ranger Captains John Sanders and Clell Morris. Bob Ransom stood behind the desk, a map of the lower Rio Grande Valley spread before them. He looked from man to man.

"Here's what we know so far," he said. "A man named Austin and his son were hung on a telephone pole right in the middle of Sebastian. Their store was burnt out, along with their house outside town."

"Anybody else killed?" Morris asked.

"Nope, just the Austins."

"Hold on, Cap'n," Maddox interrupted. "Are you sayin' they were only after the Austins? Nobody else?"

"That's the way it looks," Ransom said. "Alfred Austin, the father, was head of a vigilante group around Sebastian. I suspect it was revenge for the way he'd treated Mexicans."

"And the Mexicans just got clean away?"

"Well, that's where it gets interesting. The town marshal says there was fifty, maybe more, in the raiding party. They kept folks pretty much pinned down till they rode out."

"Fifty," Gordon mused aloud. "From what we know, they have a hundred men or less at this point. Why would they commit half their force to one action?"

The Ranger captains were not yet aware of the German conspiracy. Gordon and Maddox, in concert with General Parker, had decided that Monterrey, and a possible invasion force, was still supposition. Until the facts were borne out, there was no need to spread alarm.

"Got no idea as to the 'why,' " Ransom said. "What's important, we've got a chance at fifty of the sonsabitches. Might just be our lucky night."

Gordon nodded. "Where are we now?"

"Army's already been notified, and they're gonna redouble their patrols between here and Reynosa. I wired Jack Fox in Laredo, and he's on the move with Ranger Company B. They'll coordinate with the army up that way."

Ransom paused. His many years on the border gave him the tactical expertise to run a field operation. But everyone in the room knew Gordon spoke for the president of the United States and had the authority to override any decision. They waited for his reaction.

"Sounds good to me," he said. "What's next?"

"Cover our bases." Ransom indicated the map. "Send Company C to San Pedro and Company D to La Paloma. That'll put 'em in position if the army flushes anybody."

Gordon gave him a quizzical look. "What do you have in mind for Company A?"

"You remember where we waylaid them that first time? The night of July fourth?"

"The river crossing west of Los Indios?"

"One and the same," Ransom said, thumping the map with a thorny forefinger. "They'll think we think they won't use the same ford again. But that crossing's on a beeline south of Sebastian. I figure we'll catch 'em there."

Gordon studied the map. Sebastian was some twenty miles due north of the river crossing. He calculated time and distance, confident the rebels would not run their horses at a gallop for twenty miles. All things considered, he estimated the raiding party would reach the ford somewhere around nine o'clock, maybe slightly later. He finally glanced up at Ransom.

"We need to coordinate this with the army."

"Already got it covered." Ransom said. "Talked with General Parker's adjutant and told him you'd call him after our powwow. He'll get the word to their field units."

"Sounds like a plan," Gordon said. "So we'll have Rangers at San Pedro, La Paloma, Los Indios, and Laredo. Are we missing anything?"

"The border's like a sieve," Maddox observed with a shrug. "We've only got four companies, and that spreads us thin. The army'll have to take up the slack."

"How about transportation?" Gordon said. "We don't have a lot of time to spare."

"All laid on," Ransom informed him. "Everybody in Brownsville that owns a car has volunteered. Nothin' like killings to bring out folks' civic spirit."

Gordon looked around at the Ranger captains. "Anything else?"

Their faces were sober, almost phlegmatic, the faces of men untroubled by a dirty night's work. None of them spoke and he nodded.

"Let's roll."

Bud Grant, the rancher outside Los Indios, again provided the horses. His house had been burned down in a previous raid, and he was eager to assist in any way that would avenge the loss. Dead Mexicans seemed to him the best payback of all.

The Rangers came across an army patrol west of the ranch. There were nine troopers in the squad, led by Sergeant Ira Wilson, and he told them the alert was out along the river. His commanding officer, a Captain Bates, had spread the word that Rangers would be in the area. Three squads were patrolling the eight-mile stretch of river between Santa Maria and Los Indios.

"We heard there's fifty Mexicans, maybe more," Sergeant Wilson said. "You think they're gonna try to cross along here somewheres?"

"Doubt there'll be fifty," Ransom said. "Some of the *Tejanos* will likely peel off and head back wherever they live. Sorry bastards lay low over here till they get called out for another raid."

"But you still think the main bunch will try and cross somewheres close?"

"You know that ford about a mile upriver?"

"Yeah, you could practically wade through it."

"We figure that's the spot."

Gordon and Maddox were off to one side, listening to the conversation. Wilson glanced at them, and Gordon reined his horse closer. "Sergeant, I'm Special Agent Gordon. I work directly with General Parker."

"Yessir." Wilson seemed to sit straighter in the saddle. "What can I do for you?"

"How often do you pass that ford?"

"Generally about once an hour."

"We're planning a little ambush," Gordon said. "You happen along at the wrong time, you're liable to spoil things. Captain Ransom, what would you suggest?"

Ransom motioned off into the distance. "I'd say the

sergeant and his boys ought to stay north of the river. If they spot the Mexicans, attack from the rear and drive 'em toward the ford." He paused, his mouth curled in a wolfish grin. "We'll be there waitin'."

"That should do the trick." Gordon glanced back at Wilson. "Sergeant, do you link up with the patrol west of the ford?"

"Just now and then," Wilson said. "Mostly, it's an accident when it happens. We're not on a set schedule."

"Well, if you do, advise them of what Captain Ransom just said. We want everyone following the same plan."

"Yessir, I'll pass along the word."

The cavalry patrol turned north from the river. The Rangers proceeded west and halted a half mile or so from the ford. Ransom dismounted the men and ordered them to tie their horses securely in a stand of trees. From there, carrying their Winchester carbines, they moved out on foot. Gordon and Maddox had again armed themselves with pump-action shotguns.

The river crossing was lighted by the sallow cast of the moon. Ransom split his men, leaving ten Rangers with Gordon and Maddox, hidden in the trees on the east side of the ford. He led the other Rangers across the narrow clearing that sloped down the riverbank, and positioned them within the treeline on the opposite side. They settled in to wait.

Gordon, though nominally in charge, wisely conceded tactical command to Ransom. He realized his own shortcomings, and from talks with Maddox, he knew Ransom was versed in the ways of fighting Mexican *bandidos*. The Ranger captain's orders were for the men to stay low, firing upward at mounted riders, rather than across the clearing at each other. Under no circumstances were they to leave the trees until the fighting ended.

Not long after they'd taken position, they heard gunfire from the north. The firing quickly swelled in intensity, growing louder, clearly moving in their direction. There was no doubt in anyone's mind that Sergeant Wilson and his cavalry patrol had jumped the rebels, and were driving them south, toward the river. The only question was whether or not the raiders would try to cross at the ford.

Then, just as Ransom had predicted, the rebels thundered into the clearing at a gallop. They were silhouetted in the moonlight, those at the rear firing over their shoulders, pursued closely by the cavalry. The horsemen were wedged together, three and four abreast, and there appeared to be forty or more in their ranks. Their mounts were lathered with sweat, hooves churning at the earth, the drumming thud almost deafening. They pounded toward the river.

Ransom opened fire. His shot was instantly followed by the sharp crack of carbines and the dull boom of Gordon and Maddox's shotguns. A maelstrom of lead cleaved through the riders like an invisible scythe chopping down rows of wheat. On either side of the clearing, the treelines spat sheets of flame, the muzzle blasts turning night to day. Horses faltered, and their riders, caught within a funnel of gunfire, toppled from the saddle. Four went down, then six, then ten, then more.

Those who made it into the river were still framed in moonlight. The Rangers rose from the trees, carbines at their shoulders, hammering volley after volley into the riders. The slugs whined through the air and men pitched headlong from their mounts, splashing in a tangle of arms and legs in the shallow waters of the ford. What seemed an eternity passed before the last of the raiders gained the far shore and disappeared into the night. A final gunshot faded into a sudden, eerie stillness.

The clearing was littered with dead. By rough count,

Gordon saw at least fifteen bodies, and more in the water. A man groaned and rolled over, his shoulder shattered from a wound, his shirt dark with blood. Another man levered himself to his hands and knees, tried to stand erect, and slumped to the ground, seated on his rump. The Rangers stepped from the trees, carbines held at the ready, watching the men. Neither of them posed a threat.

Ransom walked forward. He pulled his revolver, moving from one wounded man to the other, and shot both of them in the head. Their skulls exploded in a mist of brains and bone matter, and even as the report of the gunshots faded, Gordon charged forward. He grabbed Ransom by the shirt.

"Are you *crazy*?" he shouted. "Those men were wounded!"

Ransom's eyes went cold. "Take your hand off me."

Maddox pried Gordon loose. "Easy does it, pardner," he said in a low voice. "Let's not fight amongst ourselves."

"Like hell!" Gordon shrugged him off. "We finally had a chance to interrogate somebody. Dead men don't talk!"

"Too damn bad," Ransom said with a tight smile. "The Rangers don't take prisoners, and you can like it or lump it. Them's our orders."

"Whose orders?" Gordon demanded. "The attorney general?"

Ransom turned and walked away. Maddox averted his eyes, looking toward the river, and Gordon realized he wouldn't get an answer. Not tonight, probably never.

The Rangers had closed ranks.

Hector Martinez crossed the bridge into Matamoras late the next morning. The noon hour was approaching and the plaza was busy with shoppers and tradesmen hawking their wares. He turned the corner onto Calle Morelos.

Halfway down the block, he passed the German Consulate. He wondered if Garza was in there even now, plotting strategy with Otto Mueller. One thought triggered another, and he warned himself that today was a day to proceed with caution. A mistake would almost certainly get him killed.

Gordon had asked him to redouble his efforts. Somehow he was to infiltrate the headquarters of the Army of Liberation. The intelligence he'd gathered to date had been useful, but not of a critical nature. All guesswork and conjecture, and few hard facts. He had to separate the grain from the chaff—get at the truth.

The raids of the past two nights offered a meager opening. A railroad depot destroyed and Anglos killed, two by firing squad, was the stuff of conversation, hardly more. But the ambush last night by the Rangers had sparked new anger among Mexicans on both sides of the border. All the more so since two raiders, already desperately wounded, had been brutally executed. There, Martinez told himself, was a tragedy to fire the blood of any patriot. He had only to act the part.

The house on Calle 5 was quiet. When he knocked on the door, he was admitted by the man who served as the headquarters orderly. They had met on his previous visits, and the orderly knew he was a sergeant in the Army of Liberation. Still, he was told Captain Vasquez was busy at the moment, and forced to take a chair in the front room. Some while later, Vasquez entered from a hallway that led to the rear of the house. His expression was neutral.

"Martinez," he said without offering a handshake. "What is it now?"

"*Buenos dias, mi capitán.*" Martinez stood rigid at attention. "There is talk in Brownsville of a great tragedy last night. They say eighteen *soldados* were killed."

"There is talk as well that two of my men were executed. Have you heard that?"

"Our people speak of little else. The Ranger captain, the one named Ransom, he shot them in the head as they lay wounded. *Hijo de puta*, he brags of it!"

Vasquez paled. "One day I will meet this Ransom. Before I am done, he will beg for a quick death."

"That is why I am here," Martinez said stoutly. "I spend my time telling our people of war while men die in the field. I wish to fight, *mi capitán*."

"We have had this discussion before. I need recruits, Martinez, men to replace those who were killed last night. Think of the cause, not yourself. Bring me men."

"No disrespect intended, but I weary of this assignment. I have little talent for enlisting men, and we both know it. I want to fight."

"No!" Vasquez bristled. "You will follow orders!"

Garza entered from the hallway. "What's going on here, Luis? Why are you shouting?"

"Excuse the intrusion, *mi coronel*. Martinez questions my orders and insists that he be given a rifle. I was explaining that his value is in recruiting men."

"Is that correct, Sergeant?" Garza said with a stern look. "Are you questioning orders?"

"*Por favor, mi coronel*." Martinez squared his shoulders. "I simply wish to join our comrades in the struggle for liberty. I want to kill *gringos*."

"Spoken like a true *guerrero*, Sergeant Martinez. The time will come when you will lead men in battle, and sooner than you think. Until then, you serve best by enlisting soldiers in our cause."

"If I may be permitted, how soon will we march into battle? I have lost my taste for talking of war, *mi coronel*. I want to fight."

"Did I not say soon?" Garza reprimanded him harshly.

"You will be called before the month is out. Let that be an end to it."

"*Gracias, mi coronel*," Martinez said obediently. "I ask only to take my place in the ranks."

"And so you shall."

Martinez was dismissed with a curt nod. Outside, as he walked toward the plaza, he mentally patted himself on the back. There was much to be said for truth in anger, and he'd pushed them to the edge, perhaps even further. He felt certain Garza had slipped, saying more than intended. A quick rebuke to a brash subordinate.

Granted, he had failed to infiltrate the headquarters staff. An appointment as an aide, or even a lowly field sergeant, would have provided access to intelligence on a daily basis. But sometimes, as Texans were so fond of saying, half a loaf was better than none. Tonight, after a meeting was arranged, he would have much to tell Gordon. Their first clue that an invasion was imminent. A hard fact about time.

Within the month!

Chapter Seventeen

Sunrise was a sudden flare on the horizon. Within moments dawn receded and the land was limned by fiery streamers of light. Hoary dewdrops glittered like scarlet diamonds on the grassy plain.

Aniceto Pizana waited with his men in a stand of cottonwoods bordering a small creek. There were forty raiders in the band, all of them mounted on fast horses and armed with Winchesters. A sense of camaraderie pervaded their ranks, and they felt honored to be chosen for the mission. They were there to strike the wealthiest Anglo enterprise in all of Texas.

The date was Saturday, August 7, and they were sixty miles north of the border. Two nights ago Vasquez and his band had raided the town of Sebastian. The raid was considered important, for it had resulted in the execution of a *gringo* vigilante leader. But it had been planned as a tactical diversion, to deflect the attention of the army and the Texas Rangers. The primary target, the object of today's attack, was the King Ranch.

Pizana and his men had traveled by night for the past two nights. Their line of march was overland, avoiding roads and towns, skirting outlying farms and ranches. During the day they went to ground, taking cover in dense mesquite thickets, always making a cold camp, without fire or smoke to betray their presence. The military and the Rangers had no reason to suspect guerrilla action so far north of the Rio Grande. Nor would they suspect a raid on a ranching empire steeped in legend.

Richard King, a former steamboat tycoon, began acquiring Spanish land grants in 1853. Over the next three decades he built the largest ranch in the world, encompassing a million acres scattered through four counties south of Corpus Christi. Upon his death in 1885, his daughter and her husband, Robert Kleberg, assumed control and continued to expand the operation. The King Ranch Running W brand was stamped on the rumps of more than one hundred thousand cows.

The *vaqueros* on the ranch were known as *Los Kinenos*, the King People, and they were intensely loyal. Richard King's descendants had built homes for their families, schools for their children, and four generations of *vaqueros* had grown to manhood on the vast cattle spread. There were easily five hundred *Kinenos* and none of them would be swayed by the revolutionary proclamations of the Army of Liberation. Their loyalty was not to race or ideology, but to the King family.

Pizana, waiting in the stand of cottonwoods, was not interested in recruits. He was a mile south of the Norias Division headquarters, and he believed Caesar Kleberg would be found there. Kleberg was a nephew-by-marriage to Richard King's daughter and the manager of the Norias Division. Kingsville, the main headquarters, was almost fifty miles farther north, and entirely too far for attack by a small raiding party. The ranch was so large that it was operated in divisions, with four separate headquarters, Norias being the southernmost. Pizana's mission was to kill Caesar Kleberg, one of the most prominent ranchmen in Texas.

A low whistle brought Pizana and his men alert. Jesus Murguia, a seasoned veteran of the *Revolución*, had been sent ahead to scout the Norias headquarters. He drifted through the cottonwoods, quiet as a ghost, and stopped beside Pizana. He motioned upstream.

"Just as you thought, *mi capitán*," he said. "The stream crosses under a railroad bridge. The buildings are on the west side of the tracks."

"*Bueno*," Pizana said. "How many buildings?"

"Only three. A large house which appears to be the headquarters. Another house for perhaps ten or twelve *vaqueros*. And an equipment shed for the railroad."

"Are the *vaqueros* there now?"

"*Si*." Murguia looked troubled. "I also saw an encampment of soldiers, nine men and a sergeant. And four men wearing badges. Texas Rangers, I think."

"Huh!" Pizana grunted coarsely. "The army and the Rangers rush to protect their imperialist masters. I am not surprised."

In fact, Pizana was surprised. So far from the border he had not expected to encounter either army patrols or the Rangers. But then, on quick reflection, he concluded that the King family had friends in high places. A request for protection from the Kings would not go unheeded. Imperialists had only to ask to command.

"No matter," he said with an air of confidence. "We outnumber them almost two to one. And the element of surprise is ours."

"*Si, mi capitán*," Murguia agreed. "A quick charge will put them to flight."

"No, Jesus, we will overrun them before they can flee."

Pizana ordered the men to get mounted. He led them along the creek bank, their movements screened by the broad overhang of the cottonwoods. A mile upstream they came to the railroad bridge and he split his force. Jesus Murguia would lead half the men around the south end of the bridge and he would take the other half around the north end. He meant to envelop Norias from the flanks.

The fortunes of war are fueled by fickle gods. A difference of a minute or two often spells the margin between victory and defeat. Jesus Murguia's reconnaissance, necessarily conducted on foot, had taken longer than expected. In those few lapsed minutes, critical in timing, the Norias headquarters had stirred to life. Workday on a ranch began at sunrise.

The warning was sounded by an alert *vaquero*. His shout rang out across the compound as the raiders spurred their horses around opposite ends of the bridge. The distance from the bridge to the buildings was some fifty yards, and the defenders reacted faster than the horsemen could cover the open ground. Every man in the compound was armed, and none of them evidenced the slightest doubt that they were under attack. *Vaqueros*, army troopers, and Texas Rangers opened fire in a rattling volley.

The charge was broken by a hail of lead. Four raiders pitched headlong to the ground, nine slumped wounded in their saddles, and the others faltered before a wall of gunfire. Pizana tried to rally his men, exhorting them to move forward, but they turned back even as a slug sent his hat flying. They retreated to the creek, and he got them dismounted, spread out on a rough skirmish line behind the timbers of the bridge. The exchange of gunfire became general as the soldiers and the Rangers, reinforced by the *vaqueros*, took cover in the buildings. A uniformed trooper, caught running for the equipment shed, spun around, dropping his rifle, and fell dead.

For the next hour, the raiders and the defenders traded shots in a sporadic gun battle. The rebel force was effectively pinned down, for they dared not advance across open ground in the face of heavy fire. Three more of their comrades were killed, and a soldier, briefly exposed at the corner of the equipment shed, was shot through the head. Pizana moved back and forth behind his men, seemingly oblivious to the whine of slugs, his features a study in rage. Already he'd lost men: eleven killed and five wounded, and he saw no way to storm the ranch headquarters. His jaw muscles knotted in raw fury.

Murguia joined him at the north end of the bridge. "Pardon me for speaking, *mi capitán*," he said in an apologetic voice. "Perhaps we should end a fight we cannot win."

"No!" Pizana bellowed, his eyes wild with anger. "Our orders were to kill this *gringo*, Kleberg. I will not be denied."

"We are trapped under this bridge. You know without my saying it, there is no way into that house."

"Do you question my authority?"

"Never, *mi capitán*," Murguia said. "But the longer we stay here, the greater the risk we will never leave. Time is our enemy."

Pizana frowned. "What are you saying?"

"All this shooting travels on the wind. Before long, it will draw more *Kinenos*, maybe more soldiers. We could die here for nothing."

"We are *soldados*!"

"*Si, mi capitán*, but not martyrs."

The simple force of the words snapped Pizana out of his rage. He was struck by the sudden realization that fear of his own failure was why he fought on, the shame of bungling a mission. His greater concern should be for his men, who deserved more than a meaningless death. He nodded to Murguia.

"We are leaving this place, Jesus. Get the men mounted."

A final volley was fired to hold the ranch defenders in place. Then the rebels scrambled from under the bridge and ran to where their horses were tied in the cottonwoods. Once they were mounted, they clattered downstream at a gallop, thankful to quit the fight still alive. Aniceto Pizana, far from thankful, felt the burden of leaving eleven dead men behind. And worse, his failure to kill Caesar Kleberg.

He wondered how he would explain it to Garza.

"Oldest rule there is for a lawman."

"What's that?"

"Never try to second-guess a crook."

"Crooks," Gordon said, "or revolutionaries?"

Maddox grunted. "All one and the same when you're talkin' about Mexicans."

"You should have told Ransom that last night."

"Well, like they say, hindsight's a powerful teacher. Maybe he's learned his lesson."

Captain Bob Ransom had guessed wrong when he again tried to second-guess the rebels. Late yesterday morning Ranger headquarters had been notified about the raid on the King Ranch. Ransom felt certain the rebels would make a run for the border, rather than hiding out and risk being trapped by army units. He also believed they would again use the river crossing outside Los Indios, thinking the army and the Rangers would never suspect they'd use the same crossing a third time. As the situation unfolded, Ransom was only half right.

The rebels traveled overland, avoiding roads and towns. They were sighted just once, early in the afternoon, by a farmer outside the town of Santa Rosa. The farmer was taken aback by thirty or more armed Mexicans on horseback, and he dutifully reported the incident to authorities. But the rebels seemingly vanished, and were not seen again until they clashed with an army patrol at a river crossing west of Santa Maria. The engagement was brief, occurring shortly after midnight, with one trooper and one raider killed in a running gunfight. The rebels forded the river into Mexico.

Gordon and Maddox, meanwhile, were waiting at the river crossing outside Los Indios. An hour or so later, they were notified that the raiders had broken through the army line and escaped across the Rio Grande. Bob Ransom was furious, for it was apparent the rebels had read his mind, and eluded the ambush he'd laid on by Company A. Early Sunday morning, upon returning to Brownsville, there was a message awaiting Gordon and Maddox at the hotel. General Parker wanted to see them and he asked that they come to Fort Brown as soon as possible. They took time only to have a quick breakfast.

"One good thing, anyway," Maddox said as they walked along Elizabeth Street. "Eleven of the bastards got killed up at Norias. Way it sounds, must've been a helluva fight."

"Too bad we missed it," Gordon said sourly. "Only action we saw was swatting mosquitoes."

"You mind a suggestion?"

"No, fire away."

"Ransom don't like it much, but he's under your orders. You could always override what he's got planned—like last night."

"Hoyt, I thought it sounded good myself. He outsmarted them twice before."

Maddox was quiet a moment. "I'm just sayin' Ransom's no Robert E. Lee. Next time, you might want to trust your own judgment."

Gordon laughed. "Question is, would anybody else trust my judgment? I'm not exactly an old-time border fighter."

"Well, pardner, you're learnin' fast. Damn fast."

The parade ground at Fort Brown was now a sea of tents. Only yesterday, five hundred additional troops had been posted to the garrison, and calvary patrols in company strength were on the move at all hours of the day and night. In the regimental headquarters, Sergeant Major O'Meara's expression was that of a juggler with one too many balls in the air. Maddox grinned at him.

"Keepin' you busy, Sergeant Major?"

"Aye, and then some," O'Meara said with a trace of a brogue. "What with these new lads, we've about run out of space. Any more and we'll be raisin' tents on the polo field."

"Well, why not?" Maddox said with mock gravity. "All the officers are off chasin' Mexicans. Who's got time for polo?"

"Well, sir, polo's a bit like religion. If you take my meaning."

"Not much different in the Rangers. Officers play while the troops do all the work. That the idea?"

"You'd never hear me say that, sir. Not out loud, leastways."

"Sergeant Major, you're startin' to talk like a diplomat."

"And how do you imagine I got to be a sergeant major?"

A fleeting smile touched O'Meara's eyes. Then his stern countenance returned and he showed them into the commander's office. The door closed, and General Parker, who was seated behind his desk, motioned them forward. Spread out across the top of the desk was a battle standard, or flag, two feet by four feet in dimension. He waved a hand over the flag with a look of distaste.

"Our first trophy of war," he said dryly. "Taken off the rebel who was killed outside Santa Maria last night. Captain Bates, who commands that area, had it rushed here by automobile."

The standard was white, with red and green emblems.

Across the top and bottom, painted in bold letters, were the words *LIBERATING ARMY OF MEXICO—TEXAS*. In the center was a symbol familiar to all Mexicans, an eagle atop a nopal cactus, wings spread wide, a serpent clutched in its beak. Widely used by revolutionaries, the symbol represented the struggle of the people against tyrants. The message was immediately apparent to anyone of Mexican ancestry.

"What's it mean?" Gordon said. "I'm not much on Spanish."

Parker first explained the symbolism. "They've added the word '*Texanos*,' " he went on. "In the past, it was the battle standard depicting opposition to Mexican tyrants. Now, it's been revised to include Texans."

"Just more of the same," Maddox commented. "Their handbills spelled it out clear enough for anybody. They aim to take over Texas."

"Yes, that's true," Parker said. "Actually, it's not why I asked you gentlemen to come by. I just thought you would find it interesting."

Gordon nodded. "What can we do for you, General?"

"I needn't tell you that the King Ranch has considerable influence with both Governor Ferguson and President Wilson. Do either of you have any idea as to the reason for the attack?"

"Two things bother me," Gordon said. "This is the first time they've raided so far from the border. And instead of hit and run, they seemed determined to make a fight of it. I understand it lasted an hour or more."

"Yes, that's true," Parker acknowledged. "Fortunately, I was directed to post troops around the ranch. The result might otherwise have been disastrous."

"No two ways about it," Maddox agreed. "Governor Ferguson ordered Rangers stationed there to patrol the ranch. Good thing he did."

Parker fixed him with a look. "I received a rather disturbing report, Sergeant. Your Rangers apparently roped some of the dead Mexicans and dragged them through the brush." He paused, his mouth pursed with distaste. "I'm told they even posed for photographs."

"General, there's no explaining what men will do when their blood's runnin' hot. I'll look into it."

"There is no excuse for brutalizing the dead. I think a report to the governor would be appropriate—don't you?"

"Yessir, I'll see that it's handled proper."

"Please keep me advised," Parker said in a firm tone. "Now, back to my original question. Why would they ride sixty miles to attack the King Ranch?"

"Only one thing makes sense," Maddox said quickly. "Three nights ago they hung that Austin fellow, the vigilante leader in Sebastian. Yesterday, I think they meant to kill Caesar Kleberg."

"A member of the family?" Parker said. "To what purpose?"

"Same reason they killed Austin. To show all the Mexicans that nobody's beyond their reach. Not even a bigwig *hidalgo* on the King Ranch."

"Wait a minute," Gordon broke in. "Are you talking about deliberate assassination? Targeting prominent men?"

"The bigger the better," Maddox replied. "Lots of Mexicans sitting on the fence, waitin' to see what happens. Thing like this proves the Army of Liberation won't be stopped."

"Good God," Parker said with a heavy sigh. "We can't provide personal protection for every civic leader in southern Texas. How do we know where they'll strike next?"

"No way to know," Maddox said. "The advantage is all theirs, leastways till they come out in the open and try to invade. Like we told you, Martinez says it'll be early September."

"I find myself almost hoping he's right. We seem ill-prepared to fight a small war."

Gordon thought it was a perceptive remark, and true. The army was always a step behind in guerrilla warfare, and the Rangers were no more effective. Yet a large war, a Mexican force invading American soil, played directly into the Germans' hands. The very thing he'd been sent there to stop.

For the first time, he felt a worm of doubt. He wondered if he could stop it. And even more to the point . . .

How?

Chapter Eighteen

Toro Bravo had become unofficial headquarters for the Army of Liberation. A sign, depicting a fighting bull with fierce horns, hung over the door of the *cantina*. The painting of a brave bull seemed properly symbolic for the men who led the rebel movement.

The interior was dim and cool even on the hottest days. A crude wooden bar was backed by a faded mirror with bottles of tequila and native brandy displayed on a shelf. Tables and chairs were arranged opposite the bar, and kerosene lamps hung from the ceiling. The room was utilitarian, a place where common men came to drink.

Jacinto Trevino, the owner of Toro Bravo, welcomed the business of the rebels. Everyone in Matamoras knew his establishment was a clearinghouse for information about the Army of Liberation. As the gathering place for rebels and their supporters, his *cantina* had gained a certain notoriety. He treated Augustin Garza with the respect due a man of stature.

On the afternoon of August 10, Garza, Vasquez and Pizana were seated around a table at the rear of the room. They were drinking Cuervo, the most expensive brand of tequila, distilled from the blue *agave*, a flowery desert plant. Vasquez sprinkled salt on the web of his thumb, licked it off, and downed a shot of tequila. He took a wedge of lime from a plate on the table and sucked it with satisfaction. He smacked his lips.

"What a day!" he said vigorously. "If I weren't an officer, maybe I'd get drunk. Maybe I will anyway."

"*Si*," Garza said with a faint smile. "We have come far in a short time. General Huerta would approve."

Vasquez poured another shot. "*Caramba*! I can still see the look on Austin's face when the rope was put around his neck. His *cajones* shrunk to nothing!"

"We all have much to celebrate," Garza agreed. "Think of it, the first raid on the King Ranch in twenty years. You will be famous, Aniceto."

Pizana had scarcely touched his drink. "No, *mi coronel*," he said glumly. "I lost eleven men and never got near the *gringo*, Kleberg. I take no pride in that."

Three days had passed since the raid and Pizana was still in a sullen mood. He felt he had failed, while Vasquez had struck a blow that would terrorize all Anglos. Garza had invited them to Toro Bravo as much to enhearten Pizana as to celebrate their progress. He shook his head.

"You are too hard on yourself, Aniceto. Your raid proved to all that even the mightiest *Americano* must fear our vengeance. Is it not so, Luis?"

"*Si, mi coronel*," Vasquez said readily. "Even if Kleberg was not killed, the raid itself drove fear into the hearts of the *gringos*. I salute you, Aniceto."

The door opened as Vasquez raised his glass. Hector Martinez stepped into the *cantina* and paused, allowing his eyes to adjust from bright sunlight to the dusky haze of the room. He finally saw them and hurriedly made his way back to the table. He stopped, hat in hand.

"*Buenos dias, mi coronel*," he said, nodding respectfully to Garza. "Your man at headquarters told me I might find you here."

"And you have found me," Garza said without inflection. "What is it, Sergeant Martinez?"

"I felt it important to bring something to your attention,

mi coronel. A terrible atrocity by the Texas Rangers."

Martinez placed a printed leaflet, the size of a postcard, on the table. The front of the leaflet was a photograph of three Texas Rangers, mounted on horseback, lariats strung tight from the pommel of their saddles. At the other end of the ropes were three dead Mexicans, feet lassoed together, their bodies torn and raw from being dragged through the brush. The opposite side of the leaflet bore the message, printed in Spanish:

DEATH TO MEXICAN REBELS WHO
CROSS THE RIO GRANDE.

"*Mil Cristos*!" Pizana blanched. "Those are my men. Soza. Fierros. And Lopez . . . *muerto*."

"Not just dead," Garza corrected him. "They have been savaged by the Rangers. Dragged like animals."

"*Yanqui bastardos*!" Vasquez cursed. "Those men will never see the face of our Savior. God have mercy on their souls."

The dead men would be denied a Roman Catholic burial. For decades, Rangers who killed Mexicans had made it a practice to leave the bodies for vultures, or in some instances, burn them on pyres of dried brush. The dead never received the final sacrament and their remains were not interred in consecrated ground, a burial site blessed by the Church. Their immortality, many believed, was never sanctified.

Varquez was impervious to his own irony. Nor were Garza and Pizana able to equate their own acts with those of the Rangers. In the *Revolución*, they had killed men, murdered many in cold blood, and blown others apart with cannon fire. Within the past month, they had executed Anglo ranchers by rope and firing squad, some of them little more than children. Yet they were incapable of casting themselves in the same light as the Rangers. They saw the act as bestial, an abomination.

"Sergeant Martinez," Garza said, tapping the leaflet, "where did you get this?"

"The Rangers had them printed in great quantity, *mi coronel*. They are passing them out to our people all along the other side of the river."

"These men were killed in the raid on the King Ranch, and that was only three days ago. The Rangers acted quickly."

"Captain Vasquez was right," Martinez said, forcing anger into his voice. "The Rangers are *bastardos*, the Devil's own. I thought you would want to see the leaflet *muy pronto*."

Martinez stood as though awaiting orders. His outrage at the Rangers' brutality was genuine enough; but he was there for another reason entirely. Frank Gordon, upon seeing the leaflet last night, had been appalled. He planned to lodge a formal protest with the governor of Texas, and request disciplinary action against the Rangers involved. Yet, from a pragmatic standpoint, he couldn't ignore opportunity.

Gordon saw the leaflet as a plausible excuse for Martinez to report to Garza. He thought it might somehow bring Martinez to Garza's favor, and result in a staff appointment at rebel headquarters. He had instructed Martinez to present the leaflet, with a proper display of anger, and volunteer himself for any duty Garza might require. His hope was that Martinez would at last be able to infiltrate the Army of Liberation—at the staff level.

"I am at your command, *mi coronel*," Martinez said now. "You know of my wish to further our cause. How may I serve you?"

"Quiet!"

Garza studied the leaflet with a frown. His eyes

squinted in concentration as he stared first at the mounted Rangers and then at the bodies of the roped raiders. He cocked his head, lost in thought, and finally nodded to himself, as though acknowledging some inner revelation. His mouth razored in a grimace.

"This is a sacrilege," he said, thumping the leaflet with a forefinger. "But the Rangers have outsmarted themselves trying to frighten those who would join the fight. We will turn it to our advantage."

"Advantage?" Vasquez echoed dully. "What do we gain with dead men, *mi coronel*?"

"Watch and learn, Luis."

Garza took a stub pencil from his shirt pocket. He turned the leaflet over and scratched out the printed warning from the Rangers. Then, with bold strokes, he wrote: *Basta ya de brutalidad! Basta ya de sufrir insultos y desprecios de los gringos! Viva la libertad!*

The message was short but succinct, a ringing battle cry to all Mexicans. Enough of brutality! Enough of suffering insults and contempt from the Yankees! Long live liberty!

"There," Garza said, dropping his pencil. "We will have the picture of our dead comrades reprinted at the top and the words I have written at the bottom. I will add my name as commander of the Army of Liberation."

Pizana, for the first time in days, broke into a smile. "You are brilliant, Augustin." He slapped the table with the flat of his hand. "These poor men I led will not have died in vain. The people will rally to our cause."

"*Salud, mi coronel*," Vasquez said, hoisting his glass with a laugh. "The Rangers will regret the day they printed their *atrocidad*!"

"Before we are done," Garza said in a tight voice, "they will regret many things."

Pizana volunteered to have the leaflet reprinted. Martinez, instead of being promoted to the headquarters staff, was ordered to distribute the leaflets throughout villages and towns along the north side of the Rio Grande. Despite himself, he felt a certain grudging admiration for the commander of the Army of Liberation. He thought it was indeed a stroke of brilliance.

Augustin Garza had turned the tables on the Texas Rangers.

Major Hans Eckhardt arrived in Los Angeles on August 11. He was traveling under a diplomatic passport, which identified him as an attaché of the German embassy in New York. His orders were to seek out Ricardo Flores Magon, publisher of *Regeneración*.

Eckhardt checked into a hotel near the train station. He wore civilian clothes and he was alert to the possibility of unwanted surveillance. In the course of his westward journey, he had changed trains in Chicago, Kansas City, and Albuquerque. He thought it unlikely he'd been followed by agents of the U.S. Bureau of Investigation.

After a change of clothes, Eckhardt got directions to Edendale. The small farming community was on the northern outskirts of Los Angeles, and serviced by an interurban streetcar line. On the ride north, the land became increasingly bleak and barren, almost a desert. Eckhardt, whose family estate was in the Bavarian forests of western Germany, found it all rather depressing. He wondered why the Americans prized a land so devoid of greenery.

Colonel Franz von Kleist had charged Eckhardt with a critical mission. His orders were to secure the cooperation of Ricardo Magon, and influence him to further inflame the situation on the Rio Grande border. Through *Regeneración*, the anarchist newspaper, von Kleist hoped to build support for the Army of Liberation, and incite rebellion among the tens of thousands of *Tejano* workingmen in Texas. All of this was to be accomplished in time for the invasion, in early September.

On the trip west, Eckhardt had versed himself on Ricardo Magon. The embassy staff had assembled an intelligence portfolio that revealed a man at odds with the world. A native of Mexico, Magon had first surfaced as an opponent of Porfirio Diaz, dictator of the country since 1876. In 1900, Magon and his brother, Enrique, formed the Mexican Liberal Party, commonly referred to as PLM, and established the newspaper *Regeneración*. Their strident opposition to Diaz resulted in intermittent prison terms through 1903.

Late that year, the Magon brothers went into exile. By the time they settled in California, Ricardo Magon had been transformed from a revolutionary to an anarchist. He advocated the abolishment of private property and rejected any form of government as corrupt and inherently impossible to reform. His view was that any society based on private landholdings and industrial wealth robbed common people of any hope in life. *Regeneración* spread the message that government, through control by the rich, subjugated the masses to exploitation and poverty.

Eckhardt stepped off the streetcar in Edendale. The town was a farming community, and as he walked along Main Street, he recalled that Magon rented five acres of land just outside the city limits. As a livelihood, Magon and his brother, with their families and other dedicated members of PLM, operated a peach orchard. The small farm was worked on a communal basis, with no one person holding ownership and all sharing equally. They lived the life they preached, the hallmark of anarchists.

The offices of *Regeneración* were located at the corner of Main and Fargo Avenue. When Eckhardt entered, he saw immediately that the quarters were spartan, clearly operated on a shoestring. There were two battered wooden desks at the front, and at the back of the room, an antiquated printing press. For the moment, the press was silent and several men were busily engaged in bundling stacks of newspapers. A narrow-faced man with an unruly mustache sat at one of the desks.

"Good afternoon," Eckhardt said. "I wish to speak with Ricardo Magon."

"I am Magon," the man replied. "Who are you?"

"Hans Eckhardt. I have traveled from New York for the pleasure of meeting with you. Could we speak in private?"

"There are no secrets here. Sit down, Señor Eckhardt."

"Thank you." Eckhardt seated himself in a rickety chair. "I have come to talk with you about your newspaper, *Regeneración*."

"Your accent is German," Magon said with a hard stare. "I understand the Germans are backing Huerta's man, Augustin Garza, in the Texas rebellion. Are you here in an official capacity?"

Eckhardt was momentarily speechless. "Well—" he quickly gathered his composure. "May I ask how you come by such information?"

"I have my sources," Magon said. "What is it you want of me . . . Herr Eckhardt?"

"Nothing more than that you support the movement for liberty in Texas. These are your people, Señor Magon, and *Regeneración* can speed the day to their freedom."

"*Por favor*, do not attempt to guile me with propaganda. You seek to replace one government with another, and perhaps provoke war with the United States. Why should I support your conspiracy?"

"You are a proponent of anarchy, Mr. Magon. Is not chaos, and the fall of any government, a great step toward anarchy? How could you better serve your own goals?"

"A clever argument," Magon said with a wave of his

hand. "But it begs the question in large measure. Will a rebellion in Texas open the floodgates of true anarchy? Or will it simply lead to another dictator, Huerta or someone else—a government by any name?"

"Permit me to quote your own words." Eckhardt took a slip of paper from his suit pocket. " 'The revolutionary must be willing to use terror against the state and all who support it. Violence in the name of the people!' "

"I am flattered you are a student of my philosophy. But what is your point?"

"You have struggled for fifteen years to liberate your people and free them from oppression. So I ask you now in all sincerity, Mr. Magon. Doesn't a rebellion in Texas take you closer than ever before?"

"Perhaps," Magon said vaguely. "Perhaps not."

"Then consider your own position," Eckhardt countered. "Let us presume the rebellion succeeds, and you have elected to take a neutral stance. Would your name still be spoken of with respect by those you respect? Would your people still look to you for leadership?"

Eckhardt knew that Magon was aligned with radical organizations throughout America. William "Big Bill" Haywood, who headed the Industrial Workers of the World. Samuel Gompers, the president of the American Federation of Labor. Emma Goldman, a Russian émigré anarchist whose fiery speeches championed the overthrow of the U.S. Government. And Eugene V. Debs, leader of the American Socialist movement. Intelligence reports concluded that all of these organizations provided occasional financial support to keep *Regeneración* in business.

All the more remarkable then, Eckhardt told himself, that Magon managed to publish 20,000 newspapers a week. The majority of the subscribers were in Texas and California, and by 1915 *Regeneración* had become the leading anarchist newspaper in America. Eckhardt sensed he'd struck a nerve by alluding to the loss of Magon's good name among the American radical community. These were people whose opinion mattered greatly to Magon, and he couldn't be seen as a slackard in the fight for liberty. Confident now, Eckhardt moved to close the argument.

"We both have our sources," he said. "From what I gather, you receive financial assitance from Gompers and Haywood, and other friends. Am I mistaken?"

"No, you are well informed," Magon said with a guarded look. "There are many people who applaud the efforts of *Regeneración*."

"So, then, I'm sure you wish to remain the leader in the anarchist movement. I propose you allow those I represent to further assist in your efforts."

"Are you offering me a bribe, Herr Eckhardt?"

"Nothing so crass, Señor Magon. Let us call it a contribution to the struggle for liberty."

"How large a contribution?"

"Fifty thousand dollars." Eckhardt removed an envelope from his inside jacket pocket and placed it on the desk. "And another fifty thousand with the publication of your September 1 issue."

Magon eyed the envelope. "And what message would this issue deliver, specifically?"

"A clarion call to rise up and take arms in the Texas rebellion. A ringing endorsement by *Regeneración* for the Army of Liberation."

"How do I know I would receive the final payment?"

"You have the assurance of those I represent. And we are the most ardent supporters of anarchy in America."

Ricardo Flores Magon placed the envelope in his desk drawer.

Chapter Nineteen

The train chuffed to a halt before the Brownsville depot. The engineer tooted his whistle with three sharp blasts and a cloud of steam billowed from the locomotive. Lieutenant General Frederick Funston, accompanied by his aide-de-camp, stepped off the lead passenger coach.

General Parker waited on the platform with members of his staff. Arrayed behind him was the Fort Brown marching band, buckles and buttons polished to a dazzling brilliance. Off to one side, the honor guard, resplendent as freshly painted toy soldiers, was called to present arms. The band struck up a lively military march.

"Welcome to Brownsville, General," Parker said with a snappy salute. "I trust you had a good journey."

"Tolerable," Funston replied over the racket of the band. "You didn't have to turn out the fort to greet me. It's hardly what one would call a ceremonious occasion."

"Yes, sir, though it's good for the morale of the troops. Would you care to review the honor guard, General?"

"Let's be quick about it."

Funston, with Parker to his right, walked along the front rank of the honor guard. Once a year, generally in the spring, he traveled to the various posts under his command on an annual inspection. But his trip to Brownsville was prompted by the crisis on the border, and the threat of war with Mexico. The date was August 18, with a sweltering midday sun overhead, and he was in no mood for ceremony. His review of the troops was cursory, conducted at a brisk pace.

A Ford Model-T, Parker's personal staff car, waited at the end of the platform. He led Funston to the car, and the driver, a crisply starched sergeant, opened the door. Some moments later, with the Ford puttering along in the lead, the band fell in behind, still blaring away, and the honor guard brought up the rear. Shops and stores emptied on Elizabeth Street as people turned out to watch the curious little parade. The column slowly made its way to the front gate of Fort Brown.

"Field quarters, hmmm?" Funston said, pointing to the rows of tents covering the parade ground. "How are the men holding up?"

"Quite well, General," Parker replied. "Our main problem has to do with routine medical care. The post hospital wasn't built to accommodate so many troops."

"I daresay."

Funston spoke in a precise, clipped manner. A man of short stature and keen intellect, his reputation was that of a soldier who demanded the most of subordinates. He was a graduate of West Point, and in 1898, leading a cavalry squadron, he had made his mark in the Spanish-American War. Theodore Roosevelt, a president partial to veterans of the Cuban conflict, smoothed the path to rapid promotion. He was often mentioned as a future candidate for General of the Army.

The Ford stopped in front of regimental headquarters. After the driver opened the door, Funston led Parker and his aide-de-camp into the orderly room. Sergeant Major O'Meara stood stiff as a ramrod as the officers trooped through and entered Parker's office. An orderly appeared an instant later with a large silver carafe, and Captain Hugh Willowby, Funston's aide, poured mugs of coffee. Funston settled into a chair, pulled a cigar from inside his tunic, and lit up in a blue fog of smoke. He waved Parker to his desk.

"All right, Jim," he said, motioning with the cigar. "Let's have a status report. Anything new?"

Parker seated himself at the desk. "Nothing more than my report day before yesterday. Garza and his rebels are still raising hob throughout the district."

On August 16, two days ago, Parker had submitted a lengthy briefing by telegraph. In it, he reviewed five raids in three days, with several ranches and farms burned, and four civilians killed. Army patrols, in concert with the Rangers, had accounted for seven dead rebels. The report, so soon after the raid on the King Ranch, had prompted Funston to act. He'd telegraphed back that he was on his way to Brownsville.

"This has to stop," Funston said, puffing a wad of smoke. "I've given you two thousand men over and above your normal complement. Why aren't your patrols able to intercept the rebels?"

"No excuse, sir," Parker said, in the traditional response to a commanding officer's criticism. "Although I will say we're at something of a disadvantage. The rebels operate almost exclusively at night. They're easy to miss in the dark."

"Come now, you have nearly five thousand men under your command."

"Yes, sir, that's true, but it still makes for a thin line of defense over a four-hundred-mile border. The rebels can slip across the river in a thousand different places."

"Point taken," Funston said. "Show me the disposition of your troops."

Parker unfurled a map of the Rio Grande from Brownsville to Del Rio. He used a pencil as a pointer, indicating dispositions of battalion strength at towns and villages along the four-hundred-mile stretch of river. Funston studied the map as though he might see the solution to a mystery as yet unrevealed. He finally looked up.

"You are spread thin," he conceded. "Have you considered redeploying troops from upriver closer to Brownsville? All the raids so far have occurred within fifty miles of where we sit."

Parker nodded. "The problem revolves around this much-talked-about invasion. If and when it happens, we don't know where Garza will strike." His pencil skimmed the map. "Tactically speaking, the raids around Brownsville could easily be a diversion. Garza might well be planning the invasion farther upriver—Rio Grande City or Del Rio."

"Too much river and too few men." Funston was silent a moment. "Tell me about this special agent, Frank Gordon. Do you think he's up to the job?"

"General, quite frankly, he's our biggest asset. All of the intelligence to date has been developed through his operatives in Matamoras. He has a decided talent for espionage."

"You're confident in him, then?"

"Yes, sir, I am. Of course, you can judge for yourself when he arrives. As you directed, I asked him to drop by. He should be here shortly."

"Good." Funston flicked ash from his cigar into an ashtray. "I'd like to see these handbills you mentioned in your report. Are they as bad as you said?"

"General, if anything, I'd say they're worse."

Parker gave him the postcard printed by the Rangers and the handbill printed by the rebels. Funston stared at them, the cigar wedged in the corner of his mouth, and his features knotted in a scowl. He shook his head with disgust.

"Damn the Rangers, anyway," he said tersely. "For sheer stupidity, that sets a new standard."

"Yes, sir, I couldn't agree more," Parker said. "The rebel handbills have been distributed by the thousands. Gordon's operatives report that both Mexicans and *Tejanos* are mad as hell."

"I wouldn't wonder. There is no justification for desecrating the dead."

"General, I believe it will surely come back to haunt us. One picture is worth a thousand words—and perhaps a thousand new recruits to the rebel cause."

There was a rap on the door. Sergeant Major O'Meara opened it and stood aside. "General, sir, Special Agent Gordon to see you."

Parker performed the introductions when Gordon entered the office. As he seated himself, Funston assessed him with a shrewd, penetrating glance. A moment slipped past before Funston spoke.

"General Parker speaks highly of you," he said. "I understand your operatives in Matamoras have done a commendable job."

"Thank you, sir," Gordon said. "Given the circumstances, we've been fortunate so far. Garza plays it close to the vest."

"You're convinced he means to invade Texas?"

"All of our intelligence leads to that conclusion. We believe he's assembling a force of five hundred men, maybe more. Probably somewhere around Monterrey."

"The Army of Liberation," Funston said pointedly. "No doubt armed and funded by the Germans."

"No doubt at all," Gordon remarked. "Garza meets almost daily with Otto Mueller, at the German Consulate. We suspect Mueller is a military man, an officer of some sort. He has the look of a soldier."

"And you're equally convinced this invasion will take place in early September?"

"Everything we've learned points in that direction. We're still trying to determine a specific date."

Funston thoughtfully studied the coal on the tip of his

cigar. After a time, he looked at Parker. "Jim, I'm assigning another thousand men to your command. I suggest you deploy them as a mobile reserve." He paused, his eyes steely. "Counterattack the rabble when and where they invade."

"Excellent idea, General," Parker said, clearly pleased. "I'll position them somewhere in the vicinity of McAllen. Depending on where Garza strikes, we'll be ready to move upriver or downriver. Hit him quickly, and in force."

"Good thinking." Funston's gaze turned to Gordon. "Needless to say, Mr. Gordon, the better plan would be to stop the rebels at the river. Destroy them before they set foot on American soil."

"Yes, sir, I agree," Gordon said. "I've always heard the best defense is a good offense."

"Indeed so. If you will, ask your operatives to turn heaven and earth to nail down an exact invasion date. We might just avert war with Mexico."

"I'll do my best, General."

"Splendid."

Funston thought it was a heavy burden for so young a man. But then, in a moment of vivid reflection, he remembered that day in Cuba, when he'd led the charge on Santiago. Nothing was impossible when you were young. And bold.

Frank Gordon impressed him as just such a man. A man who might yet outwit Augustin Garza and the rebels.

And most of all, the Germans.

A late afternoon sun smoldered on the horizon. The day was bright and clammy, the temperature hovering near a hundred. Puffy banks of clouds hung in the sky like balls of cotton.

The Fresnos Pump Station was located on a branch of the Arroyo Colorado River. The operation was three miles south of Harlingen and some thirty miles northwest of Brownsville. Irrigation was the lifeblood of farms throughout the lower Rio Grande valley, and millions of gallons of water were pumped each day. The Fresnos Station served farms through canals that radiated outward from the Arroyo Colorado.

Aniceto Pizana stood hidden in a tangled thicket of mesquite. Behind him, dismounted and holding their horses, were ten of his most trustworthy men. He watched the activity around the pump station, on the alert for any sign of military patrols or the Rangers. The building that housed the pumps was a large frame structure, and so far, he'd seen only three white men and four *Tejanos*. A Ford Roadster was parked outside the building.

Last night, to divert attention away from Pizana, two raids had been staged near the border. Luis Vasquez and twenty men had ambushed a cavalry squad not far from the village of Ojo de Agua. Their mission was to kill the squad of troopers, and thereby convince Texans that the Army of Liberation would actively seek out and engage military units.

The second raid was conducted by Miguel Barragan and Juan Cross, leading a party of eight men. Based on intelligence developed by Barragan, their orders were to dynamite a railroad bridge five miles north of Brownsville. They had detonated the explosives not ten minutes after the train carrying General Frederick Funston crossed the bridge. The message sent was one of contempt for military security and the army high command. Had they wished, they could have easily killed General Funston.

Pizana and his men had forded the Rio Grande shortly after the raids began. With the cavalry patrols and the Rangers diverted elsewhere, they made their way in the dark to the Fresnos Pump Station, some fifteen miles north of the border. All day they had remained hidden in the dense mesquite thicket, silent and still, nothing to betray their presence. The raid was planned for late afternoon, not long before sundown. They would retreat back into Mexico under cover of darkness.

The purpose of the raid was to strike at the heart of the Anglo economy. Farmers were dependent on the pump stations and the canals to irrigate their fields and nourish their crops. The destruction of a pump station affected scores of farmers, and brought with it the threat that their bountiful fields would return to the fallow earth of a decade ago. Terror came in various forms, and economic ruin was at the top of the list for those whose livelihood centered on agriculture. Without irrigation, the lower Rio Grande valley would be converted into a wasteland.

As he watched the pump station, Pizana still simmered over the incident at the King Ranch. He had lost eleven men in a bloody attack that, in retrospect, seemed not just futile but foolish. Even now, almost a fortnight later, the postcard of the Rangers dragging the bodies of his *soldados* played out vividly in his mind. He was determined he would not lose so much as a single man on today's raid. He would, instead, avenge those brutalized by the Rangers.

On his signal, Pizana's men mounted. They rode out of the mesquite thicket, spurring their horses into a gallop, and crossed the open ground to their front in a matter of seconds. The workers at the pump station looked around, startled by the sight of horsemen bearing down on them, and realized there was no place to run. The raiders fanned out, encircling the workers, and herded them to the front of the building. Pizana reined his horse to a halt.

"*Buenos dias*," he said pleasantly. "Who is in charge here?"

There was a moment of leaden silence. The four *Tejanos* stared at him as if he'd asked a question too profound for comprehension. The three white men exchanged nervous glances, and finally one of them stepped forward. He was stout, with a potbelly and wire-rimmed spectacles, and his jaw bulged with a wad of chewing tobacco. He cleared his throat.

"I manage the station."

"And your name, señor?"

"Seth Dodd."

Pizana nodded. "I am Captain Aniceto Pizana, of the Army of Liberation. You have heard of us?"

"Yeah," Dodd said in a shaky voice. "I've heard."

"You do not sound impressed, *señor*. What is it you've heard?"

"Nothin' good."

"No?" Pizana feigned surprise. "One time I had a disagreement with a Texan. He told me: It's like a fly walking across a mirror; it all depends on how you look at it. I was not amused."

Dodd bobbed his head. "Reckon I wouldn't've been either."

"But later I came to understand the wisdom of his words. The man who has the power dictates the terms. *Comprende*?"

"Meanin' you've got the power today."

"Yes," Pizana said, gesturing at the frame building. "I intend to destroy your pump station, señor. Do you object?"

"Nope." Dodd spat a stream of tobacco juice. "I'm not in no position to object."

Pizana motioned to his men. Three of them, already assigned the task, stepped off their horses. They hurried into the building, returning a moment later with cans of kerosene, and splashed it over the outside walls. The half-empty cans were thrown back inside, and one of them lit a match, tossing it into the doorway. The pump station went up in a roaring *whoosh* of flame.

Dodd and the other men watched as the building was

engulfed in fire. Pizana pointed to the Ford Roadster. "That is a fine automobile," he said. "Does it belong to you, *se-ñor*?"

"Yep." Dodd shifted his cud to the other cheek. "I suppose you're gonna burn it, too."

"Yes, I think so."

One of the raiders punctured the gas tank with a knife. A match flared and within moments the Ford Roadster burst into an oily ball of flame. Pizana looked on with satisfaction as the tires popped and smoke billowed into the sky. Then his gaze shifted back to Dodd.

"Are you a religious man, *señor*?"

"Methodist," Dodd said without expression. "You fixin' to kill us?"

"We are at war, and soldiers must follow orders. You understand that, don't you?"

"I understand you're the sorriest sonovabitch I ever laid eyes on. You ain't nothin' but a gawddamn murderer."

Pizana stared at him with a cold smile. "*Suerte y mortaja del cielo bajan.* Do you know the saying?"

"I don't speak Mex."

"Fortune and death come from above."

"Says you," Dodd muttered. "God didn't send no greaser to kill me."

"You will soon find out, *señor*."

Still mounted, Pizana turned in the saddle. "*Hombres*," he said addressing the four *Tejanos* in Spanish. "These *gringos* are dead men, but your lives will be spared. You have only to serve our cause."

The *Tejanos* bowed their heads, unable to hold his gaze. "Watch and remember," Pizana went on. "Tell our people what you saw here today. *Libertad* for those who join our ranks!"

Dodd and the other two white men were forced to their knees. Three raiders moved behind them with Winchester carbines, thumbing the hammers to full cock. One of the men moaned, his features stark with fear, and Dodd turned his eyes heavenward, his lips parted in silent prayer. On Pizana's command, the rebels fired.

The men pitched forward on their faces. Blood and brain matter puddled the ground around their heads, and Dodd's right leg kicked in a spasm of afterdeath. A moment slipped past, the bodies bathed in the reddish glow of flames from the pump house and the burning car. One of the *Tejanos* crossed himself as the raiders swung into their saddles.

Pizana led his men south from the Arroyo Colorado.

Chapter Twenty

The Rangers were ganged around the annex of the court-house. They stood smoking and talking under a late afternoon sun, their conversation centered on the action of last night. The general consensus was that they'd again been outshone by the greasers.

Inside Ranger headquarters, an after-action war council was under way. The three Ranger companies had returned to Brownsville only an hour before, and the officers were trying to determine where they'd gone wrong. The air was thick with smoke and curses, and no matter how many times they rehashed it, the result was the same. Their response to the raids was too little, too late.

Last night, Company D, commanded by Clell Morris, had been dispatched after reports of a railroad bridge being blown north of Brownsville. They had caught four Mexicans crossing the river outside San Pedro, and killed one in a brief gunfight. Company C, under John Sanders, had been held in reserve, expecting a call of yet another raid. The call never came.

Bob Ransom, with Company A, had gone upriver to Ojo de Agua. Gordon and Maddox had accompanied him, and outside the village they'd found something akin to a slaughterhouse. A cavalry patrol, nine troopers and a sergeant, had been ambushed by overwhelming forces, and killed to a man. The bodies were sprawled along the banks of the Rio Grande, and all the sign indicated they had been taken by complete surprise. None of them had gotten off a shot.

"Damnedest thing I've ever seen," Ransom said. "The greasers waylaid them in a grove of cottonwoods and blew 'em clean outta the saddle. Poor bastards never had a chance."

"Turnabout, all right," Sauders mused. "Jump the soldier boys on purpose, 'stead of tryin' to steer clear. Sounds like they're sendin' a message to the army."

"Could've sent a big one," Morris said. "Dynamited that bridge right after General Funston's train went by. Guess they didn't know he was on it."

Maddox laughed sourly. "Everybody in Brownsville knew. Why wouldn't they?"

"Hoyt's right," Gordon observed. "Congress would declare war tomorrow if they'd killed General Funston. I think they're biding their time."

"How's that again?" Sauders asked. "You sayin' they knew he was on that train?"

"Well, Captain, they seem to know everything else."

"Damned if they don't!" Morris said bitterly. "We only jumped four of them dynamiters at the river. Had to be more'n that."

Sanders looked at him. "You lost me there, Clell. What's your point?"

"Some of them dynamiters was *Tejanos*, and they never tried to cross the river. They're probably livin' right here in Brownsville."

"Cap'n, they're living everywhere," Maddox said. "Spit in any direction and there's a chance of hittin' a sympathizer. Not too many rootin' for us gringos."

The phone jangled. Ransom, who was seated behind the desk, lifted the receiver. The others continued their conversation as he listened, occasionally asking a question, his features suddenly stern. After several minutes, he slammed the receiver on the hook. His eyes were like cinders.

"Sonsabitches hit again," he said. "That was the town marshal in Harlingen. They burned down a pump station and killed three white men. Got away clean."

"Jesus," Sanders muttered. "When was this?"

"Yesterday afternoon. The *Tejanos* that work there took off, and nobody caught on till the canals started runnin' dry. Somebody finally went to have a look at the pump station."

"Seth Dodd," Morris said in a rueful tone. "He managed the place."

"Well, he's dead now," Ransom grunted. "Him and the other two was executed. Shot in the back of the head."

"That don't make sense," Sanders said. "I was here all last night, and there wasn't any report of anybody tryin' to cross the river. Where'd the bastards get to?"

"Maybe they went to ground," Morris said. "Might be hidin' out somewheres."

"Not likely," Ransom said. "I'd bet the soldier boys let 'em slip through. Wouldn't be the first time."

The Ranger captains fell to arguing. Morris and Sanders thought it possible the raiders were hiding out, and Ransom insisted they'd evaded the army patrols. Gordon listened a while, but he soon grew bored with a debate that would ultimately come to a dead end. Whoever was right, too much time had passed, and the chances of finding the rebels were virtually nil. He told Maddox he would see him later at the hotel.

Outside, the Rangers were still smoking and talking, waiting for their captains. Gordon walked to the hotel, and once in his room, stripped off the clothes he'd worn since yesterday. He took a long, leisurely bath, weary of chasing phantoms and rumors, wondering if he knew the truth of anything. Around seven o'clock, he went downstairs to dinner, figuring Maddox was still tied up with Ranger business. He thought it was just as well, for it was early, and he might yet catch Martinez and Vargas. He decided to call on Guadalupe.

Shortly after eight o'clock he knocked on her door. She greeted him with an engaging smile, holding the door open, and rolled her eyes toward the dining area. Martinez and Vargas were seated at the table, lingering over a last cup of coffee, cigarette smoke eddying in the lamplight. Gordon saw nothing of Antonio, and felt oddly disappointed the boy had already been put to bed. Guadalupe hurried to clear dirty dishes from the table.

"*Buenas noches*," Gordon said, seating himself. "I had hoped to find you here."

Martinez waved his cigarette. "There was so little to report, *jefe*. You already know of the raids, *verdad*?"

"Yes, I was out with the Rangers. You probably heard of the soldiers killed at Ojo de Agua."

"*Aiiii caramba!*" Vargas said with a disgusted look. "They talk of nothing else in Matamoras. The story is everywhere."

Gordon's brow knotted. "Do you know who led the ambush?"

"Who else?" Vargas said quickly. "*El Diablo's asesino.* Vasquez himself."

"And the pump station outside Harlingen?" Gordon asked. "Three men were executed and the station destroyed. Any word on that?"

"*Si.*" Vargas took a drag on his cigarette, exhaled smoke. "Garza brought Pizana and Vasquez to the *cantina* and crowed of their victories. Pizana thinks himself a *malo hombre.*"

Guadalupe took a chair beside Gordon. Martinez watched them with a lazy smile, smoke curling out of his nostrils. He knew without being told that his sister was sleeping with the *Americano* agent. Whether or not it was a good thing was not for him to say. But she was happier than at any time since her husband had been killed in the battle for Matamoras. He hoped it would go well.

"What of Mueller?" Gordon said. "Any unusual activity at the German Consulate?"

Vargas wagged his head. "Garza meets with him once a day, sometimes more. Nothing out of the ordinary."

"Have you heard any rumors about the invasion date? Do they talk of it at the *cantina*?"

"There is no talk at all. I think it is a secret known only to Garza and Mueller."

Martinez stubbed out his cigarette in an ashtray. "Maybe I could make up an excuse to call on Garza. Last time, his mouth was faster than his brain. He might slip again."

"Hector, it's too dangerous," Gordon told him. "Unless we have a reasonable excuse, it might raise Garza's suspicions. I won't let you take that risk."

"Pardon my saying so, *jefe*, but today is August 20. If they mean to invade in early September, we have three weeks, maybe less. Don't you—and the army—need to know the exact date?"

"Perhaps I'll feel differently in a week or so. Who knows, they might somehow tip their hand. Let me think about it."

"Do not fear too much for my safety. *Madre de Dios*, I'm a slippery one! I always get away."

"We'll see how it goes, Hector."

Martinez and Vargas shortly excused themselves. Nothing was said, but their sly smiles indicated they knew they'd overstayed their welcome. They bid Gordon goodnight, shaking his hand, and Guadalupe walked them to the door. She returned a moment later.

"All this talk of war." Her eyes sparkled with mischief. "I thought it would never end."

"You are the bold one, aren't you?"

"*Si*, and wicked too, *caro mio*."

Gordon took her in his arms.

Otto Mueller was seated at his desk the next afternoon. He heard voices in the vestibule of the consulate, and then footsteps approaching along the hallway. Garza moved through the door of the office.

"*Buenas tardes*," he said. "Am I interrupting?"

"No, no." Mueller set aside a pen and sheaf of paper. "I was drafting a report on your raids. How many soldiers did Vasquez kill?"

"Ten, including the patrol sergeant."

"Excellent. Vasquez has the making of a good field commander. My superiors will be pleased."

Garza was reminded again that the Germans placed great value on written reports. He wondered just how impressed Mueller's superiors would be with the ambush of a cavalry squad. Or perhaps, he told himself, Mueller was simply trying to put the best face on things until the invasion. He took a chair before the desk.

"We are planning more raids," he said. "Apart from that, there is little immediate news. I came here only because you insist on meeting every day."

"Not without purpose," Mueller informed him. "Unlike you, I must answer to my superiors, and they require detailed reports. To be precise, I need the latest advisory from Monterrey. How many men have been recruited?"

"I received a letter this morning from Hilario Hinojosa, the *comandante* of our training camp. So far, we have three thousand men."

Garza's features betrayed nothing. The actual number was slightly more than two thousand, but he felt no compunctions about lying to Mueller. He had every confidence

Hinojosa would bring the squadron to full strength by the time of the invasion. He saw no reason to concern the Germans.

"Three thousand," Mueller repeated, staring across his desk. "You were provided with sufficient rifles for four thousand men. Will you fall short, Herr Garza?"

"There will be a man for every rifle, and more. You can assure your superiors we will invade with a full cavalry squadron."

"Even so, we need far more to pose a serious threat to the American government. You assured me all these raids would draw thousands of *Tejanos* to your ranks. Why have so few enlisted?"

"We've discussed this before," Garza said. "They will rally to our cause once we cross the river in force. They merely await proof that we are in earnest."

"Not good enough," Mueller said firmly. "You must prepare their minds to accept the inevitability of rebellion. Prove you are in earnest now, today."

Garza raised an eyebrow. "How would I accomplish that?"

"Provide them with an object lesson. Kill *Tejanos* who refuse to join your army, and announce the reason. The others will rush to enlist."

"You want me to kill my own people?"

"Not in great numbers," Mueller explained. "Forty or fifty will do nicely. Sufficient to make the point."

"No," Garza said stiffly. "We do not kill our own."

"Indeed? Correct me if I am wrong, Herr Garza. When you served under General Huerta, didn't you execute prisoners from Carranza's army? Stand them against a wall and shoot them—all in the name of the *Revolución*?"

"Yes, but that was different."

"Oh, different in what way?"

"We were fighting to free Mexico."

"You make fine distinctions," Mueller said with heavy sarcasm. "You are fighting now to liberate Texas, and ultimately return General Huerta to power in Mexico. Are the lives of a few *Tejanos* too great a sacrifice?"

Garza thought back to conversations he'd had with Vasquez and Pizana. He recalled how they were infuriated by *Tejanos* who refused to join in the aftermath of a raid. Time and again, when their *gringo* masters were killed before their eyes, *Tejanos* stood mute when asked to volunteer. Their fear was but a form of treason.

Hector Martinez, the recruiting sergeant, came to mind as well. Frustrated with *Tejanos* who ignored the call to arms, Martinez had risked insubordination and demanded to be assigned to a field unit. Perhaps, in the end, the lives of a few *Tejanos* was the price required to kindle a people's rebellion. Sometimes a sacrifice was needed to serve the greater good.

"You have a point," Garza said at length. "I will order the death of selected *Tejanos*, at the right place and the right time. An example to those who refuse to join the fight for liberty."

"I applaud your foresight, Herr Garza. A commander must sometimes make hard decisions."

Mueller thought no man was immune to German logic. He wasn't fully convinced that Garza was telling him the truth about the number of men being trained outside Monterrey. But for the purposes of his communiqué to Colonel von Kleist, he could only report what he'd been told. The actual number seemed immaterial to him anyway. A thousand men invading Texas would still start a war.

After Garza left, he completed his report. He sealed the envelope with wax and took it to the counselor's office, where it would be dispatched by diplomatic courier to New York. His relationship with Erwin Reinhardt remained distant, and he often thought the consular preferred not to know the details of the conspiracy. Which was just as well, for he rarely told Reinhardt anything.

As was his custom, Mueller left the consulate early. He walked to the Bezar Hotel, where he was now on cordial terms with the manager and the staff. In his suite, he bathed, changed into a fresh suit, and prepared for the night ahead. Over the past two months, he'd grown accustomed to the leisurely pace of Matamoras, and found that he could separate his professional life from his personal life. His nights were devoted to long dinners and the convivial company of those who frequented the nightclub. And finally, to Maria Dominguez.

Late that evening, after her last show, Maria came to the suite. She still had her own room in the hotel, but for all practical purposes she was living with Mueller. One of the closets in the bedroom was filled with her clothes, and the scent of her perfume and bath salts permeated the air. Tonight, as she did every night, she took special pains to make herself alluring and desirable before she joined Mueller in bed. Her passion, though largely pretense in the beginning, was now genuine. She made love to him in ways he'd never imagined.

Somewhere after midnight, she lay snuggled in his arms, drifting on a quenched flame. Despite his stolid manner, he was an ardent lover, and generous with gifts and flowers and tokens of affection. She knew he was infatuated with her, and while she didn't love him, she felt a fondness more intense than she'd experienced with other men. Yet she was honest with herself, and readily admitted that part of it was mercenary. She thought he might be her ticket out of Matamoras.

"*Querido mio*," she said softly. "Are you awake?"

Mueller stirred. "Awake but unconscious. You've drained me of strength."

"And it is the same for me, sweet Otto. You take my breath."

"Ummm, I know the feeling."

She was still a moment. "I was wondering . . ."

"Yes."

"Do you know when you will return to Berlin?"

"No, not yet," Mueller said sleepily. "Why do you ask?"

"Well . . ." she paused, then rushed on. "I've seen nothing of the world, and from all you've said, Berlin sounds so sophisticated. I was thinking it might be fun."

"Are you serious?"

"Of course I'm serious. I couldn't bear for you to leave without me."

"Nor I," Mueller said, suddenly wide awake. "But I must tell you we couldn't be married. The Kaiser forbids foreign wives for . . . government officials."

"Who cares?" she said gaily. "I will be your mistress."

"You will?"

"Do you doubt me?"

She snuggled closer, nibbled his ear. Her hand crept lower and suddenly all of Mueller was awake. She laughed a low throaty laugh.

"Ummm, what have we here?"

Mueller groaned, his mouth thick and pasty with lust. He thought of Berlin in the springtime . . .

And Maria.

Chapter Twenty-one

On Monday morning Gordon and Maddox were summoned to Fort Brown. The day was hot and sticky, and they were sweating heavily by the time they walked into post headquarters. Sergeant Major O'Meara greeted them with a bluff smile.

"You gentlemen look a little wilted. Hot enough for you?"

Maddox removed his Stetson and mopped his forehead with a kerchief. "They're fryin' eggs on the sidewalk uptown, but it's not all that bad. I've seen worse."

"Speak for yourself," Gordon said. "I need a bucket of ice and a wet towel."

"Well, sir," O'Meara said, deadpan, "a day like today puts me in mind of the remark by General Phil Sheridan. You'll recollect he was posted to Texas after the Civil War."

"That was a bit before my time, Sergeant Major. What was it he said?"

"General Sheridan allowed that if he owned Texas, he'd rent it out and live in hell. There's many who would agree with him."

"Sheridan was a Yankee," Maddox grumbled trenchantly. "Probably a sissy to boot. Texas is man's country."

"Guess that makes me a sissy," Gordon said with a laugh. "Gets any worse, I'm liable to melt."

Sergeant Major O'Meara nodded, a sly glint in his eye.

He rapped lightly on the door of the inner office and held it open for them. General Parker was seated at his desk, an overhead fan shoving hot air around. He motioned them to chairs.

"Good morning," he said, waiting for them to be seated. "I appreciate your coming by on such short notice."

Maddox hung his Stetson on his knee. "Your message sounded like it was important, General."

"You be the judge."

Parker spread a map of the lower Rio Grande across his desk. He pointed to Reynosa, a town on the Mexican side of the border, some fifty miles upriver. His forefinger tapped along the shoreline.

"I received a report from Colonel Bullard, who commands the battalion in the area. One of his patrols spotted six boat landings over the weekend."

Gordon suddenly forgot the heat. "What sort of boat landings?"

"Quite well engineered, actually," Parker said. "On the order of twenty feet wide, with skids to maneuver boats into the water. The landings weren't there on Saturday and they were on Sunday morning. We deduce they were constructed overnight."

"Damn," Maddox said. "Take a lot of men to build all that in one night."

"Indeed it would," Parker agreed. "Colonel Bullard inspected the landings quite carefully through binoculars. Hidden in the brush, he also saw sixty boats set back from the riverbank. He estimated each boat would carry twenty men."

Gordon studied the map. "We have to assume they're planning the invasion from Reynosa. We're talking twelve hundred men."

"Something funny here." Maddox thoughtfully rubbed his jaw. "Mexicans generally operate with cavalry as their main force. Those boats sound like they've got some foot troops."

"So it does," Parker agreed. "Or the boats may be to ferry across munitions and supplies. In any event, I believe we've sadly underestimated Mr. Garza."

"By how much?" Gordon asked. "What's the ratio of infantry to cavalry?"

Parker considered a moment. "The Mexican Revolution provides an excellent gauge. Their forward elements are heavily weighted toward cavalry, usually two to one. We could be looking at an invasion force of four thousand, perhaps more."

"Up till now we've just been guessin'," Maddox said. "Appears like they've done a helluva recruitin' job at Monterrey. Four thousand men's nothin' to sneeze at."

"Unless, of course, we're wrong," Parker said. "Even with German funding, where would they obtain three thousand horses? And how would they move four thousand men from Monterrey by early September? We really need better intelligence."

Gordon glanced at a calendar on the wall. The date was August 23, which meant early September might be only a week away. "I'll talk to Martinez," he said, nodding to Parker. "We'll invent a plausible reason for him to contact Garza. Let's hope he uncovers something."

"Sooner rather than later," Parker said. "Colonel Bullard brought another matter to my attention which bears on our discussion. Are *Tejanos* actually being killed by Garza's raiders?"

"Yessir, they sure are," Maddox affirmed. "Two raids over the weekend, one led by Vasquez and the other by Pizana. Killed thirty-four *Tejanos* altogether."

"What do you make of that, Sergeant?"

"Well, sir, they made it pretty plain. Any *Tejano* that

don't volunteer for the Army of Liberation risks gettin'
killed. Serve or die, that's the message."

Parker grimaced. "The threat of death to force *Tejanos*
to join in a mass uprising. Gentlemen, I think we're very
close to an invasion."

Gordon again glanced at the calendar. A week, two
weeks, certainly no more than three. And so many un-
knowns, all too much guesswork.

Time was running out.

The sky was clear, black as pitch, the Big Dipper at its
zenith. Starlight blanketed the countryside in a silvery cast
so bright the leaves of trees glittered like fireflies. Somewhere off in the distance, the hoot of an owl broke the
stillness.

Tandy's Creek gurgled beneath a railroad bridge, then
followed a serpentine path through a landscape dotted with
brush. Luis Vasquez stood in dappled light under a stand
of cottonwoods, forty men and their horses waiting in the
shadows. His eyes were fixed on the rail line to the north.

The bridge was ten miles northwest of Brownsville.
Earlier, working with crowbars, Vasquez and his men had
removed spikes anchoring a section of rail to the cross ties.
By now, everyone knew that soldiers were assigned to
guard the railways, and their mission was to derail the train
due into Brownsville at midnight. None of the soldiers were
to leave the wreck alive.

A light pierced the darkness to the north. Some moments later the rumbling throb of a locomotive sounded as
it rattled along the railroad tracks. The headlamp on the
front of the engine grew brighter as the train approached,
misty white swirls from the smokestack fleeting skyward in
a rush of wind. Vasquez watched as the train loomed out
of the night, the dim glow of lanterns spilling through the

windows of three passenger coaches. His eyes narrowed, his mouth a tight crease.

The front wheels of the locomotive hit the section of rail that had been prised sideways from the roadbed. The front of the engine barreled off the tracks, colliding at full speed with the timbers of the bridge, and toppled into the creek like a hissing dragon. Directly behind, the coal tender snapped loose from its coupling, slamming into the engineer's cab, and dragged the coaches down a slight incline uptrack of the bridge. The coaches went airborne a moment, separating like links in a chain, then crashed to earth upright on a zigzag line. The firebox in the locomotive exploded in a thunderous burst of flame.

Vasquez and his men swarmed over the coaches. They separated into squads, some firing through the windows and others attacking through the doors. Few of the civilians were armed, but the raiders made no distinction, killing thirteen passengers already stunned by the jarring impact of the wreck. Late-night trains usually carried workingmen, and Vasquez counted it a blessing that there were no women or children among the passengers. The conductor, who locked himself in the lavatory, was riddled with bullets through the door.

The five soldiers riding guard were in the second coach. A brief fight ensued, with the soldiers taking cover behind seats, but they were outnumbered and outgunned. One was killed, another wounded in the shoulder, and the other three surrendered, dropping their rifles in the aisle. The third coach, often called the "Jim Crow" car, was segregated, the seating restricted to Negroes, Orientals and Mexicans. Tonight, the car carried two Negroes and four men of Mexican ancestry. By Vasquez's order, none of them were killed.

The prisoners were herded off to the side of the roadbed. The lanterns in the coaches were shattered, the cars quickly consumed in flame, and the terrain was bathed in eerie firelight. Vasquez placed guards on the Negroes and Mexicans, and ordered the four soldiers lined up in front of the burning coaches. He was leery of wasting time, for he had ten miles to travel to the border, and the likelihood of fighting his way through a cavalry patrol. He directed four raiders onto a line facing the soldiers.

"You are sentenced to death," he said in a strong voice. "We are at war, and as soldiers, you will be allowed to die by firing squad. Have you any last words?"

The soldiers stared at him as though unable to comprehend their sudden turn of fate. One of them, a corporal in charge of the detail, thrust out his jaw. "Yeah, I got somethin' to say. You're the lousiest cocksuckers I ever—"

Vasquez shouted a command. His men fired and the soldiers crumpled to the ground, their shirts splattered with blood. The reverberation of the Winchesters echoed through the night, and without another look at the bodies, Vasquez turned to the other prisoners. He ignored the Negroes, his gaze fixed on the four Mexicans.

"I am Captain Vasquez," he said in Spanish. "Who among you is *Tejano*?"

None of them moved. "Listen to me, *hombres*," he said brusquely. "I call on you to join the Army of Liberation. Here, tonight!"

Whether they were *Tejano* or Mexican, they all avoided his steely gaze. He pointed to one of them. "You, step forward."

The man hesitantly took a step forward. Vásquez pulled a revolver from his holster, sighted quickly in the firelight, and fired. The slug struck the man in the chest and his legs collapsed like an accordion. He fell dead on the ground.

"Remember what you have seen," Vasquez said to the

others. "Tell our people to join in the fight for liberty or they will surely die. God wills it of all!"

The raiders rode south only moments later. By the bridge, the flames from the engine and the coaches leaped higher, lighting the night with fiery brilliance. The two Negroes and the three remaining Mexicans stood huddled amidst the carnage.

Their thoughts were on the last thing said by the one who called himself Vasquez. They wondered what evil God he served.

The bridge at Tandy's Creek was two miles outside the town of Olmito. A farmer who lived nearby had seen the flames and heard the gunshots, and never for a moment doubted that it was the work of the rebels. He drove his wagon into Olmito to notify the town marshal.

Captain Bob Ransom and Company A arrived on the scene shortly before daybreak. They were mounted on horseback, accompanied by Gordon and Maddox. Off in the countryside, away from decent roads, Ransom had wanted his men mounted, and Gordon agreed. The horses were drawn from the remuda Company A kept corralled on the outskirts of Brownsville.

Ken Braxton, the town marshal, led them on an inspection of the wreckage. The engineer and the fireman had been killed when the locomotive exploded and brought down the north end of the bridge. The coaches were reduced to smoldering rubble, the remains of the passengers charred beyond recognition. The bodies of the soldiers and the Mexican lay where they had fallen.

"Helluva night's work," Ransom said, his features mottled with rage. "I count twenty-two dead, including the soldiers. Don't look like they put up much of a fight."

"Hard to say, Cap'n," Maddox observed, eyeing the

wreckage. "Way that train come off the tracks, they probably didn't have much fight left. Must've banged 'em up pretty good."

"Yeah, but you'd think they would've got one rebel, anyways. Appears to me they surrendered *muy* damn *pronto*."

"Let's not jump to conclusions," Gordon interrupted. "I want to talk with the survivors. Maybe there's something to be learned."

"I'll leave you to it," Ransom said, nodding to Ken Braxton. "The marshal tells me a bunch of *Tejanos* live not too far off. Think I'll see if they had a hand in this business."

"I'll stick with Frank," Maddox said. "Might be he'll need somebody that speaks Mex."

"Suit yourself."

Ransom rode off with ten Rangers, headed west. The first rays of sunrise tinged the horizon as Gordon and Maddox left the other Rangers to sift through the wreckage. They crossed to where the Negroes and Mexicans were standing at the side of the roadbed. Gordon nodded to the black men.

"I know you've had a bad night," he said. "But I was hoping you'd be able to fill in some details. How many raiders were there?"

"Thirty, mebbe forty," one of the men replied. "Things was happenin' so fast I didn't rightly stop to count."

"And how did the soldiers die? Were they executed?"

"Yassuh, they sure nuff was. Got pulled off the train and stood up 'fore a firin' squad. Just plain murder."

"Could you identify any of the raiders? Were any names mentioned?"

"The one givin' all the orders called hisself Vasquez. Cap'n Vasquez, and right proud of it."

Gordon and Maddox exchanged a glance. Maddox

turned to the four Mexicans. "*Habla inglés?*" he asked, waiting until two of them nodded. "Who killed your *compañero?*"

The men looked at the body on the ground. "*El Capitán Vasquez*," one of them said. "He shot Miguel with his own hand."

"Did he give a reason? Why Miguel and not you?"

"*El Capitán* asked if we were *Tejanos*. When we made no reply, he ordered Miguel forward. And then he shot him."

"Did Vasquez say why?"

"*Sí.*"

The man went on to explain. He related how Vasquez ordered them to tell all Mexicans and *Tejanos* that life was forfeit unless they joined the Army of Liberation. Miguel Gomez was killed to underscore the message.

Maddox questioned them until he had the full story. After thanking the men, he and Gordon walked back toward the bridge. Maddox shook his head.

"Like to meet this Vasquez," he muttered. "Give him a dose of his own medicine."

"Garza gets my vote," Gordon said. "Stop him and we stop the rebellion."

"Frank, I'd second the motion."

An hour or so later Ransom rode in with a prisoner. The man was Mexican, mounted bareback on a mule, his wrists secured by manacles. The Ranger detail dismounted and tied their horses in the cottonwoods along the creek. Ransom pulled his prisoner off the mule and marched him forward, followed by Braxton. They stopped in front of Gordon and Maddox.

"Meet Felix Santos," Ransom said, grinning at Gordon. "You're always wantin' to interrogate somebody. Here's your man."

Gordon looked the man over. "Who is he?"

"*Tejano* sharecropper," Ransom said. "Marshal Braxton says he's always runnin' off at the mouth about the Army of Liberation. Found some of their handbills in his shack."

"Do you think he's one of the raiders?"

"I'd tend to doubt it. All he's got is that wore-out mule and a little peashooter twenty-two rifle. His woman swore he was home all night."

"Then why did you arrest him?"

" 'Cause he supports the goddamn rebels."

"Hoyt," Gordon said, "see what he knows."

Maddox addressed the man in Spanish. Santos appeared terrified, babbling on in a shaky voice, the manacles rattling as he gestured with his hands. The interrogation went on for several minutes, and finally Maddox turned back to Gordon. He wagged his head.

"I'd judge he's all wind and no whistle. Sharecrops cotton and don't have much use for gringo landowners. Says the rebels promised to distribute the land to the people. Sides with them, but it's mostly just talk."

"So he hasn't broken the law," Gordon said. "Half of southern Texas supports the rebels, and we can't arrest them all. Let him go."

"Don't think so," Ransom broke in. "You're through with him, I'll take it from here. He's my prisoner."

"What are you planning to do?"

"I'm gonna give the rebels tit for tat. They're shootin' *Tejanos* to convince 'em to join up. Time we started shootin' a few to convince 'em otherwise."

"You can't shoot an innocent man."

"Innocent, my ass!" Ransom hooted. "Sonovabitch already admitted whose side he's on. He's gonna pay the price."

Gordon bristled. "I'm giving you a direct order, Captain. Back off or I'll place you under arrest."

"Hell you will," Ransom said coldly. "Try it and I'll bury you. Nobody arrests me."

"You're bettin' a loser," Maddox said in a hard voice. "Frank calls the shots here, and I'm backin' his play. Don't try anything dumb, Cap'n."

Ransom's features went red as oxblood. He knew it was no idle threat, for Maddox was the deadliest gunman in a generation of Rangers. What angered him most was that Maddox would stand with an outsider, but there was nothing for it. His brow knotted in a scowl.

"You'd best find yourself another job. You're through in the Rangers."

"Not likely, Cap'n," Maddox said with a sardonic smile. "I'll thank you for the key to those manacles."

Felix Santos survived the day at Tandy's Creek. He was released and rode off from the death and devastation of the train wreck on his long-eared mule. His terror of the Rangers was largely forgotten when he walked through the door of his sharecropper's shanty.

He told his wife the rebels were certain to take Texas.

Chapter Twenty-two

The train wreck acted as a catalyst in the spreading rebellion. Newspapers labeled it "The Massacre at Tandy's Creek," decrying twenty-two dead, with four soldiers and a *Tejano* executed. Editorials, fiercely jingoistic in tone, called for swift and decisive retaliation.

The following evening a mass meeting was held in Brownsville. Mayor Arthur Brown assembled more than two hundred civic and business leaders from the Rio Grande valley. After several impassioned speeches, the group drafted a petition to President Wilson demanding that U.S. troops be allowed to pursue the marauders into Mexico. The group also requested a federal declaration of martial law for the duration of the crisis. Military authorities, they insisted, should be granted supreme powers along the border.

President Wilson responded decisively. Three days later, on August 29, he ordered the War Department to post an additional thousand troops to the lower Rio Grande. Although he refused to permit U.S. forces to cross the river, he issued a proclamation recognizing Venustiano Carranza as the de facto leader of Mexico. The reason became apparent when Secretary of State Robert Lansing, on the same day, requested that Carranza assign army units to police the Mexican side of the river. The communiqué also called for the arrest of Augustin Garza, Luis Vasquez, and Aniceto Pizana.

The request for a declaration of martial law was rejected. But in a sweeping measure, President Wilson issued an edict placing local and state law enforcement agencies under military rule. The decree effectively granted General Parker authority over local police, county sheriffs' departments, and the Texas Rangers. Among civic and business leaders, there was unanimous approval of the President's quick response to their petition. The Texas Rangers adopted a stance of surly outrage.

On August 31, General Parker convened a meeting at Fort Brown. Those directed to attend were Gordon and Maddox, the three Ranger captains, and Sheriff Walter Vann. Sergeant Major O'Meara ushered them into the office, where a row of chairs were arranged before the post commander's desk. Captain Jack Fox, whose Ranger Company B was stationed in Del Rio, had not been ordered to make the trip downriver. There was a moment of uneasy silence while the men got themselves seated. Parker, who chose to stand, faced them with his hands clasped behind his back.

"Gentlemen, thank you for coming," he said by way of greeting. "I asked you here to review several matters bearing on the rebellion, as well as recent incidents involving civilians. Before we begin, are there any questions regarding President Wilson's directive about the chain of command?"

Sheriff Vann, who felt relieved by the turn of events, slowly shook his head. The Ranger captains swapped veiled glances, and it was obvious Ransom had been appointed their spokesman. "Couple things aren't too clear, General." Ransom's features were sullen, his eyes set in a squint. "What if Governor Ferguson tells us one thing and you tell us another? Whose orders do we follow?"

"You follow mine," Parker said firmly. "Your alternative would be to return to Austin until the situation here has resolved itself. Does that clarify the matter?"

"What about Gordon?" Ransom said, avoiding a direct answer. "He's been pretty free with his orders lately. Does he answer to you, now?"

"Mr. Gordon answers directly to the President. You will continue to follow any orders he sees fit to issue."

"How about Maddox?"

"Sergeant Maddox is assigned to Mr. Gordon. He does not fall under your command, Captain."

"Well, shit," Ransom said in a disgruntled voice. "Looks to me like we got too many chiefs and not enough braves."

Parker stared at him. "I understand you attempted to kill a *Tejano* at the site of the train wreck. Is that correct?"

"Somebody's got to show these pepper-guts we mean business. Otherwise they're gonna join the rebels in droves."

"I'm told you also threatened to shoot Mr. Gordon when he intervened. Is that true?"

Ransom gave Gordon a venomous look. "Some people get too big for their britches. He threatened to arrest me."

"I'll do worse," Parker said levelly. "If you kill another Mexican or *Tejano*—without justification—I will have you shot. Do I make myself clear, Captain?"

A profound stillness settled over the room. Ransom flushed, his features reddening to the hairline, and ground his teeth in silent fury. At length, he got control of his temper and lowered his chin in a barely perceptible nod. "I reckon we're straight."

"I'm glad to hear it. You and your Rangers have set a bad example for ordinary people. Summary execution of Mexicans will no longer be tolerated. Not by you, not by anyone."

The situation had become desperate. In the week since the train wreck, groups of vigilantes, sometimes abetted by

Rangers, had killed over a hundred Mexicans and *Tejanos*. Some were murdered purely for revenge, as payback for the Anglos killed at the Tandy's Creek massacre. Others were summarily executed simply because they were suspected of supporting the Army of Liberation. The color of a man's skin made him suspect.

The bloodletting had caused a mass migration. Mexicans and *Tejanos* fled in terror for their lives, crossing the Rio Grande to escape the random violence of vigilante mobs. By some estimates, more than two thousand families took refuge in Mexico, moving household goods and livestock in their flight to safety. Large parts of the countryside, particularly in Hidalgo and Cameron counties, assumed a ghostly, vacant look. The border had become a place of pervasive fear, and sudden death.

"You need to understand something," Parker said, his gaze fixed on the Ranger captains. "Every Mexican you kill out-of-hand becomes a recruiting poster for the Army of Liberation. You drive people to join the rebels."

"We could be facing a mass uprising," Gordon added. "There are thousands of *Tejanos* waiting for Garza and the rebels to invade. If it happens, it's not a matter of lending their support. They will fight."

"Greasers blow a lot of hot air," Ransom said. "What makes you so sure they'll invade? You know something we don't?"

The invasion planned for early September, and the buildup of armed forces in Monterrey, was a closely guarded secret. Gordon and General Parker, along with their respective superiors, believed that any mention of the Germans and organized military units would cause wholesale panic on the Rio Grande. Gordon trusted Maddox, but Bob Ransom was another matter entirely. The Rangers would be told only what they needed to know.

"We have nothing solid to go on," Gordon said now.

"But Garza's propaganda threatens an invasion, and we have to be prepared for the worst. Whether or not the threat's real is anyone's guess."

"Tell you my guess," Ransom said derisively. "Garza and his bunch haven't got the stomach for it. These raids are all the action we're gonna see."

"Speaking of Garza," Parker interjected. "I've been advised we'll receive no assistance from the Mexican government. They have refused to arrest Garza."

Early that morning, he explained, a communiqué had arrived from the War Department. Mexican diplomats in Washington had informed the State Department that Venustiano Carranza had no choice but to refuse President Wilson's request. The army of Mexico was engaged in fighting a civil war, and lacked the resources to patrol the Rio Grande. Nor was the Mexican military equipped to effect the arrest of bandits raiding into Texas.

"That's ripe," Ransom snorted. "Garza paid 'em off to turn a blind eye. All them damn greasers are crooked."

"Whatever the case," Parker said, "the end result will be to intensify the raids. The rebels have been granted sanctuary of sorts by the Mexican government."

When the meeting ended, Parker asked Gordon and Maddox to stay behind. He waited until the door closed, then sat down heavily in his chair. His manner seemed somehow less commanding than a moment ago. His features were gaunt.

"I couldn't speak freely, but I thought the two of you should know. I have been ordered to prepare for war."

"Ransom was halfway right," Gordon said. "Garza bought sanctuary, but with German money. He's got a free hand on the other side of the river."

"So it appears," Parker commented. "What of your agents in Matamoras, Mr. Gordon? Have they uncovered anything further about an invasion date?"

"Not a thing, General. Martinez tried, but Vasquez ran him out of their headquarters. We're at a dead end."

"Then there's nothing for it."

"Beg pardon, General?"

"I believe we are at a state of war, Mr. Gordon. Or at least, we will be shortly."

In the silence that followed, the three men were lost in their own thoughts. Yet, as though of one mind, they were all thinking the same thing. A rank admission as bitter as bile.

The Germans had won.

The landscape was desolate. In any direction the eye wandered, the terrain was bleak and hostile, filled with sand, rattlesnakes, and thorny cactus. A molten sun stood lodged in a sky barren of clouds.

Gordon sat staring out the window of a passenger coach. During the night, the train had stopped twice to take on water, and he was now some twenty miles east of El Paso. The wire from Forrest Holbrook, chief of the Bureau of Investigation, had arrived yesterday morning, shortly after the meeting at Fort Brown. Gordon had caught the noon train.

Holbrook's message was short, and cryptic in nature. He ordered Gordon to report with all dispatch to General Harold Woodruff at Fort Bliss, just outside El Paso. General Woodruff, the wire noted in terse language, would brief Gordon on the nature of the assignment. Gordon could only assume that it had something to do with the Army of Liberation. The significance of El Paso, which was over eight hundred miles upriver, remained a mystery.

The arid countryside whipped past in a blur. Gordon's mind was elsewhere, and he gave little attention to the desert wastes. Last night, though he still had mixed emotions, he'd planned to ask Guadalupe to marry him. He was certain of his own feelings, and he loved the boy, Antonio, almost as much as he loved her. He was confident of her love as well, for she wasn't one to hide her emotions. But he was nonetheless troubled by something that went beyond love and lovers. He wasn't at all sure she would marry a *gringo*.

On the long journey westward, his thoughts had alternated between Guadalupe and Holbrook's cryptic telegram. But now, as the train slowed to a halt before the depot, he was forced to set aside personal matters. El Paso was dusty and hot, a hodgepodge of buildings scattered like old dice along the banks of the Rio Grande. He had wired ahead and General Woodruff's aide was waiting for him with a Ford Model-T staff car. Fort Bliss was five miles or so north of town, and the aide tactfully deflected his questions along the way. He walked into the General's office not long after nine o'clock.

Woodruff was a tall, austere man with brushy eyebrows and short-cropped hair. "Special Agent Gordon," he said, rising from behind his desk. "Welcome to Fort Bliss."

"Thank you, General." Gordon accepted a handshake. "I was ordered to report to you by Director Holbrook. Any idea of why I'm here?"

"Have a chair." Woodruff waited until he was seated. "Sometime ago, Director Holbrook, through the War Department, asked that we keep an eye on Pascual Orozco. Are you familiar with the name?"

"No, sir, I'm not."

"Orozco was one of Huerta's generals in the Revolution. He took exile in El Paso when the *Carrancistas* defeated Huerta's army."

"Huerta?" Gordon repeated. "Does this have anything to do with the Army of Liberation?"

"We suspect it does," Woodruff said, steepling his fingers. "Huerta loyalists sought refuge around El Paso and in parts of southern New Mexico. Through informants, we discovered that Orozco was organizing loyalists into a military force." He paused, his expression somber. "Something on the order of two thousand men."

"General, as I'm sure you know, a man named Augustin Garza commands the Army of Liberation. Are you saying he and Orozco are somehow connected?"

"Director Holbrook sent us an encoded telegraph early yesterday. Here's a plaintext copy of his message. Judge for yourself."

Gordon quickly read the message. Holbrook advised that Victoriano Huerta had departed by train from New York on August 30, three days ago. Agents for the Bureau of Investigation, operating out of the New York office, had determined that he was ticketed through to Los Angeles. Holbrook suspected a ruse.

General Woodruff had been asked to check it out. In the message, Holbrook advised that Huerta had changed trains in Dallas yesterday morning, and was now traveling west into New Mexico. The Bureau was aware of Orozco's activities in the area, and raised the possibility that Huerta might attempt to make contact. Holbrook also advised that Colonel Franz von Kleist had disappeared from the German embassy in New York, and his current whereabouts were unknown. The sudden departure of Huerta and von Kleist was considered a matter of grave consequence.

"Coincidence piled on coincidence," Gordon said, looking up from the message. "Have you been briefed on this Colonel von Kleist, the German agent?"

Woodruff nodded. "General Funston has kept us apprised of the situation. Unfortunately, I have no intelligence on von Kleist's whereabouts. Huerta is a different kettle of fish."

"You have a line on him?"

"Pascual Orozco is something of a braggart. Our informants have learned he's meeting Huerta early this afternoon. Huerta plans to sneak off the train at Newman, New Mexico. That's about twelve miles north of here, right on the Texas border."

"Do you have any idea of what they intend?"

"General Funston believes Huerta and Orozco plan to attack the upper Rio Grande, while Garza attacks around Brownsville. A joint offensive, probably on the same day."

Gordon was stunned by the enormity of the scheme. His immediate thought was that the Germans were far more insidious than anyone had imagined. "The Germans leave nothing to chance," he said. "We'd be at war with Mexico within twenty-four hours."

"Yes, no question of it," Woodruff replied. "Our orders are to take Huerta and Orozco into custody. You will perform the actual arrest."

"What time does Huerta's train come in?"

"He's scheduled to arrive at one o'clock."

General Woodruff's informant was assigned the task of identifying Orozco. At Gordon's request, the detail consisted of one officer and ten enlisted men, sufficient to effect the arrest. They were trucked north within the hour and crossed the border from Texas into New Mexico. The truck was left hidden in an arroyo outside Newman.

The town was situated in a desert valley, with the Hueco Mountains to the east and the Organ Mountains to the west. There were perhaps twenty business establishments on the main street, and the population was hardly more than a thousand. The stationmaster at the train depot readily agreed to let them have the baggage room as a place of concealment. They were in position by eleven o'clock.

Pascual Orozco climbed out of a Reo Roadster shortly before the noon hour. He inspected the inside of the depot, satisfying himself all was in order, and took a seat on a bench facing the door. The westbound train arrived eighteen minutes late, and Orozco was waiting on the platform when Huerta stepped down from a passenger coach. The men laughed, comrades in war reunited, and embraced each other in a backslapping *abrazo*. Huerta's expression was that of Caesar triumphant.

Gordon emerged from the baggage room door. The officer, a cavalry captain, and the squad of troopers marched across the platform and surrounded the two Mexicans. Passengers hung out the windows of the train, staring wide-eyed with amazement as Gordon pushed through the soldiers. Orozco looked like he might bolt and run, except for the sight of so many rifles. Huerta's features went from triumphant to stoic, almost sad. His jaw muscles bunched in tight knots.

"Victoriano Huerta," Gordon said, addressing him in a formal manner. "I arrest you in the name of the United States government."

"*Que pasa?*" Huerta said. "On what charge?"

"Violation of the Neutrality Act."

The truck was brought from the arroyo within minutes. Huerta and Orozco were loaded into the back with the soldiers, while Gordon and the captain rode with the driver. Across the railroad tracks, the truck bumped along into Texas, and not quite an hour later, they stopped before the headquarters building at Fort Bliss. Orozco was marched off to the guardhouse, and Huerta was escorted into General Woodruff's office. Gordon performed the introductions.

Woodruff examined Huerta's documents and asked a few preliminary questions. But he quickly turned the interrogation over to Gordon, who was familiar with every aspect of the conspiracy. Huerta, who had regained his composure, lit a cigarette and dropped the match in an ashtray. He casually crossed his legs.

"General Huerta," Gordon said, "the Neutrality Art forbids conspiracy to commit acts of war by foreign nationals on American soil. Conviction carries a sentence of ten years in prison."

"I am a tourist, *señor*." Huerta exhaled a streamer of smoke. "I know nothing of a conspiracy."

"What of Augustin Garza and the Army of Liberation? When does he plan to invade Texas?"

"*Quien sabe*? Augustin and I are friends from another time, another life. I have not seen him in over a year."

"And Colonel Franz von Kleist?" Gordon said in a measured voice. "We know of the meetings in Madrid and New York. We know the Germans are financing the rebellion. We know everything."

A momentary flicker in his eyes betrayed Huerta. But he got hold of himself and managed a condescending smile. "You are mistaken, *señor*. I have no dealings with the Germans, and I know nothing of this von Kleist. *Nada*."

"General, you might help yourself by being truthful. For a man of your stature, ten years in prison is not a pleasant prospect. You might start by telling us the whereabouts of Colonel von Kleist."

"How can I tell you what I do not know? I am simply a tourist, nothing more. *Comprende*?"

The interrogation went on for more than an hour. Gordon tried every trick in a lawman's handbook for grilling a suspect; but it was all to no avail. Huerta was by turns indignant, patronizing, and contemptuous, and he admitted nothing. Finally, after exhausting all his wiles, Gordon called it quits. Huerta was marched off to the post stockade.

All too many questions remained unanswered.

Some inner voice told Gordon that Garza would not be deterred by Huerta's arrest. The Germans were masters of manipulation, certainly clever enough to convince the heir apparent that his time had come. Garza would somehow be induced to lead the Army of Liberation into Texas.

Gordon believed the key to the invasion was the abrupt and all too timely disappearance of a single man. A question which, if answered, might well avert a war.

Where the hell was Colonel Franz von Kleist?

Chapter Twenty-three

Progreso was a thriving farm community. The town was three miles north of the Rio Grande and some forty miles west of Brownsville. Irrigation canals crisscrossed a land ripe with all manner of produce.

On the night of September 3, Vasquez and eighty men crossed the river under pale starlight. Forty men, assigned to Sergeant Pablo Herrero, peeled off from the main formation and took cover in a stand of cottonwoods. Their mission was to act as rear guard for the strike force.

Vasquez led the other men inland. They were mounted on swift horses, armed with pistols and carbines, and a scout rode ahead to reconnoiter the way. Army units had been reinforced all along the border, and cavalry patrols were active in the area, night and day. The raiders' principal concern was to avoid any encounter with patrols on their advance into Progreso. Their retreat was planned along different lines.

The town was small but prosperous. One of the leading merchants was Florencio Toluca, who owned a large general store on the main street. A third-generation *Tejano*, Toluca was a respected businessman, the bulk of his trade with Anglo farmers. He served on the town council, and his close association with Anglos had led him to be openly critical of the Army of Liberation. He was the target of tonight's raid.

Vasquez intended to strike with swift precision. A

squad of five men stormed Toluca's home, dragging him from bed while his wife and daughters begged for mercy. The balance of the force took positions along the main street, where bands of interlocking gunfire could cover the whole of the business district. Toluca was brought to his store, barefoot, his hair disheveled, clad only in a nightshirt. He knew he was a dead man.

The store was torched. As the dry goods and flammables inside caught fire, Toluca was forced to watch the work of a lifetime consumed by flame. Vasquez reined his horse to a halt in front of the merchant.

"Florencio Toluca," he said, drawing a pistol. "You are a traitor to your people and the cause of liberty. I sentence you to death."

"*Madre de Dios!*" Toluca pleaded. "I am but a simple tradesman. I have betrayed no one. Spare me!"

"*No es suficiente, traidor.*"

Vasquez shot him. A bright rosette stained the chest of his nightshirt and he staggered backward, arms windmilling the air. His feet tangled, bare legs flashing, and his eyes rolled back in his head. He fell dead in the street.

The raiders mounted their horses. Even as the echoes of the gunshot faded, they rode off at a gallop through the business district. Lights went on in homes, and townspeople, clutching rifles and shotguns, began appearing from side streets. They found the store engulfed in flames and the body of Florencio Toluca sprawled in death. Far downstreet, they saw horsemen disappear into the night.

A mile south of town, Vasquez and his raiders collided with a cavalry patrol. Flames leaping skyward from the heart of Progreso had drawn one patrol, then another, and yet a third. In the dark, the cavalry squads headed north were taken unawares by forty horsemen riding south at a gallop. By the time the troopers got themselves oriented, the raiders had broken through and the engagement quickly turned into a running gunfight. The action moved steadily toward the river.

Vasquez rode at the head of the column. So far, with the patrols lured into pursuit, everything had gone just as he'd planned. Some ten minutes later, he saw starlight reflected on water and he led the raiders down the banks of the Rio Grande. The cavalry patrols, by now joined into a cohesive force thirty men strong, were only a short distance behind. As they approached the riverbank, Sergeant Herrero and his rear guard, waiting in ambush, opened fire. The crack of forty rifles split the night like a rolling cannonade.

Vasquez and his men turned in the river and loosed a volley with their pistols. Troopers pitched from the saddle and horses went down as the slugs from nearly eighty weapons tore through their ranks. A few, miraculously untouched, broke and ran, spurring their mounts into headlong flight. Others were wounded, some mortally, and the majority died where they fell, riddled with bullets. The riverbank, all in a matter of moments, became a killing ground littered with the bodies of men and thrashing horses. The earth was slick with blood.

Three troopers, grievously wounded, lay among the dead. Vasquez ordered them slung over the backs of horses, and then waited in midstream while Sergeant Herrero got the rear guard mounted. The rebels had lost only five men in the battle, and within minutes, the balance of the raiders gained the opposite shore. The wounded troopers, moaning piteously, were ferried across the river and dumped in a clearing in a grove of trees. Vasquez directed men to gather armloads of wood and build a bonfire. The clearing was soon lighted by leaping flames.

"Hear me, *hombres*!" Vasquez said to the assembled raiders. "Do not shrink from what you see here tonight. We leave a message for the *gringos*!"

Corporal Jacinto Talavero was selected for the honor.

He was short and muscular, broad through the shoulders, every inch the zealot as he pulled a machete from a scabbard on his saddle. The troopers, one at a time, were brought into the circle of firelight, their arms twisted backwards, and forced to kneel on the ground. Corporal Talavero effortlessly lopped off their heads.

Dawn the next morning was particularly beautiful. The pewter sky slowly lightened to a rosy hue, and then, gradually, a disc of fire emerged from the rim of the earth. The Rio Grande was soon awash in sunlight, and revealed was a sight with its own ghastly splendor. Three stakes were jammed into the sandy soil of the riverbank.

The heads of the troopers, severed clean, were wedged atop the stakes.

Gordon stepped off the train early that afternoon. Maddox was waiting outside the Brownsville depot, and his look was grim. He shook hands with a somber greeting.

Hardly to his surprise, Gordon learned that General Parker wanted to see them right away. As they turned the corner of the depot, neither of them noticed a tall man with patrician features and a commanding bearing step down from the second passenger coach. He carried a portfolio briefcase, but no luggage.

On the walk uptown, Gordon recounted the capture of Victoriano Huerta. Yesterday, from El Paso, he had sent coded telegrams to both Director Holbrook and General Parker. But now, in greater detail, he related the lengthy interrogation and the absence of any meaningful intelligence. His voice was leavened with frustration.

"So what happens to Huerta?" Maddox asked. "They gonna shoot the sorry bastard?"

"No chance of that," Gordon said. "Charges are being

filed for violation of the Neutrality Act. He'll wind up in prison."

"Well, Jesus H. Christ! Somebody ought to tell 'em what went on here last night. Maybe that'd get him a stiff rope and a short drop."

"What happened last night?"

Maddox told him about the raid on Progreso, and how the rebels had killed nineteen cavalrymen in a cunning ambush. He went on to describe how three troopers had been decapitated and their heads planted on stakes along the riverbank. A reinforced battalion, at General Parker's order, had crossed the Rio Grande early that morning. The remains of the beheaded troopers had been recovered without incident.

"Beheaded." Gordon repeated the word as though he'd heard wrong. "What kind of savages are these people? Isn't killing a man enough?"

"Not for them bastards," Maddox said gruffly. "They're warnin' us there won't be no quarter. No prisoners, no survivors."

A few minutes later they entered the post commander's office. Parker waved them to chairs without ceremony or formal greeting. His features were somehow brutalized, his eyes cold as stone. Gordon expressed his condolences about the loss of the troopers. He tactfully made no mention of the beheadings.

"Goddamn them," Parker said in an embittered voice. "There is no excuse for such an atrocity. None at all."

"No, sir," Gordon agreed. "Civilized men have limits."

"Well, enough of that for now. We have more immediate matters to discuss. Congratulations on capturing Huerta."

"Thank you, sir."

"Do you think it will have any effect on Garza? Will he call off the invasion?"

"Not in my opinion," Gordon said. "Garza's a fanatic and he's gone too far to back off now. I think he'll appoint himself as Huerta's successor. The new savior of Mexico—and the Mexican people."

"I share your view," Parker concurred. "The news of Huerta's capture was all over Brownsville by yesterday afternoon. Garza could have stopped last night's raid if Huerta made the difference. He chose instead to further inflame the situation."

"General, you hit the nail on the head," Maddox chimed in. "We're gonna have ourselves a war come hell or high water."

"So it would seem," Parker said. "I've only just received word that General Nafarrate has refused to cooperate. Nothing stands in Garza's way at this point."

The State Department had vigorously protested the Carranza government's unwillingness to police the Mexican side of the border. At the same time, the U.S. consul in Matamoras had requested assistance from General Emiliano Nafarrate, military commander of the district. Nafarrate had referred to the insurgents as "*revolucionarios Texanos*," and declared the rebellion an uprising of people native to Texas. He rejected any suggestion that the raids were staged by Mexicans, operating out of Mexico.

"Told you before," Maddox said hotly. "The Germans spread the *dinero* and bought 'em off. Nafarrate, Carranza, the whole bunch."

"I tend to agree," Parker said. "Although there's no denying Carranza has his hands full with Villa and Zapata. Still, money talks loudest, and it has the smell of corruption."

"Our hands are tied," Gordon added. "President Wilson won't allow pursuit into Mexico, and the rebels have sanctuary across the river. We're on a merry-go-round and no way to stop it."

Parker nodded. "All the more reason we need updated intelligence. We're assured the invasion is planned for early September, and I need not remind you that today is September fourth." He paused, his manner grave. "We are now at a critical juncture, and I'm forced to ask again, Mr. Gordon. Isn't there some way your agents can infiltrate Garza's staff?"

Gordon knew Hector Martinez would jump at the chance. Martinez possessed the bravado of a fighting cock and the sly aplomb of a con artist. Yet any further attempt, particularly with the invasion so close, might spark suspicion of the deadliest sort. The trade-off was risking one man's life to avoid a war with Mexico.

"I'll ask," Gordon said hesitantly. "I won't order Martinez to put himself at risk. On the other hand, just asking will probably be enough. He's a cocky devil."

"We've really no choice," Parker said in a solemn tone. "The alternative is a war where no one wins. Except, of course, the Germans."

Gordon was struck again by a thought that had nagged him for the past three days. He'd expected a wire from Director Holbrook when he arrived in Brownsville. Instead, he was left to ponder what seemed the most critical of questions.

Why hadn't they located Franz von Kleist?

Garza arrived at the German Consulate late that afternoon. One of the junior attachés had brought him a message only an hour before at the rebel headquarters on Calle 5. Otto Mueller wished to see him right away.

A servant ushered Garza into Consul Erwin Reinhardt's office. Reinhardt excused himself, nodding curtly to Garza, and went out the door. Mueller was standing beside the consular's desk, and seated behind it was a man of aristocratic bearing with chiseled features and pale blue eyes. Garza instinctively recognized him as a military officer.

"Colonel Garza," Mueller announced, "I have the honor to present Colonel Franz von Kleist of the German General Staff."

Von Kleist rose, extending his hand. "A pleasure to meet you at last, Colonel Garza. You are to be commended for your fine work."

"*Gracias, mi coronel.*" Garza accepted the handshake, trying to cover his amazement. "I hadn't expected an officer of the General Staff to visit Matamoras."

"Hardly a visit, Colonel. I have come to watch your glorious invasion of Texas. History will record no finer hour."

Von Kleist was actually there to oversee the invasion. He had slipped out of New York undetected, traveling incognito, changing trains in several cities before arriving in Brownsville. Only that afternoon, he'd crossed the International Bridge, briefcase in hand, posing as a businessman with clients in Matamoras. Though he had entrusted Mueller with the mission, he'd intended all along to be there for the invasion. World events, and a recent cablegram from Berlin, dictated nothing less.

The war in Europe gave no signs of victory. Ten days ago a battle had been fought outside the village of Champagne, in northern France. The Allies attacked with twenty divisions on a front twenty miles wide, supported by a thousand pieces of artillery. The attack was repelled, at a cost of eight thousand German casualties, and stalemate once more settled over the trenches. Kaiser Wilhelm, haunted by the specter of American intervention, directed the General Staff to take immediate action in Texas. General Alexis Baron von Fritsch, in an encoded cablegram, ordered von

Kleist to expedite the invasion by whatever means necessary.

Upon arriving at the consulate, von Kleist had learned of Huerta's arrest in New Mexico. The attack along the upper Rio Grande, under the command of Huerta and Pascual Orozco, had now been aborted. But von Kleist was nothing if not resilient, and he was determined to salvage the months of effort devoted to the Army of Liberation. Mueller, who had been advised of his arrival by coded telegram, assured him that Garza was a competent leader and a shrewd tactician. He was also assured by Mueller that the Mexican was a man of overbearing arrogance and high ambition. He thought those were the very traits needed for what lay ahead.

"We have much to discuss," he said without further ceremony. "Captain Mueller tells me you are aware General Huerta has been captured by the Americans."

"*Si*," Garza said in a rueful tone. "A sad day for Mexico and all who call themselves loyalists. General Huerta would have led us to victory."

"The exigencies of war sometimes give rise to new leaders. A man of valor makes his own destiny. Don't you agree?"

"We are military men, Colonel, and we can speak frankly. Are you suggesting I appoint myself General Huerta's successor?"

"Why not?" von Kleist said with conviction. "You organized the Army of Liberation, and it is you they will follow into battle. Who better to assume the mantle of leadership?"

Garza studied him a moment. "And after Texas, what then?"

"We adhere to the original plan. At the appropriate time, once you have overrun Texas, Germany will underwrite your campaign to defeat Carranza, then Villa and Zapata. The *Revolución* is yours to win, Colonel."

"What assurance do I have of your support?"

Von Kleist spread his hands. "You have the same assurance as given General Huerta. Kaiser Wilhelm would never stain the honor of Germany. His word is his bond."

"And you, Colonel?" Garza said. "Do you have the authority to speak for Kaiser Wilhelm?"

"I have," von Kleist lied smoothly, "and I do."

A long moment slipped past as they stared at each other. Garza finally nodded. "Four thousand men await my orders at Monterrey. Three thousand are cavalry, and their horses are being trailed even now to our base camp outside Reynosa." He paused with a dark smile. "I will transport the men by train on September 12."

"And the invasion?"

"We will cross the river on September 15."

"Excellent!" Von Kleist warmly shook his hand. "Your countrymen will applaud your daring, Colonel. Or perhaps I should call you 'General.' "

Garza shugged. "All in good time."

The meeting ended after a brief discussion of strategy. When Garza was gone, Mueller shook his head with wonder. "If I may, Colonel—"

"Yes?"

"Sir, you are a master of subterfuge. He believed every word of it."

Von Kleist laughed. " 'Deceive boys with toys, but men with oaths.' "

"How very appropriate," Mueller said. "A quote from Shakespeare?"

"No, long before his time, Otto. We can thank the ancient Greeks for the art of duplicity. Plutarch wrote that in 395 B.C."

"Perhaps General Nafarrate reads Plutarch. Not that

oaths mean anything, but he would certainly sell his soul. The man is a soldier without honor."

"Nonetheless, he serves our purpose," von Kleist remarked. "It is imperative that he not interfere with Garza's plans. How much have we paid him so far?"

"Thirty thousand, sir," Mueller said. "Our agreement was for ten thousand a month. I've arranged a meeting with him tomorrow morning."

"Very good idea, Otto. Until the invasion, we must keep our Mexican friends happy. Particularly the generals."

"Do you think Pancho Villa will honor his word, Colonel?"

"I believe so," von Kleist said. "Although it makes little difference in the end. Garza will start our war."

Otto Mueller thought they were on the verge of an historic moment. Few men experienced the sense of power, the spiritual intoxication, of starting a war. He was anxious for it to begin, the date like a beacon lighting the way. September 15.

Eleven days.

Chapter Twenty-four

Vasquez crossed the river the night of September 6. He was leading a company of one hundred fifty men, the largest strike force yet assembled. His orders were to probe the American defenses south of McAllen.

Loyal *Tejanos* in the area reported that the army's mobile reserve, estimated at a reinforced cavalry battalion, was bivouacked outside McAllen. Colonel von Kleist, in strategy conferences with Garza, had suggested that a raid be conducted in company strength. The objective was to determine the response time of American troops.

The invasion was to be staged from Reynosa, on the Mexican side of the border. McAllen was on a direct line with the staging area, some eight miles north of the Rio Grande. Von Kleist recommended that the invasion force should strike the strong point of the American defenses, the troop dispositions around McAllen. Defeat the mobile reserve, he argued, and the way was open to the interior of Texas.

The town selected for the raid was Las Milpas, six miles southeast of McAllen and five miles north of the river. Garza contended, and von Kleist agreed, that the distances involved would adequately test the reaction time of the army's mobile reserve. Las Milpas was a farm community, and the pretext for the raid was to destroy an irrigation pump station on the outskirts of the town. The

Americans would never suspect that the true purpose was to probe their defenses.

A strike force of one hundred fifty men required assembling every available volunteer. One of those called to service was Hector Martinez, who had been searching for a way to infiltrate the rebel field operations. On September 4, two nights ago, Gordon had asked him to somehow worm his way inside, and tonight he was riding with the raiders. There were four platoon leaders, and Vasquez, who recalled his determination to fight, had assigned Martinez to act as the liaison sergeant. He was in the thick of the action, and he thought it all but providential. He'd been detailed as the commanding officer's aide.

Immediately after crossing the river, the raiders encountered a patrol. The firefight was brief but deadly, for the nine-man patrol was overwhelmed by the sheer size of the strike force. Vasquez was nonetheless pleased as it would alert patrols upriver, who in turn would alert the mobile reserve outside McAllen. Martinez was dispatched with orders to post a platoon on the western flank, something of a mounted picket line, to sound an early warning in the event of a counterattack. He returned just as the main column approached the Las Milpas pump station.

"As you ordered, *mi capitán*," he said, reining his horse alongside Vasquez. "Barragan and his platoon are in place."

"Well done, Sergeant," Vasquez said. "We will draw the *yanqui soldados* into our web. Mark my words."

"I wish tonight were the night of the invasion, *mi capitán*. We would lay waste to Texas!"

"Never fear, your wish will come true, Martinez. Sooner than you think."

"Tomorrow would not be too soon for me. Am I permitted to ask when we will invade?"

"You will be told in good time. We have work to do now. *Andale!*"

The pump station was deserted. Under the light of a full moon, Vasquez directed men to break down the door. They found cans of kerosene inside and splashed it over the walls and the generator. A rag soaked in kerosene was set afire, then tossed through the door, and the building exploded into a crackling inferno. The flames leaped skyward, sparks and cinders flying, visible for miles in the night. The men cheered as the roof buckled inward on itself.

Vasquez consulted his pocket watch. In the light of the fire, he saw that something more than an hour had passed since they'd crossed the river. He thought the Yankee soldiers were slow to react, and idly wondered if a direct attack on McAllen might be the better plan on the night of the invasion. He would raise the idea with Garza, who would doubtless take it to the German, von Kleist. He told himself he could burn McAllen as easily as he'd burned a pump station.

On the retreat, Barragan was ordered to hold his position on the westward flank. Some while later, as the main column skirmished with patrols near the river, a drumming roar of gunfire suddenly erupted from the west. Vasquez immediately knew it was the counterattack by elements of the reserve battalion, and mentally marked the time. The gunfire swelled in intensity, bracketing the night in a sustained roar, and he thought it sounded like a full company of cavalry, perhaps more. He led the column at a gallop toward the Rio Grande.

Miguel Barragan and a wounded *Tejano* were the only survivors of the counterattack. Sometime after midnight they forded the river, their horses exhausted, and delivered the news to Vasquez. A cavalry force Barragan estimated at two companies had overrun his platoon and literally shot them to pieces. He'd left twenty-four dead on the field in Texas.

Vasquez revised his opinion. The *yanquis* were slow to react, but once they got into action, they were disciplined and organized, merciless fighters. He thought it was a point worth noting in his report.

Colonel von Kleist would appreciate his assessment.

Gordon emerged from Fort Brown late the next morning. The weather was pleasant for a change, a light breeze rippling through the trees on Elizabeth Street. He walked toward the hotel.

The morning had been spent in meetings with General Parker and his staff. For the most part, the discussion had dealt with last night's raid outside Las Milpas. There was consensus that it was more ruse than raid, a deception intended to test the defenses around McAllen. The staff officers thought the primary objective was to draw out the mobile reserve battalion.

General Parker took it a step further. He reminded everyone of the boat landings recently built at Reynosa, the Mexican town directly south of McAllen. In his view, the boat landings and last night's raid led to an inescapable conclusion. The Army of Liberation, he told the staff officers, was planning to invade from Reynosa. He believed their initial goal would be to defeat the mobile reserve battalion. That accomplished, the insurgent army would drive deeper into Texas.

Gordon accepted the premise. He would have preferred hard intelligence to support the theory, but no prisoners were taken in last night's raid and there was no one to interrogate. His only hope for intelligence lay with Hector Martinez, who had been called to active service with the rebels just two days ago. The timing was more than coincidence and he suspected Martinez had ridden with the raiders at Las Milpas. Yet there was no way to know until he heard from Martinez, and he couldn't hazard a guess when that might be. He felt very much in the dark.

Uptown, Gordon entered the hotel. Hoyt Maddox was attending a meeting of the Ranger captains, similar to the staff conference at Fort Brown. They had agreed to join up for lunch at the hotel and exchange notes on the morning's activities. Maddox wasn't in the dining room, and as Gordon walked back through the lobby, the desk clerk called out to him. The clerk handed him an envelope, commenting that it had been delivered by a young Mexican woman only minutes before. Gordon tore open the envelope.

The note inside was from Guadalupe. In a mix of English and Spanish, she asked that he come to her house quickly, and she had underscored the words *muy pronto*. Gordon sensed an urgency to it, for as a matter of security he'd never before gone to her house during daylight hours. He left the hotel, wondering if she'd received a message from Martinez, and made his way through the Mexican quarter of town. Housewives and children paused to stare as he approached the house and knocked on the door. Guadalupe admitted him, Antonio in her arms.

"*Gracias Dios*," she said in a breathless voice. "We didn't know if you would receive my message."

"I came as soon as I got it."

Martinez and Vargas were seated at the dining table. Gordon knew something important had occurred for them to risk meeting with him in broad daylight. As he moved forward, Guadalupe kept Antonio in the parlor and distracted him with toys. Gordon took a chair at the table.

"I don't have to ask," he said, nodding to them. "You've learned something that wouldn't wait until tonight."

"*Si*, many things for sure," Martinez said with an uneasy smile. "I have been off with Luis Vasquez and the rebels. We fought the soldiers south of McAllen."

"I thought you were probably there. Is it true he had over a hundred men?"

"Oh, yes, half again that many. Some of us returned by train from Reynosa this morning. Vasquez is very proud of himself."

"Tell me about it."

Martinez briefed him on the raid. He confirmed that the purpose was to draw out the mobile reserve and test their reaction time. His impression, though he hadn't been told, was that the rebel army would invade from somewhere around Reynosa. As for the invasion date, he'd learned nothing more, except that it would be soon, very soon. Nor had he uncovered anything about the army of thousands that would comprise the invasion force.

"But there is a curious thing," he said, one eyebrow arched. "On the train, I pretended to sleep and overheard Vasquez bragging to his platoon leaders. He told them he would report to the chief German advisor in Mexico—a military advisor."

Gordon felt his pulse quicken. "Did you get a name?"

"Not then," Martinez motioned to his cousin. "Manuel has something interesting for you."

"There is another German in Matamoras," Vargas said, clearly delighted with himself. "Mueller treats him with much respect, and I have been watching them for three days. This new one also stays at the Bezar Hotel."

"And his name?" Gordon demanded.

"I have said nothing because I only learned it today from the hotel doorman. His name is Franz von Kleist."

Gordon couldn't speak for a moment. His gaze strayed to the parlor, where Guadalupe was playing with Antonio. A thought, vagrant and unbidden, reminded him that he hadn't yet asked her to marry him. Something always intruded, another raid, desperate communiqués from Washington, the threat of war. And now, too sudden to comprehend, a mystery solved. Colonel Franz von Kleist in Matamoras.

"You've done well," he said, turning back to the men. "Von Kleist is Mueller's superior, the man responsible for the conspiracy. We had no idea where he was."

"There's more," Martinez said with a lopsided grin. "When Vasquez was bragging, and I pretended to sleep— on the train?"

"You heard something else."

"*Sangre de Cristo*, it never ends! There will be another raid tonight. The railroad bridge at San Benito."

"Will Vasquez lead the raid?"

"You know, he did not say. But he told his platoon leaders it is a very important mission. Military supplies for all the valley come over that bridge. They intend to dynamite it tonight."

"Hector, I think they're in for a surprise. The biggest surprise of their lives."

Martinez laughed. "I thought you might plan to greet them."

Gordon hardly knew where to start. General Parker would have to be advised that von Kleist was across the river, masterminding the final preparations for war. Maddox and the Rangers would have to be alerted, a trap laid on for tonight at San Benito. And with any luck at all . . .

Luis Vasquez would lead his last raid.

San Benito was thirty miles northwest of Brownsville. The bridge outside town spanned a wide arroyo, which was dry except during spring rains. Tonight, under a full moon, the wooden trestles of the bridge stood out in bold relief.

Pizana led eight men and a packhorse down the dusty bank of the arroyo. The bridge, which was fifteen miles north of the border, was the main artery for military goods shipped to Fort Brown. Pizana's mission was to totally destroy the bridge, and close off resupply of the army quartermaster a week before the invasion. The packhorse was loaded with two crates of dynamite.

The moon flooded the arroyo with light. The raiders had crossed the river shortly after dark and slipped through the cavalry patrols without incident. Dynamite was usually stable until fused, but the packhorse had slowed their ride from the border. By the cast of the moon, Pizana judged the time at almost midnight, and he figured two hours to place the charges and blow the bridge. He thought they would be back in Mexico well before dawn.

The latticework of timbers beneath the bridge suddenly erupted in gunfire. Twenty carbines and two shotguns lit the night with muzzle flashes, and a cyclone of lead whistled through the arroyo. The raiders were blasted from their saddles, tumbling like rag dolls to the ground, and the packhorse bolted west along the dry wash. A slug struck Pizana's horse in the head, and the horse reared, toppling sideways, and pinned his right leg to the ground. The back of Pizana's skull bounced off the hard-packed earth, and stars exploded before his eyes. He went limp as his horse shuddered and died.

The Rangers of Company A moved out from beneath the bridge. Captain Ransom, flanked by Gordon and Maddox, walked forward with their weapons at the ready. They watched as the Rangers approached the sprawled, motionless bodies, checking for wounded. In the moonlight, the rebels lay twisted and bloody, arms and legs akimbo, pocked with bullet holes. The arroyo looked like a charnel house, littered with men and horses brought down in the hail of gunfire. Then, abruptly, a Ranger to the front called out.

"Cap'n, we got ourselves a live one!"

Ransom, followed by Gordon and Maddox, hurried

forward. The Ranger stood over the unconscious form of a man whose leg was trapped under a dead horse. The man groaned, his swarthy features contorted, as the Ranger relieved him of his holstered pistol. Maddox, assisted by Ransom and the Ranger, freed the man's leg from beneath the horse. Gordon shouted over his shoulder.

"Manuel, up here!"

Manuel Vargas stepped from the shadowed timbers of the bridge. Gordon had brought him along in the hope he might be able to identify those killed or wounded in the ambush, particularly the leader. Martinez, who was now their chief source of intelligence into the rebels' plans, had been left behind for fear of endangering his life. Vargas quickly moved forward and stopped beside the dead horse. Gordon pointed to the man slumped on the ground.

"Is this Vasquez?"

"*No*," Vargas said without hesitation. "That is Aniceto Pizana, one of Garza's field commanders. I have seen him many times in Matamoras."

"Pizana?" Ransom said with a scowl. "Sonovabitch stood Joe Scrivner and his boys before a firin' squad. We'll just give him a dose of the same."

"Not tonight," Gordon said in a deliberate tone. "He's my prisoner and I intend to talk with him. I need some answers."

Ransom's features knotted in a mulish frown. "You're not gonna get anything out of the sorry bastard. He'd bite his tongue off first."

Pizana moaned, rubbing the back of his head. As they watched, he sat up, his eyes glazed, and slowly came to his senses. He glanced around at the bodies of his men, and then at the Rangers. His mouth set in a stoic line.

"I'll make him talk," Maddox said. "Either that or we'll leave him for the buzzards."

Gordon made a sharp gesture. "Hoyt, I won't let you kill him. Don't even think about it."

"You want information or you want a prisoner? What he knows could save a helluva lot of lives."

There was a prolonged silence. Gordon balanced the life of one man against the thousands who might be lost in an invasion. His moral aversion to cold-blooded execution was offset by an instant of hard, newfound pragmatism. He finally nodded.

"All right, do what you have to do."

Maddox knelt down beside Pizana. "*Hombre*," he said with soft menace. "You will answer my questions or I will kill you. *Comprende?*"

"*Hijo de puta!*" Pizana grated the curse. "You are all the sons of whores. I have nothing to say."

"You're sure about that?"

"I am certain."

Maddox pulled his Colt six-gun. He thumbed the hammer and placed the snout of the barrel to Pizana's temple. "Want to change your mind?"

Pizana stared straight ahead. Maddox waited a moment, then lifted the muzzle slightly and fired. The slug parted Pizana's hair crosswise and scorched the top of his skull. His eardrum burst and a trickle of blood leaked down over his earlobe onto his neck. His bowels involuntarily voided and the crotch of his pants went dark with a noxious stench. A single tear scalded his cheek.

Maddox again thumbed the hammer. "You're all out of chances, *hombre*. Got anything to say?"

Pizana talked. His voice was scratchy, the residue of courage eroded by a visceral fear. He told them of the training camp at Monterrey, three thousand cavalry and a thousand infantry, all to be transported by train. Then, with the pistol still at his head, he described the camp outside Reynosa, where the troops would be bivouacked near the border. He finally told them what they most wanted to know, the invasion date. September 15.

"Goddamn," Ransom said when it was over. "I only half believed it till now. The bastards are gonna do it."

Gordon looked at him. "Captain, I need your assistance on something."

"What's that?"

"Garza has to believe Pizana was killed here tonight. We can't let it leak that he talked."

"So what are you sayin'?"

"I want you to hide him out until he can be brought to trial."

"Save a lot of trouble just to shoot him now. Who'd know the difference?"

"I would," Gordon said pointedly. "Do I have your word?"

"Yeah, I reckon," Ransom grumbled. "We'll get him tucked away somewheres."

A detail of four Rangers was assigned to transport Pizana to Austin, where he would be held incommunicado in the county jail. Gordon convinced Ransom and the other Rangers, over their strenuous objections, to dig a mass grave on the plain above the arroyo. The bodies of the raiders were interred that night.

Aniceto Pizana, so far as the world knew, was dead.

Chapter Twenty-five

Gordon and Maddox returned to Brownsville early the next morning. Stores were opening for business along Elizabeth Street, and they had a quick breakfast in the hotel dining room. Then they walked toward Fort Brown.

Neither of them took time to shave. Their faces were dark with stubble and their clothes were rumpled and soiled. But the information they'd gathered last night was of a critical nature, far more so than their appearance. They hurried on to the post headquarters.

Sergeant Major O'Meara was an astute judge of character. He read the looks on their faces and knew immediately that it was not a time for pleasantries or small talk. He led them into the commanding general's office, announcing their names, and quietly closed the door. Parker was seated at his desk.

"Good morning," he said, motioning them to chairs. "How did things go at San Benito?"

Gordon had informed him of their plans late yesterday afternoon. As he and Maddox seated themselves, he forced a tired smile. "We hit the jackpot, General. Killed all the raiders except one, their leader. Aniceto Pizana."

"Are you saying you captured him?"

"Yes, sir, took him alive and Sergeant Maddox persuaded him to talk. It's been quite a night."

"I imagine it has," Parker observed. "When you say

Pizana talked, what does that mean exactly? How much did he tell you?"

"Everything."

Gordon briefed him on the interrogation. When he finished, Parker nodded solemnly. "You're satisfied he wasn't lying? September 15 is the date?"

"General, that's the straight dope," Maddox replied. "You might say Pizana got religion. He wasn't lying."

"It all fits," Gordon said. "We suspected a recruiting center at Monterrey, and Pizana confirms it. Four thousand men, a reinforced cavalry brigade."

"With the trains ready to roll," Maddox added. "They'll be assembled at that camp outside Reynosa by the fourteenth. The day before the invasion."

"Four thousand and more," Parker said, his features stark. "Have a look at the latest issue of *Regeneración*."

The newspaper, mailed September 1 from California, had received wide distribution along the border. Maddox translated the lead article on the front page, which was set in bold type. The article decried racial discrimination in Texas and stressed social equality for all people of Mexican heritage. The term "*revolucionarios*" was again applied to those who fought against Anglo injustice, and *Tejanos* were urged to support the Army of Liberation. The article ended with a call to action.

"Blatant propaganda," Parker said. "The publisher is the most radical anarchist in America, and he's clearly in league with the Germans. What this does is confer legitimacy on the rebels and their cause."

"Just in time for the invasion," Maddox noted. "Only a week to go and *Regeneración*'s given them a stamp of approval."

"Exactly my point," Parker said. "When Garza and his army invades, *Tejanos* will revolt by the thousands. We will be faced by a frontal assault from Garza and God knows how many guerrilla actions at our rear. Probably in the hundreds."

"What happens then?" Gordon asked. "Do you have sufficient forces to contain a general uprising? Or will it spread to the interior?"

"Mr. Gordon, it will spread like a plague. By then, of course, Congress will declare war on Mexico and our army will be on the march. All of South Texas will become a war zone."

A strained silence settled over the office. Gordon stared out the window, lost in a moment of personal deliberation. Everything he'd just heard confirmed what he had been thinking since Pizana's confession at the San Benito bridge. Four months ago, Director Holbrook had charged him with the mission of stopping a war from starting, and he'd failed. Until now, he had played by the rules, reacting to raids and German intrigue, and the end result, only a week away, was war. He decided it was time to put the rules aside. Time to act.

"We're at an impasse," he said, as though thinking out loud. "Do nothing and we're certain to have a war. I can't let that happen."

"How can you prevent it?" Parker said wearily. "What's left that we haven't tried?"

"I was ordered to use whatever means necessary to stop a war. I think it's time to try something extralegal."

"By extralegal, do you mean something outside the law?"

"General, I won't answer that," Gordon said. "At this point, the less you know, the better. We never had this conversation."

Parker stared at him. "I will not condone illegal actions, Mr. Gordon."

"By God, I will!" Maddox blurted. "Anything that

stops a war beats sittin' around on your thumb. What've you got in mind, Frank?"

"I'll tell you along the way."

Gordon rose, nodding to Parker, and walked out of the office. Maddox was only a step behind, closing the door as he hurried into the hallway. General Parker stared after them a long moment, debating whether he should notify some higher authority. Then, on second thought, he decided Gordon was right.

He didn't want to know.

"None of this is as easy as it sounds."

"That's why we came to you, Hector. We need your advice."

Gordon and Maddox were seated on the sofa. Martinez and Vargas, occupying the wooden chairs, were opposite them in the small parlor. Guadalupe watched from the dining table, where she was feeding Antonio his noon meal. Her expression was one of quiet concern.

"I do not understand," Martinez said. "Why do you wish to capture Garza? Why not kill him?"

"We're not assassins," Gordon replied. "What I want is to get him across the border and charge him with murder. The same as we'll do with Pizana."

"Pardon my saying so, but I think you made a mistake there. You should have killed Pizana when you had the chance."

"Damn right." Maddox said with a wolfish grin. "Never know what's gonna happen with a judge and jury."

Gordon had taken a chance on catching the men at Guadalupe's house. Sometimes, when things were quiet in Matamoras, they took their noontime meal at her table. Today was one of those days, and they'd just finished eating when he and Maddox arrived. He'd quickly explained what he had in mind.

"Those *cabrónes* are in mourning," Martinez said with open disdain. "The way they act, you'd think Pizana was a saint. You were wise to let them believe he is dead."

Vargas nodded agreement. He'd already told Martinez about the fight at San Benito, and Pizana's capture. But now, his features screwed up in a frown, he looked at Gordon.

"Hector is right," he said. "In honor of Pizana's death, they will not raid across the river tonight. Where you find Garza, you will find Luis Vasquez at his side."

"All the better," Gordon said. "We'll bring both of them back to Brownsville. There's no problem charging Vasquez with murder."

"Yes, there is a problem," Martinez said soberly. "These men will not allow themselves to be taken prisoner. They will fight."

"What'd I tell you?" Maddox said, glancing sideways at Gordon. "One thing to try and abduct them, and it's another to pull it off. They're not gonna come along peaceable."

Gordon laced his fingers together, considered a moment. Earlier, when he and Maddox left Fort Brown, he'd laid out the plan. Maddox had been skeptical, but entirely willing to violate international law by crossing into Matamoras. His one doubt was that they could take Garza alive.

"Hoyt, there's no other way," Gordon said now. "Without Garza to lead them, the rebels won't start a war on their own. We have to take him out of the equation."

"No argument from me on that score. Just so you understand what me and Hector are sayin'. Garza's not gonna surrender."

"If he fights, he fights. We'll worry about it when it happens."

"How will you do this?" Martinez asked. "You have never seen Garza. How will you know him?"

"We need your help," Gordan said earnestly. "Will you come with us to Matamoras? Identify Garza?"

"Of course, why not?" Martinez said with a shrug. "Where do you plan to confront him?"

"What would you suggest?"

"Do it at night. The streets are too crowded during the day. Try to surprise him."

"That brings us back to what you asked—where?"

Martinez looked thoughtful. "The *cantina* I told you about, on Calle Morelos? They'll probably gather there tonight to drink to Pizana's heroic death." He paused with a crafty grin. "Catch Garza on his way to the *cantina*."

"I will go, too," Vargas volunteered. "Who knows how many men Garza will have with him. You may need an extra gun. *Verdad*?"

"On one condition," Gordon said. "Sergeant Maddox and I will try to handle it by ourselves. You and Hector stay back unless we're outnumbered. Agreed?"

"*Hecho!*" Vargas said with a jester's smile. "We are there if we are needed. *Muy bien!*"

The meeting ended on that note. Guadalupe put Antonio on the floor with his toys and followed Gordon to the door. She waited until Maddox went out before she spoke. "Promise me something?"

"I'll promise you anything."

"No, seriously," she said, her eyes dark with fear. "Kill Garza if he tries to fight. Do not hesitate."

"That's an easy promise to keep. No need to worry."

She kissed him lightly on the lips. "Come back to me, *caro mio*. I will be waiting."

"I'll see you tonight."

Gordon left her in the doorway. He wanted to say more, but it occurred to him that he'd probably said too much. Only a fool made promises when he was headed into harm's way.

He told himself he qualified on both counts.

Dusk settled over Matamoras in a bluish haze. Street lamps flickered on around the plaza as shopkeepers closed for the night. Cafés were already crowded with people at the supper hour.

Gordon and Maddox crossed the plaza in the fading light. Martinez was waiting for them at the southeast corner, where the great square emptied onto Calle Morelos. He explained that Vargas, in his guise as a street vendor, had kept Garza under surveillance throughout the afternoon. Only a short while ago, Garza had come out of the German Consulate and walked to the house on Calle 5. Vargas was watching him now.

Martinez led them by the consulate, pointing it out as they went past. The street lamps on Calle Morelos were farther apart, and he moved quickly, concerned that two *gringos* on a deserted side street would attract attention. As they approached the intersection of Calle 5, he motioned them into the darkened doorway of a butcher shop closed for the night. Farther on, they saw Vargas posted outside the *cantina*, his vendor's tray suspended from his neck. His eyes were fixed on the house a short distance down Calle 5.

"We must stay here," Martinez said. "Many of the men who come to the *cantina* are Garza loyalists, and you cannot be seen. Someone might sound the alarm."

Maddox nodded. "Any idea when Garza will show?"

"I have no way of knowing. We can only wait."

"Hope to hell he don't take all night."

"*Si*, that would not be good."

Some thirty minutes later, Vargas abruptly quit his post

outside the *cantina*. He strolled to the corner, halting beneath a street lamp, as two men crossed the intersection from Calle 5. "*Cigarros*," he called out, as though hawking his wares. "*Cigarillos. Muy bueno tabaco*."

"Garza," Martinez hissed under his breath. "And the other one is Vasquez."

Gordon moved out of the doorway, his Colt automatic in hand. Maddox was a step behind, thumb hooked over the hammer of his six-gun, and they hurried toward the corner. Vasquez saw them, his instincts suddenly alert, and he muttered a warning to Garza. The two men stopped in the pool of light from the street lamp.

"*Alto*!" Maddox ordered in raspy Spanish. "You men are under arrest. *Abandono*!"

Vasquez reacted on sheer reflex, cursing as he jerked a pistol from beneath his jacket. Maddox fired twice, the shots not a heartbeat apart, and Vasquez stumbled into the lamppost, then slumped to the ground. As he fell, Garza pulled a revolver from his waistband and brought the muzzle to bear. Gordon's automatic roared three times, rapid blasts one upon the other, and the heavy slugs struck Garza in the chest. He staggered backward, dropping the revolver, and collapsed in the street. His eyes were open and vacant, fixed on nothing.

There was an instant of dungeon silence. Then Martinez darted from the butcher shop doorway. "*Andale*!" he rapped out. "We must get back across the bridge, and quickly. You are not safe here."

Vargas tossed his vendor's tray into the shadows, and joined them. They left the bodies under the streetlight and walked at a brisk pace toward the plaza. The gunshots would draw attention, and the immediate threat was the crowd of Garza loyalists in the *cantina*. Their lives were forfeit if they were caught.

The military authorities were no less a concern. If they

were apprehended, General Nafarrate would use the killings to create an international incident. Gordon and Maddox would be presented as rogue law enforcement officers, acting as assassins for the United States government. Martinez and Vargas would simply be stood against a wall and shot.

Halfway up the block, Vargas suddenly drew a sharp breath, "*Santo Dios!*" he said in an urgent voice. "The men there, coming out of the consulate. It's Mueller and von Kleist."

Mueller and von Kleist emerged from the German Consulate and strolled toward the plaza. Gordon recalled they were staying at the Bezar Hotel, and it appeared they were on their way to dinner. His mind reeled with the possibilities for ending German involvement in the rebel movement, and eliminating any threat of war. He made a spur-of-the-moment decision.

"Hoyt, listen to me," he said, his eyes on the Germans. "We're going to take them prisoner."

"What if they fight?" Maddox said. "Do we kill them?"

"Yes," Gordon said without hesitation. "But follow my lead and don't force a fight. I want them alive."

The Germans were approaching the corner that opened onto the plaza. Gordon and Maddox increased their pace, Martinez and Vargas a few steps to the rear. They rapidly closed the distance, with Gordon behind von Kleist and Maddox behind Mueller. Gordon jammed the muzzle of his automatic into von Kleist's spine.

"Don't stop, don't turn around," he ordered. "I am an agent of the United States government, Colonel von Kleist. I arrest you for conspiracy to incite war."

"Same goes for you," Maddox said, jabbing Mueller in the back with his six-gun. "We just killed Garza and Vasquez, so it's all over. Don't try anything stupid."

Von Kleist stiffened. "Whoever you are, you are fools.

This is Mexico, and we are traveling under diplomatic immunity. You have no authority here."

"Do exactly as I tell you," Gordon said with ominous calm. "We are going to cross the bridge into Texas. If you resist, we will kill you. Understand?"

"You wouldn't dare!" von Kleist snapped. "The Mexican government would have you shot."

"Let's hope it works," Maddox said in a rough voice. " 'Cause if it don't, Colonel—you're dead."

The evening crowds were starting to fill the plaza. The strains of guitars drifted from nightspots and the tables at sidewalk cafés were packed with diners. Gordon and Maddox stayed close behind the Germans, their pistols concealed beneath their jackets. Three uniformed *Rurales*, officers of the Mexican state police, were standing on the opposite side of the plaza, alert to drunks or troublemakers. Von Kleist glanced at them, weighing the chances, and Gordon nudged him hard in the back. They moved on through the crowds.

Ten minutes later they approached the International Bridge. Mexican soldiers, members of General Nafarrate's command, were stationed at the entrance to the bridge. Four *gringos* hardly rated a glance, for Anglos were back and forth between Matamoras and Brownsville at all hours of the day and night. Von Kleist and Mueller realized it was their last chance, and they tensed as they started past the soldiers. Maddox laughed and genially clapped his arm over Mueller's shoulder. His voice was low and deadly.

"One peep and I'll blow your backbone out. Just keep movin'."

The opposite end of the bridge opened onto Elizabeth Street. The lights of Brownsville glittered under a full moon, and Gordon and Maddox relaxed, once more in Texas. Maddox kept the Germans covered while Gordon turned to Martinez and Vargas. He warmly shook their hands.

"Hector. Manuel," he said with genuine feeling. "I want you to know I'm grateful for your assistance. We couldn't have done it without you."

"*No es nada*," Martinez said modestly. "What we did tonight was a good thing. That is thanks enough."

"*Si*," Vargas said, beaming a grin. "I think life will be dull now. *Aiiii chihuahua*, what a night!"

They walked off toward the center of town. Gordon looked around, nodding to Maddox, who motioned the Germans in the opposite direction with his six-gun. Von Kleist thrust out his jaw.

"Where are you taking us?"

Gordon pointed. "See those gates, Colonel?"

"*Ja.*"

"Welcome to Fort Brown."

Chapter Twenty-six

Sergeant Major O'Meara stood sipping a cup of coffee. Some three hours ago he'd been summoned from his quarters by the night orderly. Thirty years in the army hadn't prepared him for what he found in the orderly room. He still couldn't quite credit it.

The Germans were seated in chairs against the far wall. Their hands were cuffed in manacles, and two hard-faced troopers, their rifles held at port arms, stood guard. Von Kleist stared straight ahead, his features rigid, his pale blue eyes fixed on infinity. He looked like a man reading his own obituary.

Otto Mueller seemed dazed, somehow deflated. His thoughts were across the river, on the life that might have been, and Maria Dominguez. He wondered how she would hear of his capture, and how soon before she'd be sharing another man's bed. She was a mercenary little witch, but he would miss her ardor, those passionate nights. He regretted that she would never see Berlin.

O'Meara studied them with open curiosity. As a soldier, he was fascinated by the war in Europe, and he'd read everything written about the vaunted German army. He knew the two men in manacles were officers, and he felt a grudging admiration for the chaos and terror they'd brought to the Rio Grande. Yet he was oddly disappointed that they had allowed themselves to be captured, and not a mark on them. He thought a true German would have fought to the death.

The door to the general's office opened. Maddox stuck his head out and motioned to O'Meara. "Sergeant Major, bring 'em along. We're ready."

O'Meara led the way, trailed by the Germans and the two hard-faced troopers. He halted inside the office, shoulders squared. "General, sir!" he said in a bull-moose voice. "Would you like me to leave the boys to guard the Krauts? Wouldn't be any trouble at all."

"No, thank you, Sergeant Major." Parker was seated behind his desk. "I believe Mr. Gordon and Sergeant Maddox are all we need. Hold your detail outside."

"Sir!"

O'Meara marched the troopers through the door. When it closed, Maddox crossed the room and took a chair beside Gordon. Von Kleist and Mueller, hands manacled, were left standing before the desk. They held themselves at attention.

"Colonel von Kleist. Captain Mueller." Parker stared at them with a level gaze. "Were it within my power, I would have you taken out and shot. Unfortunately, I am obliged to follow orders."

"General, I again protest," von Kleist said curtly. "We are officers of the German Reich under the protection of diplomatic immunity. I insist we be returned to Mexico."

"Colonel, you are now on American soil, and how you got here is not my concern. I hereby advise you that you have been charged with violation of the Neutrality Act."

Earlier, von Kleist and Mueller had been interrogated at length. Apart from name and rank, they admitted nothing, claiming assignment as attachés to the consulate in Matamoras. Parker and Gordon, operating jointly, exchanged a flurry of coded telegrams with the State Department, the War Department, and the Bureau of Investigation.

Secretary of State Robert Lansing, at the direction of President Wilson, had ultimately decided on the charges to be brought. The official story was that von Kleist and Mueller had been captured while fomenting insurrection in Brownsville.

"I believe that completes our business," Parker told them. "You will be transported by train to Washington, where formal charges will be lodged. Frankly, gentlemen, I hope they hang you."

"One question, General," von Kleist said, a note of skepticism in his tone. "Is it true Augustin Garza is dead?"

"Deader'n a doornail!" Maddox woofed a great belly laugh. "Your shot at a war just went to hell in a handbasket."

Von Kleist made no further comment, as though he'd finally accepted the truth. After O'Meara and the guard detail were called in, the Germans were marched off to the post stockade. Parker waited until the door closed and then slumped back in his chair. His gaze shifted from Maddox to Gordon.

"Irony is hardly the word," he said with a cryptic smile. "You broke every rule in the book, and you'll probably receive medals. Off the record—just between us—was it really necessary to kill Garza and Vasquez?"

"Yessir, it was," Maddox said. "Any man worth shootin' is worth killin'. Wasn't like they gave us a choice."

Gordon smiled. "Lucky we stumbled across von Kleist and Mueller. Except for them, we'd probably be cashiered out of the service."

"Nonetheless, I congratulate you," Parker said. "Your initiative was exemplary, and never more timely. You've saved our nation from war."

"General—" Maddox paused with a nutcracker grin. "Speakin' for me and the Rangers, we won't mind a little peace and quiet. We'll go back to catchin' horse thieves."

"Sergeant, if I may say so, more's the pity for horse thieves."

"Yessir, you're right, just like old times."

General James Parker thought hanging *bandidos* was an acceptable compromise. Far preferable to war.

The moon was sinking westward in a starry sky. As Gordon approached the little house by the river, he saw a light in the window. His pulse quickened and he couldn't suppress a smile. She'd waited for him.

Guadalupe opened the door at his knock. She pulled him inside, throwing her arms around his neck, and kissed him long and tenderly on the mouth. When at last they parted, she was breathing heavily, her cheeks damp with tears. Gordon gently wiped them away.

"What's this?"

"Hector and Manuel were here after you left them at the bridge. They told me everything."

"Well, you know yourself, Hector and Manuel tend to exaggerate. It wasn't as bad as it sounds."

"You might have been killed."

"No, not while the light burns in your window. I'm like a moth to flame."

"Now you jest."

"Only to see you smile."

She led him into the parlor. A single lamp burned on a small table by the sofa and the house was quiet. She seated herself beside him on the sofa and he looked around at the rooms dappled in shadow. A strange sense of vacancy came over him.

"Antonio's asleep?"

"Oh, yes—" she paused with a beguiling grin—"I left him with Señora Alvarez, next door. She will keep him for the night."

Gordon glanced at her. "You've never done that before. Why tonight?"

"Because you are leaving in the morning."

"What makes you think that?"

"A woman knows these things."

"Well—" Gordon hesitated, momentarily undone by her intuition. "I've been ordered to deliver the Germans to the authorities in Washington. We leave on the morning train."

She scooted closer, slipped beneath his arm. "Hector told me how you took the Germans by surprise and forced them to cross the bridge. That was very brave of you."

"I'd say it was more on the order of luck, good for me and bad for them. Tonight was my night."

"Washington is very far away. How will you manage all that time? Aren't the Germans dangerous?"

"Not all that much." Gordon stroked her hair, the scent of her nearness somehow sweet and exotic. "General Parker assigned me an escort of soldiers to guard the Germans. We won't have any problems."

"What time is your train?"

"Not till eight."

She snuggled closer. "Then we have all night."

"Don't say it like that." Gordon tilted her chin. "You make it sound like our last night."

"I knew you would go away one day. I just hoped it wouldn't be so soon."

"No, you've got it all wrong. I'm going to take you with me."

"What?" She pulled away from him. "Take me where?"

"Not tomorrow," Gordon said, suddenly flustered. "I want you to be my wife and come to Washington. You and Antonio. I thought you understood."

"Oh, *querido mio*, I cannot do that."

"What are you talking about?"

She looked beautiful but sad, a subdued butterfly. "I am *Mejicano*, a simple peasant woman. There is no place for me in Washington."

"Of course there is," Gordon insisted. "You would be my wife."

"And would I be accepted by your friends? A woman who knows nothing of dress or fine manners? Would they not laugh at me and pity you, the man who married a peon? Tell me it is not true."

"Once they get to know you, they'll say I'm the luckiest man in the world. You'll see I'm right."

"And Antonio?" she asked, her voice clogged with emotion. "Would they accept him, let the little brown Mexican play with their children? You know they would not, and I cannot do that to my son."

"I—" Gordon shook his head. "Listen, we'll work it out somehow. People aren't as bad as you think."

"*Te amo*," she said fiercely. "I love you and I want to be with you, always. But, yes, even in Texas, people are that bad. Washington would only be worse . . . especially for Antonio."

Gordon was stunned. All this time he had just assumed there was nothing that could stand in their way. But the matter of race never occurred to him, and now, in some dark corner of his mind, he knew she was right. Texans were outspoken, perhaps more honest about their prejudice. Anyone not of Anglo blood was simply inferior.

In Washington, people were more subtle, but their prejudice was no less real. Anyone of color, mostly blacks, was consigned to menial work, porters and maids, the servant class. A Mexican, though an oddity to easterners, would still be viewed as a dark-skinned foreigner, an inferior. Guadalupe and the boy would never be accepted.

The truth was often hard, sometimes repugnant, and it

gave Gordon pause. He was forced to consider, all too suddenly, the depth of his emotion for this woman. In his witless certainty, he'd asked her to sacrifice, and now he had to ask himself, what was he willing to sacrifice? How important was she to him . . . to his life?

Somehow, though he'd never posed the question, he'd known all along.

"We'll live in Texas," he said, never more certain of anything. "I'll get a transfer, or maybe just quit. There are lots of law enforcement agencies."

Her smile was bleak. "Texas is not the place for you, *caro mio*. Whatever you feel now, we both know it is true. You would never be happy here."

"No, I've thought it through, and my mind's made up. The only place I'll be happy is with you. Nowhere else."

"What seems clear today is often our regret of tomorrow. You need time to think about it."

"You won't get rid of me that easy. I'll take the Germans to Washington and then catch the first train back here. Let's not talk about it anymore."

"*Si*, no more talk."

She took his hand and led him into the bedroom. A spill of lamplight from the parlor washed them in an umber glow as they undressed each other. He pulled her into a tight embrace, and she prayed it would not be the last time. Yet her heart told her the truth.

She knew he would never return.

The train chuffed steam at trackside. A warm morning sun, bright as brass, rose higher in a cloudless sky. Passengers hurried to board the coaches.

Gordon and Maddox stood on the depot platform. They watched as four armed troopers from Fort Brown marched von Kleist and Mueller to the express car. The Germans were manacled at the wrists and hobbled with leg irons around their ankles. The express car, where mail and other valuables were stored, was the most secure car on the train. The prisoners would be locked inside on the ride north.

"Maybe they'll try to escape," Maddox said with a dry chuckle. "Give you an excuse to shoot 'em."

"Not much chance of that," Gordon said. "I was ordered to deliver them safe and sound."

"Your bosses in Washington ought to take a lesson from the Rangers. Not a lot of justice puttin' those two behind bars."

"I think the idea is to send a warning to Kaiser Wilhelm. Let him know he can't mess around in our backyard."

"Well, pardner, no doubt of that," Maddox said. "Haven't had so much fun since heck was a pup. Hate to see you leave."

"Never know," Gordon said. "You might see me sooner than you think. I've gotten to like Texas."

"Why do I get the feeling you're talkin' about Guadalupe?"

"No reason you shouldn't be the first to know. I'm planning to marry her."

Maddox didn't believe a word of it. He'd seen white men get sweet on hot-eyed señoritas any number of times, and it rarely led to wedding bells. He was of the opinion that Brownsville, and Guadalupe Palaez, would soon be a distant memory for Gordon. He decided to keep his opinion to himself.

"Look me up if you need a best man. I'm always available for a shindig."

"Hoyt, I'd count it a honor."

Gordon extended his hand. They shook with the warmth of two men who had shared a dangerous time and found a bond that would last a lifetime. Maddox thought it was unlikely they would ever meet again, for señoritas, in his experience, were most often out of sight, out of mind. A roguish smile tugged at the corner of his mouth.

"Watch yourself," he said. "Don't let them Germans get on your blind side."

"I'll sleep with one eye open."

Gordon walked to the express car. As he stepped inside, the express guard slammed and locked the door. The locomotive billowed steam, driving wheels grinding, and the passenger coaches rocked forward, windows glinting in the sunlight. The engineer tooted his horn as the train slowly pulled away from the depot.

A place had been cleared at one end of the express car. There were four chairs and a couple of folding cots, with pillows and blankets. The soldiers would alternate guard duty, two on their feet at all times, positioned to watch the prisoners. Von Kleist and Mueller were seated, and as the train lurched into motion, Gordon took a chair across from them. His gaze was direct, impersonal.

"Gentlemen, there is one rule aboard this train. If you try to escape, these soldiers have orders to shoot you. No exceptions, no second chances. Understood?"

"Quite clear," von Kleist said with a sanguine expression. "But why would we attempt to escape, Mr. Gordon? We will be returned to Germany in good time."

"Colonel, the only place you're going is prison. Violation of the Neutrality Act carries a sentence of ten years."

"I assure you we will never be imprisoned."

"What makes you think so?"

"Diplomacy," von Kleist said with a sardonic smile. "Neither of our governments can afford an international incident. The situation is too delicate."

Gordon gave him a quizzical look. "You're talking about the war in Europe?"

"Actually, I refer to our respective leaders. Kaiser Wilhelm and your President Wilson would prefer that the

United States remain neutral. Why should American boys die to save England and France?"

"Americans died here in Texas. We can document your conspiracy with Huerta and Garza, and the Army of Liberation. Perhaps you overrate the power of diplomacy."

"No, I think not," von Kleist said. "A pact will be arranged for the deportation of Captain Mueller and myself. All quite discreetly, of course."

"Colonel, if it happens," Gordon said evenly, "take a message to the Kaiser. Tell him to stay out of Mexico or he *will* see Americans in Europe. Nothing could be more certain."

Von Kleist shrugged. "There are no certainties in war, Mr. Gordon. Look to the fields of France if you need proof."

Gordon saw nothing to be gained in debate. He rose and walked to the barred window that allowed the express guard to look outside. The countryside was dotted with chaparral and mesquite, and the sight somehow reminded him of all that had happened since he'd arrived in Texas. The death and destruction seemed to him an appalling waste, provoked by warlords who sought supremacy whatever the cost in human life. The futility of it all was marked by their failure.

President Woodrow Wilson, acting swiftly, had defused the situation. In a strongly worded communiqué, he warned Venustiano Carranza that Mexico risked war with the United States unless the raids into Texas were halted. Carranza, who at last recognized the danger to his own shaky regime, directed his military commanders into the field. Their orders were to disband the Army of Liberation.

The rebel brigade in Monterrey was now commanded by a Colonel Hilario Hinojosa. With Huerta's arrest in New Mexico, and Garza's death on the streets of Matamoras, Hinojosa deferred marching on Texas. His attention turned instead to Mexico, and the bitter civil war, and upon hearing that Carranza's generals had taken to the field, all his options were closed. He joined forces with Pancho Villa, and the Army of Liberation rode off to fight in the *Revolución*. The invasion of Texas, once all but certain, ceased to be a threat.

The train rattled on through the countryside. Gordon stood looking out the window, images of the raids, the brutality and wanton death still vivid in his mind. Yet, for all he'd seen on the Rio Grande, there was an overriding sense of vindication. A last laugh of sorts.

The warlords, in the end, were like ashes scattered to the winds.

Texas was safe.

Epilogue

Colonel Franz von Kleist and Captain Otto Mueller were deported to Germany in October 1915. Upon their arrival in Berlin, Mueller was assigned to the Western Front, where he was killed by artillery fire a week later. The German General Staff offered von Kleist a choice of court-martial and disgrace, or an honorable solution. He shot himself on October 21, 1915.

Five months later, in March 1916, Pancho Villa crossed the border with five hundred men. He attacked the town of Columbus, New Mexico, destroying property and killing civilians and soldiers. On orders from President Wilson, General John "Black Jack" Pershing invaded Mexico with a cavalry regiment. He persued Villa through the state of Chihuahua until early 1917, fighting countless skirmishes without capturing the revolutionary leader. American intelligence agencies believed that Villa's raid was yet another conspiracy instigated by German provocateurs. The stage was set for war.

In January 1917, the MI-6 British intelligence service intercepted a coded telegram from German Secretary of State Arthur Zimmermann to Venustiano Carranza, President of Mexico. In the event the United States entered the European conflict, Zimmermann proposed that Mexico declare itself an ally of Germany. The telegram offered massive financial aid and German military assistance for

"Mexico to reconquer its former territories in Texas, New Mexico, and Arizona."

The Zimmermann Telegram, as it became known, was decoded and forwarded to President Woodrow Wilson. The release of the telegram to the press on March 1 confirmed yet another foreign conspiracy and resulted in a public outcry for war against Germany. President Wilson went before Congress, and after a month of debate, the United States formally declared war on Germany on April 6. Venustiano Carranza denied ever receiving the Zimmermann Telegram, and publicly proclaimed Mexico's friendship for the United States. In Washington, the lie was accepted to prevent a war with Mexico.

General John "Black Jack" Pershing, commander of the American Expeditionary Force, arrived in France in June 1917. Forward elements were soon deployed, and by August 1918, over 2,000,000 Doughboys occupied the trenches along the Western Front. On September 26, the British, French, Belgian and American armies began a joint offensive against the Hindenburg Line, Germany's final line of resistance. By October 2 the line was broken and the Allies advanced on a wide front toward the German frontier. Victory was but a matter of time.

On November 9, Kaiser Wilhelm II abdicated the throne as ruler of the German Empire. The following day, with the German army in full retreat, he departed Berlin by train and sought exile in Holland. One day later, on November 11, armistice was declared and the guns at last fell silent on the Western Front. On June 28, 1919, in the Hall of Mirrors at Versailles, France, the peace treaty between the Allies and Germany was signed. The World War was over.

The Texas Rangers continued to patrol the border throughout the war. For a time, in the spring of 1917, there was widespread fear that Mexico, acting in concert with

Germany, would declare war on the United States. Hoyt Maddox, who never trusted the leaders of Mexico, remembered all too well the summer of 1915 and the Army of Liberation. Yet the peace held, and Maddox, who served out the war on the Rio Grande, was eventually promoted to a captain of the Rangers. He retired with honors in 1931.

President Wilson awarded Frank Gordon a commendation for valor in October 1915. The next day, though his future was assured in Washington, Gordon requested a transfer to Texas. He was reassigned to the Dallas office, and in November, with Hoyt Maddox as his best man, he married Guadalupe Palaez. Gordon adopted Antonio, and by the end of the war, Guadalupe gave him three daughters. Hector Martinez, Manuel Vargas, and Hoyt Maddox were their godfathers.

During the Roaring Twenties, Frank Gordon was instrumental in combating the resurgence of the Ku Klux Klan throughout Texas and Oklahoma. The U.S. Bureau of Investigation, under the directorship of J. Edgar Hoover, ultimately became the Federal Bureau of Investigation. Gordon, who routinely refused offers of promotion to Washington, ended his career as Special Agent in Charge of the F.B.I. field office in Houston. He and Guadalupe and their children never left Texas.

Today, at the F.B.I. headquarters in Washington, there is a plaque commemorating Frank R. Gordon. He is remembered as the man who brought peace to the Rio Grande.